ROBERTA'S WOODS

ROBERTA'S WOODS

BETTY J. COTTER

FIVE STAR
A part of Gale, Cengage Learning

GALE
CENGAGE Learning™

Detroit • New York • San Francisco • New Haven, Conn • Waterville, Maine • London

Copyright © 2008 by Betty J. Cotter.
Five Star Publishing, a part of Gale, Cengage Learning.

Set in 11 pt. Plantin.
Printed on permanent paper.

LIBRARY OF CONGRESS CATALOGING-IN-PUBLICATION DATA

Cotter, Betty J.
    Roberta's Woods / by Betty J. Cotter. — 1st ed.
    p. cm.
    ISBN-13: 978-1-59414-673-2 (alk. paper)
    ISBN-10: 1-59414-673-X (alk. paper)
    1. Family—Fiction. 2. Rhode Island—Fiction. 3. Petroleum reserves—Fiction. 4. Natural gas reserves—Fiction. I. Title.
PS3603.086846R63 2008
813'.6—dc22   2007050872

First Edition. First Printing: March 2008.

Published in 2008 in conjunction with Tekno Books.

In memory of my father
Silas Warren Thayer
1923–2006

ACKNOWLEDGMENTS

Many people helped make this book possible. I wish to thank members of the South County Writers Group and author Robert Gover, who critiqued earlier versions of the manuscript; my sister, Andrea Thayer, and my mother, Eleanor Thayer, who read early drafts and made helpful comments; my agents, Jack and Joan Ryan, who never gave up on the book; and last but not least, my husband, Timothy, and our children, Perry, Colby and Mary, who have supported my "other career" with patience and love.

CHAPTER ONE

In better times someone would have been at Kingston Station to meet her. Her father would have been standing next to his pickup, under that sprawling maple tree in the parking lot, doffing his orange hunter's cap as she stepped off the platform.

All the way from Baltimore Roberta Wilcox had imagined him. As the suburban yards and boat docks of Connecticut faded into the woods of the Rhode Island countryside, she had seen only his craggy face floating by. She pictured him waiting for her as he had so many times before in those eight years since she had moved to Maryland. She saw the hint of welcome in the creases around his eyes and imagined the brief hug that would smell of sawdust and aftershave. She knew he always arrived well ahead of the Washington-to-Boston, then waited with growing impatience for a train that never seemed to be on time. By the time she got there, he usually was on his third or fourth cigarette.

Of course it was absurd to expect him to meet her; he hadn't had enough gas to run the car in months.

Still she looked for the old maple, but its graceful canopy was gone, a stump in its place. The paint was flaking from the sides of Kingston Station. Inside its waiting room people should have been busy snuggling babies, handing off luggage or embracing one another. Instead Roberta watched as her fellow passengers shuffled out to the one bus that waited silently at the curb. They had made it to their station, but the hardest part of the journey was still ahead for many of them. A few she saw carrying luggage out of the parking lot and up the street. She knew they didn't live nearby. They were just hoping for a ride.

If he couldn't make it, her father had said, there was always Ida Kenyon, and Roberta found the postmaster packing sacks of mail into the back of a white Jeep. She was dressed like a man, in a pair of faded black jeans and a brown flannel shirt with its tail flying out of her pants. She pursed her lips when Roberta walked up. If she could have, Roberta thought, Ida would have tossed her in the back with the sacks of letters and packages.

"Alton said you might be here. Well, get in."

They headed out onto Route 138. The roads were nearly empty, although occasionally they passed a bus or a truck, its back full of riders. Like schools of fish, the cars they did see traveled together, most of them aimed south. It felt strange to be driving in the opposite direction. Roberta felt like the heroine of a made-for-TV movie rushing back to a volcano that's about to blow: headed for trouble. The landscape looked the same, but once in a while something jarred her into realizing just how different things really were. A lawn as high as a beach dune appeared out the window or a boarded-up gas station where prices hung crookedly from an overhead sign. Two-fifty a gallon, one said, which meant it had been shuttered at least a year. Now, in 2013, you couldn't get gas for less than ten dollars a gallon, if you could find it at all.

Ida was grimly gripping the wheel as the old Jeep whined at the height of third gear. The postmaster had aged since Roberta had been home last. Folds of her skin hung from her neck, and her face was a relief map of rivers and streambeds. Her brown hair, messily tied back in a bun that couldn't quite hold all of the short strands, was peppered with gray.

But when Ida turned to Roberta, her eyes were as sharp and

black as ever. "How long you staying?"

"As long as I have to, I guess," Roberta said cautiously. "Gran's getting on, you know, and could use some help."

"Seems to me May gets along all right for a woman her age."

"She does, but she's almost ninety, Mrs. Kenyon. Her rheumatism bothers her, and she's had trouble gardening, bending down, things like that. She'll be canning pretty soon, and I'll help out with that, the cooking, other stuff around the house."

Ida Kenyon looked from the road to her passenger and raised one eyebrow a notch. Roberta could almost hear her thinking, *Well, you never lifted a finger when you were living there. Why start now?*

Instead Ida said, "What about your sister? She lives a damn sight closer than Baltimore."

That was true; Paula lived in Westerly, about twenty miles to the south, but Roberta's relationship with her half-sister was more than she wanted to explain to Ida Kenyon. "Well, she doesn't want to leave her house, you know, and her husband has a job right in town."

"Young folks don't want to come back here," Ida mused. "It's not like the old days."

Roberta offered no comment. She knew Ida probably lumped her together with all the others who were leaving—newcomers who never really belonged in Coward's Hole to begin with. Hadn't she left for college and never come back? And wasn't that proof enough that she was an outsider?

"You better hope you can get back, if you have to," Ida finally said, ominously.

The August afternoon was gray and hazy. The flattened landscape was giving way to gently rising hills and forest. In the midst of scrub pines and maples stood ranch houses and colonials, looking oddly out of place in the scraggly Rhode Island woods. One after another paved roads trailed off into subdivisions, fronted by stone posts bearing signs like "Laurel Estates" or "Blueberry Ridge."

"See that?" Ida pointed a slightly crooked finger toward one of the houses. "Boarded up. Gone to hell they are, too. Nothin' worse for a house than to sit empty. All it takes is a year, and they're full of vermin and termites and every other goddamn thing. Maybe these people think they're coming back, but I won't live to see it. If they do, their houses won't be fit to live in."

"They just left?"

"Yeah. Headed south, the Carolinas, Florida, although I hear some tell Texas is a good place, with its oil fields and all. They pack up the car and a U-haul-it and go down there without a job or anything. Cheaper to live, you know. Don't have to heat the houses, and gas is a little easier to get. Up here, they get desperate. Can't get to work, can't get Junior to soccer practice or some such foolishness. So they dump the mortgage and get out of town." Ida turned onto the Victory Highway, jamming the Jeep's gears with a ferocious yank. "Soft, they are. Don't like heating with wood, being stuck in the house all winter."

Soft city people, just like me, Roberta finished the thought for her. She wondered what it was like to pack up your belongings in a truck and leave behind a home you might never see again. What did you take; what did you leave behind? *Of course,* she realized, *that is just what I've done, and my belongings barely fill two suitcases. Two suitcases and a cardboard box of papers.* Eight years of work stuffed into the back of a Jeep, and it took up no more room than a day's mail.

For she was coming home to stay, although she would never tell Ida Kenyon that. She had nowhere else to go.

Roberta turned to the window, where the landmarks of her childhood were passing by in the muggy afternoon. The entrance to the drive-in was now more tall grass than asphalt. Soon the woods would take it over completely. The screen was merely a frame that looked like the blackened timbers of a burned-out house. How many movies had she seen there, nestled in the front seat of one of Steve Reynolds's gas-guzzling American cars? But he was in the past, just as surely as that two-fifty-a-gallon gasoline.

They were on old Route 3 now. The road, two lanes of concrete divided by what once had been a neatly mowed median, had been bypassed long ago by Interstate 95. Roberta knew tractor-trailers once had roared along this stretch, and the locals had done a good business selling gas, groceries and trinkets to travelers. All that had been gone for years. Some of the businesses had hung on, kept alive by the newcomers and the few cars that strayed off the interstate. But most had closed after 95 went in, and gradually nature had taken over where man left off. If you looked carefully, you could see peeling billboards and the caved-in roof of Franklin's Luncheonette, the tangles of bittersweet its only traffic jam now.

But the Silver Pine Diner was still open, although Roberta saw only one car out front. Its aluminum sides glittered in the sunlight. And as they turned onto Jonnycake Trail, a boy walked out of Woodmansee's Store and hopped on a bicycle. The two gas pumps were still out front, but no cars stood beside them. The numbers that made up the price had long since fallen down.

"Did Cal close the gas station?"

"Lord, yes. You have been gone awhile. He couldn't get gas. No sense in having a gas station without no gas. Only the big stations get it now, in the city. Suppose you know all about that, being from Baltimore."

"I'm not *from* Baltimore; I'm from here," Roberta pointed out. She was beginning to feel more and more aggravated. Had she caught some disease, living away? This hostility to the city was worse than she remembered. "And no, I don't know all about it. Things are just different down there; I can't explain it. It was hard to get gas. But it was harder to find a place to live."

"Guess you've found one now."

"I haven't found—" But what was the use? Ida had found a sore spot, and she would pick at it until she got a reaction. Well, she wasn't going to get a reaction, not this time. "Do you know how my father's doing?"

"Alton? Same as always, I 'spect. He's in and out of the Hole more than I am some days, getting that lumber out. Sooner or later the state's going to put a stop to him. He loads that International 'til it looks like a stiff wind could tip it over. And the state doesn't like a competitor, if you know what I mean."

Roberta had no idea what she meant. Their whole conversation seemed to be woven around Ida's intimate knowledge of a world that had turned upside down since she had left. Roberta knew all about the gas crisis and the oil shortage and bad times, but none of the postmaster's observations squared with her understanding of those things. Life was different here, and Roberta had a feeling it would be some time before she understood just how different.

The Jeep's gears began to groan. They were climbing now, as much as you could climb in this wild western pocket of the state. Up and down, like a roller coaster they went, until ahead loomed Mount Laurel, the wall that separated Coward's Hole from the rest of Exeter. At the top was the old turnoff, threaded with grass and littered with broken bottles. "Scenic Overlook," the green and white state sign said. The pond it looked out upon was surrounded by the skeletons of trees. The Big Fire had taken care of that view.

As she always did, Roberta found herself jerking her head toward the overlook and the dizzying drop beyond. She could not, she knew, ever pass by it without visualizing the long drop, the blur of brush and treetops smashing by a car window and water rushing in at the bottom.

"State still hasn't fenced that off." Ida gave her a sideways glance. "No, you won't find them state workers up here anymore. What guardrails we got is rusted to hell. You should see the roads down in the Hole."

"Mmm."

"Just the other day I was telling the senator, 'Why don't you call up the state garage, get them to fix that drop-off?' But he said, 'Ida, there ain't no use in worrying about that. Not enough drivers anymore to make it dangerous.' "

Roberta's breath caught.

"But it only takes one, I says to Fred—"

"That's right, Mrs. Kenyon, it only takes one."

Ida looked grimly superior. "Roberta, I didn't mean anything. You don't have to be so sensitive about it."

They were close now. Roberta tried to collect herself before their arrival. She began to see the swamps and rock-filled woods that had given the place its unofficial name. They said the Narragansett Indians would hide behind the rocks to escape their enemies, thus the "coward" of Coward's Hole. Roberta thought that the place should have been called Idiot's Hole, for the Colonists who never caught on to the Indians' guerilla tactics. Seventy years before the Revolution, more than one subject of the king had lost his life to that ignorance, and Roberta knew some of her ancestors were among them.

They came to the junction of the Dump Road and Cook Road, and Ida pulled the Jeep beside the white cottage that was half post office, half Ida's home. It wasn't too far now; barely a mile. Ida disappeared behind the back of the Jeep and Roberta sank her head into her hands. *What in hell have I got myself in to? If she's leading the welcoming committee, I am in big trouble.*

Ida quickly unloaded the sacks of mail and hopped back in

the Jeep. Soon they came upon a faded billboard: "Laurel Cabins." Then Roberta saw the family's old tourist court, a cluster of three bungalows partly obscured by brush and brambles. Across the street was the homestead, a rambling white Cape Cod house with a bright green door and a wishing well at its side. Beyond it was the faded red barn, overgrown fields and the trail leading to her father's sawmill. How odd it all looked: The grass was calf high, and the barn's paint had almost completely peeled. It had been only a year since her last visit, but in that time the farm had taken on the seedy look of abandonment.

Later she wondered if they had seen her. Whether they had watched her paying Ida Kenyon and pulling a pair of suitcases and a cardboard box out of the Jeep. Perhaps they had seen how white her face was in the golden light of the late afternoon, all the paler against her auburn curls that were frizzing in the damp air. Maybe they had wondered why she took such mincing steps to the front door, her leather sandals crunching on the gravel driveway. But if they had watched her arrival, they did not let on.

CHAPTER TWO

They were gathered in the old farmhouse kitchen as though she had never left. Gran was at the blackened wood range, stirring jonnycake batter in a yellow-ware bowl. Standing behind the oak rocker was Roberta's father, Alton, his hands folded around a cigarette, his face cloudy but inscrutable. Paula was there, too, buzzing about the room like a darning needle, still spinning in a whirlwind of chaos and self-righteous purpose.

Gran heard the door first, put down her bowl and enveloped Roberta in a hug.

"Goodness me! You'll give an old woman a heart attack."

Roberta dropped her bags and returned the hug, feeling the curving bones of May Wilcox's back. *Why, she's shrunk,* Roberta thought with a start. Once Gran had been able to look her straight in the eye, but now she tilted her chin up to regard her granddaughter.

"You look peaked," the old woman pronounced. "You haven't been getting enough to eat, have you? I'm not sure I like that color on you, maybe that's it."

"Oh, Gran," was all Roberta could muster.

Roberta's father hung back and nodded stiffly. He was dressed up for Sunday: dark pants, a dress shirt and a string tie. His hair was almost all gray now, and his face had the soft wrinkles of a dried-up apple. "Roberta," he said with a nod as though he were meeting a passing acquaintance on the street. "Ida get you all right?"

She started to answer him, but he had picked up her suitcases and headed down the hall.

Paula barely stopped her stirring to say hello. Roberta, following her half-sister into the tiny sinkroom, was startled by how much Paula had aged. She had the beginnings of crow's feet around her eyes, and her long brown hair was laced with traces of silver. But she hadn't gained an ounce; she still wore those size-four blue jeans and a shirt tucked into them for good measure.

"How was your ride?" Paula mumbled from the depths of a cupboard she was rifling through. The room was tiny, with barely enough space for an old soapstone sink, a few open cupboards and a stepstool. *She doesn't want to look at me,* Roberta thought.

"About as good as a half-hour with Ida Kenyon could be."

"Be careful what you say because we have company."

"Not much has changed around here, I can see."

"You wouldn't know, now would you?" Paula dropped a pot lid and turned to face her. She had lowered her voice, and Roberta felt a chill at her tone. "What do you think you're doing here?"

Roberta took a deep breath and tried to keep her own voice level. "What?"

"That letter. Oh, please. Wanting to help out. I don't believe a word of it. If you wanted to help, where have you been for eight years?"

"What do you mean? I'm here every summer."

"Well, the other fifty weeks a year I've been here almost every day," Paula hissed at her. "And let me tell you it's a little different in the middle of winter when you're praying you'll make it over Mount Laurel with a car running on fumes. Sure, you come here every August and lie in the hammock and take your hikes and drink lemonade like some goddamned hotel guest.

Well, this year you're going to have to join the help in the kitchen." Paula picked one of Gran's aprons off a hook and shoved it into Roberta's hands, then gave her a jumble of knives and forks. "You want to help? Go set the table."

Roberta looked down at the apron, feeling a pang at the familiar rosebud print. Did Gran and Dad feel this way, too? The silverware was cold against her hands, and all the knives seemed to be pointing straight at her. Of course, Paula would see through the letter, the thinly disguised begging to come home. Gran would help her save a shred of pride, but not Paula. She wouldn't give her an inch. And what about Dad? That greeting didn't bode well. Had she heard a judgment underneath it, a silent condemnation? Or was she just imagining things?

Somehow, she was going to have to walk out to the dining room and set the table and make pleasant conversation with whoever caught her doing it. The dining room, shadowy in the late afternoon light, was blessedly empty. *Don't think about it, don't think about it,* Roberta repeated to herself as she laid out the cutlery.

"Not much has changed," she mocked herself aloud. How could she have been so stupid as to think things would have changed? She was still Paula's least favorite person. She was still branded for leaving . . . although, thinking about it now, it had seemed at the time the only thing she could have done.

Her mother had been dead for thirteen years when Roberta graduated from high school, but the whole town still talked about the day Jackie Wilcox drove off the side of Mount Laurel. That was what came of the sin of escape. But once you left, you could never come home. Not and have things be the same. She could have stayed and lived with the whispers, or left and tried to forget. Even Paula had moved to Westerly when she married Ray. But somehow, that was more acceptable than going off to a college so expensive your father had to sell one of his prized wood lots to afford it.

"No, things haven't changed, have they?"

Roberta didn't have to turn around to recognize that voice or the ghost of a mocking smile that followed it. She turned to find Steve Reynolds there, leaning on the doorjamb and smiling with a sort of triumph.

"So they put you to work, did they?" he said. "You look good in that apron. I always said you'd take to the domestic life, but you didn't believe me."

"Fuck you, Steve."

"Feisty! That's what I loved about you. You always thought you could kick my ass." He laughed as though he had told a great joke. "What are you doing in that getup, anyway?"

She looked down at her pantsuit and tried to hide her dismay. Its creamy linen had been crisp and chic in the morning, but now it hung limply, like one of Gran's dishtowels. In Baltimore she would have blended in with the crowd; here the silk shell and narrow-cut jacket made her look like an alien.

"I must say, that apron does something for it." He was making no attempt to hide a smile. "So seriously, Roberta, what are you doing here? You once swore you'd never come back."

"I'm just here to help out, that's all."

"I remember the day you said you were getting out." He had stepped closer to her, leaning his head down, lowering his voice though they were alone. "Over on the Queen's Pillow, smokin' sinsemilla and listening to—what was it?"

He still had a good voice, an almost silky roughness. She could finish the lyric for him. But he wasn't playing fair. He knew what he was doing, reciting the Doors and invoking that last day. She could smell that shirt of his, a musky flannel, and taste his salty skin and feel the pulse exploding in his neck. The ground was cold beneath her. When you sleep on the Queen's Pillow, your dreams become visions . . .

Focus on the conversation, she ordered herself. "Listen, Gran's getting old. She needs some help, that's all."

He was still singing, as though she hadn't said anything, his right leg moving to a barely discernible rhythm and his fingers playing pretend drums. But then he picked up the thread of their conversation, stepping back and smiling. "May. Now there's a woman who could kick my ass, even if she is almost ninety. No, you're not here to help around the house. Come'n, Roberta, what's up? You and Paula going to duke it out?"

"Wouldn't you like to know?" she said lamely. Oh, this was just great. First Paula, and now she had to face Steve Reynolds, of all people, just when she was feeling the most vulnerable. She hadn't thought about the prospect of meeting him again when she had given up her apartment and spent half her savings on a train ticket. At least, that's what she told herself.

"Have you been crying?"

"Oh, yeah. Over you."

"You have been crying. What's the matter?"

Now he was being solicitous. She hated him even more for being nice. It was easier when he was a jerk. The thought was half formed in her mind that maybe it wouldn't be such a bad idea to confide in him. Maybe he knew why Paula was being so hostile. Maybe he could—

But Gran was rushing in with a platter of hot jonnycakes, and Paula was behind her with a steaming loaf of brown bread. Steve pushed her elbow to sit down, and she felt his breath at her ear."

They gathered around the broad oak table. There was Alton, and Steve's father, Ben Reynolds, who had spent so many Sundays with the Wilcoxes that he seemed like a member of the family, even though he wasn't. There was Paula and her husband, Ray, who hung back until almost everyone else was seated before taking a chair himself. And there was Steve, who took the only chair besides Gran's that was empty. It was directly across from Roberta. Gran was still shuffling back and forth for a forgotten this and misplaced that, until someone— Roberta thought it was her father—yelled at her to sit down.

"All right, all right," Gran said, finally admitting defeat as she settled at the head of the table. "Roberta, tell the men to stop talking politics so I can hear about your trip."

Roberta made a half-hearted attempt to tell them about the crowded train, the trouble getting tickets, the ride in the Jeep. She had wrangled her spot on the Washington-to-Boston by sheer luck when a colleague at the university had to cancel his own travel plans. Still, the ticket had cost her nearly $500.

"Crowded?" her father asked without looking up.

"Standing room only. But it's cheaper than flying."

"I don't know what this country's coming to," Gran said. "Never thought I'd see the day when we'd start rationing gas again."

"We've got to get ready for the winter," Alton was saying. "Things is worse than they were last year already. We might not have any oil at all, and we might not be able to get out for food."

Although Alton was looking at Ben, the elder Reynolds was nodding back at him as though he needed no convincing. It was Steve who had stopped buttering his roll while Alton talked.

"Alton, if you think there's not enough oil for us, you've been deceived." His voice rang out sharply, and the older men looked at him as though he had taken his mother's name in vain. "There's enough oil and enough gas. The state just doesn't want us to have it. The feds are putting the squeeze on the whole Northeast. The governor's under pressure to show the feds that we're conserving. But you don't think the governor's going to give up his SUV, do you? It's easier to take it away from the little people. Instead of filling up your wood box, you ought to use next month's gas ration to get your hide up to the state house—or get the senator to take your story up there for you."

"Well, maybe that's worked for you," Alton began with a brief look in Steve's direction, "but it's no long-term solution."

Roberta suppressed a smile, knowing Alton was needling Steve, who was infamous for finagling whatever government jobs he could get.

"Why should I ask the state to give me oil so somebody else goes without?" Alton continued. "The fact of the matter is, there ain't enough to go around anymore. It don't matter how many people have gone to Florida. People up here is going to do without, and we all need to make sure we have what we need to get through."

The jonnycakes were golden and crisp, the mashed potatoes fluffy, but Roberta's fork worked its way through them in slow motion on the wheat-patterned plate. Do without food? No oil? Baltimore had shortages and gas rationing, and the price of everything was skyrocketing, but it had not been as serious as this. Leave it to Rhode Island, where politics was always mixed up in everything.

"We'll get by," Gran spoke up. "We always have. I remember during the war, when they rationed gas and sugar and everything else. We didn't starve. We've always had a full cellar, and I don't expect this year will be any different."

"It is different," Alton insisted. "We used to be able to do for our own without the state sticking its nose in. Jesus Christ, I can't even cut my own woodlot these days without a permit."

"They should be sending you a thank-you note, Alton." Ben was helping himself to more jonnycakes. "Lord knows they ain't been up here to thin out Arcadia in years. All those blow-downs are going to come back to haunt them."

Ben was talking about trees blown down by line storms and

blizzards; Roberta knew that much. Arcadia was the state forest that surrounded the farm, and the state's management of what had once been Wilcox land was always a bone of contention. Roberta had been back for only a few hours, but she was slipping back into the rhythm of their speech, their ways. Still she felt disconnected, cut off. Maybe Paula was right; maybe she had been away too long. Everything around her, the scraping of the chair legs on the maple floor, the mealy taste of a jonnycake dissolving on her tongue, the faint scent of Gran's rosewater perfume—it should bring her back; it should connect her. Still she felt like a guest, one who nods and smiles to mask the sense of being lost.

Everything seemed so small; that was part of it. The old Cape Cod was like a doll's house, and the seven of them crowding around the table seemed strangely out of scale, like teddy bears too big for their chairs. It always took a while before she adjusted to the house, before she felt at home again with its nooks and crannies and crooked floors. Now as she looked past Steve to the front hall, the doorway reminded her of a mouse hole that would lead one on a dark and dusty journey underground.

"Alton, you shouldn't be complaining about the state," Steve was saying, his mouth curled. "I hear they're writing your paycheck these days." Why did he always antagonize her father? He knew what he was like riled. "Good thing they aren't up here cuttin' wood. They'd be cuttin' into your business."

"Well, not everybody can hold three jobs with the town," Alton shot back. "Scoff all you want, Steve Reynolds. I predict bad weather coming, and I don't just mean the snow. We've forgotten what it's like to be tough. We might just learn this winter. If we can't get out of the Hole we'll be eating a lot of venison."

Gran was up, helping herself to carrots halfway across the table. "Bring on the deer, I say. We'll have mincemeat pie and venison steaks. I can remember when all the meat we had to eat was skunk and possum."

"Oh Gran, please." Paula grimaced. *She's like a child who's just learned where meat comes from,* Roberta thought. "Can't we just eat? Christ, we've been cooking all day. I don't want to hear about how bad the winter's going to be, or what the state's up to."

Roberta looked around the table and knew what Paula meant. Gran had made the brown bread from scratch, for she could see the indentations of a coffee can in its sides. The baked beans, the Harvard beets, the carrots, the ham—no one ate, or cooked, like this anymore. No wonder Paula was grouchy.

"You people who live out here are gluttons for punishment," Paula was saying. "I'm going to be snug in my oil-heated house in town, drinking my public water and walking to work. If you live way out in Coward's Hole you can't expect to be comfortable in the middle of an oil crisis." She looked at Ray as though he were about to shut her up, then plunged ahead. "If you'd listened to the state, you wouldn't have these problems. This is nothing new."

"A lot of this is news to me," Roberta said. "Dad, do you really think we're going to have a hard winter?"

"Think? I know it," Alton said, oblivious to the tight-fisted way Paula was holding her knife and fork. "Look at the acorns already on the ground, and the trees that are turning early. That wouldn't matter ordinarily, but this ain't no ordinary year. We can survive all right, I suppose, but we've got to take it seriously. If we get a foot of snow at Thanksgivin' we could be snowed in all winter, and—"

"That's all the more reason you should move into town," Paula interrupted. "What if Gran gets sick? What if you run out of gas making a delivery, and can't get home? What if—"

"What if you keep still? We're not moving off this place while

I'm alive to tell about it."

"Where would they go?" Roberta knew she shouldn't get involved, but she couldn't help herself. "Are people really moving into town for the winter?"

"Yes, if you knew anything," Paula snapped. "They can move in with us. Of course, that means you'll have to go back where you came from."

"Paula." Ray spoke at last, in a low undertone that carried more threat than volume. "I think that's enough."

"Don't shush me! You know perfectly well they can't stay here."

"I don't know any such thing," Ray continued quietly. "Why don't we change the subject? Roberta, tell us how your book is coming."

"Never mind her damn book! Nobody wants to hear about her book. It's ridiculous for them to stay way out here all winter when the state might turn off the electricity or cut off their gas ration altogether. You know that could happen."

"The last time I checked, this was still the United States of America, and a man had a right to his property." Alton had stopped eating, had folded his hands in front of him, and was staring across the table at Paula. "I'm not afraid of the state. Let them try to put me off. This property has been in Wilcox hands since before there was a United States of America, Goddammit. They can talk all they want about The Ring and all this nonsense. That's a bunch of foolishness for you people who don't know how to take care of yourselves."

The Ring? Roberta thought. What the hell was that?

"Alton, your food's getting cold." Gran spooned some more mashed potatoes onto her plate. "Roberta, we are interested in your book."

"Well, it's on hold right now." The others had stopped eating, and the sounds of clicking silverware were fading. Roberta's mind raced on, and she tried to ignore Paula's glowering presence at the other end of the table. "I need to do some traveling for my research, and it's not a good time to travel."

"You got here, didn't you?" It was Steve. He was goading her again. "So what are you researching?"

"The history of tourist cabins. There are still thousands all across the country, and I need to go out and interview their owners and photograph them before they disappear."

Steve hooted, leaning back so only two legs of his cane chair were on the floor. "Well, you don't need to travel far to do that," he said. "You can just walk across the road."

"I can't write a book about Dad's old tourist cabins. I need more than one example." Why was she sounding defensive? No one else at the table cared what she was up to. She realized with sudden embarrassment, though, that everyone was quietly following their conversation. "I won't be doing any more work for a while, until I can get a big gas allotment."

"I can just read that proposal now," Steve said. " 'Professor wants gas from the government to write about a bunch of old cabins that nobody needs anymore because nobody has enough gas to go anywhere.' I have to admire you, Roberta. I wish I'd thought of it."

As much as she hated to admit it, she knew Steve Reynolds was right. She would never finish the cabins project stuck way out here, in the middle of nowhere, with no way to get around. She had focused her entire professional life on research she couldn't finish, all to prove a thesis that meant nothing. She looked past Steve to the cold fireplace and the mahogany case clock on the mantel. It said four o'clock, but she knew that wasn't right. That clock's hands had been frozen there for as long as she could remember Now she had to mark time by them once again.

CHAPTER THREE

Sleep had not come easily to Roberta in her stifling upstairs bedroom. Now, in the bright light of the late summer morning, she looked on the bedroom of her childhood with unsettled eyes.

The ceiling was low and slanted, and the room's only window was cocked at an angle, as though some eighteenth-century carpenter had struggled to fit it into the tiny space. It was the perfect room for the Wilcoxes, who weren't especially tall, but Roberta wasn't built like a Wilcox—she was tall and big-boned like her mother, and she almost had to duck walking in. The wallpaper was still blue roses, faded and stained in spots. The white metal bed was covered in a thin blue and pink quilt Gran had made when she was a child, and its stitches barely held it together. On the wide pine floor, painted a deep brown, rested one of Gran's rag rugs. There was no closet, only a maple wardrobe with doors that stuck in the heat and into which Roberta last night had squeezed a few dresses and pairs of pants on hangers. A small maple desk and a rough pine bookcase Alton had made were the only other furnishings.

It was to this attic-like room Roberta had fled after her mother died. She had read *Little Women* and envied the March girls for having Marmie; she had followed the Ingalls girls out West and cried over Mary's blindness; she had absorbed all the gothic darkness of *Jane Eyre*. Even now on her bookshelf she could see the demarcation between the innocence of these classics and the real life she had uncovered later—the political awakening that came from Kate Millett and Germaine Greer, the sexual secrets inside *Fear of Flying,* the head rush of freedom in Kerouac's *On the Road.* There was so much out there beyond Coward's Hole, over Mount Laurel and down the road. Even at fifteen she had dreamed of setting out after it.

It was a road that had led her in a circle. She hadn't imagined it happening this way. She had spent every summer for the last eight years visiting and photographing the tourist cabins that had once been a home away from home for so many Americans struck by wanderlust. Now, with her book so close to being done, she had no grant, no money and no job. She wondered if the work that had had its start in teenage dreams was truly over.

She got up, dressed in shorts and a t-shirt and headed downstairs. Gran not only was done with the dishes, she already was hanging out a load of laundry; but she had left a warm pot of coffee and some corn muffins. Roberta settled down with both in the small room off the kitchen where the family took its meals during the week. As she watched Gran snapping clothes-pins onto billowing white sheets, she thought of what she would have been doing right now in Baltimore. Sitting in the café a block from her apartment, probably, sipping a java while read-ing the *Sun.* Gran's harsh leftover coffee made her nostalgic for the French vanilla she had grown addicted to in the city. She wondered where, and how often, one could get a newspaper these days.

"Well, if that isn't a picture."

Roberta looked up to see Paula in the doorway. She had pulled her hair back severely in a ponytail and her brow was deeply furrowed. Her normally brown eyes seemed almost black. For such a small woman, she had a way of looming when she walked into a room.

"How can you sit there and watch an eighty-nine-year-old lady hang out clothes?"

Roberta was too surprised to act polite. "What are you doing here?"

"Ray thought it might be a good idea if I stayed on this week to help out. I guess it's a good thing I did."

I'll bet, Roberta thought. She wondered if Ray ever had an idea that Paula acted on. "She doesn't want my help, and you know it."

"Oh, really? And then what are you doing here? I thought that was the motive for this surprise visit."

So that was how it was going to be. Gran, she knew, would cover for her, make her feel needed and welcome; but Paula wasn't playing that game.

"Dad has a full crew this morning and they'll be heading in for a coffee break at ten o'clock." Paula's voice had that scolding tone Roberta hated. "I was going to feed them the muffins, but I see we're on to Plan B."

Gran puffed her way through the doorway with an empty wicker basket that rattled with a few stray clothespins. "Don't fuss over them corn muffins. The cookie jar's full, and your father hates muffins anyway. Besides, there's too much to do to fight."

Gran's presence was like the thin blue of sky showing after a storm; the electricity left the air and Paula went about her business, helping Roberta with the dishes and filling the coffee pot. They passed the morning in a sort of post-storm truce, saying "Excuse me" when their sides bumped in the tiny kitchen, or passing dishes politely but having no real sisterly conversation.

Just before ten o'clock, Roberta volunteered to walk to the mill and invite the men back for their coffee break. Alton never wore a watch, and he wasn't one to cut out early if he could get one more board sawed or a few more two-by-fours stacked. But the truth was this was an errand of freedom rather than duty. Walking through the calf-high grass and black-eyed Susans in the west field and then along the shady woodland path to Sawmill Road, Roberta was alone and free. The whine of the saw grew in intensity as she passed by the old stone walls nearly buried in brush, and soon she saw a blizzard of sawdust spraying out from the mill's aluminum pipe.

Roberta leaned against a pine tree and watched the men in the shadows of the sawmill building. Alton was in the thick of it all, orchestrating the mill's movements in a deft ballet that belied his sixty-two years. He pushed the control forward with his arm, then back again sharply, and the saw sliced into the log, sending another two-by-four onto the skid. To Alton's left through the double doors Roberta could see Ben Reynolds and his oldest son, Wayne, stacking boards in a pace that kept up with Alton's. Alton raised his hand, and the sawmill engine ground down to a rumble and died. Motes of sawdust settled in the air, and the men's movements seemed to wind down, too, as they broke out of the morning's rhythm.

"Good logs, Alton," Ben was saying, wiping his hand on a rag. "We'll get a good piece of work out of them today, eh?"

"We're going to have to pick up the pace to do it," Alton answered.

"Hey, we've been going full bore all morning. I don't believe we can go much faster, unless I get Steve up here to help out. You're going to burn up the mill if you push it anymore."

"You let me worry about that. I've been running this mill for forty years and it ain't quit on me yet."

Roberta realized she was eavesdropping, but she couldn't help it. Even she had noticed how driven her father had seemed at the controls. She knew the market was good for lumber now, and Alton's was one of the few independent mills left. But as long as he had gas enough to deliver, he shouldn't be in any race to get his boards to customers: They should be waiting for him.

Wayne was looking busy in the far corner of the building, at a discreet distance from his father, who had lowered his voice so that Roberta could barely hear him. "Listen, I know you're worried about Maine, but we'll get by him," Ben was saying. "Steve can get you gas if Maine shuts you off." He said something else Roberta couldn't make out, and Alton nodded. "I'll get Steve up here this afternoon, and we'll get the day's work loaded."

Her father turned and Roberta stepped out of the shadows, hoping it looked as though she had just strode up from the road. "Hey, Daddy, coffee's on."

"Roberta." That nod again, and he spat tobacco juice. "Ben, Wayne, let's take a break."

Wayne was two years older and even more handsome than his brother, but there had never been a spark between him and Roberta; he had been married since high school and had two little girls. She regarded him now with curiosity. Wayne was quiet and shy, and Steve cocky and sure, but it was Wayne who seemed to be so much more together—married, a father, and a man who relied on hard work instead of schemes to get ahead. If only Steve were a little bit more like Wayne. Still, she hated to admit, it was Steve who attracted her. Wayne was a little too together, a little too stable. He was handsome, yes, but also a little dull.

"Welcome home, Roberta," he said with a polite smile. *Well now,* she thought. *If he isn't the first person to say that.*

Wayne probably knew exactly what their fathers had been talking about, but he would never tell her. That was the Swamp Yankee honor code: You mind your business, and I'll mind mine. Alton and Ben Reynolds had been friends for a lifetime, but Roberta knew Alton would just as soon not have had that conversation a few minutes back. If there was a way to do anything alone, he would do it.

What did it all mean? Roberta watched her father's back as he strode purposefully toward the house. She never could match her stride to his, although she had tried hard, even as a child, often breaking into a run to catch up. He was even heading to his coffee break as though a man with a gun were at his heels. There would be no asking him what and why. She would have to figure it out herself.

Something was haunting Alton, some pressure she didn't know about. What did Fred Maine have to do with it? That old dairy farmer, who had been state senator for as long as she could remember, had always been stuck in her father's craw. They had never been friends, but then she wasn't sure anyone counted himself a friend of Fred Maine. People were afraid of him, they catered to him, they did business with him, but friendship wasn't part of the equation.

When she'd headed to Smith, it had burned bitterly in Alton's heart to sell his favorite woodlot, but it was selling it to Fred Maine that hurt the most. Maine would clear-cut it, mine it for gravel, dump in a few inches of topsoil and carve the twenty acres into house lots, Alton said. Funny, but Maine hadn't done any of that; instead, he had thought of something far worse—to let it be, so Alton had to walk down Sawmill Road every day to see a full wilderness of swamp maple and oak that he couldn't touch.

So what was Maine up to now? He seemed to be controlling Alton's gas allotment somehow, or interfering with his deliveries. Whatever it was, it had Alton in a fury to get his logs sawed, loaded, and out on the road. He was not above taking risks to get the job done, that was for sure, but his risks had always been in the spirit of adventure, to be translated later into a tale of vainglory. He could brag about sawing logs so big they bent the saw's teeth, or felling giants that missed his head by a whisper of air, or packing logs so tightly the body of his International truck swayed in the wind. But though he pushed himself, he never pushed anyone else. Not the way he had today.

The men filed into the house and Roberta hung back, sinking into a wicker chair on the back porch. From here she could see that many of the farm's buildings were in disrepair. The lilac bush had all but overtaken the outhouse, the roof of which had begun to rot. Not that long ago the outhouse had served a practical purpose. Roberta was in high school when Alton had finally broken down and put in the bathroom in a small downstairs bedroom.

Ida Kenyon was right; it didn't take long for a building to deteriorate. The carriage shed did have a function—besides a rusting sleigh, it housed the family station wagon on one end and stacks of cordwood on the other—but it was leaning to the east and Roberta could see birds' nests in the rafters.

The barn, too, off near the west field, needed a new roof, and it no longer stood four-square and sturdy. Once its stanchions had been home to a small but productive dairy herd, but now Gran kept only two milk cows there and a flock of chickens in the henhouse next door.

The duck pond was empty of ducks, too, and it had been years since they had kept hogs, goats or rabbits. Roberta had heard her father boast of what a fine butcher Grampa Wilcox had been. Once Gran had served the finest hams and smoked bacon you could buy, and Grampa had traveled all over the county doing neighbors' butchering. They had kept turkeys and sold them at Thanksgiving, and Gran had even made fresh chicken pies that she peddled to stores and hotels on the shore.

But Alton's interests lay elsewhere. For him, the farm was one giant woodlot waiting to be cut. He still grew hay for the cows, and Gran planted enough vegetables to sell at an honor stand in the front yard. But the days when Wilcox Farm was almost a brand name were gone.

Roberta's mind returned to the conversation out at the mill. How bad off was the family? she wondered. Bad enough to borrow money from Fred Maine? If her father owed Maine money, that might explain some of the pressure to get the lumber order out, especially if Maine controlled his gas ration. Or it could be fear that motivated Alton—the pressure of the coming winter, the uncertainty of oil and gas shortages, the sudden need to be self-sufficient. Maybe Alton had let the farm go and he knew it, enough to wonder if he could feed them and keep them warm without the government's help.

She heard the screen door slam, and her father stepped out alone. He stopped to light a cigarette and leaned up against the porch post.

"What are your plans?" he said, without looking at her.

"What do you mean?"

"Your plans. How long are you going to stay?"

"I don't know, Daddy." Suddenly she was twelve again and he had caught her smoking in the barn. The quiet inquisition was always worse than the beating that would follow. She would never find out about his troubles; she would have to confess hers instead.

But he wasn't waiting for her to reply. "I don't need an extra mouth to feed right now. I think you know that."

"I was hoping I could be a help." She tried hard to focus on her responses. If she thought about what he was really saying, she couldn't bear it. He didn't want her at home. How could he say such a thing? Worse, how could he feel it?

"I've got too many people up here as it is, trying to mind my business." He took a drag on the cigarette. "Maybe it's time you gave up this book business for good. Why can't you just teach? It's a respectable profession."

"I could teach, but not at the university. I lost my job." If he wanted to be blunt, well, she could match him toe to toe. "Hard times are everywhere. I don't have tenure, they're cutting back, and unless I get this book done I'm not likely to get tenure, even if I find another job. So you see I'm damned if I do, damned if I don't."

He stubbed out his cigarette on the porch floor and whistled.

She tried to gather up what she had left of her voice. "Do you want me to leave?"

Alton looked away, toward the back field and the woods on its edge. "Of course it's not that," he said. "But this isn't a good time right now for you or your sister to be up here. Your grandmother and I can take care of ourselves. But we don't know what's going to happen tomorrow. You could get stuck up here for quite a while."

"Would you rather have me stuck in Baltimore?"

He wiped his brow with the back of his hand. "You might wish you'd stayed there," he said.

"I just need some time to get back on my feet. I can help Gran. I'd like to help you, too, if I could." She let the hint fall in the air like an early autumn leaf, but he didn't reply. She would have to be direct without letting on that she'd been eavesdropping. "Dad, is everything all right? Really?"

He opened his mouth to answer, but the screen door slammed, and Ben and Wayne filed out. As her father fell into step behind them, he looked back at her once, then turned and headed for the mill.

CHAPTER FOUR

The next day Gran sent Roberta to Cal Woodmansee's for supplies. It was four miles to where the store stood at the end of Jonnycake Trail, much of it uphill, and she didn't relish the thought of biking it, but the car was down to an eighth of a tank, and they needed to save that for an emergency.

Alton needed gas for so many things that their ration didn't go very far. The sawmill's motor ran on number two heating oil, just like the family furnace, and it was powered by a gasoline starter. The International took diesel, and in a pinch Alton made his own with a combination of number ten motor oil and kerosene. Nonetheless, those were petroleum fuels, no matter how you divided them, and each one was rationed. Roberta knew Alton was siphoning off the family car's gasoline for other uses, and she could hardly blame him. It all came down to what put food on the table.

She found her bike in the barn, behind a stack of fence lengths in a dusty corner, and with a backpack over her shoulders she set out into the glare of an August morning. The weather had been hot and dry, the sun relentless, and she could feel the tar give beneath her wheels.

When she and Paula were kids they had waited for days like this, when you could stick the toe of your shoe into the edge of the pavement and feel it squish like Play-Doh. Now the road gave off waves of heat that carried a strong oily smell. It was rutted on the edges and needed patching badly. But the broken asphalt of Jonnycake Trail was just one more thing dependent on a petroleum product that was scarce to come by.

She arrived at Cal's, with a sore fanny and breathing raggedly, to find her father's loaded lumber truck in the parking lot. *Now what the hell is he doing here,* she wondered. Gran had said this morning that Cal might be getting a gas delivery, after so many months of being shut down, but Alton had seemed disinterested. He must not have had enough gas to make it to Hope Valley.

The store was a ramshackle one-story building with ells built out at crazy angles. Cal and his father had just kept adding on as their business grew, and two of the wings were attached to one another like a child's line of dominoes. The main room, with its rough pine floor and glass-fronted sales case, had the appearance of an old general store. To the right was a wood-burning Glenwood range around which the men sat on rainy days and dispensed opinions and gossip like a ladies' sewing circle. Inside the ells were rows of groceries lined on shelving Cal had built from Alton's rough pine boards. The first room to the left was canned goods; beyond, what Cal called "necessaries"—everything from laundry soap to rain bonnets.

The bell above the door jangled when Roberta entered, but no one looked up. Around the stove—blessedly cold on this hot August day, and serving as a display for baskets of sweet corn—Alton was sitting with a group of men engrossed in a discussion about something. "Tell Cal you want some of that hamburg," he said when she walked in, but he barely looked her way. She saw that Steve, who was standing to one side, was clearly in the thick of it, and then she recognized a man who made her heart lurch to her throat.

It had been years since she had seen Fred Maine. Yet even from behind she immediately knew it was Maine, or maybe she sensed his presence before she saw the rounded hulk of his frame and the tufts of silver hair that touched his collar. Since her childhood she had consciously avoided him. When she saw his black Cadillac in the parking lot of Cal's or the post office, she would wait until he had waddled out and driven away before going inside.

Every child in Coward's Hole probably had had a run-in with Maine, who had no children of his own and, like most bullies, picked on the young and the vulnerable. Roberta was unlucky enough, or perhaps sensitive enough, to remember two—both of which still made her feel the helpless rage and fear of the scolded child. One time had been in this very store, and as she looked over at the glass counter she could still feel the smart of his gloved hand slamming on top of hers as she tried to count the pennies to pay for a bag of caramels. No, not today, she thought, as Steve briefly glanced her way. She couldn't let herself think about all that today.

Yet it was hard not to remember. The whole room was full of this slatternly man in the green work shirt and pants, who, even as he listened to Steve, vented a guttural sound from his throat like an animal waiting to jump on its kill. He slouched forward in his chair with a hand on one knee, a hand so damaged from some unknown fate, he always kept it encased in a wrinkled brown leather glove. Without turning to face him, Roberta knew how his lips sneered and his bushy eyebrows crawled above his eyes and his whole face convulsed with the effort to keep from exploding.

She could see his temper reflected in their faces: Steve, who loved to goad him, seemed to relish the effect he was having, and Roberta knew he would keep going until Maine's face was purple and he was pointing a leather finger under Steve's nose. Her father's face was still, a studied effort not to show the contempt in which he held his neighbor, for he was a man who believed everyone deserved respect, even if they hadn't earned it. Across from Maine sat a stranger, an attractive man in his fifties who seemed oblivious to him as he leaned back in his chair and listened to Steve rant.

She walked up to the counter, where Cal already was wrapping a pound of ground beef in white butcher paper. He creased the corners without looking down, his hands moving in quick, deft motions.

"This is good beef, but we've got to sell it today. I had to defrost twenty-five pounds because I can't afford to keep that back freezer going."

From behind her Steve was shouting to be heard. "I'm telling you, they'll send somebody here the same way they sent somebody up to Coventry. Look what happened there."

"That's fine, Cal. Why don't you give us another pound? I'm sure Gran can use it."

He nodded, but he was looking over her shoulder, to the men. "What are they going to do?" he called. "Force us off?"

"Maybe Fred should answer that." Steve again.

"If your place is paid for and your taxes is paid up, there ain't much they can do, now is there?" Maine's gravely voice unrolled like stones being kicked up by a harrow. "If they's not, that's a different story."

"Would you like anything else, Roberta? Maybe some chicken?"

Behind her Alton was speaking mildly but with a tone of authority. "We don't know that they want our land for anything. They probably want to do just what they say they want to do. The thing is, we don't have to go along with it."

"She was hoping for some stew beef."

"I just happen to have some."

"I think somebody could be doing a lot more upstate." It was Steve again. "I think somebody should be getting us a bigger gas ration, so we wouldn't be beholden to the state."

It was a direct slam at Maine, and Roberta whirled to see him jump to his feet, almost tipping his chair over in the process. "I decide who needs gas, and I decide how much they need, Steve Reynolds." His voice had the eerie control of the truly enraged, and he was pointing a crooked finger in Steve's direction. "You may think you can get special treatment because you work for the town, but there is only one person in Coward's Hole who signs ration coupons. That is Senator Frederick P. Maine, and don't you forget it." He looked at Alton, then Steve again, and lowered his voice. "Of course, if somebody doesn't want their ration coupons—"

Roberta felt her stomach churn just listening to him, but Steve seemed almost amused. "Wouldn't you like that, Fred? More ration coupons for you."

"I'm going down to town hall, Goddammit, and take you off that snowplowing list." Maine was shouting now, his voice big enough to echo off the tile wall in the back room. "When I get through with you, you won't have a pot to piss in. You've been stealing taxpayers' money for years with all those damn jobs—"

Roberta had to get away from him. She put the wrapped meat in a basket and walked into the ell, the men's voices fading behind her. She had only been home a few days and already felt her old life suffocating her. Last week she had been in Baltimore, a respected faculty member of a state university, an urbane woman who shopped in organic food markets and ate lunch in Thai restaurants. Now here she was clomping around the gritty floors of this tiny store, scouring its nearly bare shelves for something to eat while her childhood came crashing down around her like cans falling off a shelf.

Fred Maine. He had hit her hand so hard that the pennies had made red circles in her palm. She hadn't thought about that day for years, but as she recalled it now Gran's list vibrated slightly in her hand, as though a breeze had come into the room.

If someone could do that to a child, they were capable of anything. But she couldn't think about that now. There was nothing to do but read Gran's elegant penmanship and try to find each item, one by one, as she put one sandal in front of the other.

A jar of cherries. Now what did she need those for? Then Roberta remembered the secret ingredient in Gran's brownies; she must be planning them as a sort of welcome-home present. She always sent Roberta off to Maryland with a tin of them, a melt-in-your-mouth dessert that bordered on a confection. Gran had always taken such care in sending her off; ironing her clothes, picking up her favorite chewing gum, and, of course, baking brownies. Now she was welcoming her home with them. Did she know, or hope, that Roberta was home for good?

She picked up a can. Asparagus. No one in the family ate it, and if they had, it grew in a patch behind the barn each spring. She moved to the baked goods aisle and found some brownie mix and on impulse put some chocolate chips in the basket. Paula had always hated the cherries in Gran's brownies, but she loved chocolate chip cookies, so maybe they could count as a peace offering. She consulted Gran's handwriting again. Jonny-cake meal. Good Lord. Didn't they have enough of that at home? How many jonnycakes could one person eat, anyway? She looked in vain near the flour and finally found three small sacks of meal on the top shelf. Then she had a crisis of conscience: Should she take all three, or leave some for the neighbors? She picked up two and then, muttering, put one back.

The men's voices were picking up again. Mostly she heard Steve's. What was wrong with him? He wasn't happy unless he yelled the loudest. Probably that was what came from being the youngest in a family of all men. His mother, fed up with Ben for one reason or another, had left when Steve was a teenager and moved into a cabin down by Lake Manchester. She lived there still, so far as Roberta knew, but she was rarely seen around Coward's Hole. The last Roberta had heard she was working as a nurse's aide at the hospital in Norwich. Steve never mentioned her, and Roberta knew enough not to bring her up. Her disappearance—for she might as well have packed up and moved to California, for all he saw of her—had made him mistrustful and not a little bitter of what the world would do to you if you gave it half a chance.

The men's voices faded again as Roberta walked into the far corner of the store. She found toilet paper and bars of soap, although neither was of the brand Gran had requested, and most of the other goods in the back room had been well picked over. Her gaze settled on a note tacked to the wall: RATION COUPONS ARE REQUIRED FOR ALL PRODUCTS CONTAINING PETROLEUM. In tiny print was a long list, from charcoal lighter fluid to petroleum jelly, of the affected merchandise and the allotment per person, with FREDERICK P. MAINE, RATIONS AGENT signed at the bottom.

So it has come to that, Roberta thought, imagining some baby's mother pleading with Fred Maine for a diaper rash cure. What did he care? Of all the people to be meting out the village rations, they had to pick Fred Maine. Or maybe, as state senator, he got the job *de facto*. In any case, they couldn't have found a man likelier to use his power for no good than the senate's longest tenured Republican.

She wandered back through the warren of rooms. A boy, about twelve, was flipping through a rack of comic books in the main part of the store, just a few feet from where the men sat arguing. It was the same boy she had seen hopping on the bicycle when Ida was driving her home. His hair was in his eyes and his sneakers were untied, but his brown eyes and rounded face had a purity about them that made her freeze.

The comic books were smaller now, and they certainly looked thinner than when she had been a girl, and when she picked one up she found they had more than doubled in price. Must be something in the ink, she reflected, and wondered if the boy really had enough money for one or was just looking, as she had so many times at that age. She noticed his hands, which were brown from the sun and a day's worth of dirt, and glanced back toward Maine. But he had not seen the boy at the comic book rack just as, inexplicably, he had not seen her.

"If the state comes up here they'll find the butt end of a gun," Steve was saying. His tiff with Maine apparently had passed. "I'm not signing over nothing, and neither's my father. They can take the high road to hell as far as I'm concerned."

She had turned just long enough to hear Steve speak, and when she turned back the twelve-year-old boy with the brown eyes was gone. He had slipped out the door without even jarring the bell, and standing by the doorway was a tall, brown man wearing blue jeans and a deerskin vest. It was Oatley, Maine's hired hand, and Roberta realized he had been there for a while, following the conversation she had tried so hard to ignore.

"The state will do what it wants." Oatley stepped closer to the men as he spoke. "And all you Europeans who came to Coward's Hole may find yourselves with only the rocky land or only the wet land, or maybe no land at all."

Roberta had not known Oatley was still around Coward's Hole, but here he was, his face ageless and unlined although he must be pushing fifty. Oatley was an Indian of the Narragansett tribe, which still lived on its ancestral lands in Charlestown, a shoreline town about fifteen miles to the southwest of Coward's Hole.

Once the most powerful tribe in the state, the Narragansetts had seen their sphere of influence dwindle to the 1,800 acres they were granted in a settlement with the federal government in 1978. They won the land claim, but lost the war. Political shenanigans had ensured that the tribe would be the only one in the country without the sovereignty to open its own gambling casino, and the Narragansetts lived in the shadow of their more prosperous neighbors in Connecticut, the Mohegans and Mashantucket Pequots, whose casinos made millions and ensured their members homes, health care and income.

Some of the Narragansetts, sharing blood with the Pequots, had chosen to live on the Connecticut reservation and enjoy this newfound prosperity. Others clung to a strong tribal identity that kept them rooted to the Charlestown land. Oatley, however, was neither of these. Whether he had Pequot blood or not, Roberta wasn't sure, but she knew he had nothing but contempt for the prosperous Indians to the west. Yet he had not lived with his own tribe in twenty years. It seemed to Roberta he had always been with Maine, though an unlikelier pairing you would not find. Her father had hinted years ago that Maine had gotten Oatley out of some trouble once, thus the beginning of their strange bond. Roberta could not imagine how much trouble it would take to indenture someone to Fred Maine for a lifetime.

"The roll of 1880." Oatley added nothing for a moment and everyone waited, accustomed to his stentorian pronouncements. "Did your grandparents tell you about the roll of 1880? Did they tell you they tried to wipe out the Narragansett nation?"

No one said anything for a moment, although they were paying attention in a respectful way, only Steve showing slight impatience by shuffling his feet.

"I'll bite," said the good-looking stranger Roberta had spotted when she first walked in. "What was the roll of 1880?"

The others looked at him, slightly alarmed, and Roberta realized he must be a newcomer. Even she had heard this speech of Oatley's.

"In 1880 the state of Rhode Island and Providence Plantations published a roll of Narragansett Indians. A list of who we were. The state declared the tribe no longer existed, and paid off each member on that roll for a piece of our land. It was illegal. It was immoral. But the state did it, and in the mind of the state the great Narragansett tribe no longer existed."

Maine, leaning back slightly in his chair, looked as though he were falling asleep. But the stranger was at rapt attention, and even Alton looked as though he were hearing the story for the first time.

Steve shifted his feet. "Jesus Christ, Oatley, will you knock it off? I'm not a European. I'm an American, for God's sake, and so are you. All that crap happened over a hundred years ago. I'm sick and tired of being blamed for something that happened in horse-and-buggy days."

"You know what they say about those who are ignorant of history," Oatley replied.

"Yeah, yeah, we're doomed to repeat it. So beware of white men bearing trinkets." Steve, ignoring Oatley's stiffening back, stubbed out his cigarette on the hardwood floor. "Listen, we've got a real problem here. Unless we all want to freeze to death, we've got to figure a way out of this mess."

Steve appeared ready to go on, but Alton raised a hand to quiet him. "Oatley, I appreciate what you're saying. And I think you're right, after a fashion. The state can make up whatever rules it wants. You know, Fred, The Ring never came up for a vote in the general assembly. It just happened, in the way that government regulations sometimes do. One minute it was a plan in somebody's drawer. Then it was a proposal. Then it was heard at some meeting nobody bothered to attend. The next thing you know the federal government's threatening to withhold aid, and the state's digging up the fairgrounds."

So this was The Ring they had been talking about at dinner.

But what did the fairgrounds have to do with it? Roberta was now unabashedly eavesdropping.

Alton spat neatly in the spittoon next to the stove. "If we want to fend off the state, first we have to stop fighting with each other. Fred, that means you, too."

The stranger had a slight smile on his face, Roberta noted, and Maine was suddenly sitting at attention. "What sort of help would you be needing, Mr. Wilcox?" His sarcasm came out like a heavy spurt of tobacco juice. "Tell me what I can do for you."

Alton said nothing. The stranger, oblivious to the dynamics of the group, crossed his legs and looked up at the ceiling. "You know, we just have to be self-reliant. I think the less we need each other, the better. Take my solar panels, for example. I'll never have to worry about a heating oil ration as long as the sun shines, and when it doesn't, there's plenty of wood to be cut."

He had a curious way of speaking, Roberta thought. She wondered if he was a teacher. His voice was cultivated, with a trace of an accent she couldn't place, and he pronounced letters her father didn't even know existed. He was an educated man, that was certain, and he carried himself with ease and self-confidence. His hands were worn and red enough to be a worker's hands, yet the nails were neatly trimmed and a gold watch touched his shirt cuff. She couldn't tell if he had joined the men's circle for amusement or out of real interest in their predicament. He probably had so much money that the state's restrictions didn't matter. A rich man can easily get the things for which a poor man must wait in line.

"I can't wait around here all day." Maine suddenly stood up, put his thumbs in his belt loops and hiked up his pants. "I don't know where Cal got the idea a tanker would stop way up here. I'm going down to Hope Valley." As he shuffled toward the door, Oatley following close behind, the group began to break up, lost without somebody to argue with. The stranger followed them through the door and got into an old blue Peugeot that started with an ugly cough, and Steve barely acknowledged Roberta as he stomped outside, too. Wordlessly Alton took Roberta's basket of purchases to the counter and pulled out his cracked brown leather wallet to pay for them.

Maine was gone. Roberta felt the tension leave her. But the unease returned as she puzzled over the men's strange conversation.

CHAPTER FIVE

Alton kept up a breakneck pace at the mill, and for days the kitchen was a whirlwind of canning and feeding the men. Roberta found the work hard on the hands but easy on the mind, and her thoughts drifted in the steamy kitchen. Every Mason jar that came out of a hot water bath was like her future sealed up under glass. Would she still be here next winter? Would she be sitting at the table when Gran opened the relish or tomato sauce? And would all the glass jars so neatly lined up on the cellar shelves be enough to feed them, if they couldn't get out?

One morning Roberta and Gran left Paula in the kitchen with a canner full of tomato sauce and headed across the street. May, who had exchanged her housedress for a sweatshirt and an old pair of Alton's pants, wanted to get the last of the blueberries before the birds did. Buckets bounced from their necks as they walked behind the tourist cabins, heading for a field about a quarter mile from the road.

Roberta had always thought it odd that the farm was bisected so; the house and outbuildings on one side of the road, another fifty acres or so of woods and fields on the other side. Why turn a forest into a cow meadow if that meant the cows had to cross the road every night, wearing a path in the field and crossing against traffic? But of course there had been no traffic in 1728 when the house was built, unless you counted an occasional ox-cart on its way to Norwich. The farm had come first, then the road.

Gran tutted to herself as they walked by the cabins.

"Got to get your father out here to paint those, or I'll end up doing it myself." Despite her appearance of frailty, Gran was setting a brisk pace, and Roberta found herself panting trying to keep up. "If he ever gets that mill straightened out, maybe we'll get some work done around here. There's no end to things I could have him do, if I could get aholt of him for a day or two."

They had come to the first bushes, which were still dotted with fat little berries. Roberta immediately fell into the rhythm of picking, the berries making plop-plop sounds as she dropped them into the metal bucket. Her eyes lingered on the smoky blue-gray fruit as she thought of the blueberry buckle and pie Gran would make later. But the image of the kitchen brought her mind back with a jolt to the realities it held.

How strange her homecoming had been. Paula was high strung and unpredictable, and their sisterhood had always been strained. And Dad . . . well, you never knew what was going on behind the metal gray of those eyes. She still had a headache from her visit to Cal's the day before, and Alton had shed no light on the men's conversation when she saw him that night. What had they been jawing about? The state taking their land, this matter of The Ring, rationed goods—it was too fantastic to be real, yet the argument she had overheard was a far cry from the typical political wrangling that occurred at Cal's.

She watched the curls of Gran's hair frizzing on the back of her neck and felt a wave of emotion, love mixed with a sort of protective angst. Gran was the one constant since she had returned home. She was older and probably weaker, but her spirit was the same. This old woman in men's pants picking blueberries was the sun around which they all spun.

"These'll taste good this winter, don't you think, Gran?"

"If they last that long." May kept on picking with her left

hand, shooing a mosquito with her right. "It's going to take more than blueberries to get us through this winter."

"Do you really think it's going to be that bad?"

"Your father's worried, I know that much. The state keeps threatenin' to pull the plug on electricity, and they keep talking about this Ring foolishness."

"What? What is this Ring?"

"You never heard of The Ring? Ain't they doing that in Maryland? I heard it was all over the country. Forcing folks to move back toward the city, herding 'em up into the suburbs like cattle. Well, this is one woman that ain't going anywhere, I'll tell you that."

Roberta had heard of something similar in Maryland, but as she was already in the city she hadn't paid much attention to it. Still, even there she had been under the impression the program was voluntary. "Gran, they can't force anybody to move. You must be mistaken."

"Oh they can't? By the good Jesus they're trying. Between the state and your sister, I don't know which is worse. Everybody thinks it's better to live in town, so you can walk anywhere. I'm not doing any more walking than I have to at this age."

Roberta smiled to herself. Gran had tramped all the way out here with barely a shortened breath, but the idea of stomping on the sidewalks of a town was too much for her. As amusing as it was, she understood. This was Gran's home; her environment; the natural habitat of a Swamp Yankee. That's what she was really saying.

"As long as they can't force you, what difference does it make? You've lived out here for years. You said it yourself. You'll get by."

Gran stopped picking then and leaned one hand across the berry bucket, as though something waited there to be born. She looked away; for a moment Roberta thought she was going to cry.

"Oh, we'll get by all right. And we'll stay right here where we belong. But bad times is coming. I feel it, Roberta. I lived through bad times. Back in the Depression, my mother sewed sheets out of grain sacks. Some days we really didn't have enough to eat. Seems like all we et was potatoes—boiled or fried up in bacon grease or sliced cold—them, and jonnycakes. It's a wonder I can eat either one these days. Times was bad. Yes, I lived through bad times, but that don't mean I have any desire to repeat them at my age."

"But Gran, you were married and here on the farm by the thirties. You must have had plenty to eat." Roberta loved to hear Gran talk about the past, but she wondered how much of it was an old woman's embellishment.

"Not after the state come in and shut your grandfather down. After we lost the herd, that was the end of our meat and our cash. And people were scared. They stopped buying even the vegetables. That's how superstitious they were—as though brucellosis could hurt more than a cow."

How could I have forgotten? Roberta thought. *How could I bring this up again?* It was seventy years ago that May's husband had lost his herd to brucellosis, but the event ran deep in the family mythology, a seminal moment when a state agriculture official in a suit and a pair of wing tips had stolen the family's livelihood. They marked time from the moment when a deadly cattle outbreak turned Grampa from an independent farmer into a desperate and furious man. The cabins were the best he could come up with to support his family—and shortly after building them he had lost his grip on sanity, and it had been left to May to make it all work.

"Gran, I'm sorry. But it couldn't get that bad again. The world is a different place."

"Well, maybe it is. That don't mean bad times can't come again, though. That don't mean we can't suffer." She began picking again, her fingers briskly combing the bush. "I just hope we don't lose power. I don't mind not having gas to go anywhere, because I don't have too many places to go, but I sure don't want to give up my automatic washer."

From behind her Roberta heard a scratching in the grass. She turned to find not a chipmunk or squirrel, but Paula, strolling up to them with arms swinging. She had a bucket of her own and set to picking immediately, not bothering to say hello.

She joined the conversation as though she had been part of it all along. "If you want to keep your automatic washer, Gran, maybe you should come home with me. I don't know why you insist on staying here this winter. You yourself just said it. It's going to be bad, a bad winter, and you could be stranded here. There's no need of it. I've told you plenty of times both you and Dad can come live with me."

Gran had stopped picking and regarded her granddaughter quietly. "Paula, your father isn't going to leave this place, and I ain't neither," she said. "He was born here, and I was born right down the road, and I'm not going to spend my last days shut up in some house in town. And if your father ever leaves that mill, it will kill him. It's all he's got left in this world to keep him going."

"The mill! *It's* killing him, seems to me, not keeping him going. Gran, why do you have to be so stubborn? It's only for the winter. You could come back in the spring—"

"Huh! If I had a house to come back to."

"You could come back in the spring when it's warm, plant your garden and pick up where you left off. Maybe by then things will be better."

"Things isn't going to get better, because we're due," Gran said. "We've had good times for too long."

"That's my point, exactly," Paula said, but she seemed to have lost the thread of her argument. If Gran agreed how bad times were, why didn't she agree with Paula? Gran obviously understood the finer points of the family's predicament, Roberta thought with amusement, but her take on what to do about it was far different than Paula's. Paula could make fun all she wanted, but Gran was a pioneer—she had lived a hard life and saw bad times as a challenge to her self-sufficiency. Retreat was not in her vocabulary, and the more dire Paula's predictions, the more memories Gran would dredge up in comparison.

"If you came home with me, you wouldn't have to worry about any of this," Paula persisted. "It's safe in town. Everything you need is right there. You can walk to the supermarket, to church, to the park. They have a nice senior center where the ladies play whist. You would really like it, Gran, if you would just give it a chance."

"Ha! I'm not going to any eye-talian church," Gran said with scowl. She had no love of Roman Catholicism; both granddaughters knew that.

"They have a Baptist church! And besides, there's no such thing as an 'eye-talian' church. There are all kinds of people in Westerly, wonderful people, and yes, many of them are Italian. There's nothing wrong with that."

But Paula, Roberta knew, had miscalculated. She had given Gran a tangent to take off on, and soon she was on it for all she was worth. Yes, Gran said, she knew some eye-talians were nice; but they were awful "clannish," and she didn't need anybody turning their nose up at her at this late stage. Twisting her own prejudice around was a classic Gran argument. Roberta knew there was no hope Paula would get her back on the subject.

But Paula was not giving up so soon. "I still don't see why you have to be so stubborn."

Roberta, watching Gran's shoulders sag, could no longer

hold her tongue. "Leave her alone, Paula. She's already told you how she feels."

"You! You're a fine one to butt in!" Paula turned around to face her, her eyes fiery. "What are you even doing here, but making things worse and making more work for everybody? As if Dad didn't have enough to worry about without one more mouth to feed! But thinking of other people has never been your strong suit, has it?"

Roberta started to reply but Paula whipped around and headed back toward the house.

"Don't mind her," Gran said finally. "She's not herself."

I'm not myself either, Roberta wanted to snap. Why did Paula have the corner on sympathy? She had a husband and a job, two things Roberta lacked, and she was browbeating Gran, but still the old woman defended her. She felt an unexpected jealousy take root. "I don't see as she has anything to complain about."

"You don't know the half of it." Gran had stopped picking and looked winded, her face as flushed as a raspberry. "I don't think things is good between them. I see the signs."

Roberta felt at once relieved and troubled anew. Paula and Ray, having problems? The very idea stunned her. Ray was so quiet and so—devoted—to her sister that she had never dreamed they had anything less than a perfect marriage. But it would explain Paula's moodiness, and her frequent visits, and maybe even her desire for a houseguest. Nothing like company to keep a fighting spouse at bay, Roberta thought.

"What's wrong?" Roberta finally ventured. "Ray loves her so. I can't believe it."

"Yes, he does love her." Gran stopped short as though there was more to say, as though marriage required more than devotion. She had pursed her lips, obviously uncomfortable talking about this most private of topics. Gran had never been a gossip.

"She's angry with me, Gran. I don't know why. If you know, please tell me."

"She's angry with everyone. She's mad with me over this foolish idea she's got into her head about me moving down there to Westerly. Why, that's all Ray needs is his grandma-in-law moving in on him. But she won't be persuaded. Don't take it to heart, Roberta. She does love you, and she needs you, and some day, God willing, she'll figure that out."

Roberta hoped Gran was right, but she wondered. The half-sisters had always had a tense relationship. It couldn't have been easy for Paula to lose her mother when she was young, and then to have her father remarry a younger woman so soon— well, that must have been almost as bad as losing her mother. Then to have a new sister, on top of a stepmother, and to have the stepmother die too—well, was it any wonder she looked at Roberta in so many different ways, hating her one minute, feeling empathy for her the next? They'd had some good times together, when Paula was the fun older sister, but they'd had hard times too, when Paula hated Roberta for existing or wanted to be the mother both of them had lost. It was a tangled mess, but they'd had Gran, firm, loving Gran, to help them through it, to dry tears and talk sensible.

Their buckets were full to the overflowing, but Roberta hated to leave. She knew she would not have time alone with Gran any time soon, and she had so many other things to say. They began the walk back, but this time they were slowed by the heavy harvest around their necks and the intensity of the sun, now almost in the center of the sky.

"Gran, what's wrong with Dad? He seems so intense lately. He's in such a rush to get this order out. Fred Maine was arguing with him yesterday at Cal's, and he seemed to be almost threatening him. Do you think he's in trouble?"

"When hasn't he had trouble?" she replied enigmatically.

"But what kind of trouble? You must have some idea."

"I try to stay out of Alton's business," Gran said, her lips pursed. Worse than being a gossip to May Wilcox was not minding your own business. But Roberta pressed on; this was, after all, her father, not some stranger they were talking about.

"Gran, please tell me. I might be able to help."

"You can't help, child. Your father's got a lot on his mind. It costs a lot to keep this place going."

"But Ben Reynolds said something about Dad and Fred Maine. Something about gas rations. Do you know what he meant?"

"Don't know as I know anything about that."

Roberta knew she was pushing it, but she couldn't help herself. "Does he owe Maine money? Is Maine giving him a hard time?"

"Lord, you do ask questions." They had come to the road now. Gran stopped, took a breath, and glanced across the street at the vegetable stand the family filled every morning. "Somebody's been stealing my sweet corn, and I wish to God I could catch 'em in the act."

They crossed the road without looking. The conversation had ended, the door was closed, and Roberta knew little more than when she had started. She wanted to tail May into the kitchen and keep asking questions, but instead she found a seat on the back porch and began to pick through the blueberries.

As she sorted the berries she went over in her mind the conversations of the morning, keeping this and discarding that. So Paula and Ray were having trouble—well, now a few things made sense. Paula didn't want be alone with Ray, so she stayed on at Coward's Hole, yet she resented every moment she was away from home, for that was the whole point of their argument: that she wanted to stay in town.

The situation was so convoluted that Roberta wondered if

even Paula herself understood it. And she was angry and resentful, and the handiest person to take it all out on was Roberta. But why? Roberta had assumed that Paula would want her home . . . wasn't that what she had said the first day? Wasn't she pissed because Roberta was off having a life, and she was stuck driving out here to get Sunday dinner on the table? So why not be glad now that Roberta was here, and leave it at that? Why, Paula could go home to Westerly now, guilt-free. So why didn't she?

Roberta absently picked tiny stems off blueberries and tossed them aside. No, something more was going on. As the bucket next to her filled with the choicest berries, her thoughts returned to what Gran had said. The winter would be bad, the state would turn off power . . . where had she gotten that idea from? Even the men yesterday, with all their dire predictions, hadn't mentioned that. Roberta couldn't imagine why the state would turn off someone's electricity, even if resources were tight. Ration it maybe, or ask people to conserve . . . but turn it off? That seemed drastic. It was probably Gran fearing the worst. And all this talk about being stuck, that seemed silly somehow. If they couldn't get gas, well, they'd just have to plan their trips better, maybe go shopping once a month, say. And they had canned enough food already to feed an army.

But her father's trouble, that seemed real. What had Gran said? Money was tight. Well, that part was interesting, but Roberta doubted it was anything new. Each year at this time it was a struggle to come up with the money, thousands of dollars usually, to pay property taxes.

So Gran hadn't revealed much of anything. Anyone could see taxes on 125 acres amounted to a lot more than a sawmill operator made every year. Alton had been chipping away at the family farm for years to pay that bill. He had even auctioned off most of the farm equipment one year, leaving only one rusty

Farmall tractor and enough milking equipment for the small herd. This year he was probably debating whether to sell more land to Maine. Maybe that was what Maine had meant yesterday when he suggested darkly that there was something he could do for Alton.

Roberta's hands grew still, and she gazed out into the backyard's August sunshine. On the subject of Fred Maine Gran had been silent. What could he be up to? Was there something Alton had that he wanted? The land. That was nothing new—Maine was greedy for it, although he already had the biggest farm in the valley.

Was there something Fred had that Alton wanted? Maybe the gas vouchers—that seemed like a good guess, based on what she had overheard at the mill. Maine was a powerful man, a state senator; it would be just like him to pocket a few favors in exchange for a gas allotment, and then try to blackmail everyone in town who needed the vouchers. Steve almost seemed to be suggesting that yesterday. If that were the case, Alton wasn't alone. But maybe he needed what Maine had more than anyone else. He did, after all, make his living carting around logs and delivering the lumber they produced. No gas, no money; yet no money, no gas. No wonder he was in a dilemma.

The blueberries had been picked over, and Roberta felt no closer to insight than when she'd begun. She was sitting there with her hands absently in the bowl when Steve Reynolds walked around the corner and stepped onto the porch. He looked at her, slightly amused, smiling lazily as though he had expected to find her there. Despite the warmth, he wore steel-toed work boots, a long-sleeved shirt and a pair of jeans. His hair was a little tousled as though he had just rolled out from under a car, which, no doubt, he had.

"You going to make me a pie?" he finally said.

"I wouldn't make you a pie if you were starving to death."

He grabbed a few berries and popped them in his mouth, and Roberta smacked him a couple of times on his arm. "Get out! I just picked those over."

"You're going to have to do better than that if you want to beat me up." He frowned at her. "Hey, you look bored. Stop picking fights, and let's go for a walk."

Roberta hesitated. Steve drove her crazy. Maddening was the word that came to mind. But there was no one else in all of Coward's Hole even close to her age that she could imagine spending more than five minutes with, especially considering her sister was on a campaign to have her thrown out of the family. And Paula, blessedly, was nowhere in sight to stop her from getting away for a while.

She put the berries in the kitchen, and they headed out. The afternoon heat showed no signs of dissipating, but aside from rolling up his sleeves Steve made no concessions to the warmth. They headed down the west field toward the trees, walking in a path bordered by waist-high grass until they entered the cool quiet of the white pine woods. The sun penetrated here in geometric bars, and the brown needles crunched gently beneath their feet.

To the south Roberta could hear the brook making its way to the river, bubbling over rocks and between the twists and turns of its mossy shoulders. The quiet settled her mind. Steve was silent too, leading the way along the narrow woods' path and occasionally holding back a sharp branch for her to pass. Roberta knew this path from her childhood. How many times had she run through here with Gran's old German shepherd, Smoky? As they came upon the brook she could just picture Smoky, putting the brakes on cartoon-style and dunking his snout noisily into the cool, rushing water. What a friend Smoky had been when she needed one, a confidant who could never spill her secrets, a gentle pal whose daily runs gave her an excuse to escape.

They crossed the brook and headed on. The Mill River was to the northeast, down the gravel Woodlot Road that intersected with the path they followed. As they crossed the road and continued on, the sound of the river's rushing headwaters gradually faded. Roberta knew suddenly where they were headed. Down this path was the state fire tower. When its spindly supports came into view behind a stand of pine, Steve stopped.

"Want to go up?"

She craned her neck and thought about it. She wondered what Steve had in mind. She didn't want to give him the wrong idea; the last thing she wanted was to reprise their long-ago romance. *But that's silly,* she thought. *He probably doesn't want to go back to that time anymore than I do.*

The ascent was a zigzag stairway with a flimsy metal railing that was no protection from a serious misstep. As they began to climb, she felt her legs burn and her breath come quicker. But Steve had bounded up ahead, taking the steps two at a time, his work boots shaking the tower's frame. The metal made a humming noise like rails announcing a coming train. At the top Steve unlatched the entry, which opened above them like a trapdoor. He easily scrambled inside but Roberta hesitated for a second, until he pulled her in all at once with one arm, dragging her onto the platform like a fish being pulled onto the deck of boat. She still lay there after he had kicked the door shut and fixed the latch.

He bent down to help her up.

"Was that necessary? I wasn't going to fall." She wiped off her shorts and scrambled to her feet.

"I don't know. You were teetering quite a bit."

She gave him a withering look but could think of no rejoinder.

Damn him; he was always so amused by her. She looked around. The tower room was square and enclosed in glass, giving a panorama of sky and treetops. She had the discomfiting sensation that if she pressed too hard against the windows she would fall out, taking the whole tower down with her. But Steve seemed perfectly at home in this basement of the clouds.

Along the walls were built-in angled shelves, the type found in old-fashioned print shops, and on one shelf lay a clipboard. Steve began thumbing through its pages as an air traffic controller might read the report filed by the last man on duty. Then he picked up a pair of black binoculars and began scanning the horizon, up, down, left, right, in a systematic grid.

Cautiously, Roberta stepped closer to the windows. Like a movie-goer who begins to lose the frame around the screen and sees only the picture unfolding, she gradually began to take in the enveloping horizon. All around her were woods. Anyone who thought Coward's Hole would run out of firewood this winter should climb up here, she thought. The darker green was the evergreens, the paler shades the maples and oaks. Squinting, she could make out the river threading a blue vein out of Coward's Hole toward Hope Valley, and as she turned her head other features stood out.

There was the brown and rounded top of the town dump to the south, which some liked to call Reynolds' Hill. Ben Reynolds was the dump master, too, a job he had inherited from his father and effectively was passing on to Steve. To the east of the dump was Mount Laurel itself, which stood like the rigid back of some prehistoric animal. Beyond it unfolded a valley of green, dotted with the houses of suburbia.

She saw an empty space this side of Mount Laurel, and tiny figures moved on it like fleas on a dog's back.

"Are those horses?"

Steve stood before the opposite windows, aiming the

binoculars toward the west and Connecticut. He turned and passed them to her without a word. She struggled to focus them, watching the scene career around wildly until her eyes finally began to see as one again. Yes, they were certainly horses, and she could make out a riding ring and a figure inside it.

"Lucas Whitford," Steve said. "He bought the old Cook place. He has a bunch of horses, rents them out to people, people who need to get somewhere and don't have any gas. Does a pretty good business, but I keep telling him he could do better if he'd put some effort into it."

The Cook place. It backed up to the Wilcox Farm, on the northeast corner, but it had been empty through most of Roberta's childhood. She gave the horse ring one last look. Yes, it was just like Steve to think someone else was a lazy businessman.

She turned the binoculars slightly north, and a blackened stripe could be seen following the river out of Coward's Hole. It was a swath of dead trees from the fire of '36 that Roberta had heard her father tell about so many times. Alton wasn't even born when the legendary fire had swept its way from the north all the way to the sea, but his father had nearly died setting back fires in West Greenwich.

Roberta turned and saw little that was different from the view she had just scanned: lots of trees, and off in the distance the twin ponds of Lake Manchester, bisected by the highway. Then toward the south, Fred Maine's dairy farm emerged in an oasis of pine. With the binoculars she could see toy-sized black and white cows, a silo, barn and house, even a miniature tractor in a field. Then, on the farther edges of the farm, she spotted something else.

"Steve, look here."

He was writing something on the clipboard. He looked up,

half paying attention, then took the binoculars in one hand for a quick look.

"I don't see anything."

"I didn't either, at first. Look again." It had been a misty apparition, more like fog on the lenses than anything real in the distance. But then, focusing steadily, she had seen it move and change shape and rise. It was smoke.

"Oh, that." Steve seemed bored. "Yeah, I've spotted that before. That's not a forest fire. That smoke's going straight up, out of a chimney."

"There's no chimney that far out on his property. That's way south of the house and barn."

"Well, maybe he's smoking meat."

Smoking meat. Well, it was a little early for that, Roberta thought stubbornly. She took the binoculars for another look. "I wonder what the hell he's up to."

But Steve seemed to be losing interest in their conversation. He stepped behind her, took the binoculars from her gently and took another look. She was conscious for the first time of his physical presence: he smelled a little smoky himself, as though his shirt had been hanging in back of a woodstove, and the aroma was mixed in with the earthy notes of axle grease and motor oil. And something else, something sweet: the particular soap he used, a well-scrubbed smell that was fighting with all the other odors a Reynolds man collected in a day of hard work.

She felt his shirtsleeve brush her bare skin.

"Just some of Maine's business," he declared, putting the binoculars on the shelf. He came up behind her and encircled his arms around her waist.

"Steve, have you noticed this before?" she demanded, ignoring his hands.

He was brushing up against her now. "Oh, I've noticed 'it' for a long time," he said, nuzzling her neck.

"I'm talking about the *smoke.*" She brushed his hands away. "What if he was up to something? Shouldn't you investigate?"

"I'd rather investigate you." His hands were back around her waist and trying to move up her cotton t-shirt.

"Stop it. Doesn't he have to have a burning permit? What if he's doing something illegal? He'd be the first to get after you if you so much as dropped a cigarette butt in the street."

"Jesus, Roberta, I don't know." He swung her around. "Who cares? You know I'd love to catch Fred doing something illegal, but the man's wily as a fox. But it's probably nothing. If I chased after every farmer who burned his own garbage or had a smoking compost heap, I'd have the fire department out every five minutes."

"Well, I guess it must be one of those fake fires with fake smoke." She was starting to feel annoyed, and she knew she was pursuing the argument not because she cared about Fred Maine but because Steve was getting to her. His hair had smelled like pine needles. Why was she remembering that now? They had spent the whole autumn rolling around the forest floor. He had pulled off her jeans and buried his head between her legs. Now she would give anything to be seventeen again, when all that mattered was his mouth and tongue and the screaming pleasure they brought her.

But now she was thirty, and the man standing next to her fixed junk cars for a living and had never gone to college. He had no interest in all the things she had become. He had never heard of chai, had never traveled outside New England, and probably hadn't read a book since high school.

As though he read her mind, Steve kissed her, wrapping his free hand around her back as he pressed his mouth against hers. The feel of his lips, the musky smell of his skin and neck and hair, the firmness of his hand on the middle of her back, all of it was so enveloping that she didn't even struggle to get free.

It was, of course, why he had brought her here in the first place; what better place to make his move? She was truly a captive, for she certainly wasn't about to dash back down those stairs. Then the kiss was over, and the physical pleasure in its wake made her even more annoyed.

"Why did you do that?" Roberta demanded.

"Because you wanted me to."

She hooted. "Oh, and I suppose I was sending off some special female signal that only you can interpret!"

"Yeah, like smoke." He smiled. "Like smoke from a greasy hot pan."

"Let's get out of here."

"Why? No one can see us up here. You couldn't find a better place to get away from it all." He had released her, but reluctantly.

"Steve, I don't think this is a good idea. The past is past."

He backed away, shaking his head. "You know what your trouble is? You've got this idea that you're something special now, with your big professor's job and writing your book and all those hot city clothes. You're too good for me, is that it?"

"Stop shouting. You know that's not true."

"Why shouldn't I shout? Is somebody going to hear me? Maybe Maine has the place bugged! Why don't you go home and tell the family that one?"

He pulled a pencil out of his pocket, looked at it, then put it back. "We could be having a lot of fun, you and I," he said quietly. "What's to stop us? We're two adults. No responsibilities. We're living in Eden up here. We could be running around the woods naked, and nobody would ever know." He lowered his voice and put his hands on her waist. "There wasn't a day that went by that I didn't think of you. But I had made up my mind that you were never coming home, and I figured if you did you'd have a husband and kids with you. I couldn't believe my eyes that Sunday when I saw you standing in that dining room."

"Steve—"

"Listen, Roberta. I'm not stupid enough to think you're still in love with me, or even that I'm still in love with you. But don't you think there's a reason we've been thrown together again? Don't you think if there was somebody out there better you would have found him by now?"

"Maybe I have," she said. She instantly regretted it. She didn't want to have to explain any of the life she had led in Baltimore. She wanted to keep the two things separate, disconnected. Her life here, her life away; past, present, future.

"And maybe you haven't." He was regarding her seriously with those deep brown eyes. "Fine. Have it your way. But it's your loss. Sooner or later, I think you're going to come to me."

She should have been relieved, but she felt herself sag with dismay. This was not what she had planned when she got on the train. If only her body would follow the logic of her mind. If only it didn't remember that autumn in the deep pine woods. If only her mind could make her body forget about Steve Reynolds once and for all and act like the woman she had become. But it was no use. She knew she had to get out of the fire tower before she fell; she had to get back on solid ground, at least for now.

CHAPTER SIX

As the weeks wore on Roberta became reacquainted with life on the farm. In the morning she rooted out eggs from under the fluffy down of the chickens' behinds and scattered feed on the hardened mud outside the coop. In the kitchen she wrestled with sticky pie dough, scraped jonnycakes off the skillet and peeled potatoes until her hands were raw. Every afternoon she tried to get more out of the fading garden—raking up dirty mounds of potatoes, picking the last of the sweet corn, planting a fall crop of cabbage and lettuce, searching for a few ripe tomatoes. She was learning, slowly, how much work it took to keep the household going.

In September the wind turned cold and the sky gray, and one Sunday afternoon Gran said she was ready to make that beef stew. Roberta hadn't said anything when she brought the stew meat home from Cal's, but she doubted it was a good idea to freeze it after he had just thawed it out for a quick sale. Gran would not have been dissuaded anyway.

As Roberta tried to cut the sticky stew beef, she sniffed at it surreptitiously. It had that rangy smell of bad hamburger. But maybe it was just her. Gran always said she had too strong a sense of smell for her own good. She stood there at the sink counter idly chopping at it, watching as the raw meat grimed under her fingernails. Somehow, growing up, she had always avoided work in the kitchen. She always found a way to run and hide when there was work to be done—usually running with

Smoky down to the brook, which was far enough to claim she hadn't heard her name being called. She missed that dog more than she realized.

"Are you cutting that meat or mashing it?" Paula ran up to the sink and began rinsing a colander of beets.

"That depends. Are you taking a poll?"

"Don't get huffy with me. You're standing there looking out the window. It's a wonder you don't cut off a finger."

"What a pity that would be! Then I'd have to go to the hospital, and I'd be waited on hand and foot. And then you could be lady of the manor again."

Paula scowled back at her, deep furrow lines drawn above her eyes. *She really is a pretty woman,* Roberta thought dispassionately, *or she would be if she ever smiled.* She had dark, almond-shaped eyes, high cheekbones, and a thin, angular face. In a better-tempered person all that might have added up to beauty, but in Paula's face those features just made her seem more witch-like.

Now that Roberta had truly antagonized her, Paula showed not rage but exhaustion. She sighed, shut the water off and began to shake the colander vigorously. "I don't know what I did to deserve that."

"Ha!" Roberta, tired and unguarded herself, could feel her irritation building. "I come home to help, you attack me. You take every opportunity you can to put me down. And why? It's not my fault you and Ray aren't getting along."

The colander fell with a clank into the sink. "Who told you such a thing? My marriage is none of your business! Why don't you worry about your own affairs? Coming home and sneaking off with Steve Reynolds before you'd even been home a week. Look at you. You were daydreaming about him just now."

"I wasn't—" But what was the use? Paula obviously had seen her walking to the fire tower that day and drawn her own conclusions . . . which meant Gran and her father probably thought the same thing. Wonderful.

Roberta stalked back into the kitchen and put the meat in the kettle to brown. Gran either hadn't heard the tiff in the sinkroom or was exercising her discretion by turning off her hearing aid. She was mixing up some grape-nut pudding—in case Roberta's apple pie was a failure? Roberta wondered. Maybe it would be better to do something she could handle. Paula, peeling the carrots and potatoes for the stew, was obviously itching to take over. Maybe a bouquet of zinnias from the garden; a way to get out of the house. The light of late afternoon was dimming, but if she hurried there was time. Too late she pulled the garden scissors off a hook on the wall.

"Roberta, when this meat's browned put in the water and spices," Gran said. "Then we'll . . ." The old woman's voice trailed off. "What in heaven's name?"

Roberta felt her stomach lurch. Not only was she caught, but she had a sick feeling that something she had done had led to her grandmother's exclamation, and she noticed from the back door that even Paula was looking her way. She had visions of a pie made with salt instead of sugar, or stew meat burned to the bottom of the kettle.

Nothing seemed amiss when she walked back into the kitchen, except for the ominous look on Gran's face. She was leaning over the stove with a potholder folded in the crook of her arm like a newspaper.

"Touch it," Gran said.

"Touch what?"

"Touch this burner. Go ahead, touch it."

The electric coils where the stew pot lately had sat, Roberta noticed, were black, not red. Tentatively, she put her fingertips on the burner. It was as cold as a refrigerator door handle.

"Did I forget to turn it on?"

"No! Don't be silly. Try all of them—they're as cold as a skunk's nose in January."

"Maybe the stove's broken."

"Not likely. Try the light switch."

Roberta did as she was told, and nothing happened. They then walked about the kitchen, trying the toaster, peering into the now darkened refrigerator, pressing down on the electric can opener. Nothing.

"Blasted fuse box," Gran was saying. "That pie's probably ruined. I wish Alton would get here."

Roberta's father was off making a delivery. A vague sense of alarm began to spread through Roberta. But Gran, after the initial shock, seemed unperturbed. She was rifling through the junk drawer, looking for a fuse.

"I told you this could happen." Paula stood in the door of the sinkroom, her arms folded. "Now what are we going to do?"

"Oh, you, be quiet."

Roberta had never heard Gran speak that harshly. It was not the words, but the tone. She wanted to say something to calm them all down, but she couldn't think what it would be. Even as Gran headed for the cellar with a new fuse, Roberta felt the discomfort spread. They all knew a blown fuse wasn't the problem. And when Gran came back, her face was steely gray. As she returned the fuse to the junk drawer Alton walked into the kitchen. Roberta knew he could read panic in their faces.

"Power's out," Gran said shortly.

Alton took off his hat and dropped it into the rocking chair.

"I'll be damned. Well, I wouldn't put it past the bastards. I'll call Ben and see if he's got power. If he don't, I guess we know the state's made good on its threat."

"Could be a pole," Gran said, but when Alton picked up the receiver he shook his head.

"Phone's out, too."

Gran exhaled and began plodding around the kitchen, wrapping up the food and stowing it in the now dead refrigerator. For a moment the only sounds in the room were the mechanical tick of the mantel clock above the stove and Gran's white nurse's shoes shuffling from the stove to the fridge. Finally Alton picked up his hat off the chair and reached for his coat.

"I ain't going to sit here. We've got to see how everybody's doing. I believe there's enough gas in the wagon to take a little ride."

To Roberta's surprise, Gran declared she would go, too. Soon they were all piled into the station wagon, Gran in the front seat next to Alton, and Paula and Roberta in the back, taking their natural places like actors in a revival. *Here we are*, Roberta thought. *An American family.*

It was dark enough now for the kerosene lamp to glow in a front window at the Reynolds house, immediately answering their question. Ben invited them into the sitting room, and they all began to talk at once, even Paula showing signs of excitement. But Steve stood back in the doorway, regarding Roberta meaningfully. Was he looking at her in love, or lust? She wondered. But it was neither. It was impatience.

"This isn't a coincidence," he began. "Cal Woodmansee told me down to the store yesterday that some state worker's been nosing around. Trying to get people to join The Ring."

"You think that's got something to do with this?" Gran asked.

"I don't think, I know. It wasn't some car hitting a pole, that's for sure. There aren't enough cars on the road. No, this is no accident. This has got the State of Rhode Island written all over it. That's how they do it, you know. They make life more and more unbearable until you're forced to move."

"Steve has a point," Alton said, stubbing his cigar out in Ben's ashtray. "They probably figure The Ring'll look pretty good if we can't use our flush toilets or keep our food cold."

Paula looked from one to another. "Don't you think they have a point? And we don't even know if this was deliberate. Sooner or later it's going to come to this. It might as well be now, before the snow flies."

"Maybe you don't mind being routed out of your home, but I do," Steve said. "I'm going down to Hope Valley and see what I can find out."

Ben and Alton exchanged glances, and Gran bit her lip. Into the silence came Molly, who jumped on Roberta's lap with an insistent "mew."

"You better be careful," Alton spoke up. "There are plenty of people who would love to run into a truck with a full tank of gas. You'll find yourself walking home—if you can walk."

Roberta patted the cat absently. "Is it really dangerous?"

"Dangerous!" Steve's voice startled her, and Molly, annoyed, let out her claws. "This isn't some college campus. Yes, it's dangerous. People are desperate. But don't worry. I can take care of myself."

From the wall behind the couch he pulled down a shotgun and then began rummaging through the fireplace cupboard for bullets.

"We should get out of here while we can," Paula said. "Is this the way you guys want to live? Never knowing what's going to happen next?"

"That's the way I've lived my whole life, and I haven't figured out how to tell the future yet," Alton observed dryly.

But Paula was not about to be shushed. "Suppose the electricity doesn't come back on? You can't live up here all winter without power."

"That's just what they want you to think," Steve retorted. "They want you to feel helpless. The more helpless you feel, the more likely you are to take the easy way and move out of here."

"I ain't about to move," Alton said, glaring at Paula. "We've got a hand-dug well and candles and an outhouse. We'll get by. It's not the electricity that worries me. It's the gas. If they cut us off . . ." His voice trailed into hoarseness. "What will we do when there's no gas at all?"

His question hung ominously in the air. Not even Steve had an answer for it, but its very existence—the possibilities it evoked—was enough to send them all speculating to themselves. Life was going to change, whether they moved or not.

Steve left, and the Wilcoxes said goodbye to Ben. Alton drove back to the post office, where Ida lived with her elderly mother. The Kenyon house, too, was dark except for one oil lamp flickering like a firefly in a window.

As they piled out of the car, Gran refused to budge.

"Make sure you come back with the shirt on your back." She still thought Ida was lifting vegetables from the honor stand. Just last week she had sworn there were potatoes missing from the root cellar, and in fact the lock was loose enough to force, Alton had agreed. But Roberta, as much as she disliked the ornery old postmaster, doubted she could be responsible for all the thefts to which Gran attributed her.

Roberta felt an unrestrained curiosity as she and Paula followed their father to the back door of the one-story house. She had never been in the Kenyons' living quarters and wondered how the old woman lived.

But when Ida let them into the small kitchen Roberta was surprised at how warm and cozy it was. The table, covered with a red-checked oilcloth, held the remains of a plain but inviting supper of roast chicken, green beans and rolls. Ida's mother, Dolores, was rocking in a chair in the corner, working on a cross-stitch. Another hurricane lamp, not visible from the driveway, lit up the table. The room was papered in a vivid yellow print and the white cupboards appeared clean and bright even in the lamp's shadows.

Ida did not invite them to sit down, but she greeted them without her usual sarcasm. "Did you walk down here in the dark? I don't know what surprised me more, losing electricity or hearing a knock at the door."

Her mother went on sewing, although how she could see the stitches in the dim corner of the kitchen, Roberta couldn't imagine. Alton took off his hat. "We won't stay, Ida, I just come to make sure you was all right. Ben's lost power too. Probably it's all of us."

"What do you suppose it is?"

"The state, I imagine. The keep saying this'll happen from time to time. I guess maybe we better get used to it."

"Wish I'd got me a generator. When Fred said—" she stopped. "When I heard this could happen, I didn't quite believe it."

But Alton wasn't about to let that go. "Fred? What did Fred say?"

"Nothing. He bought a generator, you know, for the cow barn, that's all." She spread her hands flat against her apron and made a step toward them as though ushering them out the door. "Where's May? Did you leave her home alone?"

"She's in the car," Paula spoke up. For a moment Roberta thought she was going to say more, but Alton put his hat on. "How are you fixed for kerosene?"

"Fine, fine. My lamps are cleaned and full, got enough for every room in the house." She seemed relieved at the change in subject. "Could use some groceries, though. Last time I was at Cal's, the shelves were nearly bare. Not a very good year for the garden, was it?"

Roberta, looking again at the remnants of the night's dinner, didn't think the Kenyon ladies were starving. She wondered what that garden comment was about. It was a good thing Gran hadn't come in; she was liable to say anything.

They said their goodbyes and trailed back to the car. Paula was hooting before Alton had started the engine. "She was claiming they had a bad garden this year," she said. "Those beans looked an awful lot like yours, Gran."

Gran shifted around in the seat, clearly beside herself. "Ida Kenyon hasn't planted a garden in twenty years. She's too busy tooting up and down the road in that Jeep. I'd like to put my Social Security number on every God-damn bean that I grow."

Roberta said nothing. What, she wondered, had Maine said to Ida Kenyon about buying a generator? Did the senator know something about this outage? Enough to warn some and not others? She wanted to ask her father about it, but she knew Maine was a sore subject. She stared at the back of his head, wondering what he was thinking.

They were heading to Paula's grandparents, her mother's folks, the Teffts. They lived on the Cook Road in a small but rambling one-story house. Although the Teffts were one of the oldest families in town—they had bought their land from the Indians, it was said, and one branch of the family had been massacred at the hands of the Narragansetts—today they were poor, barely scraping a living off a three-acre lot that was all that remained of the family homestead. Since the house had been swept away in the 1936 Fire, they had lived in a glorified shack that had probably been an outbuilding at one time. Bud and Amy were old and alone, still struggling to make enough to pay their taxes though they were past retirement age.

Roberta had never been entirely comfortable in the Teffts' house. They were nice people, to be sure, and they had never done or said anything to exclude or hurt her; but she was not of them and they were not of her, and nothing could change that. Amy Tefft was a slim, pale woman with thinning salt and pepper hair that barely covered her scalp. She had Paula's sharp nose and penetrating eyes, and Bud Tefft—a short, rotund man—

resembled his granddaughter in the way he curled his lip down when he was displeased. But Roberta could see little of the perky Peggy Tefft Wilcox in the two. Mostly, they looked tired and spent, as though their daughter—or maybe just her death—had drained whatever life they'd once had.

Bud welcomed them into the kitchen, where they, too, were sitting by kerosene lamplight. Mrs. Tefft was sitting by the stove, taking up the hem in a pair of work pants. They seemed neither surprised nor interested in their guests, merely taking it as a matter of course that the whole Wilcox household would use up precious gasoline to check on their neighbors.

They sat around the kitchen table, resting elbows on its red Formica and making polite conversation. Roberta thought they were acting odd, almost wary, but no one else seemed to notice anything amiss. Amy offered them gingersnap cookies and coffee, and, having had no dinner, they ate ravenously.

"I'm going to bring that tractor back over to you before spring," Alton said to his former father-in-law. "I think the whole damned block is going to have to be rebuilt, I don't know."

"I wouldn't do that, Alton," Bud said slowly.

"Well, I think it needs it," Alton persisted.

"If it does, I won't be here to do it."

Roberta thought for a moment that Bud Tefft's girth had finally caught up with him. His declaration sounded like a death sentence.

"We're going. Selling out," Bud said. "The state's going to buy us out, lock, stock, and barrel, and give us a place to live. I figure we'll be gone by April."

Roberta inhaled sharply. So the Teffts had signed on to The Ring.

"Bud, you can't mean it," Alton said.

"I do, Alton." He sounded tired. Amy Tefft watched her husband out of the corner of her eyes, maybe for signs of wavering. But there seemed to be none. "I'm too old to be working. And I don't make enough on Social Security to pay the taxes on this place. It's not like I have anyone to save it for. The boys is all set over in New York, they're doing pretty fine, and . . . well, Peggy's gone, and I don't think Paula wants this place."

"Oh, Grampa." Paula seemed genuinely moved that he had thought of her. "I think you're doing the right thing," she added, with feeling. "You'll be so much more comfortable. And Gramma Tefft won't have to do any more sewing, unless she wants to do it. I just think you'll be so glad you did this."

Her enthusiasm made Roberta wonder if her half-sister had known all along about the Teffts' plans and perhaps even played a part in convincing them to go ahead.

"Amy Tefft, I've known you for too long to think that you really want to do this," Gran spoke up suddenly. "You think you're going to be happy in some apartment? With a bunch of neighbors? Why, you can't stand it when Bill Fenner drives his truck near your woodlot or lets his dogs run over the back field. What'll it be like when you've got a neighbor above, below and on either side of you? What if Bud wants to fix his own truck and they won't let him? What if they won't let you hang out your washing? What if they tell you how much company you can have and when you can have it?"

Amy Tefft put the mended pants in a bag and came back to the kitchen table. "We can't stay here, May," she said flatly. "We can't make the payments. Bud and me . . . we took out a mortgage on Fred Maine a few years back, 'cause we needed the money bad. And there ain't enough business up here anymore to pay our bills. Oh, you've been faithful to us, Alton, and Steve Reynolds has, too, but aside from that we haven't got too many customers. All the big accounts don't want to come way up here, too expensive to drive."

This was an incredible soliloquy from such a normally

reserved woman, Roberta thought, but she could see that Amy was speaking for her husband. In the dim kerosene light she saw in Bud's flushed face all the pride and shame that such a move would engender in a true Swamp Yankee. People in Coward's Hole paid their bills and made good on their debts, and to fail in any of that could not be lived down.

"You know what this means, don't you?" Alton asked. "It's the beginning of the end for all of us. First you go, and where will I get my tractor fixed, or the sawmill's motor repaired? And what about Fred? Even he relies on you to fix his machinery. What the hell is he thinking of? First you go, and then someone else can't make it. And that person, well, maybe they made some contribution to life up here . . . sharing this or that, helping us all get along . . . and the more people go, the harder it is on those of us who stay. Pretty soon this whole place'll empty out."

"It's not just Fred, especially," Bud said, drawing circles on the hard Formica. "He likes to make a big fuss when I miss a payment, but he keeps stringing us along. He knows he needs me, and he needs you, Alton, as much as he'd like to take our places from us. No, it was a lot of things. We're getting along in years, you know. We won't be able to stay here forever anyway. This just sort of makes it all easier, somehow."

"Easier?" Alton snorted. "Easier for who? Easier for the state maybe . . . You really want to do this, Bud? You've lived here all your life. You were born on this land. And your father, and his father before him. This place don't mean anything to that state fellow, but it means something to you. Your folks is buried up in back. Will you ever come back to visit their graves? Will you ever set eyes on the place again? Can you just go off like this and not turn around to look back? I can't see it. I can't."

Roberta had never seen Amy Tefft angry, but now she seemed furious. And in her eyes was something Roberta had never seen—desperation, maybe, or some sort of desire.

"Maybe we don't want to die on this place," she said. "Maybe I'm tired of living in this tumbledown shack with the wind blowing through it all winter. Tonight it don't even have electric lights. Maybe I don't want to spend the rest of my life taking up some neighbor's pants or letting out a dress for some woman who eats too much of her own cooking. Look at my hands. The arthritis is so bad I can't even stretch out these fingers all the way. And when I hold the needle they cramp up something terrible. That's how you want me to live, Alton Wilcox? Look at your mother. She's a lot older than I am—and you know it's true, May—and she's too old to be living up in these woods using the backhouse and filling up the wood stove in the middle of the night. And she has help. I don't. It's just me and Bud, and maybe we'd like to live out whatever years we have left in a nice, warm, snug place with new floors and new cabinets and a handyman who's just a phone call away. Besides, it's our choice, ain't it?"

Roberta could see her grandmother's back stiffen at Amy Tefft's comments about her age, and Alton stood up and put his hat on. They all made moves to put their coats on and say their goodbyes, trying to pretend that the two families—sharing so many ties—had not just had words, unminced words, about something so important to both. Paula, the one who linked them all, hugged her grandmother Tefft and whispered something to her. Then she hugged her grandfather, and Roberta heard her promise to come see them before they left.

The heater was barely working in the car. It had not had a chance to warm up, and Alton said he doubted it would before they reached home. But as they headed back down Cook Road he stopped again and pulled off the road, into a gravel driveway. Roberta looked out to see a Saltbox farmhouse, candles flickering in the back windows. This was the old Cook place that

Steve said was home to Lucas Whitford.

"I'll run in and make sure he's not leaving us too," Alton said, and Roberta added quickly, "I'll come with you." She was relieved when Paula agreed to stay behind with Gran.

Even in the darkness of the landing she recognized the man who opened the door as the distinguished stranger she had seen talking with the men that day at Cal's. He was probably in his late fifties, although he looked younger, and there was something in his face—perhaps a glint of humor in those green eyes, or that self-deprecating half-smile—that she found disconcerting.

He welcomed them into the kitchen, where candles flared from the table, the fireplace mantel and the windowsills. He and Alton talked like old friends, which, Roberta began to realize, they probably were. But Alton refused Lucas's offers to sit down and have coffee.

"Don't worry, I won't be leaving this place," Lucas said, and his eyes seemed to blink with amusement at the very idea. "But that's a shame about the Teffts. They are good neighbors. Bud helped me out a great deal when my wife was sick, bringing us wood and doing chores while I cared for her. You can't get much more neighborly than that."

"No, you can't," Alton agreed. "I just hope no one else follows in his footsteps."

"If you think it'll help, I'll talk with him," Lucas offered. "I would say whatever carrots the state is holding out will seem empty indeed when he gets down there. That's what I moved here to get away from, you know. It all seems so seductive, all those conveniences, but they can come at the expense of your soul."

Roberta thought some of this was a little too deep for her father, but Alton was nodding knowingly, and he shook Lucas's hand firmly as they said their goodbyes. Roberta tried not to stare at him, but his moss-colored eyes were burning into hers.

As they drove home, the gasoline warning light glowed like a jack-o-lantern on the dash. Outside the trees arched blackly overhead. When Lucas had said "Stop by sometime," he had been looking at her.

CHAPTER SEVEN

Three days passed, and the lights did not come back on.

Roberta paced in the candlelit living room each night, restless and distracted, her fingers plunking random keys on the piano. Too dark to read, too early to sleep. She wondered what Lucas Whitford did at night alone in his candlelit farmhouse.

What had all that been about? He was obviously flirting with her, and she rather liked it. He certainly was more charming than Steve who had thought nothing of manhandling her up at the fire tower. Subtlety was not his game. But this Whitford, despite his age, had a gallantry and an intelligence that had shined in the darkened night.

She wondered what his story was. A widower, her father had said, still getting over the death of his wife. Funny, but he didn't seem to be in mourning the night they had come calling. Alton said he had been a lawyer but had given up his practice to please his wife who wanted to move to the country. Roberta wanted to ask more, but she didn't want to give voice to the questions that burned in her. What was such an urbane man doing in an old Saltbox in Coward's Hole? Now that his wife was dead, why didn't he move back to the city? His life certainly would be a lot easier.

Part of her restlessness was the distraction of Lucas Whitford, but most of it was worry about Steve. He had not returned. Roberta was torn between an irrational anger that he would take off on such an escapade and guilt that she hadn't tried to stop him. Apparently road trips were dangerous, more danger-ous than she had suspected, and she had made a fool of herself at his house that night by not understanding the risks.

Still, it was hard to believe that Steve couldn't take care of himself. Who would want to meet up with him toting a shotgun? Maybe his disappearing act was a grand community gesture, and he would come home with news to shed light on their predicament. But somehow it just seemed like another example of his impulsive nature. He had gone off "half cocked," as Gran would say, and now they had more to worry about than losing electricity.

Ben came every day and conferred with Alton on what to do. Should they wait, or try to go find him? Was it worth using what little gas they had left to search for him? Would he return on his own? Little seemed to be accomplished by these conversations.

"You know, we could be at war again," Ben said on the third night, leaning forward intently in one of the Wilcoxes' kitchen chairs. "We could be at war and not even know it."

"What, you think they drafted him?" Alton could not hide his amusement.

"It's coming, I tell you. How long are we going to put up with this before we take over one of them countries? It's been two years of things getting worse and worse and worse. We've gone to war for less."

"Maybe we have, but seems to me if we was at war we would have heard something about it by now. No, I don't think Uncle Sam has your boy, Ben."

"Then who does?" Ben stood up and slammed all four legs of the chair on the floor for emphasis. "When he comes back I'm going to wring his goddamned neck. Alton! We've got to go find him."

Alton nodded slowly, went outside to spit tobacco juice and returned, with the same observation he made every time Ben visited. "We could search from here to Sunday and not find him. We might's well stay put."

To see Steve's father every night agonizing over the possibilities was too much to bear. Ben was a man of few words, like her father. Ordinarily he spent most of his time chewing the end of a pipe or rubbing one hand on his grizzly whiskers. He could be counted on for a dry one-word observation but little else. Roberta had never heard him talk so much in her life. At the end of each evening, his voice was raspy, whether from exertion or emotion she could not be certain.

"I think we should go see the senator," Ben finally declared.

"Don't be foolish, Ben," Alton said in a low tone.

"I don't care. There's no other way."

"He can't help you, but he'll pretend he can. And you can't afford to make a bargain like that."

"You know all about that, I suppose."

"Watch it."

"You can come with me or I'll go alone. But I'm going."

"What in hell is that going to accomplish? He can't find Steve any more'n we can. But he'll pretend he knows something, and then he'll get out of you whatever it is he wants. Before you know it he'll be your landlord."

"I don't care, if it brings Steve back! Wouldn't you do the same, if it were your child? Wouldn't you do anything to find him, or her?" He was pointing to Roberta, who tried to look inconspicuous as she checked the water heating up on the wood stove. "What do I have, besides my boys? A junkyard? The town dump? A farm that barely turns over a thousand bales of hay? What is it without them? Wayne, you know, he's got his family. He's on his own. But what would I do without Steve, Alton? Who do you think is running things over there now? Not me. He's the dump master now, for all pract'al purposes. He's learned the fire warden's job. He runs the junkyard. I come over here to have something to do. He's the one who's bringing in the money now. Smart boy, he is. And he takes care of his old man. Pretty good cook, you know. You'd be surprised. Keeps the books. Does our taxes. Last year he saved me a bundle. Reads all that fine print, you know, finds things we can do to cut it down a little. On the up-and-up, mind you. And he takes care of the house. He wouldn't want me telling this, I suppose, but he even hems my pants. My hands shake, can't do some things. He takes care of them for me."

Roberta felt torn by embarrassment and intense curiosity. She stole a glance at Ben's green work pants—yes, there it was, a line of barely discernable stitching about an inch above the bottom.

Somehow, Alton talked Ben out of enlisting Maine's help, but the next morning he took Roberta aside and told her he was going to visit the senator himself. Roberta didn't know what surprised her more—that he was going off to see Maine, "hat in hand," as he put it or that he had invited her along. She tried to fight down the feelings of panic that Maine always engendered.

Alton knew she had overheard his conversation with Ben, and he probably figured it would be better to take her than Paula, who kept pressing the family to move and might say anything to Maine. And he needed a witness; that was the gist of it. He wanted someone to hear every word Maine said. If Alton needed her help, she'd have to go, no matter how that fat bastard made her skin crawl.

"About ten o'clock he goes in for his coffee break," Alton said as they walked west toward Maine's place. "Remember: Let me do the talking."

Fred Maine lived on a sprawling farm that sloped down to Lake Manchester, with a view of Connecticut on the opposite shore. The land was rocky and steep, more suited to sheep than cows, but Maines had been dairy farmers here since the Revolution—not as long as the Wilcoxes, but long enough.

Fred Maine was inside having coffee when Alton knocked on the side door, and he let them in with a gruff hello. In the dark, smoky kitchen Roberta tried to get her bearings. The room was not unlike most of the farmhouses in Coward's Hole, but it was obvious that the senator had not kept it up since he had lost his wife, Cora. Pots and pans cluttered the sink, the floor was gritty underfoot and the smell of salt pork and dog food lay heavy in the air.

Maine shook Alton's hand, and to Roberta's surprise she noticed his hands were bare. His right index and middle fingers were stumps, and even in the dark she could tell the hand was shrunken and pink. Alton clasped the hand seemingly without noticing it, but Roberta could not take her eyes off the scarred flesh. She had seen plenty of woodsmen who had lost fingers to an unforgiving saw rig, but she had never seen anything like this.

"Shouldn't you be working?" Maine asked Alton abruptly. He brushed some newspapers off two kitchen chairs so they could sit.

"What's the use of sawing boards when I ain't got enough gas to deliver 'em?" The way Alton said it the sentence ended with only the faintest question mark.

"You get the same business ration as everybody else."

"I must not get the same as you, the way I see those milk trucks runnin' up and down the road."

"Those milk trucks ain't mine. They belong to the co-operative."

This is not going well, Roberta thought. *We just got here and already they're arguing about the rations—and that's not even why we came.* But remembering her father's admonition, with effort, she kept her mouth shut.

Alton began asking Maine about the dairy business, and they launched into a long, complicated conversation about farm machinery. Roberta shifted in her seat. She knew this was how business was done, how conversation was made, but she would never get used to it. Why couldn't they come to the point?

"How's that new generator working?" Alton was leaning back and lighting a cigarette, as casually as if he had asked about the weather.

"It works great as long as you got gas to feed it. Damn blackout's costing me a fortune."

So that had been his lead-in.

"What do you think this is all about, Fred?"

"Damned if I know. Legislature's not in session. I ain't been off the farm."

From the back room a tall presence stirred. Roberta, whose eyes had adjusted to the dimness, realized that Oatley had been sitting in the other room all the time, watching her. He sat up now and walked into the kitchen, put another stick of wood in the stove and then sat down in a chair against the wall.

Fred looked nervously at Oatley, then stirred up a tornado in his coffee cup. "What do you expect me to do about it?" he went on. "I ain't working for Roger Williams Electric, you know."

"I don't expect you to do anything about it, Fred," Alton said slowly. "I just wondered if you'd heard anything, that's all. Steve Reynolds left the night the power went out, and he hasn't been back. I wondered if you'd been to town or heard anything about him."

"Steve's missing, huh?" Something in his eye glimmered.

He's enjoying this, Roberta thought. *Suddenly he's interested.*

"He's probably on a toot somewhere. He probably got down to the tavern and drunk up all his money."

"He is not on a toot." Roberta could not help herself. Maine just loved to tear everybody else down. "He was trying to help

88

us, which is more than I can say for some people."

Maine looked at her as if he was seeing her for the first time. "Is this little Roberta? She's starting to look like her mother, Alton. You better watch out."

Alton stood up, and for a crazy moment Roberta thought her father was going to strike Maine. But Maine was still seated, smiling, looking up at Alton as though he were pleased with his reaction.

"Haven't got your payment this month, Alton. That makes you two months behind."

"You'll get your money."

"Interest is adding up."

"I can add. That's not why we come."

From the rear of the room Oatley rose, his head grazing the ceiling. He looked from Alton to Maine and then, almost as an afterthought, to Roberta. She thought his standing up was a threat, but out of the corner of her eyes she saw her father faintly smile. But Maine must have seen Oatley's rising in the same way Roberta had, for he stiffened with a new resolve.

"Why don't you go down the road?" he said.

They left then, Roberta following quickly on her father's heels. But while she expected Alton to be grimly silent on the walk home, he was garrulous, talking about everything but the strange encounter from which they had just fled. Finally she could stand it no longer.

"What was that all about?"

"I'm not sure he does know anything. But that doesn't mean we didn't learn something."

He did not elaborate, and Roberta could not stop puzzling over the cryptic remark. Learn something? The only thing she had learned was that her father was behind in his payments to Maine, and that seemed almost as important as any clue to Steve's whereabouts. If he didn't come up with the money, they would lose the farm. Then they all would be moving in with Paula whether they liked it or not.

"Dad, did you notice Maine wasn't wearing his glove? I don't think I've ever seen him without it."

"Only wears it when he goes out. Doesn't like to show his hand in public, but I guess he figures whoever comes into his own home knows him well enough to take it."

"What happened to him?"

"His hand? That was years ago. He was a kid, oh, four or five years old, during the Big Fire of Thirty-Six. He and his mother got trapped up in the farmhouse, and he ran through a break fire to get her out. His hand was burned, and he lost part of two fingers. Imagine a little boy doing something like that."

For an instant she felt a flash of compassion for Fred Maine and shame at her hatred of him. "How horrible! He must have been terrified. But what about the rest of the family? Where was his father?"

"The old man wasn't so lucky. He was down in the barn trying to get the cows, and he couldn't escape. Burned him alive with most of his stock. The sisters, they was safe at school . . . 'Course, I don't remember any of this. I wasn't even born yet. But your grandmother said Fred's been scared of fire ever since."

Alton said no more about Fred Maine, and they spent the rest of the short walk in silence. But from the creases in his forehead and the grim set to his mouth, Roberta knew her father was still back at the farmhouse listening to Maine's taunts about the loan. It killed him to owe money. If you owed someone money, they owned you—your time, your labor, your freedom.

Nothing good had happened since her arrival. This was just one more calamity she had stumbled upon. The days now were taken up with the simple work of keeping the household going, and she tried to lose herself in the tasks at hand. She brought in wood and stoked the stoves. She pulled up buckets of water from the old dug well, an ell off the kitchen that until the blackout had been boarded up. She swept the outhouse of cobwebs and, when nature called, tried not to think about the tiny black spiders who kept returning to its corners.

She found herself daydreaming about Baltimore. She would drift off and suddenly be having lunch in the little café around the corner from the university. She imagined the meal over and over: arugula salad with fresh ground pepper, iced tea with a sprig of mint, a sinfully large chocolate chip cookie for dessert.

Gran seemed to take the changes in stride. Although she was aggravated at the timing of the event, she seemed to see the loss of power as no more inconveniencing than an early frost or a surprise snowstorm. She had put to rest Alton's plans to dive back into his lumber order and quickly put him to work getting in the winter's wood, which he stacked in two cords inside the carriage shed. Then she insisted he clean the chimneys one balmy afternoon, and after that she dispatched him to the outhouse, where he rehung the door and then lifted the trapdoor in the rear to spread lime over the contents beneath.

On Steve's fifth day missing, Roberta roamed the house dusting. In the living room she slowly traced a piece of Alton's old undershirt over the fireplace mantel and around the objects found there, the small loving cup that her grandfather had won in the county woodsman's contest and a china moustache cup with a funny curled lip. She dusted the Victrola that once played scratchy 78s, the console TV that now stood silent, and the top of the upright piano, where rows of ancestors posed in silver and gilt-edged frames. A hand-colored studio portrait from the 1960s showed Peggy Tefft, Alton's first wife. It was hard to reconcile that graduation picture with the thin, unsmiling woman in the photograph next to it. In this photo the woman, bundled up in a cloth winter coat, was holding a baby in a blanket, almost as though she were offering her up to the highest bidder. Perhaps she had been sick then and no one knew, Roberta thought.

Roberta dusted around the photos mechanically but quickly, saving for last the eight-by-ten portrait of her mother on her wedding day. In the gold filigree frame Jacqueline Miller smiled back at her daughter. She was alone, wearing a mantilla-styled veil and a rich silk gown that fell in folds from her full, curvaceous frame. She had a heavy mane of dark hair, and her radiant smile showed white teeth and full lips. But it was the deep brown eyes that held Roberta's gaze. They seemed to be watching her in all their deep mystery.

Roberta put the portrait back. She had long since removed every particle of dust from the elaborate frame.

She had promised Gran she would go to the dump before it closed. This was a chore she didn't mind because it was a rare chance to drive the car. The family had not yet found an easy way to get the garbage cans the half-mile from Wilcox Farm to the dump. Alton said the short trip would leave him enough gas to get to Hope Valley the next time a tanker came in, but next time they would have to find another way to get there. Roberta had taken on the job, and surprisingly Paula didn't protest, probably because she hated all the mess of rinsing the recyclables. In Westerly, they had garbage pickup, she pointed out.

It felt good to drive the station wagon. Roberta could imagine that she was free and independent again, even if the illusion only lasted the ten minutes it took to drive to the Dump Road, leave the garbage, and drive back. The old Chevy wagon was a far cry from the Honda, but at least she was in motion; and here there was no one else on the road to worry about, no lanes to change, no parking spaces to jockey for.

The dump was a mountain of refuse just past the Reynolds farm. Ben Reynolds owned it and leased the land to the town, which was why he was the dump master. It was hard to tell where the Reynolds junkyard ended and the landfill began. The field south of the Reynolds house had once been home to a small dairy herd, but now all that grazed there were the rusting bones of cars and trucks and heavy machinery.

The dump was deserted and the dump shack empty when Roberta pulled up. That was no surprise, given that Steve was still missing. She was used to driving up and hearing his music blaring from the window of the shack, usually some vintage All-man Brothers tune. But today the dump was silent, save for the wispy sounds of stray papers skipping across the ground and the last dead leaves rustling in the woods nearby. Even the row of white-bellied sea gulls huddled atop the dump shack made no sound as they waited for the first scent of fresh food.

Roberta began to sort and toss the recyclables, sending metal cans and glass bottles crashing into the green Dumpsters lining the edge of the property. They had so little trash now, just two bags a week, and even fewer recyclables. It was so difficult to get to the store that Gran was more likely to make a soup than open a can of soup, or unseal her own spaghetti sauce instead of relying on store-bought.

She put the recycling container in the back of the station wagon and reached for the bags. She dreaded this part of the chore, now that the state had outlawed plastic trash bags. It meant dumping the refuse in a trench near the mountain of trash, so someone could sort through it all before it was buried, and putting the soiled but empty bag in a recycling can. Inevitably it also meant spilling discarded food or eggshells onto one's shoes and reaching into the bag with bare hands to dig out the last pieces of garbage. It was certainly an effective motivator to recycle. Gran heaved most of the leftovers into the compost heap, but it was the messiest stuff that ended up here—the meats and oily foods that wouldn't break down. Some people just tossed this stuff over a wall, but Gran was adamant there was nothing worse than discarded bones to attract vermin.

"Don't forget the plastic bag rule."

Roberta turned toward the empty gravel apron. Steve stood outside the dump shack, leaning against the doorjamb with his arms folded in mock censure. He looked pretty much as he had that day in the fire tower, wearing old jeans and a green flannel shirt with the sleeves rolled.

She ran up to him and hugged him, forgetting their awkward truce in her surprise. She stepped back and grabbed a shirttail that hung loose from his pants, tugging it in consternation. "Where have you been? We've all been worried to death about you. Does your father know you're home?"

He laughed that rich, throaty laugh that usually made her speechless with aggravation. But she could only stand there and marvel at his presence. He was back, as suddenly and unceremoniously as he had left. He must have been in the dump shack the whole time, watching her, although she could not see him.

He grinned broadly. "I meant it about those plastic bags."

"Steve! Don't be maddening. Tell me where you've been."

"It's a long story. And, yes, my father knows I'm home. Don't think I didn't regret worrying him every minute I was away." The smile was gone and a shadow fell across his face. "I have a lot to tell you, Roberta, and it isn't all good news. But I don't want to tell you here. I'll pick you up tonight after dinner. Now let me help you empty those bags."

CHAPTER EIGHT

It was still light when Steve drove up in his Olds Cutlass. Roberta had not taken literally his promise to pick her up, figuring he had burned too much gas with his past week's adventure to take the car out again. But there was his pride and joy, with its cream-colored landau top glowing white in the sharp angles of the early evening sun. He opened the door for her, and she sank back into a brown vinyl bucket seat and easily fit her legs under the dash.

They drove south, back toward Hope Valley, and Steve was silent. She could feel him pushing the car to go faster up Mount Laurel, power shifting as they neared the top. Fifty-five. Sixty. Seventy. Roberta watched the needle move in tiny jerks clockwise around the face of the speedometer. They were descending now, but Steve hadn't let up on the accelerator. The needle read eighty now, and still he said nothing. Roberta forced herself to be quiet too, wondering what game of nerves he was playing with her. She could feel the engine vibrating under the strain. Eighty-five, and still the Olds took the curve at the bottom of the hill. They were nearing ninety, and the engine was beginning to knock.

"Damn gas." As abruptly as he had sped up, Steve slowed the car, which whined as the needle began to move back to fifty-five. Then he slowed and turned onto Arcadia Road with the elaborate care of a suburban father squiring his family around the neighborhood.

"Sorry about that." He turned to her for the first time since she had gotten in the car. "I just wanted to see what she could do. I just wanted to remember that I could still do that, if I wanted to . . . I didn't scare you?"

Now she was pissed. "You scared me half to death! How much gas did you burn back there, anyway? And where the hell are we going?"

"I told you I had some things to tell you," he said patiently, not answering her questions.

They drove to Arcadia Pond. Once the shore had been a family beach with a snack stand and restrooms and lifeguard chairs, but now all that remained were two foundations barely visible in the sand. Steve parked in an asphalt lot rutted with holes and deteriorating speed bumps.

"Remember the time I pushed you off that dock?"

Roberta could taste the sudden pouring of pond water into her mouth and feel the weeds that tugged at her ankles. If she closed her eyes she could see the beach that day: the shrieking children splashing; Steve's mother in a one-piece aqua bathing suit, reading a paperback on a blanket; the line of fidgeting, sandy bodies on the hill beyond the beach, waiting for paper baskets of French fries.

"You were such an asshole."

He laughed that deep roar again. "You have to admit it was funny."

"I didn't know how to swim, and after swallowing all that water I ended up getting a very nasty virus."

"I'm sorry about that, okay?" He looked serious again. "But that's not what we came here to talk about."

He leaned his arm across the back of the seat and began to tell her about his absence.

His drive that evening the power went out had been uneventful; he had met few cars on the highway, and it wasn't until he was on the interstate heading south that he realized Hope Valley's lights were out, too. He got off 95 and drove toward the village, where he found dozens of cars parked at the old tavern on Route 3. Inside people were scurrying about, and Jack Foley, the tavern owner, was trying to keep everybody sated with food and drink, although his stoves wouldn't work and the only illumination came from the dim emergency power lights at each exit.

Gradually Steve got his bearings. Residents were coming in and out, looking for information. Tavern guests hovered in the hallways, shouting questions into cell phones. They were looking for other places to stay, places to get gas, stores that might have food. They seemed to gravitate toward Jack.

Roberta vaguely remembered him, but Steve sketched in the details—a leftover from the counterculture who was pushing sixty but still wore a ponytail and Levis shined thin by the years. Hard to believe he was now the town council president, but everything comes full circle.

Steve slipped on an apron and began to pour drinks. Jack was relieved to leave Steve in charge, and soon the innkeeper was huddled at a corner table with a stranger.

"Listen, we don't want to play games here." The stranger's voice was an undertone that Steve tuned in, like a radio station running on low power. "You know why I'm here. Things are only going to get worse for you if you don't cooperate."

Jack was shaking his head. "It's not going to work, Tony. People don't want to leave their homes. This whole Ring idea is asinine. If the government had put its money into alternative fuel, hybrid cars and such, we wouldn't be in this fix."

"I don't make federal policy. Do you understand me? Do you understand?"

The man called Tony was starting to lose control of his volume, and Steve could hear the conversation without straining. But then just as quickly, his voice smoothed out.

"It's very simple. We can't guarantee gasoline delivery down here. We can't guarantee electricity. You need to cooperate, and the state will be behind you all the way. But if you buck us on this it's going to be bad, Jack, very bad."

"What do you want me to do?" Foley hissed, gesturing over his shoulder. "Go out there and tell everybody that we don't know when the power's coming back on? Tell 'em they might as well sign up for The Ring now? You know I can't do that."

"I know there are political exigencies, Jack—"

"Damn the politics!" Foley's voice rose and then he checked himself. "Damn the politics," he repeated in a whisper. "Who do you think I am? Fred Maine? I'm a man of principle. I was elected on principle, and I'm not going to bail on these people now. They don't want to leave. Can't you get that through your head?"

The state official had no time to reply, because Jack had kicked back the chair and stalked behind the bar where he began furiously washing glasses, pushing them down into the suds until Steve thought they would shatter in his hand. All the while he glared over at the table where Tony still sat, sipping a Diet Coke that had grown sweaty and pale in front of him.

"His name is Anthony Piccirelli," Steve told Roberta. "He works for the state. Has some title. I can't remember it. Foley hates his guts. He's just the opposite of Jack. One of those government types, thinks he knows what's best for everybody else.

"You were gone when all this started," he added. "Last spring was when the feds first started talking about The Ring, and then the state really came down on the towns. Wanted them to change zoning laws, make it more difficult to build in rural areas like Coward's Hole. But not all the towns would go along with it. There was a movement, a backlash if you will, to do away with The Ring altogether, regardless of what the feds wanted. And Foley was the ringmaster. He got the council in Hope Valley to pass a resolution condemning the whole idea as unconstitutional. Not all of the towns went that far. They didn't want to lose state aid. But Foley made enough of a stink about it he got on the TV news."

Roberta still didn't see what the big deal was. What did the state care about a couple of town resolutions? They didn't have the force of law.

"For The Ring to work, everybody has to sign on," Steve continued. "If the state doesn't get participation from everyone in the county, the feds won't count it. And if the feds don't count it, the state doesn't get credit in its gas allotment."

"I don't understand," she insisted. "What's this got to do with the power being out?"

"Roberta, coal may be high and the nuke plants may be in trouble, but we've still got one of the most reliable electric systems in the world. This was a planned outage."

"But why? Why would the state go to all the trouble of turning the power off and keeping the reason a secret?"

"I already told you. It all goes back to The Ring. In three weeks the state is going to sweep through here on a campaign to get people to sign up for it. And they want to make sure people are as cold and frustrated and hungry as possible when they get here."

Roberta exhaled. Poor Jack Foley. He was feisty and independent and probably a bit too liberal for most people in Coward's Hole, but he had the area's best interest at heart. She was sure of it. What a bind he was in. If he fought the state and stood up for his beliefs, he might be doing the right thing, but in the short term everybody would suffer for it.

"Well, now what? Do you think they'll just keep the power off forever?"

"Nah. They just want us to stew a while. It's a form of torture. You never know when it's going to happen again. Don't you get it? If people never know when the power's going out, it's even worse than if it goes off permanently."

"Steve, what are we going to do about it? They're not going to turn the power on until they're good and ready."

"Who needs their damn power? You know, some places, they're forming cooperatives. Using the mills for power again, selling their neighbors electricity; building windmills . . . there's all sorts of things you can do if you put your mind to it."

"Before winter comes?"

He didn't have an answer for that one. He fished into his pocket and pulled out a cigarette. They sat awhile, looking at the darkening water. Roberta's mind raced. She had thought of the power outage as a temporary inconvenience. Not like the gas shortage, which everyone knew wasn't going to go away. Oh, how could they live without both? She was so tired of tepid sponge baths and sitting in the outhouse in the damp of early morning. The kerosene lamps at night gave her a headache, and their light was too dim to read by. And outdoors it still stayed light until six-thirty, and it wasn't truly cold yet. What would they do this winter, when the sun set at four-thirty?

"One good thing came out of my little vacation. I managed to corner Foley and get the snowplow contract this winter," said Steve, who apparently was thinking of winter, too. "So I'll have that gas, at least."

The snowplow contract. It seemed ridiculous to Roberta that the town would waste money plowing roads no one ever used anymore, but it was important to keep the main routes clear in case of emergency. At least that was how Steve explained it. And he had told her before that the government was generous with his gas allotment, which meant he would have some to share if someone needed to get out of Coward's Hole in a hurry.

It was dark now and they could barely see the shadows of the pines on the pond in the gauze of moonlight. Their tiny world looked like any other corner of the state, winding its way toward autumn on a stiff evening breeze. But it was a moon in eclipse that spun on its own, no longer tethered to its mother planet. A moon alone was a forbidding place. It could support life for only so long.

Steve had begun to brush his hand against Roberta's cheek, and then he leaned over and pulled her to him in a backward embrace. He had yanked her out of the water the same way that summer she was twelve, while she choked and spat and furiously kicked her legs. Now he kissed the top of her head and slipped his hand underneath her sweater. His hands were smooth and surprisingly warm, and they easily found her breasts.

She felt warm and sleepy, slipping down into a familiar ritual of pleasure that required no thinking. She turned around and they began to make out a little. His lips tasted like dark, red berries, heavy and spicy and warm. Tonight she sensed no axle grease or motor oil or even wood shavings, just the deep musky smell of his moustache and his hair and the folds of his neck. She began to wiggle out of her clothes and press herself closer against him, as though he were the only refuge against a rising panic.

"I wanted to remember if I could still do this, too," he said into her ear. "To drive fast and make love and do all these things we did before the world got so crazy."

He began to undress her. She let his hands move along her skin, but she was not so sure as he. It had been a long time since they had been a couple. When he started to whisper again she shushed him. She didn't want to think too much about what they were doing, about why they were doing it, or what had come before. Soon her clothes were off and she was sitting on top of him, lost in a haze of warmth that at once seemed familiar and strange. Their bodies were bone white in the moonlight, and the radio buzzed in the background with a staticky voice she could not understand. But it was over too soon, too soon for her, and she wondered what had happened to that summer when they had rolled in the woods like animals.

She squirmed back into her clothes. Had she really sighed aloud, or just in her head? Across the pond the pines cast jagged shadows on the water. In the middle of the pond was an island covered in more pines, with a tiny beach of stones.

"Are you going to tell everybody?" she said finally.

He misunderstood. "About us?"

"Nooo. About what happened in Hope Valley."

"Oh. I don't know. You okay?"

What could she say? Surely he knew it could have been better, but maybe he didn't.

"Maybe this wasn't such a good idea."

"I thought you were into it."

"I was . . . look, a lot's happened in the last twelve years, you know, with me, and with you, and maybe we can't just pick this thing up again."

"What's happened? Are you with somebody? No. Am I with somebody? No. That's all we need to know, right?"

"That's a little simple, don't you think? You have no idea what's been going on in my life, and I guess I don't have any idea what's been going on in yours. There's just all this baggage."

"So fill me in."

"You don't want to know. Really. What does it matter?"

"You're the one who thinks it matters. So, come on, fill me in. Name names. Tell me all about it."

So she told him, in as abbreviated a way as she could; all those casual lovers in college, then the move to Baltimore and the years with Jordan. He was hard to explain, especially to someone like Steve. You could describe a man by what he did for a living, what kind of car he drove, even the music he liked or how he spent his idle hours, and still miss the mark. She did the best she could, and finally it came down to the only thing that really mattered. "He wasn't the one. I thought he was, but he didn't think he was. We were together a long time, Steve. Seven years. I just ignored all these little things that didn't fit, until one day he added them up himself, and he was gone."

Steve seemed to be listening intently, stroking the steering wheel with his hands as she talked. "He didn't know you," he said finally.

"Maybe."

This was the part where Steve was going to assume that he did know her, and she really didn't want the conversation going down that road. He *did* know parts of her. But that didn't mean he was the one, either. He knew where she came from, but Jordan knew the person she had become—or had made herself into. The twain might never meet, she thought. Maybe no one would ever know her completely. And even if he did, that didn't mean he would care to stick around.

Steve started up the car. As they drove away, she looked over her shoulder for one last glimpse, but the moon was shrouded completely now, and everything behind her was black.

CHAPTER NINE

Roberta swam underwater to a white light in the distance, a glowing orb in tangled eelgrass that drew her onward. But the harder she pumped her legs, the farther away it seemed, until it was only a pinprick in the distance. Still she swam on, though her lungs burned and the grasses around her turned into fingers that pulled and grasped at her legs. Now the light ahead, round like a flashlight, was growing larger. She had tried so many times to reach it, but this time she knew she could make it. Then the hands winding around her became black snakes, fat and slithery and strong as pythons. She screamed, but water rushed into her mouth, bitter and foul, washing away every effort to make a sound.

"You did a damn fool thing."

The sentence echoed in her head, as clear as if God had whispered it in her ear. In place of the white orb, the light of early morning spilled under her window shade. She shuddered, shaking herself awake. Slowly the room unfolded itself from where she lay under the worn patchwork quilt.

"I told you not to go to him." The voice that had whispered in her ear came clear to her again, this time through the floor-heating grate. Its impatience was punctuated by the clang of pans and cast-iron stove burners being slammed down. The voice was Gran's.

Roberta, awake now, leaned up on her elbows. Through the grate came the familiar smell of bacon fat spattering on the griddle. Voices weaved in and out, as the partners in conversation moved about downstairs.

She heard a low mumble that she recognized as belonging to her father. "It couldn't be helped. As soon as the state pays me for this last order, we'll be square with him."

"You'll never be square with him. He'll keep stringing you along, like he always does. I thought you had more sense."

"Listen, Ma, I've got to put food on the table. There's no room for pride up here now."

"And to think you stood here and warned Ben about him! All the while knowing you had done the same thing."

She heard a door slam; Alton going out to the mill. She washed her face with cold water, dressed hurriedly and went downstairs for a breakfast of oatmeal and hot tea. Gran, having a cup of tea too, volunteered nothing. Paula sat at the table writing a letter. Roberta watched them both with unabashed curiosity. How many secrets were they keeping? Not just from her; from each other? The whole house was entangled in half-truths and mysteries.

"I want you girls to help me clean the cabins today," Gran said. "Looks like we might have company."

Paula, who was leaning almost her entire body over her stationery in an effort to hide its contents, looked up and quickly folded the paper in half. "Why are we cleaning the cabins if Dad already boarded them up?"

"He'll have to unboard them. Some state workers are coming up here. Ida told me so. There's no one else around here in a position to rent out rooms. Lord knows we could use the money."

Roberta put down her teacup with a clank. "Did you say state workers?"

"Yes. Ida said they'd be here soon. Three of them. We better get cracking. There's a lot to do."

Gran was already up, gathering dishes and stacking them in the sinkroom. Roberta wanted to grab Gran's apron ties and pull her back in the kitchen. She looked at Paula, to gauge her reaction to this latest development. But Paula was meticulously folding her letter in thirds and putting it in an envelope. Roberta could tell her mind was not on the cabins or Gran or some mysterious state workers coming to town. It was already at her letter's destination, watching as it was unfolded and read, waiting anxiously for how it would be received.

The floor of the porch on cabin number one creaked dangerously when Gran stepped onto it. Roberta and Paula, loaded down with buckets, mops and brushes, looked at each other. Perhaps in one thing they were united: this was not what either sister had planned to do today.

"Damn mice. Don't know why those barn cats can't come over here once in a while." Gran was kicking something away from her feet as she struggled with the door lock. The door finally gave way with a groan.

From the steps Roberta could see dimly inside the cabin. Boxes, bags and old tools were scattered and stacked everywhere. Not visible were the trim bed and bureau, the rocking chair or nightstand. As they followed Gran inside, Roberta realized that every available surface was covered in junk. Car parts, Christmas boxes, shopping bags, a wheelbarrow tire, lawn rakes, seed flats, bolts of fabric; by both variety and volume, the accumulation was stunning. Roberta and Paula stood with their cleaning supplies still in their arms, for there was nowhere to put anything down.

"We'll have to do a little tidying up first," Gran said casually. "I wish your father wouldn't use my cabins for a tool shed." She began aimlessly clearing spaces as dust motes exploded into the air. As she moved things about, the tattered remains of the chenille bedspread and a stained bureau runner began to emerge into view.

"Gran, there is no possible way anybody is ever going to pay to stay here, ever, ever again." Paula spoke loudly, as though Gran were across the room. "It would take us weeks just to clear this stuff out of here. And even then, this place is old and filthy. It needs new linens, rugs, curtains. It needs wallpaper and paint. I can't imagine that the heaters still work. You'd probably burn the place down if you turned them on."

"Oh, it's not bad."

Gran began dragging things out of the cabin and onto its tiny lawn, and there was nothing to be done but follow suit. The sisters pulled out the wheelbarrow tire, the rakes and the tools, and soon their hands were grimy and their clothes dusty. They started a pile for the dump that grew into a toppling mound next to the porch. They ripped down curtains and stripped linens. They coughed and sneezed, sweeping mouse droppings and cobwebs and miscellaneous dirt from under every piece of furniture. Gran set the pace, tossing boxes and bags through the door with an almost cheerful abandon.

"We're probably going to get Hantavirus," Paula grumbled. "We'll all come down with it together. We won't be able to get to a hospital, and they'll find us here all in a pile, like in one of those Ebola stories."

Gran ignored her.

"We don't have mouse droppings in town, and we don't have rats, which these droppings just might be from, and if, God forbid, we ever need to go to the hospital, it's right around the corner," Paula went on. "And anybody who has any of these tourist cabins in their backyard has had the good sense to turn them into a garden shed or burn them down. Unless, of course, some professor comes around and tries to convince them they're some national treasure."

With effort Roberta ignored the dig. For a few brief moments she and Paula had been comrades trying to break through to their stubborn grandmother. As she always did, Roberta had forgotten the bond would not last long. They continued to work, until finally Paula sat in the now-empty rocking chair with a gesture of surrender. "Just who did you say was coming out here?"

"Oh, some state men," Gran answered vaguely. "Coming the first of next week."

"The first of—" Paula sounded as surprised as Roberta felt. "We can't have these cabins ready by next week. Are you out of your mind? We've spent hours just clearing out one cabin. I can't imagine they're going to share one. We're going to have to clean all of them."

"Paula's right, Gran," Roberta put in. "This is too much to do in a week. You didn't promise them, did you?"

"Promise them? I ain't ever met them to promise them anything. I heard down to Woodmansee's that they were coming, that's all, and that they were looking for a place to stay. We'd be the logical choice."

"Gran, you haven't rented out rooms, or the cabins, for years. There must be somewhere else they can stay."

"Roberta, I don't want them to stay anywhere else. Why should somebody else get their money? God knows we need it as much as anybody."

Roberta sighed and tossed a ragged bath mat out the door. There had to be a better way. She had some money of her own, although not much. Just enough to help Gran once in a while and keep some for a sort of stake when she was on her feet again.

But what good would that money do if they lost the farm? Could she live with herself if Maine took it away for want of a few hundred dollars? She had no idea what Alton owed, but it couldn't be that much if Gran was intending to pay it back with a few weeks' rent on the cabins.

Maybe it was as simple as that. She would offer Maine whatever she could, and he could keep it, as a sort of binder, on the condition he give her father more time. Then, when Alton finally got his state check and could repay his debt, he would do so, with no one being the wiser. And Maine would get a few hundred dollars in extra interest. How could he say no?

"Roberta, it's started to rain," Gran called out from the next room.

Their cleaning efforts of the morning lay in soggy heaps on the leaf-strewn lawn of the cabins. Paula brought the station wagon around and began stuffing the discarded items in the back to take to the dump. Roberta hurriedly helped her, all the while wondering how much gas was really in the tank. Once the needle got that low, you never really knew what it meant. Sometimes it would dive from the eighth mark to the red line without warning, and you'd find yourself stranded if you weren't careful. They had to keep enough in the tank to get to the gas station again. Paula, however, didn't seem concerned, and even volunteered to drive over to the dump after lunch. Good. Let her be the one to use up the gas. Alton would have a fit.

That would be a good time to get away to run her suddenly urgent errand. She would have to walk, so she would need to go before dark. But she could not get away until after lunch because any earlier and her absence would be noticed. But if she went too early, Maine might not be there . . . milking time. That would be her chance. He would be in the barn, so even Oatley never need know of her visit. But she would be cutting it close. She might have to bring a flashlight, for if the interview went well, she would be walking home in the dark.

The day passed interminably. After lunch Gran headed to bed, where she spent almost the entire rainy afternoon. "She's wearing herself out," Paula complained, eyeing Roberta as though it were her fault. "She's too old to be doing housework."

As penance, Roberta fixed a simple supper of tomato soup and grilled cheese sandwiches, and Gran did not protest when she brought it to her on a tray in the living room. It was still drizzling when Roberta slipped out the door and headed for Fred Maine's.

By instinct she headed out to the west field and through Maine's woodlot, the same one her father had sold twelve years before to pay her way into Smith. It had always been Roberta's favorite part of the farm, and Alton's. Maybe it was the canopy of oaks and maples that arched like a cathedral over the dirt woodlot road. Maybe it was the dark center of the woods, where Indian legend had it that the Narragansetts' queen had slept on a Rock of Dreams to divine the future of her people. Whatever it was, there was a reverence here in this rocky forest, where the Narragansetts had moved in a dance of stealth behind the boulders, always the watchers, never the watched.

Rain dripped on her nose from the trees above. Ahead she could see a break in the trees where she would cross the road to Maine's. She was only a minute or two from confronting him.

CHAPTER TEN

Two yellow squares glowed on the side of Fred Maine's barn like the occluded eyes of a monster. Down the rocky dirt road Roberta walked, her sneakers slipping on the wet rocks in the road's gullies.

Maine's black Cadillac, with its senate license plate, was backed up next to the house, facing out toward the driveway. In case he needed a clean getaway? The open doors of the barn spilled light onto the road and the grass as Roberta walked along the side of the barn. The element of surprise, she felt, was somehow integral to her mission. She didn't want him to have time to think of a way to say no, or ask something in return.

She expected to see Maine's hulking form bent over in the stalls, but Oatley stood at the barn door, as though he were expecting her.

"Evening."

"Hi, Oatley." She felt silly suddenly. What should she say to him? Were they passing the time of day, the way he would with her father? Maybe she could get away with being casual. Maybe he wouldn't ask too many questions.

"You walked in the long way."

So he had heard her.

"I came through the woodlot, then across."

"I know. That's not your land."

She misunderstood him for a moment. "I know Mr. Maine owns it, but—"

"Nobody owns Coward's Hole. But you Europeans think you do." His face was expressionless, but she felt he was laughing at her. "Ever spent the night in those woods?"

Of course she hadn't, and he knew it. But then she realized she had once, with Steve. She felt her face redden. "Oatley, I'm looking for Mr. Maine. Do you know where he is?"

"When you sleep in Coward's Hole, make sure your head's on the Queen's Pillow. You never know what dreams you'll have when your head's on stone."

Our heads weren't on stone, but we were stoned, she thought, but she was too impatient to be amused. She hadn't counted on having to get by Oatley. Too late she was remembering how much he loved to remind the world that his people had been here first. If she tried to brush him off, it would come back to haunt her, but if she let him talk, she'd never get a chance to confront Maine.

"Answer me one question, Roberta." He was leaning on the barn now, eyeing her with clear amusement. "How can you stand coming back here? Back with all of us who just aren't good enough for you."

Christ. He sounded like Ida. "Screw you, Oatley. Tell me where Maine is, or I'll go find him myself."

He smiled, scratched his elbow and nodded up the hill. He had made her mad and now he was satisfied.

She headed down the road again, this time as it wound up a hill and between Maine's two south fields. Here the cows lately had clumped together to graze. Her breathing came hard. Oatley's teasing had ruined whatever focus she'd possessed. The path struck out through the woods and became darker in the shadows of the tall pines. She saw Maine before he saw her, as she had hoped, but the sight of him knocked the speech right out of her.

He was behind the iron fence of the family cemetery. Down

on one knee, he scrabbled around with a trowel in front of Cora's grave. He was weeding, she realized, pulling out handfuls of grass and chokeweed and tossing them into a neat pile next to his shoe.

He turned around then and saw her. Whether he was startled or not, she couldn't tell, but he wasn't happy. "What do you want?"

What did she want? Everyone who came here wanted something. She had to know it, state it confidently, not stammer, not be unsure. He despised the weak, she knew.

"I've come to give you some money, some collateral." The word had just now popped into her mind. "For my father's debt. I understand you're waiting for your money."

He seemed about to laugh; something in his mouth was twitching. He raised the brim of his hat, scratched his head and then stopped.

"Can't get over how much you look like your mother."

If he had wanted to stop her dead, if he had wanted to twist her guts, he had known just what to say.

"I'm here because of my father." If she just kept saying it, maybe he would get it. "He owes you some money, I understand. I'm willing to give you some money in exchange for some time. I give you five hundred dollars; you give him five months. And no one's the wiser."

He spat tobacco juice. "Your mother was a tramp. Where was she off to that day they found her? I heard she was leaving home. Pregnant with somebody else's baby. Fine fix she was in."

Roberta steeled herself. She had heard all the stories before: Jackie was leaving Alton for another man; she was pregnant; the man was married; she was desperate . . .

"She was a busybody, too," Maine was going on. "Was on that damned pollution committee tried to write me up for my chicken manure. Got the DEM down here and everything."

"Mr. Maine—"

"Senator Maine. Senator. I fixed her." His tone had taken on a reminiscing quality, and he was looking over her head, through the trees. "Got a law passed. Now no damn town can have a goddamn pollution committee or any other such fool thing without the general assembly's say-so. That was, oh, twenty-five years ago."

Roberta didn't know what to say. She had no idea that Maine had ever had contact with her mother, or that her mother had been involved in politics.

"Senator Maine, about my offer. It's five hundred dollars cash. Right now. I have it here, in my pocket. We can shake on it now."

"Oh, we can shake on it now, can we?" His reverie was broken. He suddenly saw her again, remembered the interruption of whatever he had been doing. Maybe he was seeing Jackie Wilcox, too. "Get the hell out of here. What are you doing on my land, you little imp? Don't you know I've got more money 'n that in my pocket right now? What do I need you giving me money for? Alton owes me money. Anytime he wants to pay up, you send him on over." His voice was booming now and his face was reddening. "I don't need no goddamned woman's money. Tell your father to be a man and stop sending his women over here to do his dirty work. Go on! Get out!"

He was walking toward her, waving his arms. Roberta instinctively stepped backwards. She scrambled in her mind for something to say, some stand to take, some ground to regain. But it was useless. She was a fool, and he knew it. It wasn't money Fred Maine wanted; it was to have Alton Wilcox by the balls. Her idea had been ridiculous.

She stumbled back down the path, by the barn whose doors were now shut, and up the hill toward home. She had to get home in waning light, and she had to get a hold of herself, too. Only this time she wouldn't walk through the woods that Oatley called Coward's Hole. It was too dark for that.

She came in through the back door. A kerosene lamp smoked on the dining room table. She hung up her dripping trench coat on a hook in the hall and tiptoed into the living room, where Gran was asleep in the easy chair. She found Alton in a rocking chair by the cook stove in the kitchen, taking off his boots. He looked old and tired. Bent over in the chair; he was fixing his socks as he uttered a barely discernible groan.

So this much must be faced. She had probably made things worse for her father, and Maine would waste no time telling him.

"Dad."

He looked up, nodded and leaned back in the rocker. "Kind of wet for a walk. What's wrong with your grandmother? Paula told me she overdid it this morning."

"She wants to get those cabins cleaned up." Roberta took the telephone book off a ladder-back chair by the door and sat down.

"Couldn't you talk some sense into her?"

"Paula tried, Dad. She's got this idea she's going to rent the cabins out to some state workers. They're really a mess, you know."

"I know. She won't let me tear 'em down." Alton rifled through his pockets, finally locating a cigarette pack in the front of his shirt. "She don't look good, Roberta."

Engrossed in her immediate troubles, Roberta had barely given a thought to Gran. She had seemed tired and, yes, it was unusual for her not to perk up after a nap. Now Roberta felt worse. Not only had she poked her nose into Dad's business, but she had neglected Gran. This conversation with Alton had steered hopelessly off course. He had given her an opening with the talk of the cabins, and she had blown it.

She decided to plunge ahead anyway. "Dad, I have something to confess." Alton looked at her, obviously jarred by the last word. "I went over to see Maine about your loan, to see if I could straighten it out. I offered him money, but he wouldn't take it. I think I made things worse."

"What in hell? You did what?"

She told him the story, choking it out the way a teenager might report a truancy episode. Something in her stopped short of one detail—how much she had offered Maine. The money was still wadded up in her coat pocket, and she had this crazy vision of her father turning out her pockets and seizing upon the bills like a contraband flask of whiskey.

"I don't know what you expected to accomplish."

"Dad, I'm so sorry. I had no idea Maine would react that way. I thought the money would tempt him. I thought it would buy you time."

"Don't you know anything?" Alton had stopped rocking, and an ash hung dangerously from the tip of his cigarette. "You can't tempt Fred Maine. You can't buy him; you can't persuade him; you can't trick him; you can't win. Don't you think I would've tried the same thing? You think I'm some kind of a fool?"

"No, Daddy." She closed her eyes.

"I should've just given him that lot behind the cabins. That's what he's after. Given him the whole damn farm, for that matter. Ever since your grandfather's troubles Maine's been after it. Now I got your grandmother on me about it and you stuck your nose into it, and neither one of you know what you're talking about."

He walked over to the stove and dumped his cigarette into the fire. "I told you the other day not to say anything about that visit to Maine." His voice was booming now, and Roberta fought the urge to run out of the room. "Listen to me. Isn't it enough I'm feeding you and giving you a roof over your head? Isn't it enough I'm working my tail off trying to keep this place? If you want to do something, take care of your grandmother for Chrissakes instead of leaving her and going off half-cocked minding someone else's business."

Roberta got up and ran down the hall, but there at the other end was Gran. The old woman was wrapped up in a floral duster, her arms around her stomach and her face contorted in a frown. She didn't seem to notice Roberta's red eyes and looked past her, as though she was having trouble focusing.

"Roberta, could you heat me a bath? I can't seem to get warm. Funniest thing."

Roberta, who wanted to do nothing more than to run upstairs, turned on her heel and headed back to the kitchen. Her father sat in the rocker with his back to her as she heated a kettle of water on the cook stove. *A watched pot never boils,* she thought. How many times had she heard Gran say that?

She carried the bubbling water to the bathroom, where she mixed it with cold water from the tap. Once in the tub Gran seemed to relax a little and leaned back, so quiet that Roberta feared she might slip into sleep. But Gran began to speak quietly, almost in a trance, never looking up to see if Roberta heard her.

"I'm all tuckered out. Didn't think I'd be worried about making a living at this age, but what can you do? I guess we got to take it and like it."

Roberta helped Gran get out of the tub, dry off, and dress for bed. She tucked the old woman in with the sadness of a mother who bids her child goodnight for the last time. There was no help for it; she would have to leave. But she couldn't tell Gran. Instead she put her lips against her grandmother's papery cheek and hugged her extra tight.

CHAPTER ELEVEN

Roberta burned nearly all the kerosene in the lamp that night, and she did not come down to breakfast until she had spent another two hours clacking away on the old Royal typewriter. Her laptop, rendered useless without power, sat idle in the corner as her fingers got used to the manual.

Gran seemed her old self when Roberta finally made it downstairs. Breakfast had been made and the dishes cleared and washed, and Gran was sitting in the kitchen rocker working on some needlepoint. "Silly thing, feeling poorly," she said. "I guess I needed a good night's sleep. You must have needed it, too."

"I should say so." Paula was leaning on the sinkroom door. While Gran's comment had held a trace of concern, Paula regarded her half-sister with the usual enmity. "We could have used you around here this morning, but you were too busy writing the Great American Novel."

"I had something I had to do." Roberta brushed past Paula and took down a coffee cup from the cupboard. She knew Gran had kept the coffee warm for her, and she guessed some muffins were probably waiting for her on the sideboard. *And yes, Paula, I am famished after all that work, even if you don't think it's work,* she thought.

"I've got something you have to do, too," Paula announced. "I want Gran to have a rest today. So after you get off your fanny, you can get the men some coffee and doughnuts."

"I'd be happy to." Roberta knew that wasn't the answer Paula was expecting, and it almost gave her pleasure to be agreeable. Nothing was going to ruin her mood today. She found cranberry muffins right where she expected and sat down for breakfast. The men wouldn't be in for at least a half-hour. She'd be the willing servant, and then she could sneak off to the post office. She'd be back in time to help with the noon meal, or dinner, as the Wilcoxes called it, and anything else Gran or Paula might have in mind.

As it turned out, Gran had a bill for her to mail, and even Paula, after hemming and hawing, handed over an envelope that Roberta quickly saw was addressed to Ray. They had been apart for weeks now and she was curious about their correspondence, but Paula's unusual trust in her overcame her curiosity. The envelope was heavy, though, she noted. A long letter.

An old black Cadillac was taking up two parking spaces in front of the post office. Maine. Roberta stopped. Now what? Well, there was nothing to do but go forward. She couldn't let Maine stop her now that she'd made up her mind. She strode into the tiny foyer of the post office, which was no more than an annex to Ida's house.

Inside the narrow entryway was a wall lined with post office boxes, and around a corner in a second room was the service window. Ida stood behind it, elbows on the wooden counter, nodding her head at something Fred was saying. From the back Roberta could see Maine gesturing wildly about something, his arms going up and down on the counter for emphasis. He was dressed in saggy pinstriped pants, a matching suit coat and loafers that were turned over at the sides. Heading up to the state house, no doubt, or maybe to town hall. Wherever he was going or had been, he was plenty stirred up.

"You know what I call it. Bribery. It's against the law to bribe a public official, did you know that, Ida? You know what the penalty is for bribing a public official?"

"No, Fred, I don't."

"It's a felony, that's what."

Roberta shifted her foot. This could take a while. She shuffled the envelopes impatiently; she wanted to get them on their way. A barely perceptible sigh escaped her. It was bad enough having to deal with Ida, having to flatter and thank her to death. But having to wait seemed too much. What was the population of the town? A few hundred? A line at the post office didn't seem possible.

"I might have to do something about it, collect that debt early . . . Are we holding you up, young lady?"

Roberta's mind had just been retracing the conversation. Maine's harmless ravings suddenly had an eerie logic to them. Bribery. Debt. He was talking about her.

"I said, are we holding you up?" He turned back to Ida, muttering. "Don't have no more sense than her mother."

"I'm waiting to mail something." Roberta felt her jaw clench. All that determination she had needed yesterday suddenly steeled her in a burst of adrenaline. "I'm a paying customer. Are you?"

"A paying—?" Maine turned fully around to face her. "Yes, ma'am, I am a paying customer. I'm a state senator and your elder, and I'm in line ahead of you, and it seems to me someone in a position such as yours should show someone such as me a little respect."

Roberta felt her hands tighten around her mail. She wasn't even sure what they were talking about any more, but she was going to get him away from that window if she had to push her way past him. "Don't tell me who to respect. You're nothing but a two-bit loan shark, trying to bleed money out of every poor hardworking person you can find."

"Isn't that interesting. Ida. Did you hear what she called me? Well, maybe I am a loan shark. I guess that's what your father will think when he finds out what he owes me now. You flashing that money around yesterday, did you think I'd fall for that? He'll pay me that and a lot more before he even touches the principal. Ida, you're my witness. Roberta here isn't even denying she tried to bribe me yesterday. That's a felony, you know. Someone like you, without a record, maybe you'd get community service, I don't know."

Roberta shrugged. Instinctively she felt he was bluffing. The last thing Fred Maine would want would be a detective nosing into his loan agreements. But her hands turned to ice when he mentioned her father's name. He was going to make it worse for Alton, just as she had feared, and it was all her fault.

Her silence seemed to infuriate him more, but before he could speak again Ida broke in. "Why don't you mind your own business, Roberta Wilcox? Why did you come home, anyway? Seems like your sister is the one taking care of May, while you're running up and down the road with Steve Reynolds. She had us in stitches the other day, talking about your pies. Now you're nosing your way into the senator's business. Just like your mother. Used to come mooning around here, subscribing to all those beatnik magazines, Mother Earth Journal or whatever it was called. Pity your grandmother couldn't make something of you, but she got stuck with those Miller genes. I always said she should've sent you back to your own people. Look at you. You ain't even combed your hair."

Ida gave a final derisive snort. Roberta, stripped naked, her very soul held up to scrutiny and found wanting, her mother ridiculed, stood paralyzed. Somewhere she found the strength to walk forward and place the mail on the counter, with a ten-dollar bill. Ida, her mouth pursed in ill temper now, weighed and stamped the manila envelopes with fury and dumped them into a canvas bin, then took the letters and tossed them into a nearby pile.

She could not go home. She stumbled along the stone wall she had found, following its perpendicular turn to the north, hacking her way through fiery red tangles of poison ivy and sumac. The path was covered in pine needles but narrow, and she had to push her way past brush.

She had stumbled on the back way to the Cook Farm, and those horses must be Lucas Whitford's. The yard was empty except for the horses, which had heard her somehow and were beginning to clump at the western corner of the riding ring. Three heads and pairs of eyes greeted her, and as soon as she walked up to the fence they began to nuzzle her coat and her hand, looking for a treat.

"You've made some friends, I see." Roberta had not heard anyone approach, but by the sound of the voice, she figured it was a few strides away. How startled she was to see Lucas in a green checked hunter's coat nearly at her elbow. He smiled with the corners of his lips and the crinkles around his moss-colored eyes. "They are shameless, aren't they?"

"Yes." Roberta didn't know what else to say. She thought of what Lucas must be seeing as he regarded her. Surely her hair had not improved any since her melodramatic episode of sobbing, and by now it was probably interlaced with prickers from her hike through the bushes. And her eyes—they were not brown anymore; they must be two red puffs. What must he think?

"We met the night the power went out."

"Yes. Roberta. Hi."

"I saw you one day, walking in the woods. I would have hailed you, but I didn't want to scare you."

"I do like to walk. But I can't imagine you scaring anyone."

"Ha! Well."

They were silent. The horses had wandered away now that

they had determined Roberta wasn't carrying apples in her pockets. She looked around the farm. It had changed so much since she was a child. The horses' stalls, painted white with red trim, were new, as was the riding ring. The saltbox house had been in sad shape when she was young, and it had been empty for many years, but in the light of day Roberta could see its outside was encased in new shingles, and its chimney looked squarer than she remembered it. A tidy man lived here, one who took care of his things. Nary a leaf could be found on the back lawn. Across the ring and through a door Roberta caught sight of the stables. The floors were wood, bare of straw, and a saddle lying neatly inside looked freshly polished. But the man himself did not look excessively tidy, just pleasant enough, with brown hair mussed a little in the wind and streaked with gray, and dressed casually in a pair of tan work trousers and LL Bean boots.

"I find that wind chilly, don't you?" he said. "How about some tea, a little lunch? I was just getting ready to eat myself."

Indoors was as neat as the yard, with the vaguely masculine smells of saddle soap and tobacco hanging in the air. He motioned her to sit in a captain's chair at the dining room table, which was the only piece of furniture that had been given over to disorder: bills were wedged between salt and pepper shakers, and a basket full of junk—nails, tape, postage stamps— rested on a place mat.

"I'm afraid I don't have any lemon," Lucas was saying as he brought her tea over in a mug. "But I do have cream, if you like it that way."

While he warmed up soup they talked for a while about the deprivation of the past few months. Lucas, it appeared, rather enjoyed the sacrifices that he had made. It fit with the plan he and his wife had made fifteen years ago when they moved to Coward's Hole. They had prepared well to live on their own;

the front of the house was equipped with solar panels, and between that and the wood he cut from the farm, it cost him nothing for heat or hot water. The horses, however, were another matter, he admitted.

"They were really a hobby of my wife's, and since she died, I got rid of the trailer and I don't show them anymore," he said as he sliced some late summer tomatoes. "But they are beautiful animals, and they need the proper care. It's hard to get a vet up here. And a farrier? Forget it."

Roberta was intensely curious about his wife who could be seen in a small black and white photo on a shelf behind where Lucas stood. She was short, with a petite build, obviously well suited for riding horseback, and the hair beneath her English riding cap was a white-blonde. Roberta had known dozens of girls like her at Smith. Rich girls, girls with skin like porcelain and flawless manners—with hearts as empty as a paper Valentine. It was wrong to prejudge the woman, but she couldn't help it.

"Why do you keep them?" she asked.

"I promised Meredith. Those horses were her babies, so I guess in a way they were like our children. I couldn't part with them now. But it is difficult sometimes."

"Steve Reynolds tells me that you hire them out."

"Oh, that." He looked up from his slicing. "I do let people ride them sometimes, people I know well. But they are valuable animals, and I don't let just anyone near them."

She could not help smiling. "He seems to be under the impression that you could have a thriving livery here if you put your mind to it."

His laughter was a low, soft chuckle. "I don't see that happening." He served her the tomatoes on a bed of greens with a cup of corn chowder, and Roberta could not wait for him to sit before she dove in.

"But enough about the horses," he said as he served himself.

124

"Tell me about you. You look like you've had a bad morning. But I've said something too personal. Please forgive me."

"No, it's nothing really, just silly. I'm afraid I'm not the most popular person in town right now."

"I can't imagine why."

Against her better judgment she told him about her father's troubles with Maine and the encounter at the post office. She repeated the words, all the ugly ones, that had been flung at her earlier that morning, and by the end her eyes had begun to fill and she was clutching the tablecloth with one hand.

"They sound like cruel and insensitive people," he said. "But you can't worry about what other people think. You know what Emerson said. 'What I must do is all that concerns me, not what the people think.' Self-reliance. So many other parts of that essay are quoted, but I think that sentence really sums it up best, don't you?"

"I am so sorry. I—can't believe I just did that. Oh, this is terrible."

"Don't be sorry. I'm glad you found your way here."

She took a Kleenex from his hand and vigorously blew her nose. "It seems like my father's spent his whole life trying to get out of Maine's clutches. He pays off one debt and ends with another. He sold his favorite woodlot to Fred to pay my way through school."

"Fred Maine. He's got half the town in his pocket, and I never could figure it out. I had been here maybe six months when he came over one day. I was out back with Bud Tefft. Bud had brought his shingle mill over, and we were making shakes for the back of the house. Maine drove up in that Cadillac of his and waddled out to the backyard." As he warmed up to the story, his voice started to take on a Yankee twang. "Bud saw him first, and his face went white. I thought he'd cut his finger off. But there was Maine. Started acting all friendly, welcoming me to the neighborhood. Then he says, 'If you ever need a hand, a little extra cash, drop by.' Well, I told him normally when I needed a loan I went to a bank. Bud had stopped running the shingles through, and all you could hear was the slip-slip-slip of the belt going around and around. Fred didn't say a word, just turned on his heel and walked away."

"He must have figured you were doing so much work on the house, you needed money."

"Of course. He knows better now, though. He knows I'd have to be pretty desperate to ask him for a favor. And Ida, she's another one. When Meredith was alive she refused to go to the post office. She was convinced Ida hated her. I said, 'Honey, Ida hates everybody. It's her religion. If you want to get her goat, just go in there and be nice to her.' But she couldn't bring herself to do it."

Roberta found it odd she had something in common with Lucas's late wife. She quickly changed the subject. "I love that you quoted Emerson. I taught the Transcendentalists."

He looked up with interest as he began to clear the table. "Really? Where?"

She told them about her six years at the University of Maryland, her cabins project, and the non-renewal notice. "That, and some other things, sent me back here."

"I wouldn't feel singled out if I were you. Many lives have been interrupted these days."

They chatted until Roberta's tea grew cold, and then Lucas took her back outside to show her his latest project. Behind the barn, next to a stream, was a gristmill that had stood on the property for nearly 250 years. In the spring he hoped to grind corn into jonnycake meal, just as the Cooks had done for most of the nineteenth century. "I'd like to get Bud up here to help me with the grinding stones, but he's wrapped up in this moving idea," he said. "I honestly don't know what he's thinking."

For someone who preached independence, Roberta thought, *Lucas sure relies a lot on his neighbors.*

"And some day, if I find time, I might make maple sugar," he was saying. "I hear it's not easy, though. You have to tap a lot of trees to get so much as a pint."

They walked back up the hill toward the barn and the riding ring where Roberta said goodbye. Again, he shook her hand with his suede work glove, and he told her to come back any time, an invitation Roberta thought sounded sincere. As she walked back home through the shadowy forest, warmed by the tea and his comforting words, Roberta decided she had found a kindred spirit for the first time since her return. And she could not remember suddenly what it was she had intended to do when she got home.

CHAPTER TWELVE

Roberta expected to be grilled about her absence, but the back dining room was empty when she walked in. Plates of crumbs sat on the table uncleared, Gran's red-checked apron was slung over a chair, and the coffeepot on the sideboard was cold. Where was everybody? It was so unlike Gran to leave a mess behind. Once they had had a chimney fire and while Alton clambered up on the roof with a garden hose, she had stayed in the house to finish washing dishes.

When Roberta rounded the corner into the kitchen and found pots still on the wood range, she began to feel an icy panic crawl up her spine. Then she realized it was only the whoosh of air stirred up by Paula, who had dashed in behind her.

"He's here," she hissed. "Gran's in there with him." She motioned to the front of the house. "Oh, I wish Dad was here."

Roberta headed for the living room. So Fred Maine had made good on his threat after all, but instead of harassing her father, he was bringing his blackmail to her sickly grandmother. Her visit with Lucas seemed far away now. She tried to remember what Emerson had said, but it was gone from her mind. So much for self-reliance.

But in the living room she found not Fred Maine, but a younger man with glasses and a slightly balding head. He was wearing a dark green sweater vest and a yellow flannel shirt, but he looked more like a man who wrote hunting regulations than one who followed them. He turned and rose as she walked in, extending a hand.

"Mr. Pick'relli, my granddaughter, Roberta," said Gran.

"Anthony Piccirelli," he offered, gently correcting the pronunciation. "State of Rhode Island Office of Intergovernmental Affairs. Pleased to meet you."

So this was Steve's demon. His eyes, faintly hazel, looked harmless behind his wire-rimmed glasses. His sleeves were rolled up to the elbows. Roberta would not have been surprised to learn he had a pocket protector beneath his sweater vest.

"Your grandmother and I have been having just a wonderful conversation about our new state program," he said. "Perhaps you've heard of it."

Roberta shrugged. She had an overwhelming urge to make up some excuse, but forced herself to sit down on the hard-backed chair across from the sofa.

"Rocky Hill Apartments," Piccirelli was saying. "And the beauty of it is, it's close to all the services you need—shopping, movies, jobs, a hospital, doctors, dentists. And it will be on the bus line! So you can go anywhere. No more worrying about getting around. And you have guaranteed public utilities. Heat, electricity, hot water, even cable TV! And, there's more."

Roberta wanted to laugh out loud. How had Gran sat through this? But she was soaking it all in with a prim little smile. Paula, meanwhile, was still leaning in the doorway, a look of constrained panic on her face.

"The fairgrounds will retain many of their rural characteristics," Piccirelli was saying. "The state, you see, understands people like you. We know what you like about living, uh, way out here, and we've done our best to replicate that. Everyone at Rocky Hill will have barn space for chickens, cows and horses. You'll have access to a garden plot in what used to be the main ring. A farmer's market to buy fresh vegetables and fruits, if you don't want to garden. Hiking trails. A shooting gallery."

His voice droned on. Roberta looked down at the worn maroon carpet, which had been beaten so many times that only a single layer of threads held it together. Everything in the house was like that—hanging on by threads that were stronger than they realized.

"This is really the appropriate option for people who have chosen a rural lifestyle," Piccirelli was saying in his most stentorian voice. "The state will make sure residents of Rocky Hill Apartments have every comfort imaginable."

"And you'll serve watery oatmeal three times a day," Roberta snapped. "And if anybody tries to dig their way under that electric fence, a friendly guard will be on hand for a little target practice."

"Roberta!" Gran shook her head.

"I can't help it. This is ludicrous. You're not listening to this nonsense, are you? What is this, a concentration camp?"

Gran threw her a dark look.

"Well, what would you call it? Little chicken cubicles . . . I mean, it's ridiculous."

"I can assure you, Miss Wilcox, that Rocky Hill Apartments is being constructed using the finest construction methods, and of course, with native lumber provided by your father."

"My fa—" She stopped short. So this is why Alton had been in such a hurry to get his lumber delivered. This was his state contract, and the project was probably under a tight deadline. But why would he sell to people he despised so? Was he that hard up for money?

Paula turned on her heels and left. Had she known? But, of course. Alton was in a hurry to get his lumber sawed because the state was pressuring him; they wanted to get this apartment complex up as soon as possible. And he probably didn't want to advertise the fact he was playing a part in this charade.

Gran offered Piccirelli a tray of molasses cookies. "Mr.

130

Pick'relli has a lot to tell us, and all our neighbors. So he's going to be staying with us for a while."

And that was the rest of it. Gran had snagged her tenant.

Anthony Piccirelli, shuffling his papers, looked somewhat abashed. "You have to see it to understand it, Miss Wilcox. Rocky Hill will be a wonderful place to live."

"So was Siberia."

"Coward's Hole may seem like Siberia this winter, if you don't get your power back." There was a flash of acid in his tone, and then it was gone. "But that's why I'm here. To explain things. We believe in educating the public."

Steve's story of Foley's conversation with Piccirelli came back to her now. "Is that really why you're here? Are you sure you aren't here to sign us all up because your program needs more numbers? The governor sent you down here to do a job, didn't he?"

"Yes, I am here to do a job, one I'm proud of. A job, I might add, that would make your life a lot easier."

She snorted. "Mr. Piccirelli, where do you live?"

"Cranston. Edgewood, actually."

Roberta had a flash of the suburb, a series of tiny lots outside Providence that had been developed in the 1930s and 1940s. "In a nice Dutch Colonial. Hmm. I can just picture it. Little garden plot, a rose bush in the front. Would you leave that house to live in some apartment building the state tacked together in a few weeks?"

"I won't have to leave my home, Miss Wilcox. I already live within The Ring. Cranston is a densely populated city, with public water, sewers and other services. By living in close quarters, we are doing our part to conserve energy."

It didn't add up. She wondered how much this project was costing the state.

"It's not just water and sewers. It's electricity," he continued.

"At the fairgrounds we can build an energy-efficient building, cut down on waste. And don't forget the gas used by commuters. We're trying to get everyone to live closer together. Ultimately this project will save everyone money."

"And I suppose you're not burning up any gas tooling around Coward's Hole."

"Oh, I have a natural gas vehicle. An amazing thing. And I won't really be tooling around, as you put it, since I'll be staying here instead of commuting from home."

Roberta looked over at Gran, who had perked up again at the mention of Piccirelli's sleeping arrangements. "We had a cabin all cleaned up for you, but there's no heat out there," she said. "I think we better have you stay in the main house for now. I'll get Alton to help you with your bags after supper. You missed dinner, but supper's at five o'clock."

So Anthony Piccirelli, the state's official ambassador of The Ring, came to stay in the Wilcox household. He took the only remaining bedroom upstairs, which he slipped in and out of each day with his ring binder and sheaves of papers. Inside, Roberta figured, were maps and mechanicals detailing the wonders of a housing project being plopped onto the state fairgrounds. Just remembering its ramshackle buildings and bare, bumpy, and often muddy fields made her cringe.

Roberta would have laughed it off if it hadn't been for Gran's behavior. From the start she treated Piccirelli like royalty, and Roberta had assumed it was because he was a paying guest. But after a few days she started to wonder. He had paid his bill in full for the month, so there was no need to overdo it. She began to wonder if the old woman hadn't fallen under the spell of The Ring.

"What is the matter with Gran?" she spouted to Paula. "We have to cook for this idiot, and heat water for his baths, and

I-don't-know-what. And forget about privacy. He's right across the hall."

"Maybe he'll find the rural life not to his liking," Paula suggested. "Maybe he won't like running out to the backhouse at six a.m. or hanging up his wet socks behind the wood stove every night."

"It hasn't seemed to faze him yet." Roberta paused and then added darkly, "I hope you haven't been encouraging him. Gran doesn't belong down there, and you know it."

"And she does belong here? With no electricity, no hot water, no bathroom? I wish she'd just come home with me. It would solve everything."

"It would not. It would kill her. And so would moving to his Rhode Island concentration camp."

"I don't know as it's as bad as you seem to think, but don't worry. I haven't been 'encouraging' him, as you put it. You know I'd rather see her at home with me in Westerly."

Roberta let it go, but later she wondered. It would be just like Paula to try to move Gran to some state apartment, all in the name of creature comforts. She had no proof that Paula was lying, but she had no proof she was telling the truth, either.

Alton seemed unimpressed by the new boarder. The first night he had shaken hands with him, asked what his business was in town, and that was all. Piccirelli, for all his knowledge about Alton's business, acted as though they had never met. If he was doing business with the state, and Piccirelli knew that, it seemed logical they would at last make casual conversation about it. But they never did in Roberta's presence. She thought it strange and fought the impulse to grill her father on his latest contract. The truth was she was still wary of him after his last outburst.

She should not bother to care about any of this. It would only bring more trouble. But she couldn't help it. Each day she eagerly awaited the mail, hoping to hear word of a grant, and at the same time despaired over what she would do if the letter of acceptance came. For despite the tensions in the house, too much unfinished business remained for her to pack up and leave.

There was Gran, who seemed to need her more and more. Although May still did most of the housework, the new conditions seemed to be wearing on her. At night Roberta heated water for her bath, and the old woman sank wearily into the tub with bony knees, arms and legs that seemed to grow more sticklike every day. Roberta remembered not long ago when her grandmother had been plump as a pillow, all big stomach and soft edges. Now her flesh hung off her in wrinkled folds. She was eighty-nine, but Roberta wondered if more than old age was slowing her down.

There was Lucas Whitford, and her mind had no analysis for that. He stirred her as no one had since Jordan in Baltimore and she didn't want to think about him. Lucas and Jordan had so little in common. Jordan was her age, a child of the city who loved nightclubs and dark bookstores and avant-garde theater. He was funny, too, in a sort of self-deprecating way, and he loved to tell stories about his own failings as though they were strengths. Really, she hadn't had anything in common with Jordan, either.

But she didn't want to think about Jordan. She wanted to think about Lucas. As she lay in bed at night she imagined him peeling off her clothes right there in the horse stall, a pile of hay under her. He would look like . . . what? She imagined him virile and forceful. He would be in good shape, from all that horseback riding; she tried not to speculate on what a late fiftyish man really looked like naked. His body would be hairy and lean, she decided, and his arms would be strong enough to pin her down against the rough boards of the stable.

And there was Steve, who wanted her but didn't understand her. It had been three days since that night at the pond, and Steve hadn't been around at all. She was annoyed at him for staying away and annoyed at herself for being annoyed. It had been a mistake, that night by Mill Pond. You couldn't just pick up where you'd left off with someone, not after twelve years. Their lovemaking had been awkward and stupid and unsatisfying . . . so why was she thinking about it all the time?

She had not seen Steve or Ben since Piccirelli's arrival, and slowly it occurred to her they might not know he was here. Steve also might have learned more since that night at the pond. He was out and about more than any of the rest of them because he drove the school bus. She should go see him—to find out what he knew and share this new development.

No one was in the Reynolds' house. She decided to check the backyard and the dump. The dump didn't open until noon, but Steve could be over there working anyway. She headed down the road again, but found the dump, too, deserted. Back at the farm she saw smoke, a tiny column, coming from a shed.

"You're a sight for sore eyes." Steve was coming out of the shed, carefully shutting the door behind him. He came over to her and kissed her lightly, and she instantly felt guilty. But why? She hadn't done anything.

"What are you doing in there?"

"Oh, just a little chemistry experiment. Nothing you'd be interested in. But I do have something to show you."

He took her by the hand and led her to the huge old red barn, which once had been home to the Reynolds' dairy herd. He opened the double doors to a dim cavern lit only by streaks of sun leaking through the boards. Roberta smelled motor oil, sawdust and dirt, and something else she couldn't define— some chemical, maybe old pesticides.

As her vision slowly adjusted to the dark, she could see eyes everywhere, watching her, only they weren't eyes exactly. They were large globes that reflected the weak bars of sun. Headlights. On cars. Jammed into the barn fender to fender, door to door, so close a body could barely pass between them, but not so close that their paint and chrome touched. Sports cars from the sixties, coupes from the thirties and forties. Cars from the fifties, with fins. Cars from the twenties, with rumble seats. They stood together, facing all directions, making a mosaic of aqua and gray and fiery red and powder blue.

Roberta did not know what to say. Steve was looking at her intently. Whatever she said, she knew, he would measure finely, and she would be judged on what she thought of all this.

"Where . . . where did they come from?"

Steve laughed, then put one arm around her. He seemed like a car salesman about to expound on the virtues of his inventory. "The junkyard, where else? And there's more where these came from. I've been restoring them. Piece by piece. The ones on this side"—he pointed to their left—"are done, and these over here are works in progress. Aren't they beautiful? It takes almost a year to do the basics, and then it can take years after that to fine-tune it all. I guess even the ones over here aren't really done-done, if you know what I mean."

"You must have been working on this since high school."

"Nah. Not that long, but close. At first it was just something to do, you know, after I finished the Cutlass. I sort of cut my teeth on that car. Learned what to do, how to do it. I kept working on it after it didn't need work. So I thought, I'll find some other vintage wreck, maybe a 'vette or a Mustang or something. And we had some, but in terrible shape. But then I got interested in all of them out in the junkyard. They all have . . . personalities, I guess you'd say. The next one I did was that one way in the back, the '54 Plymouth. Lot of people collect those, but I dunno, it's not my favorite. Then I decided to do a real old one, so I turned to the Model A. That one there actually was my grandfather's. It was easy to get parts for. You know, you can go on the Internet even and get them, and they have clubs and stuff."

"You have a computer?" Roberta was incredulous. How had he gotten that by Ben?

"Yeah. Well, it's not working now, obviously."

Roberta's eyes had grown used to the darkness, and the cars about her began to take form like stuffed beasts in a diorama. Although the stalls were gone, on the barn's walls still hung the tools of a dairy farmer—milk cans and pitchforks and hay bale hooks.

Between the studs Steve had hung old magazine ads, in which Plymouths and Dodges and Cadillacs climbed scenic hills and reposed beside famous landmarks, in each one a well-coiffed woman riding shotgun.

Roberta found herself as drawn to the ads as she was to the cars Steve had restored. She walked up to one, a white convertible with lipstick red seats, driven by a woman in a long, flowing scarf. Where had she seen that car before? Where was it taking her? Why did the sight of it stop her cold?

"You like that?" Steve had walked up behind her; she could feel the warmth of his breath on her hair. "That's a '61 Thunderbird. You can tell by the rounded taillights. One of the last really big cars."

"I used to know someone who had one, that's all." Driving excitement, the ad said in big italic letters. She turned to him, feigning brightness. "So? Which one is your favorite?"

He didn't notice her dilated eyes, the flush to her cheek. No sooner had she asked the question than he was dragging her by the hand to the rear of the barn and a long-finned, pale green car. "You know what this is?"

"I haven't the faintest idea."

"A Pontiac Starchief. A relic of the fifties. Look at those fins. Makes that Thunderbird of yours look like a compact. Check out the length of this hood. And the ornament! Did you see that? An Indian chief. Know why it was called a Starchief?" He didn't wait for her to answer. "After Pontiac. Not just Pontiac, Michigan. The original Pontiac was an Indian chief."

"I wouldn't show that to Oatley."

Steve laughed. "Don't worry. Pontiac was an Ottawa, not a Narragansett."

"Well, it's something." With effort Roberta focused on the reason for her visit, and something occurred to her. "What are you going to do with all these cars? You can't drive them anywhere."

"That's just it. They're even more valuable now."

"How do you figure that?"

"What did people do with buggies, when the car was invented? What did they do with the rotary phone, when touch-tone became popular? Did they save them? Nooo. They threw them away like yesterday's newspaper. Gone. In the dust heap."

"Gran still has a rotary phone."

"May's not most people," he said impatiently. "Now follow my thinking here, hon. Most people throw them away, but then something happens. Twenty, thirty years pass, and that which was once obsolete is suddenly in hot demand. A collectible. Worth big bucks."

"I don't get it. People already collect old cars."

"But they won't be soon. If you can't find gas to get to work, you think you'll be getting gas to drive to a classic car meet? Of course not. These things are going to become dinosaurs *again*. And I'll be ready."

She didn't bother to point out to him that this had been his hobby for years, and it only had just occurred to him how to profit from it. Never mind that he'd be fifty or sixty before his plan would reach fruition, if it ever did.

"Steve, I hope you're right. Listen, I came to tell you something, and I guess it's all connected to this. Anthony Piccirelli showed up the other day, just as you predicted. My grandmother took him in as a boarder. He says he's going to stay a few weeks."

"Jesus." His expression had fallen so much, Roberta felt sorry for an instant that she had told him.

"Yeah. He's hawking this Ring, this apartment thing in Rocky Hill. He's using Coward's Hole as his home base, and he's going to be driving all over, from Foster to Hope Valley."

"Jesus Christ! What did I tell you?"

"Listen, Steve, we need to warn everybody about this guy. I think you're right about him being a snake. He's going all over the place trying to sign people up, like some aluminum siding salesman. I'm just afraid if people start going along with it, they'll force us holdouts to move, too."

"That's what I've been trying to tell you." He playfully pretended to strangle her. "Come on, let's have a cup of coffee. Maybe we can come up with something."

"There's something else," Roberta said, as they began to walk toward the house. "He says Dad's been sawing lumber for this Ring. Did you know that?"

Steve stopped at the barn door and looked off into the woods. "So that's what he's up to. You know, my father and Alton haven't been getting along. They had a disagreement about something, but Dad's like a steel trap. I can't get a thing out of him. Maybe Dad got wind of where all the lumber was going and they had words about it. But hey, money's money. Do you really think it's a big deal?"

"I don't know. It just doesn't seem like my father. He hates the state and everybody connected to it. He must be desperate to work for them."

139

The house was still empty. Ben, Steve said, had gone to Woodmansee's to put in an order. The dusty grandfather clock in the corner ticked loudly, Molly noisily bit at a flea as she licked her coat, and Roberta sat across from Steve at the kitchen table, stirring her coffee. She was too conscious of the quiet. It brought back with a flood what she had seen in the barn, and she didn't want to think about that.

Steve gulped his coffee and looked around, then gazed back at her. "When Dad gets down to Woodmansee's, it could be hours before he gets back," he said.

"Really."

"They get to jawing, you know."

"I have to get back."

"No, you don't."

He took her hand and led her upstairs.

She had never been inside his room, even when they were dating. She was struck by its lack of personality. Outside he had his cars and his tools, the barn and his cars, and even the dump shack had some adornment—a Playboy calendar he had tacked to the inside of the door. But here the walls were bare, and the room gave no impression that it was anything more than a transient's place to sleep.

They began to kiss. *I'll just do this*, Roberta thought, *and I'll forget everything else. I'll forget about Piccirelli and my father and that picture out there in the barn.*

The wool blanket was scratchy under her neck, but at least this was more comfortable than the car, where the steering wheel had dug into her back and she had felt like a teenager. When Steve unbuttoned her blouse and put his mouth to her breast, she closed her eyes and suddenly an image of Lucas loomed over her. She tried to focus on Steve but it was no use.

The man whose hands caressed her and whose skin rubbed against hers was Lucas, and beneath her head was stable floor.

She knew she was moaning and saying unintelligible things, but there was no turning back. Now was all about a built-up need that she hadn't felt the other night, and a need that certainly hadn't been met. Steve was rocking against her, skin to skin, and he wasn't even inside her when she came, squeezing her legs around him in a spasm that surprised even her. After that, she didn't mind that it took him only a few thrusts.

"I guess we came up with something," he said.

She tried to laugh. The Lucas fantasy was gone, and in its place was a flood of guilt and the specter of what she'd seen on the barn wall. She nuzzled next to him, hoping he would offer her something, some comfort, some gesture. But he had no idea what her need was. All he saw in the barn were cars.

He got up and put his pants back on. "Listen, I hate to throw you out of bed, but I've got my kindergarten run coming up."

"Oh. The bus." She hurriedly dressed and followed him downstairs, secret relief flooding her.

"I haven't forgotten about Piccirelli," he said, as they left the house. "I've got some things in mind, but I need to think about them first."

And that was all. He headed for the school bus, and she walked home. The only thing she knew for certain, the only thing that had never let her down, was this place.

She didn't know her own mind when it came to Steve or Lucas. Her father was a mystery, her mother a ghost. Gran—yes, she was the rock that held it all together, but even she was mortal.

Now someone wanted to take home away, too. So many of the new people already had left. Probably it didn't matter how many more of them abandoned ship; but the old families, the ones whose ancestors had settled Coward's Hole . . . if they left, it would be only a matter of time before the area had so few people the state would turn off power permanently. Then they would be like that old village in Arcadia, Lewis City, where only cellar holes and stone walls stood now. She could see Wilcox Farm grown up like that, trees filling in the pasture, and the empty house collapsing in on itself, until all that was left was the name of a place on a map.

CHAPTER THIRTEEN

The next afternoon, without thinking about where she was headed, Roberta struck out for a walk in the woods.

As she walked deeper into the woods she began to keep her eyes out for hunters. She was wearing Alton's orange blaze hat as a precaution. Better to look ridiculous than get your head blown off.

What had gotten into her yesterday, sleeping with Steve again? He represented everything she had tried to escape. He had no ambition that she could see, at least not the kind that would take a person out of Coward's Hole. Yesterday, lying in that austere bedroom, she wondered how a man could live that way. So much of him was a mystery. His mother, for example. He never talked about her. She lived only a few miles away, and yet Roberta hadn't seen her in years. It was as though she were dead.

She had come to a clearing. In a corner was a fence of iron rods that enclosed a small cemetery. She leaned on the top rail and wondered if she should go in. She knew most of the epitaphs by heart. *Desire Tefft*, read one, *Gone but Not Forgotten*. The writing on the stones was filled in with moss and rounded by centuries of weather. Two or three hundred years was a long time to survive the elements, even for stone.

The small cemetery was full of dead children and young men and women. They had all lived at Lewis City, and something had happened to them, something that had finally convinced their parents to pack up and move on. For there were few elders in this graveyard.

She closed her eyes and tried to imagine the village: the squat one- or two-room houses, the gardens of corn and potatoes at their doorsteps, the sheep and cows grazing on what was surely cleared land for miles to see. An old woman—maybe forty-five, but looking haggard, as old as Gran—stepping to the stone doorsill and dumping her dishwater. She calls out to a young woman bent over a hoe in the garden. "Desire," she is saying, "when are you going to—"

Roberta opened her eyes. It must have been an illusion, the figure she saw, not an old woman or her daughter, but a young man, leaning against a tree by one of the cellar holes and holding a gun pointed to the ground.

She called out "Hallooo" and made a big to-do of rustling her shoes in the leaves, and the man, or the boy, whirled around and aimed at her.

"Put that down." She hated to sound like a schoolteacher, but everything about him irritated her. He was lying in wait at a place she counted as sacred, and worse than a hunter, he was a careless one, with his untied boots, oversized flannel shirt and sloppy pants as much a sign of this as the gun he'd pointed. "Put the gun down and put the safety on, unless you want to spend the next five years at the Training School."

Something about that threat must have hit its target, for he dropped the gun and clicked the safety back on with his right thumb. "You don't have to get antsy. I wasn't going to shoot you, for God's sake."

"What did you think you were doing, aiming a gun at me?"

"Just wanted to make sure that—just wanted to see who you were, that's all."

As she walked closer to him, she decided he was either a young fourteen or an old twelve. He wasn't broad and husky like some boys of that age, but he had about him the air of fearlessness that some adolescent boys get when they grow tall enough to look their fathers in the eye.

"Is your father around here?"

"What do you mean by that?"

Strange response. "Just thought he might be out here hunting with you, that's all." He wasn't supposed to be hunting alone, but she figured she wouldn't push the issue. He might have been afraid she was a game warden. His father had taken off, probably running after that stag she'd seen a ways back, and he'd told the boy to keep a sharp lookout.

Something about the boy was familiar, under the brown paint he had smudged on his face for camouflage. "I've seen you around here before. Not here. I mean, I saw you that day at Cal's, looking at comic books."

"What of it?" They were cocky, his responses, but only at first blush. Just below the surface Roberta swore she could see a small, quivering animal caught in somebody's sights. "I go into Cal's a lot. So does everybody."

"What's your name?"

"What's yours?"

She took a breath. God bless his mother. "Roberta. Roberta Wilcox. Now you. What's yours?"

"Roberta Wilcox," he repeated. "Your father's the one with the sawmill. He's been delivering lumber down to East Greenwich. I hear them talking about it at Cal's."

"Yes, that's right. I bet you hear a lot in the store, don't you?" Suddenly it occurred to her that this strange boy might know more about what was going on in town than she did. Especially if he kept that steel trap of his shut all the time. The men probably forgot he was there most of the time.

"Well, since you won't tell me your name, I'll have to pick one for you. How about Deerhunter?"

"Who said I was hunting deer?" A small curl appeared at the corner of his mouth. "You know deer season hasn't opened yet. I was just out hunting a little pheasant, that's all."

"With that thing?" She pointed with disdain to the gun, of which she still was keeping a wide berth. "That's a muzzle-loader, Deerhunter. You know that as well as I do."

"Does the job. What about you? What are you doing here? Don't you know it's dangerous to be in these woods this time of year?"

"That might be why I'm wearing this." She tipped her father's hat to him. "I like to come here, that's all. Did you know this used to be a village? Lewis City, they called it. Dozens of people lived here, until something happened, and they all either died or moved away."

She had captured his interest. The face of bravura had fallen, and he glanced around the forest as though seeing the vestiges of Lewis City for the first time.

"That over there was the mill, probably to grind corn. The houses are there, and over here." She pointed and his gaze followed hers. "If you go back the way I came, you'll run into a clearing and a cemetery where a lot of the people from Lewis City are buried. You'll see some of them died around the same time. Some people think a smallpox epidemic took out most of the village."

"So why do you come here?"

"I don't know. It's half fascinating, half sort of creepy. It's a mystery. We'll probably never know what happened, but I like to come here and imagine."

Maybe she had overdone it. She could see a shiver run across his shoulders. She wondered if he could imagine the past as she did; if he could see Desire Tefft in the garden and her mother with the pail of dishwater. Or if his mind had conjured something uglier, like a young boy dying of smallpox.

146

A thought occurred to her. "Aren't you supposed to be in school?"

His face shut down and his hands tightened around the gun. "What are you, Roberta Wilcox, the truant officer?"

"No, but it is a weekday." She cursed herself for saying it; she should have stayed on the topic of Lewis City. At least he had dropped his guard then. "Don't worry, your secret's safe with me. I don't care what you're doing out here as long as you don't blow some poor fool's head off."

His eyes narrowed. For a crazy minute he reminded her of a younger Maine. "Don't you have someplace to be?"

"I think I was just asking you the same question, after a fashion. Yes, I do, Deerhunter, and this is it. I told you, I like to come here and hang out sometimes. Usually it's pretty peaceful." She reached into her pocket and his gun arm tensed again. "I was going to have a little picnic on that rock over there. You can join me if you want."

At the sight of food all the sternness in his face melted away. He put his gun against the tree and followed her to the flat rock that stood on a slight rise. They sat, and she passed him pieces of cheese and apple she had sliced and wrapped in waxed paper. He ate slowly but intently, and he seemed so hungry she passed most of it to him while nibbling on one sliver of cheese so he wouldn't notice what she was doing.

"I like sitting on this rock because you can kind of see the whole layout of the village. I used to come here when I was a little girl and pretend I lived in the village. I made up the houses in my mind and gave the people names. Names, you know, that I got from the cemetery."

The apple and cheese were gone, but he held out his hand expectantly. She found a box of raisins in her other pocket. "Do you really think they all died of smallpox?"

"Oh, I don't know. That's just a story I've heard. I might

have gotten it twisted up. It might have been diphtheria. It really doesn't matter anyway. The point is they're gone—a whole village, a ghost town."

"Kind of creepy, isn't it?"

"Yeah. I think what fascinates me is that something that was once so vibrant, so stirring with life, could just disappear." She was talking to him like an adult, she knew, but he had not taken his gaze off her. He was eating the raisins one at a time, savoring them along with her words.

"Sounds like my neighborhood."

"What do you mean?"

He looked away suddenly. "Oh—nothing. Just a lot of people have moved way, that's all."

"You must live in one of those new plats off Jonnycake Trail. Ida was telling me how a lot of people just up and left their houses. It must be sad to see your neighbors move away."

"Yeah." He crumpled the now-empty box. "Listen, I'm sorry I gave you a scare. But thanks for—for the snacks. I've got to get back. Homework."

"Wait—Deerhunter. What's your name?"

But the boy in his baggy shirt and pants had grabbed his gun and dashed off toward the setting sun, leaves kicking up behind him as he ran.

Chapter Fourteen

The next day the power came back on. Roberta was in Gran's room, dusting around pots of cold cream and old tubes of lipstick when the lamp with the frilly pink shade erupted in a splash of yellow. For a moment she kept dusting; then it hit her.

The blackout was over. Perhaps it was no coincidence that the toilet worked, the laundry could be washed, and the electric lights shone now that Piccirelli was living at the farm. At least that was Steve's take on the situation, and although she saw it as just another sign of his paranoia, Roberta had no better explanation of her own. They had no newspapers, and the TV newscasters were silent on the subject, lending credence to Steve's argument that the power outage had been local all along.

Alton shut the mill down for a week. Roberta assumed he had used up his gas ration and was waiting for the next allotment, which always came at midmonth. But little was said about the sudden break in routine.

Ben, Wayne and Alton no longer appeared at break time, and Alton set off each morning across the road, where he was hard at work on the cabins. Something—either Gran's nagging or his own determination to get Piccirelli out of their hair—had lent a new urgency to repairing broken windows and replacing worn shingles. Some mornings Ben would help him for a few hours, but most of the time Alton worked alone, and Roberta followed his progress out the kitchen window, wondering what it all meant.

After the cold of early November, Indian summer had blossomed once again. It was warm enough to walk with a light coat and no gloves, and the sun lit up the nearly bare branches of the trees. On such a morning Roberta crossed the road with a thermos of coffee, her excuse for interrupting her father.

"If this weather keeps up I'll be done by tomorrow and ready to paint," Alton observed.

"I can help." She felt briefly guilty, knowing her offer was not entirely altruistic. But it was, maybe, if you looked deeper. She did want to help her father, just not with painting.

"Don't tell your grandmother that. With that power back on, she's got plans to turn the house upside down in the next couple a days. The fall cleaning, you know."

Roberta didn't want to know. It seemed they had been cleaning something ever since she arrived home, and still there was always something to be done.

"She hasn't said she needs me." She cast about for something else to say. Why was it always so hard to talk to her father?

"You have been helping out quite a bit." He was looking away from her, over the nearly empty coffee cup to the fields and woods behind the cabins. "Maybe she could spare you."

It was as close as he would get to asking her for help, she knew, and she felt secretly thrilled. "I'll tell her. I'm sure she won't mind. What about everything else? The inside? Are you really moving Piccirelli out here?"

His eyes flashed at her. She had asked too many questions; run over him when she should have proceeded slowly, gently. But he said only, "That's up to the ladies. I've done my job. If you want to get it all cozy-cozy for Mr. Pickado, go right ahead. But I don't think he'll like it none unless I can get a wood stove out here."

The next morning May had no objection to Roberta working on the cabins, though Paula eyed her suspiciously when the subject came up.

They made quick work of the priming. The cabins were so small that they started on opposite sides and soon found themselves meeting up. For a while Roberta worked and forgot everything that weighed on her mind. But she realized that if she didn't talk to her father soon, they would be done working together and the opportunity might not come again.

Her father was kneeling in front of the porch on cabin number three, painting the trim with a narrow brush. She found another brush and joined him, washing the spools in a deep shade of green.

"How's that book coming?" Alton said finally.

She had had all sorts of opening lines planned, but the book had not entered her mind.

"I'm trying to get a grant to finish it. I can't really work on it that much here. I've got to get out and do some more research." She had told him this dozens of times, but she didn't know what else to say.

"Maybe Steve Reynolds is right. Maybe you should just walk across the street. I could fix one of these up for you. You could bring your typewriter out here."

She looked at her father in amazement. She had never thought of such a thing, but it had enormous appeal. Write the book about tourist cabins in a cabin, surrounded by all that miniature kitsch.

"Build you some bookshelves," he was saying. "As long's it's daylight, you could work out here in peace and quiet."

Bookshelves. It sounded heavenly, but Roberta knew it was a no-no. "Dad, you shouldn't change the cabins. Believe it or not, they're old enough to have historical value. Someday they could be on the National Register."

He chuckled. "The only register I care about is a cash register. Let's get some paying tenants out here. The cabins are looking pretty sharp, I'd say."

"Are you going back to the mill tomorrow?"

Alton didn't answer right away, just busied himself cleaning his brushes.

"That depends on a lot of things," he said. "Hand me that can of paint, will you?"

"Do you think you'd have to time to help me paint the inside?" She so wanted him to stay out here with her. "The two of us, we could paint them all in a day."

"I'd like to, Roberta, but I've got orders to fill." That dark look had come over his face again. "Gas ration's coming in tomorrow. We've got to make up for lost time."

"Dad, why did you ask me to leave?" The question had just come out of her mouth unbidden. Maybe because he was packing up, getting ready to walk back across the street. Maybe because she couldn't stand the question hanging in the air between them.

"There's things you don't understand."

"So help me to understand. Is it something I've done? Is it—"

He stopped her, his hand clamping on her forearm like a vise. "There's things you don't understand," he repeated. "I'm doing the best I can. I spent my whole life worrying about you girls. I just can't right now. The whole world's turned upside down. Go out, live your life, Roberta. This isn't the place for you."

If only she could remove the veil of words, if only he could say what he meant. *Say it*, she thought desperately. *Say you love me. Say it isn't my fault.*

But the moment had passed. A car had pulled up to the house and Alton turned to watch as Fred Maine got out and knocked on the kitchen door. Roberta could see Paula pointing across the street, obviously agitated.

"Now what the hell does he want," was all Alton said. He left the brushes and the paint cans on the sawhorses and loped across the street.

Roberta froze. Maine was ambling toward Alton, his hips rolling in a double limp, his left hand in his pocket. From across the road his face was inscrutable. Alton had slowed to a walk and the two met by the rock in the front lawn. Roberta watched from the cabins. Paula stood still behind the door screen, but the men's voices were just the gravelly rumblings of two Yankee men who spoke in monosyllables or not at all, and Roberta doubted if Paula could hear any more than she could.

They talked for a few minutes, and then Alton inclined his head ever so slightly toward the mill, and they were walking away together, headed for the path.

"What was all that about?" she asked Paula, when they met at the door.

Paula started to say something, then apparently thought better of it. Her face was slightly flushed, but that could have been from standing over the stove. "Fred Maine. What a jerk," she finally said.

Maybe Paula had heard something after all, but she was making an obvious effort to brush it off. Roberta felt her stomach tighten. Everyone knew more about what was going on than she did.

Paula went back to the laundry. During the power outage they had washed clothes by hand in the kitchen sink, a dreadful job but a necessary one. Now that the washing machine was working, there was a lot of catching up to do. Roberta cleaned up and took the heavy laundry basket outdoors.

As the clothesline began to sag under its burden, she turned and looked wistfully toward the back woods. Lucas would be riding today. It was a good day for it: mild for November, with no breeze and a strong sun. She would go after lunch. For a while she would forget about her father and that damned Maine. It was not hard to get away. Gran was napping after the morning's exertion and Paula, who seemed just as tired, was in the living room reading a woman's magazine. Roberta would have to be home in time to help take in the clothes and make supper, but that gave her . . . oh, three hours at least.

She found Lucas in the barn as though he were waiting for her. He expressed no surprise at seeing her, but quietly began to saddle up a second horse. Roberta regarded the sleek quarter horse with apprehension. It had been years since she had ridden horseback, and that had been on the old farm mare that was so old she could barely trot. These horses were lean and muscular, and they always looked as though they were just waiting to take off on their own. Lucas seemed to sense her nervousness and helped her up, all the while talking to the horses in a low, soothing voice.

They set out on a dirt road toward the river. The trail was narrow but well kept, and the horses picked their way along it with sure feet. Lucas had given her an orange hunting vest like his to wear, and Roberta wondered if they would see the boy. The trail they rode on would circle toward Lewis City if they rode far enough. It was another school day, but somehow she doubted Deerhunter was in school today, either. She would have to ask Steve about him; surely he would know if a boy Deerhunter's age hadn't been getting on the bus.

Lucas stopped his horse where a stream ran under the trail, and they dismounted so the horses could drink. They sat on the old stone abutment on the roadside. The trees above were almost bare, although a stray leaf or two glittered from the late bearing oaks. Birds chirped despite the lateness of the season. Roberta felt Lucas's coat brush hers.

"Did you and your wife ride much?"

"Every day. Sometimes twice a day."

Roberta searched for comforting words but couldn't think of anything that didn't sound inane. Finally she said, "You must miss her very much."

"Yes, I do. I guess you're no stranger to loss, are you? But it's hard to get through life without such sorrows. Tell me about your mother. I've heard she was a beautiful woman."

Of all the things she had heard about her mother, Jackie Miller's beauty was something that always went unspoken—although Roberta knew it was true. She felt grateful to him for saying it, for making it real, if only for the brief moments of their conversation.

"She was beautiful," Roberta said slowly. "She was tall and dark, with brown eyes. I remember her softness, mostly, but that's because she was my mother. I know others remember her differently."

"You alluded to that the other day."

"Well, I guess no one in Coward's Hole had ever seen anybody quite like her. She was a little . . . exotic looking, almost. But there was nothing exotic about her lineage. She was plain old English, like the rest of us."

"So why was she considered such an outsider?"

Roberta considered a moment. "Because she was one. Her family was from Worcester, Massachusetts. I know that sounds silly. It's not that far away, after all—but she was different. She wasn't anything like my father. Her life, her background, her education—" Roberta stopped, struggling for the right words. "She was a stranger, Lucas."

He urged her to continue, and she complied. She told him how her mother had come into town about the time Alton lost his first wife, Peggy Tefft. She had been hired to teach school, renting one of the cabins across from the farm.

"Some people called her a communist," she said, laughing at the absurdity of it. "I mean, this was 1979, and people in

Coward's Hole were still defending Nixon. The Civil Rights Movement never hit here. And here was my mother, talking about open classrooms and letting her junior high school kids read Eldridge Cleaver. She was a complete heretic. She might have been Jane Fonda, for all people talked about her."

"An odd match for your father," Lucas observed.

"Yeah. If you thought of her the way other people saw her, she probably was. And she was younger than he, eight years younger. But she was kind and—and mothering, and Dad needed a mother as much as a wife. Paula was five when Peggy died. I think my mother fell in love with Paula before my father, and that made the difference."

Lucas sighed. The horses made snuffling noises behind them but seemed content to sit in the unexpected sunshine. "I can't imagine being widowed twice. My heart aches for him. Once was incomprehensibly hard."

"I'm sorry. You probably don't want to hear all this."

"No, I do. Please finish."

This was the hard part, the part Roberta thought about all the time but gave no voice to. It was easy to remember Jackie as a kind and gentle mother. It was harder to think about the woman they said she had become, the woman she was that day in 1988 when her car left the highway at the top of Mount Laurel.

"People said she was having an affair. It sounds like a cliché, when you tell it. He was a school textbook salesman staying in the cabins. Supposedly . . . supposedly, she was following him out of the Hole when the accident happened."

"It must have been so hard for you."

"I was five, in kindergarten. I remember coming home on the bus. The bus passed a fire truck, they say, but I don't remember seeing it. I just remember getting off the bus and walking through the house, which was as still as death, calling for my mother, my grandmother. Then I found them, Gran, my father, Paula, sitting in the living room, not saying anything, just staring and staring at me as though they couldn't imagine how to tell me."

He squeezed her hand. His shoulder was warm and inviting, and when he put his arm around her, she involuntary leaned into it, a shelter from the cold. But it was she who looked up and kissed him, and if he was surprised, she could not tell in the firmness of his kiss back.

They mounted the horses and continued on deep into the woods. Soon they came upon Lewis City, and it was even more desolate and foreboding than the day before.

"Lucas, let's go back."

They rode in silence to the barn and put the horses away. The stalls were redolent with straw and the saddles' rich leather, and a hint of pungent horse droppings. She sneezed and forgot all about her earlier fantasy, and it was just as well, for Lucas led her by the hand through the yard, into the back door and up the stairs to his bedroom.

It was a room of simple but elegant colonial design. The bed was a four-poster, probably antique, covered by a white embossed coverlet. The walls, too, were white. On the floor was a circular braided rug of blues, reds and fawns, and the only other color was Lucas's red velour bathrobe, which sat folded on a chair. The room was impossibly neat, the wood bureaus well dusted and the wide pine floor spotless. There were no window shades, only white linen curtains that Lucas drew carefully against the sun.

He was a slow, gentle and careful lover, and Roberta felt herself blossoming under his touch. Freed by the knowledge of his age—and perhaps the idea, wicked as it sounded, of his gratitude—she relaxed, and soon found herself in a slow but escalating passion.

He seemed to celebrate every part of her, and for someone who had always thought herself too big, too tall and too broad to be attractive, his precise attentions were a revelation. His hands lingered on her breasts the way one might caress a piece of ripe fruit, and then moved to the parentheses of her hips and what lay between. She was glad of her roundness, the possibilities of her concave belly and slight fullness; all those nerve endings, all those miles of electrical impulses to be touched and discharged, all that skin. She was not fat or even overweight; it was more the way she was shaped, her rounded build and broad shoulders and wrists. But with his exacting touch, Lucas seemed to be celebrating it all, and too quickly to hold back she broke open in a bone-crunching spasm.

Perhaps he was slow and careful with her to cover up any of his own inadequacies; but if he had any, Roberta did not notice. For his own pleasure he was swift, strong and unsparing, although she was still catching her breath. Afterwards he got up quickly and left her in that all-white bed, despairing now about the fate of that embroidered bedspread and white sheets.

She was too lazy to get up yet, though, and her eyes swam around the room. Against the far wall, near the door where they had walked in, was a portrait in oil. It was Meredith, dressed in hunting cap and jacket, her smile thin and aristocratic. Roberta thought in horror of his perfect wife watching her moments of abandon. She could not imagine Meredith in her place, yet she had been, thousands of times. Meredith and Lucas, husband and wife, had had their own language of passion, their own secrets and rituals, their moments of ecstasy that probably made Roberta's encounter with Lucas seem silly and careless. She tried to lean up on her elbows, but fell back, too tired to study Meredith or try to live up to her. She felt herself drifting under that white coverlet, her spent passion retreating through her body like a sleeping potion.

The last of the afternoon light was a golden gauze behind the curtains when she awoke. Disoriented, she thought she was in Gran's old featherbed, with the sun setting in the west behind her. But out this window was only a reflection of lightened sky, the eastern mirror of sunset. She was not home.

She found Lucas downstairs, making dinner. Her regarded her with a sort of detached amusement. "Hello, sleepyhead."

"Lucas, please. You have to take me home—drive me. Now. I had no idea it was so late."

"I was hoping you'd stay. I was frying a steak."

"Stay? Oh, no. No . . . you see, I have to help Gran with dinner, and chores, and—it's a problem if I'm not there."

"Well, of course. I'll take you in the Peugeot."

He seemed disappointed, and Roberta cursed herself. How could she have fallen asleep? And what would he think—that it hadn't meant anything? Oh, she was bungling this as usual.

In five minutes Lucas had her home in the driveway. The windows of the house were empty of light. Roberta dashed out of the car, barely saying goodbye. The kitchen was still and dark, and no one waited for her arrival. She walked down the long hallway to the other part of the house, its sides tunneling in darkly toward her. Something was at the other end of this tunnel, this dark vortex moving her on and on.

She found it in the living room, where no light shone, but people's shadows moved imperceptibly, posed as they were around the room like wax dolls. There was Gran in her chair, Paula on the piano stool, Ray standing beside her—what was he doing here?—and against the wall a family of Reynolds: Steve, Wayne and Ben, all standing stiffly as though they weren't breathing.

But they were waiting for her, and as she entered the stage, the bodies moved and shifted and came to life. They all looked to Ben, the one who had been appointed to speak, the one who could find his voice.

"It happened this afternoon, Roberta," he began quietly, and as soon as he spoke, she knew it was a story she had heard before. "He was coming over Mount Laurel at an awful clip. The International rolled and he was thrown out. I'm sorry. He didn't make it."

CHAPTER FIFTEEN

They buried George Alton Wilcox on a cheerless, rainy November afternoon in the family cemetery.

I returned, and I saw under the sun, that the race is not to the swift, nor the battle to the strong, neither yet bread to the wise, nor yet riches to men of understanding, nor yet favour to men of skill; but time and chance happeneth to them all.

Roberta could not imagine why Paula stood next to her now. For two days she had not spoken to Roberta. When they passed in the hall, she stiffly flew by, and her questions and entreaties met with a silence that was far worse than any sharp words ever could be. In a time when a sister could be a comfort, when a common grief could bring them together, they were farther apart than they ever had been.

Wisdom is better than weapons of war: but one sinner destroyeth much good.

The rain dripped down over her scarf and onto her hair. They began to sing "Amazing Grace." Then it was over. Roberta turned around and moved through the small crowd, not hearing the whispered condolences, brushing past the hands laid on her arms, her shoulders. Maine was standing in the same place, expressionless, as though waiting for her.

"You've got a lot of nerve coming here." With effort she kept her hands steady at her sides.

"I'm sure I don't know what you mean. Your father and I have been friends since we was children. I come to pay my respects, that's all."

Suddenly Ida Kenyon was at her side as though she had been summoned. "Get along now, Roberta. There's no call accusing the senator."

Roberta stared ahead at Maine, who was ignoring her. "Tell me where he was going. I know you know."

"I haven't the faintest idea."

"Now, Roberta, we all know you're upset, but there's no need of this." Ida was pushing at her elbow, trying to move her, but Roberta shook her off like a fly.

"You were one of the last people to see him alive. You came over here that day and stood on the front lawn, and then both of you went out to the mill. You were talking business. I have a right to know what it was about."

Maine lifted his chin a little, his cold eyes regarding her. "I already told you. I don't know where Alton was headed anymore'n I know where your mama was going the day she died, and the sooner you reconcile to that fact, the sooner you're going to be able to get past this, if you know what I mean."

Her voice was frozen, and all she could utter was the word "No," and she flung it at him like a weapon and lunged forward. But Ida wormed herself between them then and began a high-pitched wail. "Oh, somebody help me. She's gone crazy! I tell you she's gone crazy!"

Roberta struggled to get past the wriggling Ida, but it was no use. As her neighbors ran back to them, she realized Steve had his hands on her arms like a vise.

They brought Roberta into the house, and she dimly heard Ben Reynolds brusquely sending Maine on his way.

Gran, cold and shaky from an hour standing in the rain, had taken to her bed. When she was sure that Gran was asleep, Roberta left her side and closed the bedroom door. Paula was sitting at the dining room table drinking a beer. She rubbed her fingers along the side of the glass, although the scum was on the inside, not the outside. The elbows of her black sweater were planted on the table, and she stared down at the white lace tablecloth as though reading something there.

Roberta pulled out a chair, the weight of the day collapsing into her lap as she sat down. She had come to the end of some road. For now it was just she and Paula, and their sick grandmother in the next room. She had braced herself for many things when she came home in August, but not this. Nothing like this.

She knew they should talk. She should say something. "Where's Ray?"

"Upstairs."

"When's he going back?"

"Tomorrow, I guess." Paula continued to move her thumbs on the glass, rubbing something invisible away.

"Are you going with him?"

Paula looked up then, her eyes narrow and black. "No. Any more questions?"

Roberta sighed. She wished Paula would explain, or at least unburden herself a little, but her older sister had never been one to bare her soul.

"What about you? You going back to that boyfriend in Baltimore?"

Roberta was so surprised Paula knew about Jordan that she stared at her, unable to respond. If she knew about Jordan, what else did she know? Or was she just a lucky guesser?

"There is no boyfriend in Baltimore," she said finally. "At least, not now. And no, I'm not going back. I don't have a job, for one thing. For another, somebody's got to take care of Gran."

Paula said nothing. Roberta expected a jibe, some sarcastic reference to her ineptitude. But Paula seemed too preoccupied for verbal jousting. She took another swig of her beer before she answered. "Do you think I should go home?"

"I think you should do what you have to do. I figured since Ray came back, you two had patched things up."

Paula was looking out the bare window into nothing. Roberta saw that she was crying. She did not sob or even hold her lip, just let tears streak down her face like some method actress who has finally learned how to bring tears to her eyes.

"It's complicated," she said.

"Maybe you're making it more complicated than it is."

"Right on, sister. It's all my fault."

"I didn't mean that," Roberta said. "I just mean that with a man and a woman, sometimes it's simple. Either you love each other or you don't. And you move on from there."

"Is that the simple arrangement you have with Steve?"

"I don't have an arrangement with Steve." *Jesus, Paula is not going to open up easily,* Roberta thought. "So which is it? Do you love him, or don't you?"

"This isn't about love. When you're married there are some fundamental things you have to agree on, and right now Ray and I are about as far apart as two people can get."

"Maybe it would help if you were living in the same town," Roberta said, and immediately regretted it. But Paula seemed not to have heard her.

"I liked my life the way it was. But Ray's never satisfied. He keeps pushing me to have a baby . . . and I just can't see it. I mean, it would change everything. I'd have to give up my job. I'd be chained to the house. I'd never get a chance to do what I want to do. I'd end up like her." She jerked a thumb toward May's bedroom door. "I don't want something . . . in me, making me fat and sucking all the energy out of me."

Roberta tried to hide her shock. It was the most absurdly selfish thing she had ever heard, but at the same time it was vintage Paula, who was probably afraid the baby would ruin her figure and spell the end of her independence. "I don't think it's that bad," she ventured.

"How the hell would you know?"

"As well as you, I guess." Roberta paused. She had not given much thought herself to the question of having children, but then again she had a lot more time left to think about it than Paula did. "Obviously it's never happened to me, but I guess it's one of those transcendent experiences that makes up for whatever physical discomfort's involved."

"Oh, stuff your transcendence. You sound like Ray. I'm so sick of hearing how beautiful childbirth must be. Give me a break. I've walked through the maternity wing at the hospital when a woman's in labor. You can hear their screams all the way down the hall."

"Maybe you could adopt."

"Adopt? And get some cocaine baby or some son of a serial killer? No thanks."

Roberta stiffened. Sometimes Paula was so outrageous, she had to be called on it. "That's an awful thing to say. Some of the kids waiting for families may be troubled, but that's all the more reason to give them a good home. And I don't see how there's that much difference between a coke addict mother and somebody who refuses to have children because she doesn't want to go up a dress size."

"Hey! At least I know better than to keep spitting out kids every time I get a new boyfriend! I knew I shouldn't have confided in you, Roberta. You have never had the least bit of sympathy for me. Ever since you came home, you've done nothing but cause trouble around here. If you were half a help, I wouldn't be stuck up here."

"You're stuck up here because you're having trouble with your marriage," Roberta reminded her. "You like to paint yourself as the selfless, dutiful daughter, but the truth is that this is all part of some ultimatum you've laid down with Ray."

"Listen, sister, this is about more than my stupid marriage. Don't you know anything? She's dying in there. We might as well dig her grave right now if she stays here because we aren't going to have enough fuel this winter to keep warm. Do you honestly think I would use Gran to get my husband back? Are you out of your mind?"

If she hadn't been so tired, if she hadn't just buried her father and gone a round with Fred Maine, Roberta might have known better. But she kept going. "No, I am not out of my mind. You just admitted you came here to punish Ray. If you were really concerned about Gran, you would have been grateful I came home to help instead of fighting me at every turn. But no. All you think about is yourself. You're so afraid she'll pay attention to somebody besides you. Ever since we were kids—"

"Ever since we were kids! Oh, here we go! Ever since we were kids I've been doing the lion's share of the work around here. Ever since we were kids you've been the chosen one. Smith College. Graduate school. Do you know how they struggled to keep you in school? Do you? Did you know that—"

Roberta heard a little cry, and a thump, and she turned around to see Gran's bedroom door half open and the old woman half slumped against it, her face flour white. She ran over. Paula was right behind her. Roberta put her arms around the old woman while Paula cradled her feet, and together they got Gran back into bed. Roberta felt the bones poking through her grandmother's skin. She was so thin, so thin, but nothing seemed broken. Gran was whispering something she could barely hear.

"She's saying, 'Don't fight,' " Paula translated, looking at her sister from the footboard.

"We're not fighting, Gran," Roberta said. "You're very tired.

If you need to get out of bed, please ring the bell I left you. Don't get up, okay? Paula, get a towel and warm it up behind the stove." To her surprise, Paula obeyed, and soon Roberta had slipped the warm terrycloth under the blankets and wrapped it around Gran's legs. They talked to her in soothing tones, and in a half-hour Gran was asleep again, her breath coming in thin, open-mouthed rasps.

The two sisters returned to the dining room table. Paula looked over at Roberta. She looked as spent as Roberta felt: Her face drained of color, her fingers nervously working the tablecloth. They could fight, scratch, claw at each other, but they could not deny that they shared Gran, just as they had shared a father.

"Paula, fighting isn't going to solve anything, and it's not going to help Gran."

Paula let out a sigh. "I always wanted to have a *normal* family. You know. A mother, a father, two kids related to both of them."

"We have to take what's been dealt us."

"You're starting to sound like Gran." Paula's voice had that old sarcasm in it, but without the furious energy of their exchange a few minutes before. "What is it she always says? 'I guess we'll have to take it and like it.' "

Roberta laughed, a short, dry laugh that felt like it was being squeezed out of her. "I never really knew what that meant."

"I guess it means that we might as well smile through our troubles because there's nothing we can do about them."

Perhaps it was spiritual, this philosophy of Gran's, but it seemed so passive, so defeatist. They didn't have to take it, did they? Couldn't they fight back? They didn't have to let Fred Maine push them around. They didn't have to let the government tell them what to do. Most of all, they didn't have to tear each other apart.

But Paula's voice moved swiftly on, still fueled by her

167

intensity. "This is it, you know. This is all we have, our only chance in life. If you're not doing what you really want to do, you'll never get a second chance."

Roberta thought about that a moment. She hoped Paula wasn't going to ask her what she wanted because at that moment she had no idea. She thought of Lucas and Steve, of Gran, and of her father lying in the west field. It didn't matter what she wanted. Too many things held her in place here, like magnetic poles.

"Well, if you love Ray, don't let him slip away. There has to be another way."

"I don't know what that might be." Paula got up, indicating the conversation was over. "I'll sleep in Gran's room tonight, on the cot," she offered. "I don't think we should leave her alone."

For years Gran had gone to an elderly physician across the line in Connecticut, but when he had died she had sworn off doctors forever. In the morning Roberta would have to work on finding someone to come to the house. She wouldn't take it and like it; she wouldn't let May die, not without a fight.

The next morning Anthony Piccirelli announced over a stack of pancakes that he would be holding a meeting at the grange hall Saturday. Everyone was invited, indeed encouraged, to attend, he continued, and he would personally see to it that anyone needing a ride to the hall got it. Roberta, Paula and Ray listened quietly to his announcement. Gran was still sleeping, and Roberta would bring her breakfast on a tray when she awoke.

She wondered what Piccirelli was up to. If he had something to tell them, why didn't he just come out with it? But he was sitting there like a Cheshire cat, smiling into the pie slice he had cut into the pancakes. The meeting would be at seven in the evening, and the ladies of the grange had agreed to provide some light refreshments, he said. It would be to everyone's advantage to come.

Paula raised an eyebrow at Roberta. "I'm afraid we won't all be there, since someone has to stay with my grandmother," Paula said. "But I'm sure Roberta can report back to us."

"You don't think she'll be well enough to go?"

Piccirelli seemed much more concerned about her absence than her illness, Roberta thought. "If you want to get her well enough to be out and about, maybe you could help us find a doctor who makes house calls."

Piccirelli seemed to give this serious thought. "Perhaps we can arrange something," he said, but he could not resist adding, "Lack of medical care is one of the hazards of living way out here, I'm afraid."

Paula began clearing plates and Roberta went to check on Gran. She found her still snoring gently, but her cheeks were pinker than they had been the previous night, and Roberta decided that, at the very least, lack of sleep was part, if not all, of the woman's problem.

After breakfast Paula and Ray left together to get the mail. Roberta was idly flipping through a cookbook when she saw Lucas on the other side of the storm door. She nearly pulled him into the kitchen.

"Oh, I am so glad you came. It's so good to see you."

He put his hands on her waist. "I hope it's not too soon. We really didn't have a chance to talk yesterday."

"I know. I wished we could have."

"I came to offer whatever I can. A shoulder to cry on, if you need it." He looked at her with those dark green eyes, and crying was the farthest thing from her mind. "Or I can chop wood or milk the cows, if you'd prefer."

She laughed. "Just sit down and talk to me, please. Steve filled the wood box yesterday, and Paula and I can still milk cows." Why had she mentioned Steve? She wished suddenly she hadn't. "I was just thinking I don't know what to do with myself."

They sat at the oilcloth-covered table, and with his right hand he began to caress her cheek. He must have meant it in sympathy, but she was taking it in a decidedly different way. How could she, the day after burying her father, be thinking of this? But there it was. The body responded; it knew nothing of right times and wrong times. She grabbed hold of his hand. "I wish I could go home with you."

"Come, then. No one will know, and what business is it if they do?"

"I can't." She explained about Gran, and he furrowed his brow in concern. "Maybe this afternoon, if Paula gets back."

"You need to do something to forget your troubles. I think it would be good for you."

"Mmmm." She was imagining just how good it would be when the front door slammed and there was a great flurry of boots kicked off and coats hung up. Paula rushed into the kitchen, and stopped, confused, when she saw Lucas.

"Oh. Hello." She seemed preoccupied as she looked from one of them to the other. "Roberta, we got a letter from the town about Dad's will. I don't understand it, but it doesn't sound good. Something about a lien—"

She handed it over, and Roberta read quickly through it, wondering what it meant. *What nice vellum this was typed on,* she thought irrelevantly. The black type on creamy paper included a salutation to both Roberta and Paula, which confused her even more.

"I don't mean to intrude, but I am a lawyer. If you like, perhaps I could interpret it for you," Lucas offered. They looked at him, as though they had forgotten he was there.

Paula shrugged. "It's all right with me. I can't understand a word of it."

Lucas read through the letter once, then again.

"Your father apparently did leave a will, and it is scheduled for probate court next week. That's routine." He paused, looking to see if that had sunk in. "All wills must be probated," he explained. "It's a routine process and, barring any unusual debts or problems, usually takes only a few months. The hearings take place at town hall."

"Do we have to go?" Paula asked.

"Oh, yes. Your father named you both his executors, or co-executors. You will be responsible for paying his debts and settling his estate. You must go to the probate hearings."

"So this is pretty routine, right?" Roberta asked.

"So far, yes. But it seems your father did have some debts. Someone already had filed a lien on the farm, before he passed away. That will have to be cleared up before the estate can be settle d."

"But it doesn't say anything about that," Roberta insisted.

"It does, but it doesn't say who filed the lien. You—or your lawyer—will have to go to town hall to find that out. But your father must have known who it was because he would have been notified while he was living."

Roberta was getting a heavy feeling in her stomach. She knew who had filed that lien, and looking at Paula she knew that her sister did, too. The nightmare just would not end. Even in death, her father could not escape Fred Maine.

"How much of a big deal is this lien? Could it really screw things up?" Paula demanded.

"I'm afraid I don't know. It depends on the amount of the debt and how much the estate was worth. If you can't repay the debt, part or all of the estate might have to be sold to settle it."

"You mean sell the farm?" Roberta felt her skin growing cold, as though someone had left open a door. It was her father who had left it ajar, a nice back door for Fred Maine to walk right into their lives. It was too late to shut it now.

Paula grabbed the letter out of Lucas' hand and began scanning it, as though trying to find his interpretation in the neat lines of pica type. "Maybe this is for the best, Roberta. We can sell the farm, split whatever money's left, and I'll take Gran back with me to Westerly. You can go back to Baltimore, or on that trip you were going to take."

Roberta was appalled. How could they just roll over for Maine and sell the farm? She could almost feel the earth shifting beneath her. This was the only home she had ever known. For all the misgivings she'd had about returning, she couldn't imagine the farm owned by someone else.

"I don't think that's what Dad would have wanted," she said.

"Maybe he shouldn't have signed his life away to Fred Maine, then," Paula countered. "I can't imagine any other way, Roberta. Gran can't keep the farm going, and I certainly don't want to stay here." She seemed to have left Roberta out of the equation entirely, as though it were inconceivable that she could run the farm.

Paula turned to Lucas. "How long will it take to settle this? Can't we just put the farm up for sale and pay off Maine? Then get our money?"

"It depends," Lucas said slowly. "Either the judge would have to order that, or you would both have to agree to it. I assume your father left each of you the property equally." He looked from one Wilcox daughter to the other. "If you both want to sell, I can't imagine it would be too complicated, as long as you can find a willing buyer."

"Whoa." This was all going too fast; Roberta felt an urge to grab her sister before she ran out and put a for-sale sign on the front lawn. "I can't agree to this. Dad's body's barely cold, and you're talking about selling the farm. How can we sell this place, when Dad spent his whole life trying to keep it in the family?

And trying to keep it out of Maine's hands. It broke his heart when he sold that woodlot to him. I can't imagine what he'd say if he could hear you talking now."

"Oh, aren't we high and mighty? Don't tell me about that woodlot. He sold it because of you, Roberta. So save your speeches. Face it. Dad's not here to work the place, Gran's too sick to do it, and we aren't in a position to do it either. You have to be practical."

Roberta felt an almost disapproving look come from Lucas, but her head was at full boil by now and it was too late to stop. "Practical! What's practical about dragging Gran down to live with you in Westerly? Unless maybe you're hoping to get your hands on her inheritance, whatever that might be. And what's practical about selling valuable land that's only going to get more valuable? No, forget practical. This is really about you, Paula. You can't stand the idea that maybe I could run this place and take care of Gran."

"You? You've been lost ever since you came home. You barely knew how to milk a cow a few months ago. You always were spoiled, and you still are."

"Well, if you call being the family outcast 'spoiled,' maybe I am," Roberta said icily. "But I know one thing. This house has been in our family almost three hundred years. I'm not going to be the one to sign it away to some stranger."

"So instead you're just going to let Gran die here." Paula let the words hang in the air, then spun on her heels and stalked out. Roberta, still seething, looked over to find Lucas regarding her oddly.

"I didn't know there was so much animosity between you and your sister," he said.

Roberta didn't answer him immediately. She wanted to break something, and she was trying to calm herself down. A few hours earlier she would have bet Paula was on the verge of giving in and going back to Ray. Now she wasn't sure. Maybe her troubles with Paula were just beginning.

"So now what do I do?" she said finally. "I can't let her sell this place, Lucas. And my grandmother doesn't want to leave. It would be a horrible thing to do to her, at her age."

"It's not going to be good going into a probate hearing with this unresolved."

"Can you help? Oh, I know this isn't your specialty, but I think I'm going to need a lawyer. And I'm embarrassed to admit I can't afford to hire one."

"My specialty was civil litigation, mostly to do with the environment. But I can't imagine it's that difficult to settle an estate."

"Please, Lucas. My grandmother's sick. Honest to God, I don't even know how we're going to pay for the groceries. Whatever help you could give us would go a long way."

Lucas took the letter with him, and Roberta felt a small measure of relief. However difficult it would be fighting Paula over disposition of the farm, she could relax a little, knowing that she wouldn't be entering the battle alone. But she felt weary. There were too many battles to fight now.

CHAPTER SIXTEEN

Anthony Piccirelli's village meeting loomed, and after that would come Thanksgiving. It was hard to think about either one when Gran lay in bed all day, too weak to come to the kitchen table or dress and bathe herself. They'd had no luck finding a doctor to visit her, and Roberta could barely help the old woman to the bathroom, never mind into the car for a trip to town.

Lurking behind her fears for Gran's health were other, more practical matters: food, grain for the animals, gas to get to town, and above all, money. Although Lucas had reluctantly agreed to begin investigating their probate troubles, the town had yet to hold a hearing, and Alton's money lay in a credit union in Hope Valley, as out of reach as if it had been in a Swiss bank vault.

When Roberta wasn't sitting in a vigil beside Gran's bed, she paced about the kitchen, her mind darting from one worry to another. How much gas did they have? Could they get into town if they had to? How long would the chicken feed and grain hold out? What would they do about groceries, especially for Thanksgiving? The cellar stairs were lined with row upon row of glass jars, and the root cellar was full, but neither would provide a turkey.

It occurred to Roberta that this was the first time since she had returned that the depth of their predicament had really hit home. Before, there had always been someone else responsible. Her grandmother did most of the cooking and took care of the animals, and her father earned the money, carted home the groceries, and dealt with the gas and oil rations. Besides the credit union, she had no idea where he kept his money. She even slipped her hands under his mattress, but she found nothing but cold bedsprings.

In the late afternoon of the Thursday before Piccirelli's meeting, Steve came to the back door and walked in without knocking. He found Roberta sitting at the table, jotting notes on the back of an old envelope.

"Haven't talked to you much. Figured I needed to check on you. I'm sorry I've been such a stranger."

She demurred. She had not really noticed his absence. She had so many things on her mind, she couldn't even think about this evolving love triangle she had started. With Steve she adopted a casual friendliness that would not be too encouraging but also not too remote, so he wouldn't confront her about her feelings but might not be so inclined to act on his.

"You know, if you need a turkey I can get you a turkey," Steve yelled from the dining room when Roberta went to get coffee. *He's reading my list,* she thought, aggravated. She came back into the dining room with the coffee cups, and leaned against the doorframe, shaking her head.

"Even I know you can't hunt wild turkey this time of year. Turkey season's in the spring."

"Yes, but Thanksgiving's in the fall."

"Steve, you'll get your fool head blown off. Or you'll get arrested."

"If I were a fool, that might be true, but I'm not. I've been hunting turkey in these woods for years. You have to know where to go, and when. You go late, at dusk, and you go over behind the Ledges, or in back of the dump, or somewhere else that's posted against deer hunting. Then at least you know won't get your ass shot."

"It's illegal," Roberta reminded him. "And plus, it's dangerous. You could run into somebody jacklighting deer at that hour, or some fool as crazy as you."

"I can take care of myself. It's the other guy that worries me. Some hunter who doesn't know a muzzleloader from a musket. Some kid who's out testing his first rifle . . . that reminds me. You haven't seen a boy around here, have you?"

Roberta stopped stirring her coffee. Deerhunter. In the frenzy of burying her father and taking care of Gran, she had forgotten all about her strange encounter at Lewis City. Now it hit her with a pang. Where was he, and was he all right?

Steve repeated his question. She shook her head as though shaking out cobwebs. "I saw him, over at Lewis City, right before my father died. He had a muzzleloader. It was right before deer season opened. Tall boy for his age, wearing baggy clothes. Maybe twelve or fourteen. Do you know him?"

"That's Niles Porter. Lives over in the Laurel subdivision. Rides my bus. He's actually fourteen, goes to the junior high." Steve was staring at her intently, as though there were something he hadn't told her. "I can't believe you didn't tell me this before."

"Well, I've been a little preoccupied," she snapped. "But what about him? Is he okay?"

"I don't know," he said slowly. Steve seemed to be mulling over the news of her encounter as though it might change what he had been about to tell her. "I ran into him the other day when I was headed to the fire tower. Scared me half to death. He was cutting across your back field, and, yes, he had a muzzleloader. I almost fell over."

Roberta felt the clammy chill of alarm. "Was his father with him?"

"That's just it. He was alone. You know, I haven't seen any sign of life at his house in months, but he gets on the school

177

bus every morning, same as always. I wonder . . ." He stopped and sipped his coffee, which by now was lukewarm. "I just wanted to tell you, in case you were out walking. Damn fool is going to blow somebody's head off with that thing."

"Maybe you should tell the game warden." But as soon as she said the words, she regretted them. "You know, he was awfully hungry. I gave him all the snacks I had in my pocket. He was just ravenous."

"Let me think about it. In the meantime, you be careful."

Roberta felt no fear of the boy, but now her concern for him had grown. If he was in some kind of trouble, she and Steve might be the only ones who knew it. Her encounter with Deerhunter—even now it was hard to put a name to his face, although she knew it to be Niles—had had a dreamy quality about it, but Steve's story brought it back into focus. He seemed to be a boy who needed some adult guidance, and Roberta, although she had no experience in the field, felt suddenly that she was meant to be that adult.

"I saw Paula at the post office the other day," Steve said, pointedly changing the subject. "When is she going home? I figured Ray would have to get back to work."

"You and me both." She told him briefly about the probate letter and Paula's desire to sell the farm. "I don't know what to do. My only hope is that Ray will talk some sense into her."

"It would be a helluva shame if you sold this place." Roberta felt warmed by his words. Steve, more than anyone else, would understand how she felt about home. "Your father must be spinning in his grave."

"And his father, and his father before him." She took the coffee cups to the sink, and Steve rose to go. She knew he would go check on Gran before he left. The two of them shared a teasing rapport that was surprising, given the difference in their ages. Gran liked to say she would give him a run for his money if he were a few years younger, and Roberta bet it was true.

She was drying the cups when Steve came back. His face was white and he grabbed her shoulders.

"How long has she been like that?"

"What? I don't know. Days. I told you she needs a doctor."

He dragged her into Gran's bedroom and even Roberta, who had been tending her closely these past few weeks, was taken aback. Her grandmother, her head sunk into a goose-down pillow, was gasping for breath. Roberta rushed over and put a hand on May's forehead, which smoldered. She couldn't tell if she was gulping air or trying to get out words, but the old woman was moving her mouth and clawing at the sheets.

"I'm going to get help," Steve said, already halfway out of the room. "Roberta, elevate her head. Try to get her fever down." And with that, he left Roberta alone with the ashen-faced woman who looked like she was fighting off death with her flailing hands.

"Can't . . . breathe . . ." May was strangling out the words. "Can't—"

Roberta swung into action. Somehow she propped Gran's head with a second pillow and then, on instinct alone, she cracked a window. Cold air rushed in, but the stuffy sickroom odor was beginning to dissipate. "That damn wood stove," Roberta said, mostly to herself. No wonder the woman couldn't breathe, with all that carbon monoxide swirling around. She opened the damper and the fire kicked up, but at least the smoke was swirling up the chimney instead of into the room.

Gran watched her with big eyes. What else was she trying to say? Roberta wondered. From the bathroom she brought a cool washcloth and gently blotted the perspiration from May's face. She would have to close that window soon or she'd make the old woman sicker, but for now the fresh air seemed to be helping her breathe. She was still rasping, but her inhalations were slower and deeper. The look of panic had left her face, too. Either she knew she was out of immediate danger, or she had resigned herself to something.

"Oh, Gran, hang on," Roberta said. "Steve said he'll get help, and I know he will." But to herself she wondered where. His car had headed west, toward Connecticut. She had thought he would go to the ambulance barn and come back with an EMT, and she wondered why he hadn't. It certainly would have been quicker.

The alarm clock on Gran's nightstand seemed to move in a swirling haze. Darkness was coming on. Gran was not so much struggling with death as sinking into it; and every moment Roberta felt that her grandmother was slipping from her. *The fight in her is gone,* she thought. *She just can't struggle anymore.*

Damn Paula. She realized her sister was out God knew where, and she had no idea when she'd be back. For once Roberta was the one home, left waiting. The realization tasted of bitterness and guilt.

She took Gran's hand, still steamy and damp, and pressed it between her own. She had shut the window, and now the room was beginning to feel close again, the air pressing in instead of flowing through as it had before, cold and clear. Roberta snapped on the rose-shaded lamp on the bed stand and Gran's eyes glowed next to her. They were trying to send the message her throat could not, and Roberta, as though trying to speak that same language, gazed into them, not knowing what to say.

"The trunk," Gran said suddenly between the deep gasps that came with each breath. The sound of her voice was so unexpected that Roberta jumped a little. "Look—"

"Gran, don't talk," Roberta forced herself to say. The words intrigued her so that it was all she could do not to coax her to say more. "There's plenty of time for that. After Steve comes—" She did not really believe what she was saying, but just then she

180

saw headlights swing into the yard, washing over the window in a quick yellow arc.

It was Steve, and he had a woman with him. Neither he nor Roberta said anything for a moment, and when the woman did not introduce herself, Steve made an offhand gesture and said, "Roberta, you remember Jessie, my mother."

"Uh, of course." She shook the woman's hand, just removed from a mitten of rainbow-colored yarn. "How nice to see you again." She hoped her tremulous smile hid her deep shock. Steve, who had renounced all contact with his mother after the divorce, had summoned her for help, all for May's—and Roberta's—sake.

"Where's the patient?" Jessie finally said, and Roberta snapped from her reverie and led them to the bedroom door. She explained about May's difficulty breathing, her apparent fever and the open window's having improved her condition.

"I'll examine her. It might be easier if you left us alone for a few moments."

Steve and Roberta reluctantly retreated to the living room, where Steve plopped down on the piano stool.

"Steve, I don't know how to—" Roberta started to thank him but he scowled and looked away, then he began tapping on the lower registers of the piano keys. "You didn't have to do this."

"What do you think I am, Roberta?" He spun around. "Do you think I'd let my own pride get in the way of helping May? That woman lying in bed in there is ten times the woman my mother could ever hope to be. She has more right to claim me as a son than Jessie Reynolds ever will. But if Jessie can help her get better, maybe that's part of the debt she owes May for standing in for her while she was off finding herself twenty years ago."

It was funny, the things she and Steve had in common. May had been surrogate mother to both of them, in her fashion.

Still, Steve's bitterness came as a shock. Jessie had kind eyes and a gentle manner. How sad that she had felt she needed to give up her family to "find herself," as Steve put it. Maybe she and Jackie Miller had something in common, too.

"I hope it wasn't too difficult. I mean, persuading her."

He made a noise of disgust. "I didn't need to persuade her. She didn't even seem surprised to see me. Greeted me in that brisk, matter-of-fact way, as though we'd parted the best of friends only the day before."

"Oh, Steve." She felt empathy for him, but it was tempered by what she could only describe as jealousy. Steve, at least, had a chance at reconciliation. He was just refusing to take it. *At least your mother's still alive. If I could trade places with you I'd know how to forgive.*

"I just hope she's got something in that witch's bag of tricks that's going to help May."

Paula walked in suddenly, still wearing her coat, gazing from one of them to the other. In her arms were the paper bags she had forgotten to drop in the kitchen.

"Damn Cal Woodmansee. He had me waiting around all afternoon for a shipment of meat he said was coming, and it never came, and on the way home I ran out of gas . . . Who's in with Gran?"

Roberta explained Gran's sudden decline and Steve's errand to fetch his mother. Paula's face darkened, and she let the bags slide onto the coffee table.

"You should have taken her to the hospital." She was looking at Steve, but Roberta felt the words were aimed at her. "What can your mother do for her here? I told you she was getting worse."

"I didn't have enough gas to get her to the hospital, Paula, for your information, and besides, I doubt she would have survived the trip. My mother went to Yale for five years. She's as good as any doctor around here."

Steve colored as his mother appeared at the door, snapping her bag shut. The last thing he would want her to hear were words in her defense, but Roberta thought they were probably the truest things he'd said all night. He might be bitter and resentful, but he wasn't going to let Paula degrade his mother, and that, Roberta thought, was a sure sign he still loved her.

"She has pneumonia," Jessie said without preamble. "Of course, I can't X-ray her lungs, but with the fever and the way she sounds, I'm virtually certain. Her lungs aren't in great shape to begin with. Does she smoke?"

Almost in unison they shook their heads. Gran had stopped smoking years ago, but even that information would never pass her lips—or theirs.

"Well. I can leave you an antibiotic, but she really needs to be on oxygen. If Steve can get me to Norwich, I can get a tank from my office."

"Oxygen?" Roberta said it as though it were an exotic substance. She knew she sounded dumb, but she couldn't help it. "How does that work?"

"Don't you think she needs to be in a hospital?" Paula interrupted. "We can't take care of her here. She sounds like she's at death's door."

Jessie looked at Paula, said nothing, and replied to Roberta's question. "It's a compressed gas system. It extracts pure oxygen from the air so it's self-replenishing. You just have to make sure you don't lose power. If I had a tank with a battery pack I'd get that for you, too, but they're scarcer than hen's teeth."

Paula had left her coat on, and now she was pulling on the top buttonhole with her thumb. "It sounds very complicated. We aren't nurses."

"It's quite simple, really," Jessie continued, regarding her. "I'll give Steve a lesson before I send him back. Just keep it away from any sources of heat. It's really not a good idea to be running that wood stove with oxygen around. Do you have any other way to heat the house?"

"Oil," Roberta choked out. "We have a small ration, though. My father died, you see, and we haven't—"

"Alton? I'm so sorry to hear that. Steve didn't tell me." She looked at him once, reproachfully, and spoke again to Roberta. "Paula is right, she probably would do better in a hospital, but I think transporting her would be very problematic. She's weak, and, let's face it, she must be—what, ninety?"

"Eighty-nine," Roberta supplied. "But up to now she's been so active. It's really only been since this summer that she's slowed down."

"Well, she may snap out of it. If we can get her on oxygen and get the pneumonia under control, she'll at least have a fighting chance. But you girls are going to have to keep a close eye on her. She needs twenty-four-hour nursing care. If Steve—if I can get a ride I'll be happy to come back and check on her next week."

"I can give you a ride." Roberta whirled to see Ben Reynolds walk into the room holding one of Alton's ironstone coffee mugs. Suddenly it all made sense. Paula had run out of gas, and Ben, who probably had been hanging out at Cal's, had given her a lift home. He had helped himself to coffee, and then heard voices. Now Steve, Ben and Jessie, who probably hadn't been under the same roof in twenty years, were crowded into the tiny Wilcox sitting room. Roberta and Paula looked at each other, and the room seemed to implode in the silence.

"I seem to be rescuing stranded women tonight, Jessie," Ben finally continued. "First Paula and now the former Mrs. Reynolds."

"I'm not stranded, and don't call me that," Jessie snapped. It was the first hint of what might be another side to her. To Roberta she seemed so motherly, but she had a fierce independent streak. No wonder she hadn't lasted as Ben's wife.

"Now don't get your feathers ruffled. I thought maybe I could give you a ride home to get that oxygen tank you was just talking about. I got a half a tank in Coventry yesterday, and I might as well burn it up driving beautiful women around town."

Jessie was having none of his flattery. Her face was impassive and even her hair bun seemed to have tightened. "Thank you anyway, Benjamin, but Steve already volunteered to take me back. So if you'll excuse us."

With that, she and Steve departed, and they seemed to leave any icy breeze in their wake. Paula rolled her eyes at Roberta as she followed Ben back out to the kitchen. "Good God," she hissed. Roberta could only nod in response.

As Piccirelli's meeting approached, there was the problem of what to do about Gran. Steve suggested asking his father to sit with her, and early Saturday evening Ben came over with a week-old newspaper he had bought at Woodmansee's and a bag of black string licorice to substitute for his cigars, since Roberta had banned smoking in the sickroom. Roberta thought she detected a new glint in his eyes these days, as though he knew the punch line of a new joke. She couldn't imagine what was making him so jovial.

They rode in Steve's Cutlass. Paula and Ray sat in the back seat, and no one made conversation. In the summer they could almost have walked to the grange hall, but the days were growing shorter and it was already too dark for that. Although the ride was only two miles, it seemed to pass interminably.

She saw many people she recognized, and a few she did not. Ida Kenyon was there with her mother, who was even thinner and more wrinkled than Ida. Along the fringes sat the newcomers, mostly thirty- and forty-somethings who were well, but casually, dressed in LL Bean fleece jackets and khaki pants.

She did not see Lucas in the crowd.

It was after seven before Piccirelli appeared from a back room. With him were three men Roberta had never seen before, dressed in brown or blue blazers and striped shirts. Piccirelli had added his favorite yellow sweater vest to this uniform, and he walked up to the podium at the rear of the room so slowly and casually that Roberta wondered again at his self-assurance.

"Good evening," he began. His voice had neither the loud notes of the overly assured nor the tremor of the shy. It was natural, just loud enough, and as slow and even as if he had been talking to Roberta over a cup of coffee. "I welcome you all here tonight. We seem to have a good turnout. I recognize that this is probably the first time you all have been gathered together in quite a while, so I thought I would give you a few minutes to socialize. I hoped you enjoyed the time."

Boy, is he smooth, Roberta thought.

"I'm Anthony Piccirelli. Some of you may have met me already, and others will soon enough. My title is Director of the Office of Intergovernmental Affairs, but that's just a fancy way of saying that I do whatever the governor tells me to." He paused for a thin ripple of laughter. "I've had the pleasure of living in your village for the past few weeks. Those of you who have met me know a little bit about why I'm here, but let me review it for the benefit of those I haven't met."

Piccirelli went on to discuss the Ring program and its many advantages and listed a few people who had signed on to it. The names of Bud and Amy Tefft were no surprise to Roberta, but others were, including the Rices, a poor family who lived in a trailer farther up Cook Road, and John Woodmansee, Cal's brother. Heads seemed to crane up and around as neighbors tried to get a glimpse of the fallen among them.

Piccirelli cut the lights and brought out a slide projector from the podium. Soon the grange's stage curtain began to move

186

with images of what Piccirelli was calling "the lifestyle of tomorrow."

"The main riding ring is being preserved as a garden plot," Piccirelli said, after pointing to the buildings in the rear. "Some of the units will overlook it, while others will be clustered around a duck pond to be built on the property."

"It'll be a muddy mess in a week," somebody called out from the audience, but Piccirelli ignored the comment and switched to the next slide.

Roberta saw a skeleton of a building, with yellow earthmovers in front of it. "This unit is shaping up to be done by spring," Piccirelli said.

There was more: a slide of the governor in a hard hat walking the property, a small building and a windmill that Piccirelli said would generate the project's electricity, and a fanciful drawing of people gathered in front of a bandstand, clapping and smiling. Roberta felt her attention drifting. Then the lights snapped on and Piccirelli began to talk. It was a moment before Roberta realized his subject was no longer The Ring.

"The federal government is announcing this evening a major revision in the gas and oil rationing program," Piccirelli said. "The changes are necessary to ensure that our energy is disbursed fairly and to those who need it most. Beginning next month, citizens will be awarded points based on conservation. Those who live closest to the urban area and within The Ring will be given higher points than those who do not."

He paused. A ripple of comment flowed through the room. Before the crowd's discontent had a chance to erupt, he was speaking again.

"I know this is not what you want to hear. But it is further evidence that the feds, not just the state, are dead serious about Ring policy. The government wants to discourage people from living far from their employment or the nearest population center. Beginning next month the gas ration will be reduced to ten gallons a month for residents of this area. The oil ration is being reduced even further, to fifty gallons a month. The oil will be distributed in allotments of a hundred gallons every other month, to cut down on inefficient deliveries."

The crowd seemed to have been rendered speechless. But Piccirelli, still speaking in as calm a voice as if he were addressing the Rotary Club, had more to say.

"This rationing will be complicated in Rhode Island by another problem with which you should now be intimately familiar. Since early this fall electrical service in the state has been irregular at best. We have relied too long, and too heavily, on fossil fuels to power our plants, and we import too much power from other states. Now one of those power plants is in serious disrepair, and another one that was supposed to go on-line two years ago is still incomplete. We need to find a way to reduce demand. Building energy-efficient housing is one way we can do that."

Piccirelli paused to take a breath, but in that instant he lost his hold on the crowd. From a folding chair to his left a man jumped up, his voice erupting in the tiny hall.

"We're not moving!" he shouted, and the ripple of assent began to grow into a chorus around him. "This is America! You can't relocate us like a bunch of cattle! Why don't you tell us the real reason for all this nonsense. Maybe the governor and all his pals, maybe the mayor of Providence, are scooping up all the ration cards for themselves and their buddies. I bet that's it! Maybe you have to be in the Mafia to get a tank of gas. What about those boys on Federal Hill? I bet they're still driving their Caddies. What about our friends in the state house? Do you see them sitting at home in the dark? Not on your life!"

Piccirelli regarded him with an almost bored expression. "I can assure you that no favoritism is taking place. You might want to ask your senator, Mr. Maine, about that. He is subject to the same rules and restrictions as anyone else. Isn't that right, Senator?"

Maine was standing up in the back of the room, behind Piccirelli, leaning up against the wall. His expression betrayed no reaction to the exchange. He seemed to be weighing his reply.

"The good people of Coward's Hole certainly don't want to move down to East Greenwich," he said finally. Everyone seemed to be waiting for more, but he simply crossed his arms and looked away.

"Fred! Tell them to increase our ration, Fred!" It was Cal Woodmansee. "People are having trouble getting to my store, never mind Hope Valley. I can't get deliveries like I used to. I got Thanksgiving coming up, and people want turkeys and cranberry sauce . . . and I ain't got any! As soon as I get meat or vegetables in, they're gone. And I need batteries and paper goods and soft drinks. The food companies don't want to hear it anymore. They aren't going to stop all the way up here. And half the time when I go down to Hope Valley to stock up, them shelves is bare too. So what am I supposed to—"

Piccirelli had found a small gavel on his lectern and had begun pounding it, with short, firm whacks. "I can't solve individual problems, Mr. Woodmansee. Your case is a sterling example of why life in Coward's Hole is going to get more difficult, not easier, as time goes on. I am only the messenger here. This policy was made in Washington. Residents across the country are dealing with these very same issues. Here in Rhode Island, of all places, we should be able to find easy solutions to our dilemmas. This isn't Texas, after all."

A man in a polo shirt and Dockers stood up slowly. "No, this isn't Texas. In Texas they have oil fields in their backyard, for one thing. For another thing, the urban 'Ring' in these bigger Western states stretches for hundreds of miles. The only 'off-limits' areas there are already uninhabitable. It's easy to set up a 'Ring' if everybody's in it. It's those of us in the East, who are trying to maintain a rural lifestyle, who are being punished unnecessarily."

"This isn't a punishment, but I am afraid it's very necessary." Roberta detected a new edge to Piccirelli's voice.

"We are in the middle of a crisis. If we don't set up rules that apply to everyone, we will have the situation like what the earlier gentleman described. This may not be palatable, but it's fair. The people who travel the most are being discouraged from doing so."

Piccirelli's command of the meeting had deteriorated and his head began to bob from one speaker in the audience to the next. One by one they protested the new limits, each telling a story—of gas used up on shopping expeditions that left them empty-handed, of oil running out on a cold November night, of sick relatives who couldn't afford to drive to the drugstore or the doctor. Finally a woman stood up, clutching a red purse in her hands. Roberta craned her neck behind her to see the bowed head of Amy Tefft.

"Bud and me signed up for this new apartment, in The Ring," she began, her fingers working on the pocketbook strap. "We went down there last week."

Her voice was almost a whisper, but it echoed off the walls as though she were shouting.

"The old horse ring was still there—a pile of mud it was. They say it's going to be a garden in the spring, although I can't picture it," she went on in her rambling way. "The apartments—well, it was hard to tell what they'll amount to. They're framed up and all, a bunch of plywood, but they look like chicken coops now. Then they've got this row of windmills, I guess that's where our power's supposed to come from. They say they're in a hurry to get this thing up, but there waren't nobody there while we was."

"Don't do it, Amy," somebody shouted from across the room.

"I guess we don't have a choice now. We signed over our property. And from what I've heard tonight, we wouldn't be no better staying here. We might not do either one. You never know. If we can find a way, we'll go out to New York to be with our sons. They ain't bothering the farmers out there yet, no matter what this man says."

Roberta saw Wayne Reynolds stand up. He was across the room, but he seemed to be speaking right to Amy, as though he held her twitching hands in his.

"Mrs. Tefft, you aren't going to leave us. If you and Bud need a place to stay we'll give you one. We'll build you a new house if we have to. But nobody's leaving here who doesn't want to. Except maybe this Mr. Piccirelli here."

The residents began to clap and cheer. The men pounded their work boots against the floor. In the back of the room, Fred Maine stood, still leaning against the wall, a faint smile working its way across his face. Roberta felt chilled as she realized she was the only one who had seen it.

CHAPTER SEVENTEEN

That night they returned home to find the stunning news of the last two hours playing itself out on the TV.

Paula came into the living room with a cup of coffee.

"Looks like you're stuck here for a while," Roberta said. It was a conniving thing to say, but she couldn't help it.

"Why is that?"

"Well, just that you better hope you have enough gas to get home. And doesn't Ray have to get back to school? You don't want to wait too long."

Paula looked at her. "You know very well I'm not going anywhere until that probate hearing next week. But Ray is going, tomorrow in fact."

Roberta could not tell from her sister's tone if she was relieved or if she would have preferred to go home with her husband. For herself, she felt a stab of dismay. She would have liked to suggest that Ray stay and Paula go. She had come to rely on him with Gran.

"But when I do go, I'm going to ask Gran to come with me," Paula continued. "Oh, I'm not foolish enough to think she'll say yes right away. But I would never forgive myself if I didn't try."

"She's bedridden! She's on oxygen! She can't go with you."

"I live five minutes from the hospital," Paula argued. "This may be her only chance to get the medical help she needs. Roberta, she's dying in there. Listen to her! She isn't going to get better on her own."

Roberta eyed her sister with a new wonder. The truth was that, with the oxygen, Gran seemed to be holding her own. But for some reason Paula was determined to take her away.

"She might not make it to Westerly," she said. "At least here she's in her home, in her bed, where she wants to be. I won't let you move her."

"Well, we'll see." Paula, clearly unmoved, was making no concessions.

Ray did leave after breakfast Sunday. Roberta felt that her last ally was walking away from her. "Try to talk some sense into her," he whispered to Roberta at the front door, while Paula was putting a bag lunch in his car. "She's not going to come home until this is resolved."

Paula returned to their earshot, and he spoke in a normal tone. "I'll check out the ration situation at home, and I'll be back for Thanksgiving. If I can get Alton's ration cards straightened out, maybe we can get an oil delivery up here."

Roberta left them alone to say their goodbyes and went to see Gran, who had just finished breakfast.

"There's no need of that," the old woman protested as Roberta fluffed her two feather pillows. Her head was sunk into their depths, and her face had taken on the appearance of a dried-apple doll's. "I've got to get out of this bed and start helping you girls."

"Don't worry about us. Just try to get your strength back." Roberta sat on the edge of the massive feather bed, and May folded one warm, wrinkled hand into hers.

"Tell me about the meeting."

Roberta did her best to explain the new rations without alarming Gran. She tried to make it seem like more of the same, but Gran was watching her shrewdly. "You're worried about this, aren't you?"

"A little. I wish—"

"You wish your father was here. Well, so do I. I also wish I could get out of this bed." May shifted and let a groan escape. "I'm sick of being tied to this foolish thing." She tugged on her tubing for emphasis.

Oh, she can be stubborn, Roberta thought with despair, *even in the face of a granddaughter's pleadings.* Then Gran turned to her and smiled, as though they already had changed the subject.

"Tell Mr. Piccirelli he better not mess with me, or he won't get any more jonnycakes."

Roberta tucked May in again and carried away her breakfast dishes. In the kitchen she found not Paula, but Steve, who had helped himself to a cup of coffee. He was pacing near the door and his coat was still on, although Roberta could see his cup was almost empty.

"What's up with you? Haven't you heard of knocking?"

"Where's that Piccirelli? Is he here?"

"He left early this morning." Roberta set down the dishes and took a good look at Steve. His face was ashen, and the hands cradling the white coffee mug were shaking. "Steve, I don't want any trouble."

"Neither do I. Do you know where he went?"

"I have no idea. I don't know where he goes. Are you mad about last night?"

"You bet your ass I'm mad about last night. I'm so pissed off I'd like to—" He stopped and sank into the rocking chair. "They came last night and broke into my shed."

"What?"

"State troopers. Wayne's wife saw them. They broke down the door. They flashed a warrant in front of her face and then proceeded to ransack the place."

Roberta, who had assumed he was mad about the meeting, felt her head begin to swim. "What would state troopers want in your shed? Are you drying pot in there?"

He laughed. "I wish. No, I'm not drying pot in there. I was working on a little chemistry experiment. Somebody, probably our friend Piccirelli, must have gotten wind of it."

"Why do you think Piccirelli cares about what you do in your shed?"

He shifted forward in the rocking chair and put both feet on the ground. "Roberta. Pay attention. There's more going on here than this stupid Ring program, can't you see that?"

He's talking in riddles, Roberta thought, *and the more questions I ask, the worse it gets.* "Tell me what you were doing in that shed, Steve Reynolds, and don't get smart with me."

"Ever hear of wood alcohol? They used to make it up here, oh, a hundred years ago. Big distilleries on the river. They put wood in large ovens, and the vapor that was produced was condensed into acetic acid and wood alcohol. It's called 'destructive distillation.' The acid was shipped in barrels to textile mills down the river, and the mills used it to make dyes."

"That's a fine history lesson, Steve, but I fail to see what it has to do with a bunch of state troopers breaking into your shed."

"I'm getting to that. Now think a minute. What's wood alcohol? Methanol. And what's one use for methanol?"

"As a fuel? Or is that methane?"

"Methane's a fuel, but you are correct. Methanol is, too. And a damned good one, I must say. Doesn't pollute the environment the way gas does, with smog and all that. Even if it spills into the water, it causes less harm than gas. Gets you great acceleration, and it's even less flammable. There's just one problem."

She couldn't help sharing his enthusiasm, as much as she wished he'd get to the point. "And what is that?"

"It's corrosive to metal and rubber. You can't just pour it in a gas tank and go. It doesn't work in the internal combustion engine. You need to build a fuel cell. But it's already being done, Roberta. There are methanol vehicles driving in the Indy 500. The feds have a whole fleet of 'em."

"So let me guess. You're experimenting with building one of your own."

"I hadn't gotten that far. I was still trying to distill the wood alcohol. But that was the general idea, yes."

"So what's the problem with this burst of ingenuity?"

"I don't know. Maybe they thought I was making whiskey. Or maybe they're afraid I'll come up with a cheaper way to gas up the car. Think about the gas tax. Billions a year."

Roberta began to laugh, and even though she could see his brows knitting together, she couldn't stop. "Steve, I can't imagine you puttering around in your backyard is any threat to the national treasury."

"Okay, smart ass, then why did two state troopers knock down my shed door and walk off with all my distilling equipment?"

She had to admit she had no answer. It was just another surreal moment in what had become a whole season of them since she returned home.

He began to pace again. "It's an awful big coincidence that Piccirelli calls this meeting and drags the whole town out, and then, when they think no one's around, the state cops raid the place."

Piccirelli did seem anxious to get everyone to go to the meeting, but Roberta hated to concede the point. "Piccirelli had an announcement to make. Besides, not everybody was at the meeting. You said Wayne's wife saw them."

"She stayed home with the kids, and they'd all walked over to my house. I think she surprised the hell out of 'em."

"So you think Piccirelli tipped them off."

"She's finally catching on."

Roberta still couldn't figure out how Piccirelli would know about Steve's experiment and, even if he did, why he would care. Didn't the state have bigger problems than somebody tinkering in his backyard to make an alternative fuel? But Steve remained unswayed. Piccirelli, he insisted, had to be behind the nighttime raid, and that was all the more reason why Roberta should give her lodger the boot.

"I can't afford to get rid of him," she protested. "Right now that's the only money coming into the house. Lucas says the probate judge might give us an allowance, but I have no idea how much."

"If you need money, I'll give you a loan. Anything's better than keeping that Judas under your roof."

"Thanks, but no thanks." The Wilcox family had taken out enough loans, she thought.

The week before Thanksgiving, Lucas picked her up in the Peugeot and they drove to town hall for the probate hearing. Roberta's heart lurched when she sighted Fred Maine, sitting next to a man in a black suit and a thin tie. Lucas was dressed for the occasion, but barely: He wore a tweed suit jacket with a brown plaid shirt, and Roberta thought he looked too much like a country lawyer to inspire much confidence. Paula sat in the back of the room and barely nodded when they walked in.

"In the matter of the estate of George Alton Wilcox," the judge intoned, and Roberta sat up straighter. Papers shuffled and the judge began to read. As the letter from the town had said, she and Paula were to be co-executors, and they raised their hands when he asked if they were present. He nodded curtly and continued.

She heard disjointed words, phrases she did not understand, then Gran's name, and Paula's and Ben's. Alton had left Paula the farm, with a life lease for Gran, and the mill and a small parcel of land would be Ben Reynolds's. So Paula, who

197

desperately wanted to sell the farm, now owned it—except she had to let Gran live out her life there. Roberta would have admired her father for such a move, if not for the rest of it. He had left her out entirely.

Lucas was staring intently ahead. He seemed about to say something when Maine's lawyer stood up.

"I represent Senator Fred Maine, who has a lien against this estate," he said.

"How much?" the judge asked.

"Fifty thousand dollars, your honor."

"Is there anyone else present who has a debt against this estate?"

Silence. *Fifty thousand dollars.* Roberta felt her throat catch. The farm was as good as gone.

"Mr. Whitford, what say you?"

"Your honor, I need time to ascertain if the debt can be paid without selling the decedent's property."

"You represent Paula Wilcox Brown?"

"Uh . . . no. I represent her sister, Roberta Wilcox."

"She's not an heir. Who represents Paula—what was her name? Brown?"

"I don't have a lawyer, your honor," Paula said from the back of the room.

Roberta looked up at Lucas, alarmed. He had warned her any split between the sisters would complicate things. Now he seemed frazzled; an errant clump of hair was hanging over one eye. He was still in the crouched position, half sitting, half standing, as though he didn't know if he had the judge's permission to address him.

"Ordered advertised for two weeks," the judge finally said. "More debtors may turn up. I have a couple of letters here—business debts, they look like. Young lady, do you understand your responsibility in all this?"

Roberta turned around to see Paula stand up. "What does this life lease mean?"

"If the will stands, it means your grandmother can live out her life on that property. Do you understand?"

"Then how can we sell it to pay our debts?" Paula countered.

The judge looked exasperated. "You may not have to. Mr. Whitford, approach."

Lucas diffidently walked up to the table that served as the judge's bench, and they began to whisper. Roberta, try as she might, caught none of the hissed words, but the judge's tone was impatient and Lucas seemed confused, hardly the masterful lawyer she had imagined he would be.

After the conversation, the judge continued the matter for two weeks, and it was over. Roberta followed Lucas to the car in a daze. Dimly she was aware of Fred Maine smirking in the back of the room as she left. *Damn him,* she thought. Fifty thousand dollars! What had happened to the few thousand dollars she assumed Alton owed Maine? Just how long had her father been in debt, anyway?

They rode silently back toward Jonnycake Trail. Lucas watched her with what looked almost like pity. Finally he put his right hand over her left and said, "I'm sorry. I had no idea what was in your father's will. I really didn't have time to do a lot of homework before the hearing."

"I don't understand."

"Apparently your father wanted to make sure the farm wasn't sold out from under your grandmother. But why he left it to Paula and not the both of you, I have no idea. As co-executor you do have some power, but ultimately Paula will be calling the shots."

Roberta sat immobile. The pain that had washed over her the night of her argument with her father was back, only this time it was more like a tidal wave, and she was going under. So it was true. The lies that she had told herself, the excuses she had made for her father—the pain, not her rationalizations, held the truth. Her father had never loved her.

She had humiliated herself trying to save him. She had come home and swallowed her pride to try to make amends. She had suffered for so many years, following at his heels for whatever crumb of affection he might leave her. When her mother died, he was the only thing standing between Roberta being someone's child and an orphan. Her grandmother had given her love, but it was her father's affection she had desperately fought to win.

For years Paula had been her competition. But now she wondered if all along her competition had not been her very self. She had lost because Alton would never love, or acknowledge loving, the daughter he had made with Jackie Miller.

Roberta felt herself hunch over, racked with sobs. It was not money, it was not the farm, it was not the business that she wanted. It was only her father's love. But he had left her nothing. He had named her and Paula executors to avoid a legal challenge, maybe, or out of some vague obligation. But he did not trust her with the farm, and he did not think she deserved any money. Not that there would be any money to bequeath, when Maine got done with them.

Lucas pulled the Peugeot over onto a sandy turnoff and wrapped his arms about her. She was only vaguely aware of his embrace. She was beyond comforting. She had lost her mother to death, but she had never doubted her mother's love. But to have her father die, then reject her so cruelly even after he was gone, was too much to bear. What was a daughter whose father did not love her? Who was a child with no loving parents? She willed herself to disappear. She had nowhere to put her need, her pain, and it was a burden too ugly to carry.

"Roberta, Roberta." Lucas was stroking her hair. "People do

funny things when they write wills. They forget how long forever is. Maybe he was angry with you, you had had a spat . . . it doesn't mean he didn't care for you. Maybe he was afraid you weren't interested enough in the farm to keep it. After all, you had made a home in Maryland. He might have thought you could provide for yourself. He didn't exactly leave your sister the farm outright, either. And you know as long as May's alive, you'll be able to stay."

She was crying too hard to talk. His words were empty, cheap, obligatory. They could not touch the truth of her pain.

"Maybe he was trying to keep Maine's hands off the farm somehow," Lucas continued. "He probably got some bad legal advice."

Instinctively Roberta rejected Lucas's theories. She had heard the language of wills, on TV and in books, and she knew people could use them to express their love. But there was no love in this last will and testament. Its words echoed coldly in her head. Not even Gran . . . oh, what would she tell Gran?

For the first time Roberta remembered the old woman lying in her bed, her life hanging on the whir of the oxygen machine. She would have to tell Gran something. She would have to give voice to this pain, or else hide it again, buried deep in a heart too used to being stuffed with such emotions.

"Take me home, Lucas," she said finally.

CHAPTER EIGHTEEN

It had turned cold, unusually so for late November. The curled brown oak leaves littering the ground were rimed with frost each morning, and a thin crust of ice covered the animals' water. The last flowers of autumn were black sticks in the west field. The darkness crowded each end of the day. The air carried the snap of winter.

Not since Alton's passing and Ray's leaving had anyone split the lengths of wood her father had left piled in the carriage shed. Roberta put on a pair of Alton's old suede gloves and set out. The ax hung in the rafters in the carriage shed, barely within reach.

Her aim was good, but her stroke was not. The ax stuck in the oak, sending her reeling forward, almost into it. She swung the ax again, and this time the wood split cleanly, its halves falling to left and right and the ax cleaning hitting the block below.

She thought she heard laughter. Maybe Alton really was watching, but if he were, would she hear him? Could ghosts make noise in broad daylight?

"Bravo." She looked up to see Steve, a shadow in the carriage shed's broad doorway. His arms were crossed, but hanging from one hand was a freshly plucked turkey.

It looked so much like a rubber chicken that Roberta wanted to laugh aloud.

"Where on earth did you get that?"

"Oh no, I get the first question. Where did you get that swing?

You look like you're playing overhand croquet."

Of course, he had to find her doing something stupid. He couldn't show up when the wood was freshly split and stacked, so she could casually say, "Oh, that? I chopped it myself. You don't think a woodsman's daughter knows how to chop wood?"

But he had probably caught the whole performance, closed eyes and all. It was like him to hang back in amusement, watching her gingerly pick up the ax, take a few practice swings. At least she could change the subject. "Is that what you used on Tom there? A mallet?"

"I hope you don't think this is funny. I risked my butt shooting this damn thing. I was up at three a.m. and stalked a flock of 'em practically to Maine's doorstep. I almost got my head blowed off."

"Maine tried to shoot you?"

"Nooo. Somebody in the woods was using me for target practice. But I got in a few shots of my own. Well, don't let me keep you from your work. You've got a lot of chopping there."

She leaned on the butt of the ax, casually, as though she needed a break. "What am I supposed to do with that thing?"

"Gut it and dress it and stick in the oven. You don't expect me to cook it, too, do you?"

"Well, you could have cut off the head and feet at least." She laughed, a little of the tension of the past weeks escaping her. She absently turned back to the pile, as though looking for the perfect piece of oak.

"I'm glad you think this is so funny. I was out there worried you weren't going to have any Thanksgiving, and you're out gallivanting around with some senior citizen."

She looked up. "What?"

"You heard me. I saw you the other day parked on the road, all cozy with that gentleman horse farmer who's old enough to be your father. I almost choked."

"It's not—" She stopped, trapped. What could she say? It wasn't what he thought, at least not then. She had been crying her heart out, and Steve thought she was giving the guy a blow job. But the essential truth of what he said was there, and that she couldn't dispute.

"I can't believe you! We were talking, for God's sake! I was upset! I just found out my father disinherited me, and you think I'm making time with the guy!"

"Alton disinherited you?"

"Yes, if you must know. At least that's what it looks like. He left everything to Paula, the mill to your father, and gave Gran a life lease."

Steve let out a low whistle. "I don't think my father has any idea about the mill. He wouldn't take it anyway. He knows it belongs to you and your sister."

"Thank you, Steve, but the mill is the least of my problems. All I know is Maine has a lien on the place, and if we don't come up with fifty thousand we're going to have to sell."

He whistled again, but his eyes were still hard. "So your senior citizen friend was offering you a shoulder to cry on."

"He's my lawyer."

"Nice try, Roberta. I'm not stupid. You've been spending plenty of time over to his place. You know there are no secrets in this town."

"I don't know what you're talking about."

He changed the subject. "So what's this about a lien? Your father owed the senator money?"

"Yeah." She let a sigh escape and put the ax down. "I thought it was a few thousand, maybe, but Maine apparently has some note he signed for fifty grand."

"That's unbelievable. You'd think if he needed that kind of money he'd just go to a bank."

"His credit wasn't the best."

"With this place as collateral? Come on."

"He mistrusted banks, always did."

"And he trusted Maine more? No, it doesn't add up."

"Well, Lucas is looking into it. He's going back to town hall. Said he has to check a few things out."

" 'Lucas'? That's what you call him?"

"That's his name, Steve."

"Awfully cozy."

"Look, I don't want to talk about this. There may be . . . *something* between Lucas and me, but I really don't think you need to know about it."

"Oh, I don't, don't I? So it's okay to lead me along like a donkey while you're humping Grampa down the road? Jesus, Roberta, he's old enough to be your father. Or maybe that was the attraction."

Roberta could feel all the grief of the past few weeks boiling inside her, taking a new form. Lucas was the only thing, the only private and special thing, she had left. And now Steve Reynolds was twisting their relationship, perverting it, turning it into another one of her failures. As much as she had begun to doubt the affair herself, Steve's derision only made her defend it the more.

"Get out of here. You don't know anything about it. You have to reduce everything to some twenty-second episode in the back seat of a car. Maybe you find it a little bit threatening that I might be having a good time with somebody who knows what he's doing."

Steve was absently swinging the dead turkey, and for a frightful moment she thought he was going to hit her with it. "You're making a big mistake."

She was sorry, truly; but she felt hardened to everything he was saying. He was like them all, seeing things in her that weren't there and expecting things she couldn't deliver . . . and failing to see what she truly needed. She didn't know what to say. She ran into the house, hoping he would leave, but he was right behind her, letting the aluminum door slam behind him.

"I think you better go," she said.

"I'm not going anywhere. I deserve some answers."

"Steve, I don't want to talk about this."

"Roberta, you must know—"

Behind him the door slammed again, and Lucas walked in and hung his plaid coat on a peg. He was taking off his boots when he looked up at them. Roberta could hear only her own breathing, which had not stilled from the run into the house.

"That's a nice turkey," Lucas finally said. "They're hard to catch."

"I chased it all the way to Maine's place. I wasn't about to let it go."

Lucas smiled thinly. "Looks like you brought it to the right place. Bring it outside. I'll cut off the head."

"After you."

Roberta ran to the window. She saw Lucas pick up the ax and run it over the grinding wheel, sharpening it. So that was the problem, she thought irrelevantly, and then: *Oh my God, they'll kill each other.* They were talking. She saw their mouths moving, ejecting little puffs of air. What could they be saying? Steve had yet to let go of the turkey, but then suddenly he swung it around onto a sawhorse and Lucas raised the ax above his head, chopping off first the turkey's head and then its feet.

Steve and Lucas came inside and helped themselves to coffee. Roberta found herself chattering uncontrollably, bringing cups and cream and sugar cookies, filling up the kitchen with her senseless commentary.

"What time's Thanksgiving?" Steve asked, turning to her.

For a moment, she had no idea what he meant. She wanted to say "Thursday," but then she realized he was asking her what time she was serving dinner—and, by implication, what time he should show up. Lucas had finished his cookie and was watching her as well.

"Uh . . . I don't know. How long do you think it will take that bird to cook?" She had put it in the refrigerator with a barely disguised revulsion.

"It's got to be twenty pounds, wouldn't you say, Lucas?"

"Oh, yeah. Figure twenty minutes a pound."

"That's almost seven hours!"

"Better get up early," Steve said, smiling.

"Steve, I hadn't figured on making a big dinner. I don't even know if Ray will make it back."

"He'll be here. Count me and Wayne's family and the old man in. Lucas makes seven, and Paula and Ray nine, and it's eleven with you and May. Make it lucky thirteen if you're going to have the Teffts."

This was an elaborate joke they were playing on her; it must be. Roberta felt a flash of malice. "Haven't you forgotten someone? Why not invite your mother while you're at it?"

He didn't bite. "Maybe I will, but I doubt if she'll come."

"Steve, this is ridiculous. We can't cook for thirteen people, especially with Gran sick abed."

"I'll send the old man up to peel potatoes Thanksgiving morning. And you know Ray will show up, and he'll probably bring some food from town. Come on, Roberta, it wouldn't be Thanksgiving if we didn't eat at Wilcox Farm."

"I'll make my famous mushroom soup. I haven't poisoned anybody lately." For a moment she thought Lucas was winking at her.

"So it's a date."

Steve stood up, and then Lucas pushed back his chair. They had arrived separately, but they were leaving together. She carried their empty coffee cups to the kitchen sink and looked out to the carriage shed where the unsplit wood still lay in disarray. She hadn't gotten anything accomplished after all.

On the night before Thanksgiving, Roberta collapsed into her cot in Gran's room just before midnight.

Her mind would not shut off. That morning they had found the hasp ripped off the root cellar door, and the bins of carrots and potatoes markedly lower than Roberta had remembered. Paula thought probably an animal had gotten in—it wouldn't be the first time, especially with black bears returning to Coward's Hole—but it didn't feel like an animal raid to Roberta.

Paula had just given a short laugh and said, "Gee, maybe it was Ida."

After her mind had worked its way around that disturbing episode, it meandered its way to probate court and then dodged back to the scene a few days before with Steve and Lucas. She had not seen either one since, and tomorrow they would both be at her table, eating her food, eyeing her for signs of . . . what? With both of them here, which Roberta would she be? With Steve she was worldly, wise, and sarcastic; with Lucas, a piece of her deeper self came out, sensitive and wounded and longing for love.

Roberta had begun to drift off when she heard the pounding. She threw on her robe and parted the curtain. A big truck was in the yard, its engine rumbling and its lights sending a yellow beam through the flying snow. A plow driver who needs a cup of coffee, maybe, she thought, running numbly to the door.

"Jesus! I could have waked the dead before you got up! Hurry up, get your clothes on and come with me."

It was Steve. He was bundled in a quilted down jacket and a red plaid hat with earflaps. He had stepped into the kitchen but he was slapping his gloved hands together impatiently. His moustache was coated in snow.

"Go with you? Where?" Roberta wished she would wake up; even talking was a struggle.

"I don't have time to answer questions. I had to leave the damn truck running; it's hopped up on homemade diesel because the state hasn't come through with my gas. Look, I need your help. Would I ask if it wasn't important? Now hurry up. Throw on something warm, and get a thermos of coffee."

Roberta ran upstairs to her room, found a pair of sweatpants and a turtleneck to throw over her long underwear, and then put on another sweater for good measure. By now she was awake enough to realize what he was asking her to do. Gran. She would have to wake up Paula. Someone would have to sleep with Gran downstairs.

Paula was a sounder sleeper than Roberta, and Roberta nearly had to drag her downstairs to Gran's bedroom. "But where are you going?" she asked over and over. Roberta pretended not to have time to answer, too embarrassed to admit she had no idea.

Steve had heated water and mixed it with instant coffee and filled a thermos. He was pacing in the kitchen when she finally came out and nearly dragged her out the door before she put her coat on.

"Gloves and a hat," he ordered, and she complied.

Steve's Mack truck was so high off the ground, he had to give her a boost to get her in the cab. Inside, it was steamy and loud, and the cracked seat felt scratchy beneath her sweatpants. The exhaust stack was belching foul black clouds into the snow. It was that homemade diesel: motor oil mixed with kerosene. She'd seen her father make it.

He backed the truck out onto the highway, put the plow down and headed east, back toward town.

"If you needed a spotter, you could have got your brother." The more awake she got, the more annoyed she felt. He was dragging her out at one in the morning, and she had to get up at five to cook that damned turkey.

"I don't need a spotter."

"What the hell did you just roust me out of bed for?"

"You'll see. Watch that edge there; let me know if I come too close to a mailbox."

"See! You're using me for a spotter."

"Roberta, I would never use you."

It was a gentle rebuke that struck its target soundly. Steve was pulling on the gears, and the old Mack truck began to inch its way up Mount Laurel. She felt the gears grate as Steve downshifted, trying to keep the ten-ton truck under control.

"Watch out for the bridge," Roberta finally said as an abutment loomed ahead.

"I see it." He had begun to slow down, and then to Roberta's surprise he turned the snowplow left into Laurel Heights, the truck barely making it through the stone pillars at the development's entrance. The plow scraped away snow on the winding street, each house it passed black under the streetlights. The umbrella of light the lamps threw seemed to come from nowhere in the swirling snow.

"What a job you have. There's barely a soul who lives here anymore. And you get paid for this."

"I'm not here to plow." He stopped the truck with a gnashing of gears near the end of the cul-de-sac and turned off the engine. "We're walking from here. I don't want him to know we're coming."

"What? Who?"

"See that house over there? Near the end of the street?" Beneath the streetlights she could barely see the colonial he was indicating, the pillars of its farmer's porch rising like statues in the snowfall. "A family lived there until October. Mother, second husband, a couple of kids. But then something happened. Like almost everyone else on the street, they moved away. All but one."

"All but one family?"

"No. All but one child. They left their boy behind."

Roberta felt the jagged edge of the upholstery cutting into her legs. Even in the murky light cast by the street lamp she could see that Steve's face was white, and suddenly it all came together.

"Niles Porter. My God."

"I've been watching him. He does pretty good. Gets on the school bus every day at the end of the street. He doesn't look like he's starving. I've been leaving him food in his mailbox. He doesn't know it's me, of course. But it's always gone the next night. His clothes seem to be clean. He's a smart kid. Street smart, almost. But you should see his eyes. They're haunted, or maybe hungry . . . he's careful. Probably his parents left him here for a reason. Can't have anybody stealing their stuff, you know."

"I can't believe this. Why didn't you tell someone?"

"Tell who? The state? They'd be up here in a second, and he'd be in some foster home, where God knows what would happen to him. No, I've watched over him as best I can, but you don't want the authorities getting a hold of him. He doesn't need some damned social worker analyzing him; he needs a home."

"So what are you going to do?"

"I don't know. I've sat back as long as I can, Roberta. It's cold, and he doesn't have any real way to heat that house. I know for a fact there hasn't been an oil delivery to Laurel Heights in months. I've never seen lights on. Probably he couldn't pay the bill or is afraid he'll be discovered. There's a couple people still living out on the other end, but even they don't know he's here. I keep thinking it's time we took him back with us."

He looked at her as though he expected an argument, but Roberta was already reaching for the door handle. "Hold on!" He grabbed her wrist and she felt the strength in his hand. "We can't just sweep in there. That's why I brought you. I figured . . . you'd know what to do."

"I don't know what to do any more than you do, Steve, but if everything you've said is true, we've got to get him."

"I know that, but how? I don't want to scare him. You know he's got a gun. And I think he's the one who shot at me that day I was turkey hunting."

Roberta shuddered. The temperature of the cab had plummeted as soon as Steve cut the engine. The cold reality of what he was asking her to do began to sink in.

"We could wait till daylight."

"I know. We probably should. But I can't get him off my mind. Maybe it's the cold, or the first snow. I just have a feeling he needs some help."

That clinched it. Roberta hopped down from her seat and began to plow through the calf-high snow to the house. Steve was right behind her, his flashlight casting a pale beam in the swirls of white. She was heading out on this mission blindly, without thought. Something propelled her forward: the same thing that had sent Steve out in the middle of this storm. She lifted her fists to the door, pounded and yelled, just as Steve had done at her house only a half-hour before. Instinct told her Steve was right; it was better for Niles to hear a woman's voice calling his name in the middle of the night than a man's.

A door was unlatched and opened slightly, a dark head appearing in the wedge. In the dim backlight from the recesses of the house she could see that Niles wore a flannel shirt and pants, as though he had been up, although his hair was tousled and his face wore the confusion of sleep. His mouth was thin and grimly set, but the hardness in his face was not matched in his eyes. They were the same dark pools Roberta had seen so many times in the mirror. Veiled yet beseeching and hungry, they were the eyes of an orphan.

"Niles." She spoke only his name not because she could think of nothing else to say, but because she felt she was meeting someone whom she had always known.

He said nothing, looking beyond her to Steve, whom he appeared to recognize. Roberta could feel Steve impatiently shuffling behind her, but her instinct told her this encounter could not be hurried. Another reason Steve had brought her.

"Do you like turkey?" she finally said. He did not answer but continued to watch her, so she felt safe in going on. "Steve caught a wild turkey the other day. We're going to have it tomorrow"—*if I ever get home, she thought*—"and we'd like you to join us."

"I can't," he said finally.

"Listen, Niles, you can't stay here anymore," Steve began, and Roberta elbowed him.

"What Steve means to say is that he knows you're alone, and nobody should be alone on Thanksgiving. That's why we thought you might like to come home with us, to have dinner."

"I can't come home with you," he repeated in the same monotone. "I can't walk that far."

"You can't—" Roberta looked at his face for any signs of facetiousness, but couldn't find any. "You don't have to walk. We have the truck."

Suddenly the boy stepped aside and swung the door open, and Roberta realized he had meant his remarks literally. He was leaning on the door and his left foot was off the floor like a flamingo's. It was wrapped in what appeared to be layer after layer of gauze, so that for a moment she thought he was wearing a cast. Then, just as she made a move to step inside the door, he fell into a heap on the hardwood floor.

"Oh, my God, Steve, look at him."

Together they stepped in and bent over the boy, whose face was ghostly under the glare of the flashlight. Steve began to feel his pulse, touch his forehead, listen to his heart with an ear to the boy's chest. "He's passed out, but I think he's okay," he said finally. "Let's see if we can get him to a couch."

Steve picked up Niles, and Roberta cast about the hallway with the flashlight. The living room was to their right. The room, as far as she could tell, was reasonably neat, but it was almost as cold as outdoors, with green logs sizzling weakly in the fireplace. Roberta found the couch, which already was made up with a pillow and sleeping bag, and Steve placed Niles gently on it.

"Oh, God. That day when I was hunting—"

He didn't have to finish. Roberta looked down at the clump of fabric wound around his ankle. It was soaked in red.

"It wasn't your fault. Get me another pillow."

Roberta placed a hand on the boy's forehead and he began to stir. "We've got to get him home. It's freezing in here."

"Go see if you can round up some clothes for him. When you're done with that, I'll go warm up the truck."

Roberta felt her way through the dark, the flashlight's beam leading her on. In what must have been Niles's room, clothes lay crumpled on the floor and the bed had been stripped to its sheets. He had been sleeping by the fire to stay warm. She could not tell which clothes were clean and which dirty, but she began piling what she could into a backpack she found on the floor, her hands cramping in the cold.

"Come on, Roberta, we've got to get this kid out of here."

She swept the flashlight around the room one last time, and then she saw it on a bureau: a family photo, framed in teak. A woman, a young girl, a balding man, and Niles. The father was tall, smiling a crooked but superior smile, and wearing a polo shirt and khaki pants. Then there was Niles, on one side of his mother, looking hard into the camera without a smile.

"Roberta, Jesus Christ!"

She scrambled downstairs, and Steve headed out to warm up the truck. She kneeled on the floor and gazed into Niles's face while she waited. He was conscious now but his face was contorted in pain, and she was not sure if he knew she was there. She began to whisper in a slow monotone, hoping the sound of the words, as much as their meaning, would get him through. "It's all right. Just hang in there. We're going to get you out of here, and into a warm bed. We'll get you something for that pain. Don't leave us, buddy."

Don't leave me, she wanted to say. She felt she had waited her whole life to meet this boy. She could not fail him.

"You made it home that day," Niles said. It was the first sign he had recognized her.

"Yes I did, Deerhunter, and I'm not afraid to say I was scared out of my wits. It got dark awful fast, didn't it?"

"Sometimes when I go into the woods, it's like time stops."

How many times had he gone back to Lewis City, hoping to find her there? How many times had he given up in the waning light before dusk? She should have looked for him. She should have done something. "Do you like going there?"

"I don't know. I like the quiet. But in a way it gives me the creeps."

He had probably been chasing Steve on purpose, she thought. Anything for human contact. This kid was begging to be saved, and the two of them had been too dumb to realize it.

With a stamping of feet Steve returned. "Sonofabitch! If you hadn't taken so damned long upstairs—"

She jumped up. "What's the matter?"

"Truck won't start. Damned homemade diesel. That's why I

left it running at your place, but I figured . . . Christ! I've got to go work on it some more."

She could hear the truck's engine strain, whine, then die. She rubbed her hands on the boy's legs, trying to warm them and carefully avoiding his wound. She felt a flash of annoyance at Steve. Yes, he had saved the boy, but he had shot him, too.

She walked to the door and began to shout his name, her voice thin in the rising wind.

"Steve, how far is home?"

"Oh, three miles as the crow flies. What? We can't walk out of here. The kid can't even walk across the room."

"What if we got a sled? Couldn't we pull him? We can't stay here."

"The kid must weigh over a hundred pounds! You want me to drag him up the mountain? Are you crazy?"

"We'll both do it. Come on. Look in the garage; I bet you anything there's a sled in there. Who brings a sled to Florida?"

Steve was mumbling under his breath, but he headed to the garage, and soon he was back with a wooden toboggan. "Even better," Roberta declared. "We'll have to bundle him up. Come on, help me get an extra pair of pants on him. I'll go look for a coat."

Soon they had dressed Niles in another layer of clothes, a down parka, a hat and mittens. Steve carried him outside and placed him on the toboggan, where Roberta had lain the sleeping bag. They zipped him into it, put the pillowcase full of clothing beneath his head, grabbed the reins together and set off.

It was rough going from the start. The snow was heavy and wet and they seemed to be working against it, wending a narrow path down the middle of the street. The flakes blew like stinging needles, straight at them, making it hard to focus on where they were going.

Niles was awake now. The cold seemed to have numbed the

pain, and Roberta could feel him watching their backs.

"So what happened to you, anyway?" Steve asked conversationally, as if they were two hikers comparing broken legs in a bar.

"Rabbit hole. Stepped in it yesterday when I was out . . ."

"Out hunting," was what he was going to say, Roberta thought, until he thought better of it. His guard was not completely down.

"Rabbit must have been armed," Steve said.

"Yeah, well, I wish I'd shot it back."

"You won't be saying that after you taste that turkey I got."

Niles turned his head back as though the truth had dawned on him, but he said nothing. They were on the highway now and had begun the gradual ascent that signaled the onset of Mount Laurel. Roberta struggled to keep up with Steve. She was wearing an old pair of hiking boots, and already she could feel the dampness seeping into her wool socks and her toes cramping from the cold.

"I think I'm getting frostbite."

"It's thirty degrees. You don't get frostbite at this temperature."

"It's freezing, isn't it?"

"Shh. You'll scare the boy."

They trudged on. Even Steve seemed winded, and their steps were slower now. Each time they pulled on the toboggan's cord, it seemed to want to slide backwards. Roberta imagined with horror it sliding over the edge of the mountain; was everything in her life reduced to the threat of that possibility?

"Steve."

"Umm."

"I'm sorry about . . . you know."

"No, I don't know. What have you done to be sorry about? Or maybe I don't want to know."

"Don't make this harder than it is."

"An apology isn't an apology unless you really think you were wrong."

"I'm sorry you found out about Lucas. I didn't mean to hurt you."

"Oh." And he let out an exhalation of frosty breath as they stopped at the summit. "You're sorry I found out, but not sorry you did it."

"I am sorry I did it. No; I'm not sorry I did it, exactly, I'm just sorry it happened when it did."

"Well, when you figure it out, let me know."

They were on the downhill side of the mountain now. The toboggan, pushed in a new direction by the forces of gravity, crept up on the backs of their boots. It was just as difficult trying to get the sled safely downhill as it had been dragging it uphill. And while they inched their way down the other side of Mount Laurel, the snow blew up the side of the hill in angry gusts that scratched and burned their cheeks. Roberta looked back nervously at Niles, whose chapped face was the only thing exposed. "His face is blue," she yelled into Steve's ear. "How much longer do you think it will take?"

Steve took the flashlight from her and looked back, then leaned toward her. "You're right. He doesn't look good. Let's try for my house. It's closer."

CHAPTER NINETEEN

They carried Niles in together, Steve holding him in his arms, Roberta cradling his head. If her eyes had not been so blinded by the zigzag of falling snow she would have sworn he was blue. But he was breathing and his eyes were open now and gradually, as they peeled off the wet layers from his body and wrapped him in wool blankets, the color flowed back into his skin. With the warming of his blood, the moans of pain returned.

"Get him some aspirin," Steve barked at his father, "or something stronger if you can find it."

Ben came back with Tylenol with codeine. Roberta read the label nervously—it had been prescribed to Ben only six months before—but Steve snatched it out of her hand.

"I'm not going to poison the kid, for Chrissakes. Let's give him one, and he should fall asleep."

Steve turned out to be right. Niles fell asleep on the sofa, and the adults slumped around the kitchen table for a cup of coffee.

"I don't think I've ever been so cold in my life," Roberta said, clutching her cup but not drinking.

"That's a tough walk even in daylight," Ben offered. He turned to Steve. "Why don't you tell me what this is all about?"

Steve told the story as he would many times in the next twenty-four hours, but he spared no details for his father. When he finished, Ben looked from one to the other.

"You realize you're going to have to report this," he said finally. "Not only does this kid belong in the custody of the state, but it looks like you shot him."

Roberta felt something clutch in her stomach. Steve was right—the last thing this boy needed was to be taken away by a social worker. But Ben probably had a point.

"I'm not letting the state take that kid," Steve said.

"What if somebody finds out? You can't keep him forever. His parents will come back, and you'll have some explaining to do."

"His parents will be the ones with some explaining to do!" Steve slammed his hand on the table. "Leaving a kid that age alone for that long. It's a wonder he's still alive."

"If he doesn't make it, it'll be because somebody was hunting turkey out of season and shooting at people, not because his parents went to Florida." Ben got up for the coffeepot.

"He shot at Steve," Roberta put in, surprised to find herself defending him. "It was an accident, and he certainly isn't mortally wounded. Sleeping in a cold house with no food was just as dangerous to him."

Ben kicked his legs up on the chair next to him. "Well, if that kid dies here, you'll have even more explaining to do."

You mind your business, I'll mind mine. How many times had Roberta heard versions of it in her own family? "He won't die here because as soon as the sun comes up I'm taking him to my house," she said. "So you won't have to worry about it."

"Don't get your drawers unhitched. I'm just pointing out that there are complications. And what if you do bring him to your house? That's even worse. You've got that state fellow right under your roof."

Piccirelli. She had not given him a moment's thought. But Ben was right—of all the people she didn't want to explain Niles Porter to, it was Anthony Piccirelli, who was so by-the-book he'd turn in his own mother if she didn't license her dog.

Steve seemed to be far away, leaning back in the old kitchen chair with its two legs off the ground. "We've got to think up a story. Dad does have a point. Tomorrow's Thanksgiving, and half the town will be up to your place."

"He's a friend, visiting. Someone's nephew. A guest." Roberta was thinking aloud, and her suggestions sounded hollow to her. "I don't know. Why can't we just tell the truth? Or a version of the truth. His parents are away and you're babysitting him, and he accidentally got shot in the woods. You don't know for certain you did it anyway. Everybody's been cooped up with the storm. They're not going to know how he got here."

"Somebody'll figure it out," Steve said. "But the one we have to fool is Piccirelli because most people aren't going to want to get involved enough to report us."

"This isn't like one of those strays you're always bringing home," his father persisted, eyeing Molly as she rubbed against Roberta's leg. "You can't just bring a kid in from the cold and adopt him."

"Who said anything about adopting him? What would you have me do? Leave him down there in the subdivision to freeze to death?"

"No," Ben admitted. "But just keep in mind this is temporary."

Roberta picked up Molly and tucked her into her lap. "Getting our story straight is the least of our problems. We've got to get this kid some medical attention."

The hint dropped in the air like a dust mote, but neither Steve nor Ben took it. Steve would not meet her eyes, and Ben got up and began fiddling with the wood stove.

"All right, you two. I don't know what the story is about Jessie, but you both know she's the only medical help around here these days. And you know as well as I do that she saved Gran's life a few days ago. We've got to get her to look at this kid. That wound needs to be dressed, and he probably needs X-rays."

Still Steve looked into his lap, as though the answer to his mixed-up parentage lay there, ready to get them all out of this embarrassing conversation.

Ben turned from the stove and began stirring his coffee, the spoon clanking loudly on the side of the cup. His eyes, half hooded, had a sadness she had never noticed before.

"All right, Roberta, this is the way it is." He sat down across from her while Steve continued to look away. "It took a lot of guts for Steve to go fetch Jessie the other day. He did it for May, and he did it for you. You have to understand how he feels. He was fourteen when she lit out of here on some tide of women's liberation. He was still a boy who needed a mother. Wayne was a little older, you understand, and maybe it didn't hit him as hard. But for Steve it was like he lost her, like she was dead. And I guess it was that way for me, too."

Roberta closed her hand over his, and he made no move to take it away.

"He grieved her. That's the only way I can describe it. And then he put it away somewhere and forgot about it because that's what you have to do. Now it's all coming back to him again. Once these feelings come out again, all that grief and hurt, it's hard to stuff it away. If he goes back to see her—well, it's ripping him up. It's ripping him right up."

Steve's face had reddened into splotches, like tomatoes splattered on linoleum. But Ben seemed not to notice. "If you want, I'll go get her," Ben finished. "But I doubt she'd come back with me."

"I'd go get her myself, but I barely know her," Roberta said, then turned to Steve. "Look. You risked your life up there to get us up over that mountain. I know how much you care about that kid. Think of him." It occurred to Roberta suddenly why

Steve had so much empathy for Niles, but she thought better of giving voice to the observation. "I'll go with you, if that would help. But we've got to do something."

Steve jumped out of his chair and walked to the door, where he watched the snowflakes coming at the glass like salt being thrown over someone's shoulder. His voice was barely audible above the storm. "I haven't got the plow. The Cutlass would never make it. I might be able to get your father's bucket loader going in the morning, but it'll be one hell of an uncomfortable ride."

She finished her coffee and volunteered to curl up in the armchair near the boy, to keep an eye on him. Before she knew it Steve was jogging her shoulder, and she opened her eyes to find a thin streak of dawn leaking under the shades.

Niles was awake, too. He was quiet, his eyes wide, like a newborn's tracking a mobile. For a moment Steve and Roberta looked back at him, not saying anything.

"How you feeling, buddy?" Steve finally managed.

"Okay, I guess."

"Do you remember how you got to Oz?"

Niles wrinkled his nose, not laughing at the joke. "Do you have a bathroom?"

Steve helped him up and took him hobbling down the hall while Roberta sat in the chair, hugging herself.

Steve left at dawn to work on Alton's bucket loader, which was parked down at the sawmill. The machine, left unwinterized and untended since Alton's passing, wouldn't even turn over. But Steve had drained enough oil from the sawmill's motor to make another batch of diesel, which, if it worked, should be enough to get the pickup to Jessie's and back. Within no time the pickup was running and Steve had driven Roberta and Niles to the Wilcoxes'.

Paula had the turkey in the oven and vegetables simmering

on the stove when Roberta walked into the kitchen with Niles. She stood with a wooden spoon in mid-air as they trooped indoors—Roberta, who had been gone all night without explanation, and a teenaged boy Paula had never met, hobbling on a homemade crutch.

"Where have you been? What on earth?"

"Don't say anything, Paula." Roberta gave her sister what she hoped was her best evil eye. Nothing could be said in front of the boy. Explanations could come later. "I'm going to put him in Dad's bed. Get ahead of us, please, and take down the covers." Paula seemed about to do as she was told until she looked down the hall and went white.

"What's this I hear about a sick boy?"

There was Gran, standing as straight as she could and leaning on the table in the hall. She had ripped out the oxygen's tubing, freeing herself at last, and dressed herself in slacks and a polyester shirt, even adding a string of beads around her neck. She had made an attempt to pin up her now-white hair, and she was wearing a smear of lipstick.

Roberta had almost forgotten about the other patient in the house. But now here she was, either making a recovery or a valiant attempt to fake one. And as they all stared, Niles's face was growing whiter from the strain of standing.

Somehow Roberta convinced Paula to help her bring Niles to Alton's bedroom and they got the boy into bed. She felt exhausted from the effort of just helping him into the house. And the day had just begun—this day of thanks that promised to be a minefield from start to finish.

But now, as she fussed with Niles's covers in an attempt to avoid the confrontation yet to come, she heard sounds of someone coming in the kitchen door. It couldn't be company; it was only midmorning. But it was Ray. He had finally made it home, only to find the whole household hovering over a young boy in the old iron bed that had been his father-in-law's.

Ray kissed Paula, but she stood stiff and unmoved. "Ray, for God's sake, where have you been? I've been worried sick about you."

"I know, I know. I had no way to get you a message. I ran out of gas in Hope Valley. Finally I made it to the Tavern and Jack Foley gave me enough to get home."

"First you don't show up yesterday, then Roberta runs off with Steve in the middle of the night. I've been through the mill, worrying about the two of you."

"Paula, believe me, I'm sorry. Jack's phone's been cut off. I guess he couldn't pay the bill. But everybody is fine, honey, except . . . this young man here."

"Hurt my foot," Niles said shortly. "Stepped in a rabbit hole."

"But you look pretty fair," Ray said to Gran, taking in the clothes and jewelry. "It's good to see you out of bed."

"Good to be out of bed. But now we have another patient."

"What's this all about?"

Paula, too, had shifted her attention to the boy. "Yes, Roberta, what is this all about? Who is this boy and what happened to him?"

Roberta stuttered for an explanation, but then she saw Niles's eyes on her and she felt a new resolve. "He lives in Laurel Heights. His parents are away . . . for the weekend, and he's hurt. Steve and I picked him up last night. The plow broke down and we had to drag him to Ben's in a sled."

The drama of Niles's rescue, as she had hoped, eclipsed the thinness of her story. Even Paula seemed impressed. "You walked across Mount Laurel last night in a sled? I can't believe it. You're lucky to be alive. Where is Steve, anyway?"

She explained about the motor oil he'd taken from the mill and his errand to fetch Jessie. When she was done, they all just stared at her, as though seeing her in a new light. But Gran seemed to see more than the rest.

"Why don't you all go into the kitchen and have a hot drink," Gran suggested, and as they filed out of the bedroom, she led Roberta into the sitting room and out of the boy's earshot. She didn't have to say a word. One look, and Roberta let the whole story out.

"Something else, isn't it, when parents will go off and leave their children." Gran had pursed her lips into a grim line. "He can stay here as long as he wants. Jessie'll fix him up. She did a job on me, that's for sure. Now don't you worry about Mr. Piccirelli. I'll take care of him. If he wants the jonnycakes to keep coming, he'll know enough to mind his own business."

Roberta, as tired as she was, couldn't face more coffee, but she went into the kitchen and poured cups for the others. Ray sat at the head of the table with the air of someone about to deliver bad news. He jangled his spoon in his coffee cup, took it out and put it back in again.

"Oh, for God's sake," Paula said. "What is going on? Out with it."

"I went to the courthouse to check on the ration coupons," he said slowly. "The clerk says we've been cut off."

"Cut off? You can't be serious." Paula's voice had risen an octave.

"Because Alton's dead, you can't get any more ration coupons in his name. Somebody has to qualify as the new head of household. I brought the forms, but from the way they read, the estate has to be settled before we can get any more gas or oil up here."

"That can't be." Roberta instantly thought of Lucas. He would fix this somehow. "There must be emergency provisions, or something. I mean, people die all the time. What if he had a widow? Or young children?"

"If you lived in The Ring, you'd be all set. But since you

don't, the allotment can't be transferred until there's a new property owner."

Roberta's head was swimming. The state was everywhere in their business. Maybe Steve was right. No gas, no oil, no money, no food . . .

The door slammed again. *This snowstorm certainly hasn't slowed anybody down,* Roberta thought grimly.

It was Piccirelli, all bundled up in a suede coat and knitted green scarf that Roberta thought looked suspiciously like her grandmother's handiwork. He had slapped the sides of his boots together and was standing in the doorway of the back dining room, looking from one face to the next with an almost cheerful expression.

"Happy snowstorm!" he said. Roberta saw he was smiling broadly. Had she ever seen more than a wan, sarcastic grin from him before? "And happy Thanksgiving! My, if this isn't like that famous song. 'Over the river and through the woods.' All we need is a sleigh."

Four faces looked grimly back at him. Finally Paula spoke. "We'll need a sleigh if we can't get any more gas," she said. "The state just cut off our ration because our father died. What do you say about that?"

Piccirelli hung up his coat on a peg. "Well."

"And I ran out of gas trying to get here last night and had to spend the night at the Tavern," Ray chimed in. "I got some gas from Jack Foley, but I don't have enough to get back to Westerly."

Piccirelli stood there, unfolding his scarf. It *was* her grandmother's work. Roberta would recognize those fine herringbone stitches anywhere. Now when had she done that?

"If it makes you feel any better, I'm stuck here, too," Piccirelli said quietly. "A truck that runs on natural gas is a marvelous invention, until you need to refuel and you're too far away from the station."

Gran was up, getting another coffee mug. From the kitchen table they could hear her opening and closing pot lids. "We'll have a big Thanksgiving dinner and then you can nap all afternoon. Wait till you taste my gravy."

"May, shouldn't you be in bed?" Apparently Gran's condition had just dawned on Piccirelli, who sat down and began shoveling spoonfuls of sugar into the coffee she had brought him. "You're looking much better, I must say."

But Ray, who still had a set look to his mouth, was not about to let the subject be changed. "Mr. Piccirelli, perhaps you didn't understand Paula. The state just cut off our gas and oil ration completely. A clerk told me that we can't get any more until Alton's estate is settled. That could take months."

"Doesn't sound right, does it?"

"You must know someone who could straighten this out," Paula pressed. "It must be a mistake. What will we do?"

"Perhaps you should reconsider whether to stay on here," Piccirelli said quietly. "I've said before, living here will not be easy."

It should have been an idyllic Thanksgiving: the mounds of snow outside the window; the smell of roasting turkey mixing with the aroma of steaming brown bread; the oak logs in the old wood cook stove snapping and crackling. But here they were, talking about the possibility of being stuck here with no oil or no gas, or worse, leaving the farm altogether.

There seemed no reply to Piccirelli's comments. Gradually they all left the table. Piccirelli retired to his room while Ray began to help Paula and Gran with meal preparations. Roberta, getting ready to set the table, was relieved when Lucas came in. He was shaking off snow from the top of his plaid hat to the rubber toes of his boots, and snow clung in the folds of his coat like mounds of ice cream.

"I came the back way," he said, stomping and shaking at the doorway. "Must be two, three feet in the woods. It's a clingy snow, too, and I kept brushing against the trees."

"Don't worry about the floor." She gave him a quick kiss, glad suddenly that Steve hadn't returned.

"You look tired. Did you get the turkey in early? You could have taken a nap, you know."

"No. It's a long story. Paula did the turkey." She helped him off with his coat, and he left his boots near the door. She walked into the sinkroom, and he padded after her in his gray wool socks.

In a whisper she told him the story of her late-night adventure. "Steve says we have to be careful who we tell. The state might come and take him. I want you to go in and see him later, Lucas. He looks like a lost fawn. I can't even think what might have happened if we hadn't gotten there when we did."

Lucas was watching her quietly, his arms folded across his chest. "Steve is at least partly right. If the state found out, they would take him, because that's the law. Oh, Roberta, you can't keep the boy here. You don't even know for sure that he's abandoned. Besides, he's injured. You've got to report this."

Roberta, reaching into the high cupboard for serving bowls, stopped and looked back up at him. "You can't be serious."

"I'm perfectly serious. You've got to call the police, or social services. This boy isn't some stray animal you've brought in from the cold. He's a juvenile. He's somebody's kid."

"That 'somebody' happens to be down in the Sunshine State with the boy's stepfather. That 'somebody' left her fourteen-year-old boy alone to fend for himself. You can't possibly think I'm going to do anything that might reunite her with him."

Lucas pressed his lips together. He reminded her of a principal she'd had in school once. "Roberta, use your head. This isn't your business. Maybe you and Steve got a rush out of rescuing this kid, but you can't keep him here. He doesn't belong to you."

"And who does he belong to, Lucas? A mother who doesn't give a damn about him? A stepfather who feels the same way? The state, which will put him in some foster home in Providence? Use *your* head. This is about simple human decency. This boy deserves a safe place to stay, where people care what happens to him."

"I couldn't agree with you more. But what constitutes a safe place is not up to you, Roberta. It's up to DCYF. Now if you're not going to call them, I will."

Their voices had been rising steadily since they retreated into the tiny sinkroom, and Roberta stood up to see Paula standing in the doorway, her mouth slightly open. Now it was all out. There was no way to protect Niles. Roberta felt defeat seep into her bones. Why had she ever thought she could keep people's curiosity at bay?

"Roberta, I think Lucas is right. We'll just bring more trouble on ourselves if we keep that boy here."

"Oh, Paula, shut up." It was the only thing she could think of to say. The bowl clanged on the floor but did not break. She heard the door slam, and looked across the kitchen to see Steve, alone, shaking snow off his hair. Why would he leave his mother out in the pickup? Then she realized. Jessie hadn't come.

"She wasn't there. I drove to her office in Voluntown, and she wasn't there, either." Steve was talking to Roberta, but he gave a curt nod to Lucas as he spoke. "She must have got invited somewhere for Thanksgiving. There's fresh tracks out of her drive to the main road. She headed west toward Connecticut. She might even be at the hospital, but I didn't have enough gas to chase her all the way to Norwich."

It was already noon, and before long the other guests began arriving—Ben, Wayne with his wife and the girls, Ida Kenyon and her mother, and Bud and Amy Tefft.

As Roberta sat at the other end of the table, the closed door to Alton's room burned in the back of her head. Just beyond its thin panels lay Niles, asleep, she hoped. Below the clatter of silverware and the mumbled "thank yous" as dishes were passed, she thought she could hear his raspy breathing and the rustle of blankets as he turned over. Gran, Lucas, Steve and Ben knew he was there too, but Piccirelli and the Kenyons—the people most likely to make something out of it—had no idea.

"Best gravy I ever had," Ida was saying, looking at Gran. "I always said you had the touch, May."

Gran winked at Roberta and smiled.

"Well, I'm just glad we got out of the house today." Ida's mother, chronically deaf, spoke in a near-shout. "If Steve hadn't come to fetch us, we'd be eating pork and beans for dinner."

"You never seem to have any shortage of fuel." Piccirelli, reaching for more turkey, was looking down the table at Steve. "I see you out quite a bit."

"No thanks to you and your bunch of goons." Steve winced as Roberta nudged his shin with the toe of her left clog. "I've been driving around town on homemade diesel. Last night the plow broke down because of it. I almost froze to death trying to get back here. Then I had to drain oil out of the sawmill this morning."

"I don't follow you. What is this homemade diesel?"

"Motor oil and kerosene. Works if you can get it. Knocks the hell out of some engines, though."

"I imagine that's quite polluting."

"Listen, Mr. Piccirelli, I had twenty miles of roads to plow last night, and I couldn't be worried about pollution. As it is, I didn't get to half the town. The town guaranteed me a certain allotment of gasoline this year for plowing the roads. I don't get paid, see. I just get the gas. Well, now I'm not even getting that."

Piccirelli was buttering a roll and looked across at Ida as he spoke. "Gas is scarce. Only the most densely populated areas are guaranteed of getting it. The more it has to be transported, the more wasteful it is. But you can't be taking matters into your own hands, Steve. I can't imagine this homemade diesel is legal."

"God forbid we should come up with a way around the state. Is that why you turned the state police on to me the other night? Afraid I might be cutting in on your action?"

The room had grown quiet as everyone followed the conversation. Roberta heard an exhalation from behind her, soft and muffled by the door. But just then Lucas cleared his throat.

"May, I think you are looking wonderful. Truly. I'm so happy to see you up and about."

"You can thank Jessie Reynolds. She's turned into quite a healer, that woman." Roberta groaned inwardly. Lucas had thought he was on safe ground, but he had merely hit another one of Steve's buttons. She looked to her right, where Ben held his fork suspended above his plate and was staring outdoors, his thoughts lost in the snowdrifts.

She followed his gaze to where the sun was spreading a thin yellow light, like yolk over the mounds of white. Then she saw what had drawn his gaze. It was the black cloak of Jessie, swinging in the breeze as she headed up the back porch to the door.

"Shit." She had not thought she said it aloud, but now everyone was looking at her curiously. She got up, nearly knocking over her chair. "Forgot something," she muttered and headed for the kitchen.

But Roberta had forgotten about Wayne. When she walked into the back room, he was hugging his mother, and Jessie was greeting her grandchildren for the first time.

It was Paula who, with a nod of her head, got Jessie's attention. "Here's Roberta. She'll get you a place setting. We're so glad you could join us after all."

Roberta didn't know why, but Paula had smoothly explained her appearance and given Jessie the subtle hint to be quiet. Across the table Jessie looked up at her and raised one eyebrow, and Roberta nodded.

It was nearly dark before Piccirelli had gone to his room and the Kenyons had left. It was then that Jessie quietly slipped into Niles's room and examined him. He was in pain, and the wound was still seeping, but she found no evidence of infection. The bullet had passed above his ankle bone, tearing tendons but leaving the bone intact. She left antibiotics and warned that he would be on crutches for at least six weeks.

"How are you? How's your ankle?"

He shrugged, but Roberta noticed his cheeks had color again. "Okay. Do you have any batteries?"

"What?"

"Batteries. For my Gameboy. I brought it with me, but the batteries died about a month ago."

Roberta looked at Steve. She saw a ghost of a smile under his moustache. "Not on me. But you could watch TV. I could put you on the couch for a while."

He helped Nile s out of bed, and when he came back he sank onto the bed.

"You look like you could use a little nap."

"I'm all right."

"I'm sorry about Jessie. I mean, I know this is hard on you. But maybe it's for the best."

He said nothing. Clearly he didn't want to talk about it, and suddenly she was aggravated.

"That was a close call today. I mean, with Piccirelli and the Kenyons, and Niles in here the whole time. Steve, what are we going to do? Everybody seems to think we should hand this kid over to the state."

"I can't have that on my conscience."

"Me either. But what are we going to do with him? Sooner or later his mother will reappear, don't you think?"

"We'll worry about that later."

"Maybe we should try to get in touch with her."

Roberta walked over to her father's small roll-top desk, turned the key and opened it. "Maybe Dad had some batteries. Isn't that sad? That Gameboy was probably his only companion after his mother left, and now even that doesn't work."

She began to open tiny drawers and sift through the desk's nooks and crannies. She had looked all through the desk once before, for her father's passbook and ration card, and come up with little of interest. One drawer held the stubs of lumber pencils, bills of sale, receipts; another was full of household hardware, everything from curtain hooks to tiny picture nails.

"I wish you hadn't gone after Piccirelli today. I mean, I agree with you, but Jesus, we don't need to get him riled up."

"I can't help it, Roberta. He pisses me off. I'm out there before the sun's up this morning draining the oil pan in the sawmill, freezing my you-know-whats off, and he was probably still in bed. He's got this holier-than-thou attitude. I mean, who appointed him as our moral conscience? Wait 'til he needs to get out of here in a hurry. He'll be begging me to cook up some of that diesel."

"Well, we've got to come up with a story. We can't keep Niles a secret forever." She sifted through piles of paper, trying not to linger on her father's elegant, Palmer Method handwriting. "Maybe we should say he's a relative."

"We'll tell him he has some rare, contagious disease. You know how fastidious the guy is. He practically polishes those fingernails of his."

"We should tell him he has some rare disease unique to Coward's Hole." She kept searching as she spoke. Tax bills, check stubs, a statement from the Fox Saw Company. Her fingers worked quickly. She hadn't really looked too carefully last time, she realized. It was too hard; she could still smell her father in this room, a mix of cigars and flannel shirts and sawdust.

"What's that?" Steve said. He was standing behind her, and he pulled something from the pile, a large piece of paper, rolled up and tucked way in the back of the desk. As he slowly unfurled it, Roberta caught the fine lines of a surveyor's map, and next to Steve's right thumb the legend, "Roberta's Woods."

"Oh, my God."

"What the hell is it? Is this yours?"

"No. I don't know." She helped him flatten it out, her hands moving slowly in fan-like motions, like an iron. The legend said Joe Riddle, Surveyor, and "20.2 acres, more or less." *Roberta's Woods.* For a moment she could see her father standing there on the Sawmill Road, driving a pair of twitch horses into the right-of-way for that last load of cedar he had cut there so many years ago. Her stomach had been tied into knots watching him.

"Roberta?"

"It's the tuition lot. That's what he called it." Her voice caught. *Roberta's Woods.* Was it a cruel joke, or a gift? "He sold it to Maine when I went to college. To pay the tuition."

"Well, he must've bought it back, looks like."

"No. He couldn't have. This must be an old survey."

"Roberta, it's says 2012. He had the land surveyed last year."

She followed his finger to the map. There it was, another fine inscription. What was Alton doing having Fred Maine's land surveyed for him? Maybe this wasn't even his map. Maybe the joke was Maine's, not her father's. Another taunt.

From across the house came Paula's high-pitched laughter.

"You better put this in a safe place," Steve whispered. "I don't know what it means, but if I were you I wouldn't be advertising it."

Roberta rolled the map up quickly, snapped the elastic back on and put it in a drawer of her father's bureau, underneath a pile of flannel shirts.

"Where is that lot? Over by the sawmill?"

"The story is that the first cabin burned down in a forest fire, and then the Wilcoxes moved over here. My father always had a sentimental attachment to that land. He and my mother were going to build their own house over there, but of course that never happened."

"I knew he'd sold a woodlot to Maine," Steve mused. "I can remember my father talking about it. When my mother left, my father joked that he and your father should build a cabin over there. He didn't think it was so funny when Jessie bought a cabin of her own down on Lake Manchester."

He was still calling her Jessie. Would he ever call her "Mom" again? "Well, I'm sure he would rather have moved down there with Ben than sold the lot off to pay my tuition bill. He certainly griped enough about it when it happened. That was all I heard about for the four years I was in school. It got so I hated to come home."

"Hey, Roberta, I know your father used to get your goat, but I think you're exaggerating. He was crazy-proud of you, that you went to college. It was all he talked about."

"Hey." Steve gathered her up and let her cry. "I don't know what this means, but we'll find out," He said into her hair. "I have a feeling that map is yours in more ways than one."

CHAPTER TWENTY

Winter had gotten a head start and showed no signs of letting up. The temperature began to plummet in early December, hardening the top of the Thanksgiving snowfall into a dirty crust.

Christmas would come, as it always did, despite their desperate circumstances. On the second Saturday in December, though Roberta had no idea how they would manage to feed people and give presents, they began to decorate the house.

Steve cut down a scraggly white pine from the east meadow and dragged it across the snow and into the house. It was a pathetic thing, and her heart constricted with a sudden pang for her father. He had always been one for chopping down the spindliest, scrawniest, droopiest pine tree, with needles too long and limp to hold ornaments without sagging, and with a trunk and branches dripping with pine pitch. It was not that they lacked trees. It was more that he couldn't bear to cut down something good—a nice, shapely Balsam, for example, or a sturdy Fraser fir—that cut a pretty figure outdoors and might be good for lumber some day. He couldn't abide the waste of a tree, cut down, put into water and then dragged outside to die a few weeks later.

Roberta met Steve at the door. "Is that the best you could find?"

"If I had a way to get them here, the woods are full of better ones. But as long as I'm the one hauling the tree in, this is what you get."

"It's better than the one we had last year," Paula said, then suddenly turned away. "I'll get the stand."

She rushed into the cellar. Of course, Paula was upset too. Ray had left the day after Thanksgiving. Ben had given him a ride to Cal's, then he had hitched a ride with a trucker passing through on Route 3. He had classes to teach, after all, and Paula wasn't disposed to going with him.

"There." Paula stood up and triumphantly held forth the lights, now magnificently festooning her neck and arms. "All set."

Paula and Steve circled the tree with the lights until they stretched from the pine's shaggy top to its sweeping bottom branches. Now the tree actually didn't look half bad. It was holding the weight of the strings better than Roberta would have guessed. Steve plugged them in, and the tree glowed with greens, blues and reds. The lights were so fat, much bigger than the white minilights that had come into vogue. The room seemed to blossom under their festive glow.

"Quite an improvement, wouldn't you say?"

"Niles, don't you want to help?" Roberta looked over and saw the boy absorbed in another video game. Its low beep-beeping was an undercurrent to their conversation. He only stopped playing when his batteries went dead.

"In a minute."

"Come on, buckster, put the game away," Steve insisted. "Help me out with these high branches."

Roberta had to admit they made an odd family tableaux. The half sisters with their guarded exchanges, Steve who was her off-and-on-again boyfriend, the little boy who belonged to no one, and the matriarch Gran in the center of it all. All they needed was Piccirelli to show up. She was glad he was out of the house, glad he wasn't going to steal this moment from them.

She looked up then, out the window, just to make sure his truck wasn't in the yard, when she saw Fred Maine's black Cadillac coast into the driveway. *Good God, I've summoned the devil.*

"Fred Maine just pulled up," she announced.

"Now what on earth does he want?" Gran was pulling herself out of the rocker.

"He probably saw my truck," Steve said, and Roberta wondered what that meant.

Maine came to the front door, as though he knew where they were. No one ever came to the front door.

"Afternoon, R'berta." Maine had his hat off and was winding it clockwise with his fingers. Behind him was his tall shadow, Oatley. She was so surprised to see the two of them standing on the stone stoop that for a moment she didn't know what to say, but then she recovered and invited them in.

They squeezed into the living room, Oatley ducking on the way in.

"Decoratin' your tree, I see," Maine began. "Them's nice lights."

"The Christian Christmas." Oatley dropped the words like two leaky bags of garbage. "Quite a ritual. Do you know there are Narragansetts that actually celebrate Christmas? Down at the Indian Church. They converted when the white man came. Can't see how you can call yourself a Narragansett and worship some white god."

Roberta caught Steve's eye.

"Hey, Oatley, put yourself to work, will you?" Steve tossed him the star and Oatley easily reached over and put it atop the pine tree. "I knew I was waiting for you to show up for a reason."

"Hello, May, you're looking fine."

"I'm not deaf, Fred. Yes, I'm much better. Take off your coat and sit a while. I'll get some pie."

"No, no, no, can't stay, can't stay. We're bringing some news, folks, and we've got other people to see." Nonetheless Maine had settled himself onto the sofa next to Niles, who quickly scooted as far away from him as possible. "Been down to Cal's. Just heard some news."

"Well, for Christ sake, Fred, tell us what it is." May was half way out the living room door, probably on the way to get pie anyway, but she stopped, suspended, unsure whether to leave or not.

"Yes, those are mighty nice Christmas lights, ain't they, Oat?"

"If you care for that sort of thing."

"Haven't done a tree myself in quite some time, not since Cora passed on." At that Maine seemed to almost tear up, but then he caught himself and looked around the room again. "The lights add a lot to your electric bill, though."

"Mr. Maine, let Gran go get the pie. It won't take long. Come in here, I have something of my father's I want to show you."

Maine perked up then. He hadn't expected a diversion. He probably really did want a slice of Gran's famous pie, and whatever Roberta had to show him had to be of some interest if it had to do with Alton. Paula was looking at them both quizzically, but Roberta winked at her as though it were all part of some ruse.

Gran and Paula headed to the kitchen, and Roberta brought Maine into Alton's old room, dragged out the map, and fanned it out on the bed, careful to cover the legend "Roberta's Woods" with her left hand.

"Does this look familiar?"

"That's the woodlot Alton sold me years ago, so you could go to college." He looked at it with a curious pleasure. He traced the ragged finger of his gloved hand over the contour lines. "Where'd you get this?"

"He had a survey of it done last year. Do you have any idea why?"

"He did, did he? What the hell for?"

"I was hoping you could tell me. Seems like he had plans for it."

"What kind of plans? After all, I owned it."

She wondered if the past tense was a slip of the tongue. "I don't know, Mr. Maine. I thought maybe you might."

"Don't know a damn thing about it. But that was Alton for you. Always dreamin' bigger than his wallet."

"I can't imagine he'd pay to have a survey done for property if he didn't at least expect to own it."

Maine turned away and headed for the door. "People do funny things. Now look at this, here comes your grandmother with a custard crème pie. Oh, my, my."

Roberta slipped the map back in the drawer. Maine had ended the conversation. He must know more about the map than he was telling. Or maybe he just hadn't expected it. She wished for once he'd just tell the truth. What difference did it make? Alton was dead. His rival was gone, and there was no need to hoodwink him out of something anymore.

They sat at the dining room table, ate pie and drank coffee, and talked of nothing. Finally, after two slices and a refill of coffee, Maine sat back and folded his hands across his flannel shirt.

"Well, folks, it's like this. Roger Williams Electric is about to pull the plug again. Enjoy those Christmas lights while you can because in a few days Coward's Hole is going dark, and I don't know when we'll have power again."

"Oh, Jesus." Paula buried her face in her hands.

"What's this all about, Fred?" Steve demanded.

"Can't say. I was at Cal's when this government type came around, some friend of Piccirelli's, and made the announcement. Me and that lover man of yours, Roberta, were dispatched to tell the neighbors. So here I be, telling the neighbors."

He meant Lucas. Christ. She saw Steve's eyes grow hard.

Gran began gathering up the plates and forks. "Now Fred Maine, I don't believe you don't know more'n that about it. Seems to me a state senator would have some 'in' or other. Now suppose you tell us what all this is really about. What's the state hope to accomplish, making honest folks' houses go dark?"

"I swear to you, May, on my dear wife's grave, I know nothing more than I just told you." Roberta looked at his solemn face and for once she believed him. "It doesn't make a whole lot of sense to me, either. This is going to be tough. Oil burners won't work without 'lectric ignitions. Water pumps, same thing. Now you take me, for instance. I've got this space heater in my bedroom. Helps me get through the night. Now I'm going to have to go back to tending a wood stove every night."

"We're already doing that," Paula snapped. "What I don't like is losing the lights and the refrigerator. I suppose we can put food outside, but then the animals are liable to get into it. Somebody already broke into the root cellar." She looked pointedly at Maine, but he handed back that same vacant, grave look that had convinced Roberta earlier. "And what are we going to do when spring comes?"

Steve drained the last of his coffee. "I'll tell you what we'll do. We'll do what they did a hundred years ago. Come tomorrow the old man and me will head out to Lake Manchester. We've got some ice to cut."

There was no telling how much time they had. The next day Paula and Roberta did three loads of wash and hung it all over the house, behind stoves, on bed footboards and over quilt racks. Then they scrubbed the kerosene lamps and hunted down candles.

After lunch Lucas rode up on one of the mares, trailing another behind him, with two pairs of ice skates in a saddlebag. Within minutes Roberta had added a layer of long underwear, bundled up in hat, scarf, coat, and mittens, and was riding with Lucas toward the lake.

They took the horses down by the sawmill and then cut through the tuition lot. Deep in these woods her father used to set up a saw rig when he had logs too heavy or cumbersome to get out with the twitch horses. That was the only reason anyone would want to get through these woods, and it was odd that Maine had kept the lane so neatly cleared when he obviously wasn't doing any logging.

"This is the lot my father used to own," she told Lucas. They had stopped on a rise after he waited for her to catch up. "He sold it to Maine to pay for my freshman year at Smith. Even though I had scholarships, it was tough on him. He could barely afford to buy my books, never mind our share of the tuition."

"Looks like Maine still uses it."

"It does, doesn't it? You know, I think my father may have bought it back from him."

"What gave you that idea?"

She told him about the map, the legend "Roberta's Woods," and Maine's reaction to it. "I don't know if he was telling the truth or not, but he seemed mighty interested—that is, until I started asking too many questions."

"I'll do some checking. In the meantime, look around some more. If your father bought that lot back, he had to have put the deed somewhere."

Lucas skated like he did everything—effortlessly, with a glowing sexual energy that belied his age. Roberta followed his lead and they danced in ever smaller arcs, until she stood still in his arms on ice that was doodled by the marks of their swirling blades. In the distance she saw a lone cabin, about the width of two rooms, with a cozy curl of smoke trailing up from its chimney like a balloon's tail. This was where Jessie Reynolds lived.

"Look at that," he said, following her gaze. "Don't you wish nobody was home? We could sit by the fire and thaw out our toes—and whatever else is cold."

"That's Jessie's place. Steve's mother. I don't know how she lives out here in the winter. Look at the laundry. It'll be like shoe leather before she brings it in the house."

"I admire a woman who can live on her own. Now that's living. She's too far away to be bothered by anybody. Just the woods and the animals to keep her company. Now that's Walden. Right here in front of us."

"I thought Walden was out on the Cook Road."

He laughed, a little too heartily, she thought. "Touché! No, I'm not living half the life that woman is. She's pared it down to the basics. She's got food. She's got shelter. And that's all she needs. My two-story monstrosity is no mark of simplicity, that's for sure."

Roberta stepped back and looked at him. "Would you really want to live like she does?"

"Sure! Why not? Maybe when I retire. Not that I'm not already retired." He laughed again. "But to see if you could do it, Roberta. A man's test of himself."

Roberta shuddered. "Jessie Reynolds has nothing. She disowned her husband and her sons, and until this Thanksgiving she had not even seen her grandchildren. She spends her whole life working, not contemplating the universe. She gave up everything in life that's meaningful to pursue her medical career. I don't think she's happy. I think inside she's probably the loneliest, most miserable woman on the planet. And she did it all to prove some point."

"Roberta." His voice rose in surprise. "That doesn't sound

very liberated of you. Do you think she should have stayed at home with that dour old Swamp Yankee husband of hers? Scrubbing pots and washing floors?"

"Don't talk about Ben that way." She felt a flash of loyalty that she hadn't known was there.

"It seems to me she did what was right for her," he continued. "She was just being true to herself."

"True to herself? She had a husband and two children. While she was being true to herself, her boys were growing up without a mother." She realized she was shouting.

He seemed faintly amused. "They don't seem any worse for wear."

"How would you know? You and Meredith never had children. What do you know about being a parent?"

"I know enough to know when it's none of my business." His tone had lost that playful quality and turned brisk. "Like with that Niles boy. You don't have any children either, Roberta, as much as you'd like to pretend to the contrary."

" 'lo, Roberta, Lucas!" Steve shouted. "Put those skates away and give us a hand. Playtime's over."

CHAPTER TWENTY-ONE

It was Christmas Eve when the power finally went out. They were sitting in the dining room over a skimpy dinner—sliced ham, canned green beans from the summer, and fried potatoes—when a pop came from the living room. The Christmas tree bulbs had exploded, probably from a power surge, and then the house went dark.

Thus began what Roberta thought of as the Dark Time. Throughout January and February, even as the cold waned and the snow cover finally receded, their lives took on a gray and shadowy cast. They ate colorless meals mostly made up of potatoes and pale canned vegetables. At Christmas Steve shot a duck, but it was tough and greasy and nothing like the turkey dinners of years past.

Roberta felt dirty. The house, so poorly illuminated, was no longer as clean as Gran would have liked, especially with the wood stoves sending a fine film of soot everywhere. They had begun flushing the toilet with buckets of water from the well, because it was just too cold to use the outhouse, and heating water for baths was such a pain that sometimes Roberta simply sponged off with a face cloth in the sink. Life was a struggle, but she felt as if she'd given up the fight.

In late February Piccirelli disappeared for a couple of days. Roberta told Lucas when he came in for a cup of coffee the next day. Maybe Piccirelli had headed out to Cal's, and some state worker had given him a ride back upstate. Maybe he had decided to chance it and head back to Providence to refuel. Or maybe he was just tired of eating dry toast.

"Don't be so sure he's gone," Lucas said.

Roberta felt instantly defensive. Why did Lucas always disagree with her lately? "What makes you so sure? I'm telling you, he's been gone for twenty-four hours. Unless you want to start dragging the river, my money puts him back in Cranston with the missus."

"His job's not done here yet, Roberta."

"Says who? Who knows what he's doing here, anyway? All this Ring nonsense. He hasn't signed up a soul in months. He might as well be selling encyclopedias."

"That could be the point."

"Do you think he'll send someone after me?" They had forgotten about Niles, who was sitting at the far end of the table reading a motocross magazine Steve had unearthed at the dump.

Roberta looked at Lucas and then Niles. "Do you mean to a foster home? Don't you worry. None of us would let that happen to you, unless that was what you wanted."

"Uh, Niles, why don't you go help Mrs. Wilcox with the dishes?"

Niles made no motion to move. Such a funny boy, Roberta thought. Moving him was like moving a rock. She could never get him to do anything, yet at the oddest moments he would be there to lift something heavy, hand her a pair of scissors, or even sometimes put a hand lightly on her arm. His ankle had healed, and he could bound out of the chair like a jack-in-the-box, if he only had the will.

"Niles, do as Lucas says," she said finally, and then added, "I think Steve recharged some batteries for you last night. If you help out, maybe I can get him to bring them over for you later."

That did it. The Gameboy motive. He was up and out of his chair, and soon they heard May coaching him on the proper way to dry a glass. Lucas leaned back in the chair, his arms folded over his gray plaid shirt and his legs crossed. "Roberta?"

"Mmm?"

"I did something you probably wouldn't approve of, but it was necessary." He didn't wait for her to react. "I wrote to the boy's mother, and this morning I got a reply. She and her husband intend to return in the spring. I explained the situation as best I could, and she gave me a release to be Niles's guardian. That means he can stay here, Roberta, and everything is legal. But it also means she *is* coming back."

"What?"

"I'm sorry, Roberta," he said gently. "But you know the alternative. Sooner or later someone at the school or with the state would have found out, and that would have been much worse. At least this way you don't have to always be looking over your shoulder, wondering when she was coming back."

"What is she going to do with him?" She choked out.

"Apparently they haven't been able to find work in Florida. Things there aren't as wonderful as people imagine. They're coming back and they're going to try to make a go of it here."

So at least he would be nearby. She wouldn't be taking him away . . . "Oh, Lucas." She whispered, aware Niles was still in the next room. "I suppose you're right. But I can't bear turning him over to her. She left him alone. It was just horrible. Couldn't you report her? Couldn't we get custody?"

"I don't know who you mean by 'we,' but I doubt it. You don't have any standing. If you were his aunt or sister, for example, you might have a chance. But you're just a neighbor. You're single. You don't own this house. You really aren't in a position to be adopting a teenage boy."

She wrapped her arms around herself. It was always so damned cold in the back dining room.

"And there's something else, Roberta." Lucas continued to

talk in an undertone. "I don't think you should be hanging out with Steve Reynolds. There are things you don't know about him. I would hate to see you or the boy get in over your head."

"What are you talking about? I've known Steve my entire life. He may not be the most orthodox person in the world, but I certainly don't think he's a bad influence, particularly on a fourteen-year-old boy who could use a father figure."

"Roberta, I'm trying to help you. Reynolds may be mixed up in something you don't want to be involved in. Anthony Piccirelli wouldn't have spent all winter up here to recruit tenants for a housing complex. There's a lot more at work here than you could ever imagine."

"Maybe you should concentrate on your own problems instead of inventing some for Steve."

"Roberta, I don't know what you mean. This isn't an argument between us. It's some advice, and I hope you take it."

"What I mean is it's been three months since my father died, and his estate's still not settled. If it wasn't for Piccirelli's board, we would be broke. And you still haven't given me an answer on that map I found in my father's desk."

Now his jaw was set. "Roberta, I told you from the beginning that these things take time. A quick settlement of the estate would have given it all to Paula, and you certainly don't want that. It can take a year for a will to go through probate. And as for that map you found, that's all it is—a map. Wishful thinking by a man who wanted to reclaim a piece of land. I haven't been able to find any evidence in town hall that Alton ever bought that land back from Senator Maine or had the legal right to develop it."

"Lucas, I know my father. He wouldn't have paid a surveyor—or anyone else—a dime on a pipe dream. He was a Swamp Yankee through and through. He must have at least thought he had the right to develop that land, or he wouldn't have had it platted out."

Lucas sighed and pushed himself back from the table. "I'll look again, if it makes you happy. But meanwhile, I wish you would value my advice. I'm telling you Steve is mixed up in something, and it isn't good."

He walked out and Roberta, peevish, did not say goodbye. She had managed to convince Lucas she didn't believe his story about Steve, but now that he was gone she found the doubts rush fresh into her mind. There was only one way to find out. She grabbed her parka and gloves, but before she could make it out of the house alone Niles begged to come with her. Of course, he wanted to pick up those batteries.

The snow was long gone. A January thaw had taken care of that, but the bitter cold had quickly returned. Roberta watched her breath stream out in white puffs and heard her lungs working, almost panting as they headed up the Reynolds driveway. The Cutlass was there, parked next to the pickup.

She walked on ahead to the old barn, where one of the double doors lay ajar. Steve was in there, and she could hear him talking before she could see him, talking on the phone. She didn't know the barn was wired, but maybe he had a cell phone.

"I gotta get some more, or I can't finish." There was a pause. She heard his feet shuffling in grit on the floor, and she motioned to Niles to keep quiet. "I've got other sources, you know. This isn't the buyer's market you think it is." A longer pause this time, and one of Steve's cats rubbed suddenly against the boy's leg and meowed; did Steve hear it? "You know what you are? A price gouger, that's what. I've been doing business with you a little too long, too." She heard him sigh and realized he was off the phone, and she was standing there just outside the door, like Nancy Drew spying on a jewel thief.

"Hey." She tried to sound casual.

"Hey yourself. Hi there, Niles." He looked distracted still, and his brow was a black angry squiggle. "Look what the cat dragged in . . . or who dragged in the cat. What brings you two out in this cold?"

She motioned to Niles, who was petting the cat. "Looking for those batteries."

"Oh, yeah! Damn! I forgot. You guys want to go for a ride?"

"A ride? Where? I mean, sure. Sure."

"Come here, Princess." He swept the cat up in his arms. "Is Princess hungry? Mmm, you smell like you've been over at that Wilcox barn again."

"I'm glad you're not talking that way to me."

She expected him to make a joke then, but he didn't. He simply put down the cat and headed to the Cutlass. Soon they were speeding out on Jonnycake Trail. Roberta noticed the gas gauge was nearly on E but he made no attempt to conserve, his tan work boot keeping the pedal almost completely depressed.

"When was the last time you were in town?" he finally said.

Roberta laughed. "I don't remember. Christmas?"

"You'll find it slightly changed, my friend."

"Where are we going?"

"I've got some business to take care of. You need anything?"

If Gran knew she was heading to town without giving her time to make a list, she'd be furious, but Roberta's brain didn't seem to want to work. As much as she knew they needed things, she kept coming back to the dark look in Steve's eyes and the crazier-than-usual way he was driving. Business to take care of . . . buyer's market . . . it all had to be connected. As they headed off the highway, Roberta saw a clump of people huddled near the overpass, their breaths floating like puffs of cotton.

"What are those people doing?" Niles asked.

"Waiting for the bus," Steve explained. "From Westerly. It's the only way most of these people get to work these days. Looks like it's late today, though."

The Tavern seemed deserted. Steve looked around nervously after he parked the Cutlass, then he saw Jack coming out with a huge black Lab on a leash.

Jack ushered Roberta and Niles into the bar, poured them sodas, and sat down at the table. In the corner of the window Roberta caught a brief glimpse of the Cutlass. Steve had pulled it into a shed, and now he was tying the Lab up near the shed door.

"What's taking him so long?"

"You can't leave a car out these days without its tank getting siphoned."

"Is this how you live all the time? Do you hide your car every time you drive it?"

"If you want to keep it you do." He took a Camel out of a pack in his pocket and lit it. "Rationing. I allow myself just two a day. I think now's as good a time as any."

Steve came in, poured himself a soda from the tap and sat down. For a while no one said anything.

"You going up to the trail today?" Jack looked at Steve.

"Got to. I've got a little problem, though, I was hoping you could solve. Roberta, Jack and I have to talk business. If you want, give Niles a tour of the place. Inside, I mean. You don't have any guests, do you?"

"Nah. Check out the view from the honeymoon suite. Take the stairs down the hall, go up two flights and look for the second door on the left."

She could hear the men's voices start up again as they headed toward the stairway. Well, if she had any doubt that Steve was doing something illegal, that should seal it. At the very least he was hiding something.

She found the honeymoon suite easily and opened the door, expecting to find a room of lush colonial beds and antique highboys. But the room, which stretched nearly the entire length of the third floor, was empty. White curtains hung from the windows, and she motioned Niles over to the glass, which looked out over the river and to the other side. Roberta shivered. She didn't like the honeymoon suite or this place; it was cold and empty and gave her the willies.

"Can we go now? I want to go back and get my batteries."

"Not yet. Steve has some business to do. We have to give him time to talk to Mr. Foley."

"That's all you guys do around here is talk. Why don't you ever do anything? You let that state guy live with you. Why don't you just kick him out? And you let Paula push you around all the time. I don't see what everybody's so afraid of around here."

"That's enough, Niles. Sometimes adults have to talk about things. You can't always take matters into your own hands."

"Oh, is that why you let Lucas tell my mother where I was? I bet you'll just hand me over when the time comes. Anybody else would do something about it. But you just sit around and let people push you around."

So he had overheard the conversation with Lucas. "Niles, I'm sorry about what Lucas did. I didn't know he was going to write to your mother, and I certainly would have tried to stop him if I did. But he is right. We have no legal right to keep you. If your mother had found out we were hiding you, it would have been bad for both of us."

"So you're just going to let her take me back, like nothing happened."

"I don't know, Niles." She leaned against the windowsill wearily. "That's what I was hoping to talk to Steve about. I thought he might have an idea. I hadn't really counted on you coming with us, but now that you're here, I suppose it's best that it's out in the open. After he gets done with Jack we'll ask him what to do."

Their voices were low but she could make out Jack's. "Are

you sure this is going to work?"

"I haven't test-driven it, no, but in theory it will."

"If anybody finds out, you'll have worse problems on your hands. What are you going to do meanwhile?"

"I need some gas. My ration's done for the month. I was going to try to get some off of Woodmansee's brother, if he's got any."

"Wait a minute." She heard a chair scrape and realized that Jack was headed their way.

Steve grinned at her. "What did you think of the honeymoon suite? You want to try it out?"

"Not unless they get a mattress up there. It's empty."

Jack walked back in, handed Steve a piece of paper and sat down. "Had to sell some of the furniture. Antique dealer offered me some money for it. I couldn't refuse. Steve, that'll get you what you need. You folks want some lunch? I've got chili on special."

"If that's the same chili that was on special last week, no thanks." Steve shook Jack's hand good-naturedly. "Listen, I've got to go up to Woodmansee's. Do you think Niles could hang out here? We won't be gone long."

"Sure. I'll make him a PB and J sandwich. How's that sound?" Niles nodded and he seemed to brighten at the prospect of hanging out at the Tavern. "Then I've got something verrry interesting to show him."

Steve retrieved the car and they headed up Potter Road, over the bridge and out beyond the village. Roberta saw laundry stiff in the wind, a couple of dogs sitting on a stoop, some cows grazing. She was relieved Steve had brought her along. Now was her chance to tell him about Lucas's letter and how Niles had reacted. "It's just a mess. I could strangle Lucas, but I suppose he was right."

"He could have consulted with us. It's none of his business.

That's what I hate about that guy. He's always nosing in where he doesn't belong."

"Be that as it may, we still have a situation on our hands. Niles is freaking out. I don't think he wants to see his mother. He's mad at her for leaving him, and who knows what he'll be going home to?"

"Well, they aren't coming back tomorrow. We'll think of something."

He turned the car down a narrow dirt road through tall pine trees that cast a canopy of shadow across the hood. "I have to take care of a couple of things. I'm going to let you out of the car for a few minutes. I need you to keep a lookout."

"You're dropping me off?" She was incredulous. Lookout for what?

"I'll be nearby. You're not in any danger. I'm going to leave you my cell. I have on a beeper." He gave her a number. "The cops come up here sometimes to patrol." He stopped the car at a bend in the road. In a field was an old farmhouse boarded up, a barn that had collapsed into itself, and a rusted hay baler. "Wait behind that barn. I'll be back in ten minutes tops. But if you hear or see somebody, beep me. Okay?"

Roberta was too stunned to protest. She stood by the dirt road, feeling like a teenage girl who's just been dumped by her date. The Cutlass roared off to the west, clouds of dust and stone billowing out behind it. And then she was alone.

The minutes dragged on. Her hands and feet were cold.

She was proud of herself when she caught the sound of the car engine again, but something about it wasn't right. It was coming from the wrong direction, from the north. She turned to see a flash of white grill in the distance. She ran to the old barn and hid behind it. The roar grew louder and she realized it was a truck, not a car, and when she saw the side she immediately knew whose it was. Piccirelli's.

The truck nearly skidded to a stop, and Roberta felt her heart hammer faster. But he had not seen her. He got out, walked to the roadside a few steps away, and began to pee. Roberta willed her body to be one with the rough barn boards. She heard steps again and realized someone was with him; another man, peeing. Was this some sort of thing men did? They walked back to the truck but didn't get in. *Oh, dear God in heaven,* she thought, *I don't want to explain why I'm hiding behind a barn watching them take a leak.*

"Is this where you saw it?" Piccirelli's voice.

"I think so. I'm not sure. It was damned dark last night, no moon."

"There's tracks over there. They look pretty fresh."

"Too small. Those are car tracks."

"Probably a customer." Roberta felt the cold plastic of the cell phone in her jacket pocket; she could dial it, but Steve's first impulse would be to rush over here, and that might be worse. But he had said to call . . .

"We're so close, yet so far. I feel like I'm chasing a phantom."

"He's good. I could've told you that."

"Nobody's that good. He's got to trip up sometime. He's got stuff hidden away all over this place."

She heard a door open, then close, and a match struck. Piccirelli's friend was having a cigarette. Piccirelli, she knew, didn't smoke.

The other man took a drag, then exhaled hard. "You talked to Oatley?"

"You mean the Indian?"

"Yeah. You think he'll help us?"

"He knows every inch of these woods, that's for sure. He took me all over Coward's Hole one day. Didn't say much. He just takes it all in. He probably knows more than we do about the thing. But I doubt he'd tell us too much."

"Every man has a weakness. What's his? Maybe he needs a new ration card."

Piccirelli laughed softly. "I don't think a ration card would do it, Dennis. The man doesn't even own a car."

"We could get him a car cheap enough."

"Dennis, focus, focus. What good would it do to get a man a car, if he can't get enough gas? And if you're beholden to him for gas, it's a bribe you pay over and over again. The next thing you'd know, he'd be driving it over to Foxwoods."

"He'd be the only one there."

"Oh, no he wouldn't. He'd never come back, is what he'd do. That's what happens, you know. People get over there now, and they can't get back. They lose everything they have, and they can't afford that sonar monorail thing they built. They get desperate, sell their cars . . ."

"All right, all right. But maybe he's a gambler at heart. Maybe if we promised him a ride over there. You know, a free turn in the magic mobile here."

"Nonetheless, Dennis, this is not getting us what we need. We need information. We need a tip. We need something solid, not somebody's hunches."

"Speaking of which, we better get going."

Roberta heard two doors slam and the truck start. Her ears could follow the trail of its sound, headed in the direction in which Steve had disappeared. She began to press the keys on the phone, dialing the same number, over and over. But as she looked toward the cutoff she heard a car engine in the opposite direction, from whence Piccirelli and his friend had come. A damned logging road, and it was busier than the Seekonk Speedway. But it was the Cutlass. Steve had somehow circled back.

"Listen, I know I was more than ten minutes, but—"

"Steve, we've got to get out of here." She ran over to the passenger side and got in, putting her head in her hands. "Piccirelli. And some guy. They went—the way that—"

Steve didn't wait to hear more. He jammed the shift into reverse and floored it, accelerating backwards until the trees were rushing by in a cinematic blur. The car skirted back around a curve like some drunken fish Then Steve braked suddenly, backed into a clearing, and turned around. The trail linked up to Potter Road again and the tires gripped the asphalt in a sudden squeal. Roberta looked over to the console. The needle on the tank was hovering just below F.

"They won't find anything amiss, thank God," he finally said, taking his hand off the shift. "Why didn't you call me?"

"I was afraid you'd come rushing into a trap. But then they headed up where you'd gone . . ."

"What the hell is he doing up here, anyway?"

Roberta's head felt like it was in a winch. If she told him everything she had heard, would she be abetting something that was really wrong? Or, if she didn't tell him, would she help Piccirelli get the goods on someone who was probably her friend, her neighbor, one of their own—maybe even Steve himself?

"I don't know," she said finally. "They stopped for a minute . . . and they were talking about looking for something. I don't know what."

"That sonofabitch. I told you he was up to no good. Everybody thinks he's gone home, and he's around spying on everybody."

"I didn't say he was spying. I don't know what he was doing."

"What did he say? And didn't you say 'they' before? Who was with him?"

"I don't know. Some guy. Dennis something."

They headed back to the Tavern. Niles seemed like a different boy. His color had returned, and he had an eager look about him. The sullen teenager had been banished, and he was a boy again, full of news. He chatted away in the back seat, oblivious to Steve's sullen mood.

"Jack took me out to the dam. He has this great idea. He's going to hook it up to a steam turbine again, like when it powered the mill, and make electricity and steam heat for the whole village!"

CHAPTER TWENTY-TWO

The story burst out of Niles. Foley was applying to the federal government for a permit to use the dam. The only hook was that the feds—Niles even used that word, obviously quoting Foley—wanted to make sure that the dam didn't block the Atlantic salmon from swimming upstream. "Conflicting federal priorities," Niles repeated. So Foley was trying to design a fish ladder.

"But once he gets that going, he says it's a cinch to hook up the old mill houses around the tavern. They could get their heat and their electricity from hydroelectric power. He said years ago the mill used to supply steam heat to dozens of homes in the village. He said the pipes are still under the road."

"I heard he was up to something," Steve said. He was silent a moment as he turned off Route 3. "He owns most of those houses, you know. He's not getting much in rent from them now, but if he has steam heat and electricity to offer, people are going to be bidding against each other to live there."

"Well, it's not going to help us any," Roberta reminded him.

"Don't be so sure. It's a great idea, when you think of it. Anywhere there's a river, we could generate our own power."

"Can I go back there sometime?" Niles piped up. "Jack says I could help him build the fish ladder."

Roberta murmured, "We'll see." Steve had gas now, but she couldn't imagine he would want to cart Niles back and forth to Hope Valley very often. It was too bad Steve couldn't think of something closer to home to keep the boy occupied.

"I don't see why the feds don't let him do it," Niles continued. Roberta realized she was hearing a modified version of everything Foley had told him. "But maybe Senator Maine can help. He's going to get him to write to these people, ferks, to see if they can give him a permit."

"F-E-R-C," Steve murmured to Roberta in an aside. "Federal Energy Regulatory Commission. They'd have to give him the permit to generate electricity. But if somebody objects, on environmental grounds, say, they'll reject it."

"You seem to know a lot about it."

"Foley likes to talk. I hope he doesn't get mixed up with Maine, though. Maine doesn't get involved in things unless there's something in it for him. He's as liable as not to do something to stop the project, especially if he thinks Foley might make some money."

As they approached the house, Roberta noticed something stuck in the front lawn. Her first thought was, "How did anyone ever get that thing in the frozen ground?" Then her eyes registered, and she read what it said: For Sale.

"Sweet Jesus, Roberta, where did that come from?" Steve pulled the Cutlass into the driveway. Without a word Roberta bounded out of the car and into the kitchen.

Paula was standing near the far window, as though she had been peeking out of the curtain. Roberta, about to go off on a rant, stopped short. Her sister stood there, her eyes almost soft in the early afternoon light, her arms wrapped around her stomach as though she cradled something there. Something about her—the way she stood leaning against the wall with her hair loose about her face, or the liquid look to her eyes—was different in a way Roberta couldn't fathom. Now that she thought about it, Paula had been looking odd for the past few weeks.

"It's time," Paula said. "I know you don't want to sell, but I talked to Lucas, and he agrees with me. It's the only way to settle this thing."

Roberta, still trying to get breath back into her lungs, heard Steve and Niles follow her in the door.

"What about Gran? Where will she go? This is her home. How can you sell your own grandmother's home?" *Lucas agrees with me,* she had said. Roberta was not sure what appalled her more: that it could be true, or that Paula would use him as an ally.

"There's something you should know." Paula stepped out of the shadows behind the cook stove and into the middle of the kitchen. "I'm going to have a baby. I mean, Ray and I are going to have a baby. So you see, the clock is ticking. We need the money."

That look to her eyes; of course. But when? When Ray was up at Christmas. That would put Paula a little over two months along.

"I'm happy for you," she said, hearing the stiffness in her own voice. "But I don't think you need to sell the family homestead to have a baby. Besides, you can't sell without my signature. I'm still the co-executor."

"That's a formality. Lucas says we can straighten all that out."

Lucas says, Lucas says . . . Roberta gripped the back of the rocking chair, trying to hold it steady. "Formality or no, I'm not signing. Daddy must be spinning in his grave right now. You know this isn't what he intended."

"Roberta, be reasonable. What are you going to do up here? You can't stay. We're out in the middle of nowhere. People can't live like this anymore. You can't get to work; you can't get out to get food; you're stuck! We need to get out now, while we can."

"So who do you think's going to buy this place, then? If I'm such a fool to stay, do you think you'll find someone to pay you for the privilege?"

"Somebody will buy it, if just for the timber. Probably the state. And it will be for the best, really." That patient tone, that *explaining* tone. "It's the land that's worth something, not this old broken-down house."

"This old broken-down house!" The chair clunked to a halt. "This old broken-down house has stood for almost three hundred years! Don't you feel it, when you walk through it? Can't you see them all, hear them all? All those Wilcoxes. Wilcoxes who were subjects of a king! Wilcoxes who fought in the Revolution! Wilcoxes who lived and died, who *made us*. Doesn't that mean anything to you?"

Paula smoothed the front of her shirt; Roberta could see a slight bulge underneath it, not enough to be conspicuous, just enough, if you knew Paula, to foretell a change to come.

"That's an old, tired story, Roberta. And so what? So what if people lived in this broken-down house for three hundred years? Does that mean we have to molder away here for three hundred more? Look at this place. It needs a paint job. The sills are bad. The ceiling upstairs leaks, the wallpaper's stained. You can romanticize it all you want, but this is nothing but an overgrown shack that's seen better days. We'll be lucky if someone takes it off our hands."

Niles was looking alarmed, and Steve hung back awkwardly, not sure if he should stay or go. Roberta veered for the door, stumbling past them. The stake was not so deep in the ground after all. One tug and it was out, but the abrupt yank did nothing to satisfy her rage. She took the sign over to a rock in the yard and began bashing it until only shards of kindling were left.

"Take it easy, Roberta." Steve was trying to take a shattered piece of wood from her hands, but she flung it across the lawn and into the brush. Paula and Niles stood on the lawn, watching her dumbly, and Gran had come to the door, a look of questioning on her face.

"I will not take it easy." She took a breath and tried to regroup. "I will not take it, period, anymore. I will not take having other people decide what is best for me and this family. I will not take all these secrets, and lies, and—and *machinations*. I am going to find out once and for all what is going on here, and I am going to do something about it." A thought had occurred to her, some time between pulling up the "for sale" sign and flinging its last remnants across the yard. "I need to borrow your car."

"Roberta, I don't think you're in any shape to be driving around—"

"Can I go?" Niles shot over between them, inches from her face. "Can I go too, please?"

But she brushed him aside. The last thing she needed now was a teenage boy getting in the way.

"Watch out for second gear; it sticks. Don't drive like I do. And for God's sake don't use up—"

But she was in the Cutlass and turning the key, and the roar of the engine drowned him out.

She saw no one on the road. In the back of her mind she remembered all those warnings Steve had given her in Hope Valley, about people who would try to hijack you just for your gas. But there wasn't a soul out on this late February afternoon. She pulled into the town hall parking lot beside a police cruiser.

The town clerk did not look up right away, and even when Roberta explained what she wanted, she hesitated before she answered.

"Do you know the plat and lot number?"

"No," Roberta admitted. "But I know it adjoins our property.

I mean, my father's property."

"So your father was a seller once." She opened another drawer and began flipping through the cards. She had not asked Roberta her name, but flipped quickly to Alton's name on a three-by-five card. "He's sold a number of lots over the years. Look here. See if any of these fit the bill."

Roberta obeyed, but she had no idea what she was looking for. Each card had only the name of the seller, the date and the plat and lot numbers. The woman passed her scrap paper and a small pencil, and she jotted down the numbers. The woman had already lifted a bound volume out of the stack and slid it on the table.

"I think this might be it," Roberta said, pointing to the card. "This lot was sold in 2001, the year I went to college."

The woman raised an eyebrow but made no comment. She flipped through the pages. "Here we go. George Alton Wilcox to Maine Development Co."

Roberta's heart sank. That must be the senator's. "Do they still own it? Is there any way to check?"

"All you have to do is look in the tax book." The woman disappeared into the front office and returned with a small staple-bound booklet. She thumbed to the M's. "That's funny. There's no Maine Development Company in here at all. Maine, Fred . . . he has one, two, three lots. That's all his farm, though. I don't see this parcel. Well, let's look up Maine Development again."

She thumbed through the cards in the file drawer. "Here. Maine Development sold the parcel two years ago. To something called Miller Land Company."

"Did you say—Miller?"

"Ummm. Here it is. July 5, 2003. Maine Development Company to Miller Land Company."

Roberta sat down on one of the hard wooden chairs. The

room, with its peach-colored cement blocks, was weaving sickeningly in front of her. She gripped the table and forced herself to look. But the deed was signed by a name she had never heard of. Alton's name was not mentioned. The sum, written in figures and words, was large enough to read from across the room. Fifty-five thousand dollars.

"Are you okay?" The clerk looked at her for the first time. "Let me get you some water."

"Drink this. You're Alton's daughter, aren't you? I thought I recognized you." The woman sat down next to her. "It's none of my business, but does this have anything to do with your probate trouble?"

It occurred to Roberta then that the woman of course knew her; she was also the probate clerk. "My father owed Maine fifty-thousand dollars. I'm trying to find out why. I think I just got my answer."

The woman turned back to the book. "There's a mortgage recorded for fifty thousand. That must be the amount owed in the lien."

"But is it my father? How am I going to find out? I never heard of this man here."

"David Brewster? He's a lawyer. Hold on a minute." After a few minutes the woman came back and gestured her to follow. In the front office they sat before a computer. "Secretary of State incorporation records. They're all on-line. There you go." Roberta looked at the screen. *Miller Land Company. George Alton Wilcox, President. David Brewster, Financial Agent. Purpose: residential development. 2003.*

"Looks like he owned it all right. But it's not mentioned in the will, huh?" The woman was flipping through another filing cabinet. *This place is an archive of my life,* Roberta thought. She would not have been surprised if the woman produced her father himself, the punch line to a public records magic act.

"This is your father's will. It's dated 1995. That's quite a few years before he bought back that land. I'm surprised he didn't update his will. Did you find any other papers in his box?"

"His box?" Roberta asked dumbly.

"His box. His safe-deposit box, at the bank."

"I didn't know he had one. I haven't even found his bankbook. He did all his business at the credit union in Hope Valley, but Lucas Whitford said he only had a small account there."

"Honey, are you sure?" The woman was dialing the phone as she spoke, punching numbers with a long apricot-colored fingernail. "Extension sixteen." She spun around. "Lonnie? It's Kay. I need a favor. Didn't you say Alton Wilcox used to do his business with you? Do you have an account for him? Sure." After a moment she began jotting something down on a piece of memo paper. "Try Miller Land Company." She wrote more and Roberta felt herself begin to sweat again. Then she hung up.

"You're going to have to go up there. But it's too late today. They're getting ready to close."

"But what did she say? Does she have any idea?"

"Just go up there, hon. Ask for Lonnie." She handed Roberta a piece of paper with the name Mid-State Credit Union on it and an address. "Maybe you'll find some answers."

CHAPTER TWENTY-THREE

It couldn't be too late. Roberta headed out on the highway, trying to remember which exit to take. It had been so long since she'd been up this way.

She guessed and took the Coventry exit, and found the credit union about a mile down the road, between a gas station and a boarded-up tile shop. She stood at a fake wood counter and shuffled her feet and cleared her throat. Finally a woman came out of a back office.

"You must be Roberta," she said before Roberta could explain herself. "We're just closing up. Let me lock up, and I'll take you in the back."

Lonnie led her down a narrow corridor to a row of metal boxes. "Your father was such a nice man. He used to bring me a coffee from the doughnut shop across the street every time he came."

Roberta stared at her. Were they talking about the same person? "You knew my father?"

"Oh, sure. He did a lot of business here." Lonnie lifted a metal box from the wall and carried it into a small adjoining room. "You're the college professor, right? He used to tell me all about you girls. He was so proud of his daughters."

Roberta smiled politely. Her mind reeled. She could not, in her wildest imagination, conjure up her father bragging about her to a stranger.

"I have to stay with you," Lonnie said, sitting down at the

table. "It's bank regulations in cases like these. But you go ahead. I won't be nosy."

Roberta opened the box and came upon a pile of papers. She lifted them out and spread them in front of her. But now, confronted with the possibility of what they might contain, she felt her fingers freeze. Everything already had changed. Her father. Talking about her and Paula.

"What did he say?"

"Excuse me?"

"My father. What did he say about us? I'm sorry, but that's not like him. He was an old Yankee, you know. He didn't talk much to—to people he didn't know well."

"Alton? Oh, heavens. He *was* a Yankee, wasn't he? He was a funny one, too, you know? He was always kidding. Well, he liked me, I guess, because my father's from down your way. They went to school together. So I guess he talked to me maybe more than he might some people. But he would just come in, you know, pass the time of day, ask about my family. He always said how smart you were, down there teaching at that college. And Paula too, working at the hospital. He was just sorry you both didn't have a mother."

On top was a sheaf of documents. Life insurance. Roberta flipped through the pages quickly. Ten thousand. That would have paid to bury him in a real cemetery, with a small headstone. She opened a white, business-sized envelope. It was a letter on heavy stationery. She skimmed quickly to the bottom. It was signed by Fred Maine.

Roberta felt that cold sweat on her hands again. She wiped them impatiently on her jeans. She started again. *Dear Alton,* the letter read. *This is to remind you that the balloon payment on your mortgage is overdue. If you do not remit the full amount of the loan in thirty days, I will be forced to take legal action.* There was more, a reference to property that Roberta immediately recognized. The letter was dated the September past.

So Alton did owe on the land he had bought from Maine. Roberta sighed and picked up another envelope. It was thick and held closed with a rubber band, which she snapped off impatiently. Inside were dozens of pieces of paper, covered in her father's familiar handwriting. Numbers, abbreviations, red check marks. *25 brls, Sept. 5. $500.* Each sheet had a similar mark, written in pencil, her father's usual flowing penmanship cramped with haste. Then another envelope, also closed with elastics. This time she cracked a nail opening it. Then out fell the money.

It was the biggest wad of bills Roberta had ever seen. Not tens or twenties or even fifties, but layer after layer of one-hundred and five-hundred-dollar bills. They fanned out on the table like a pile of grass clippings. Roberta looked up at the woman who sat across from her, and for a moment neither spoke.

"Oh, my," Lonnie said. "Well, people do use safe-deposit boxes to keep cash sometimes. Seems silly, seeing as how they lose the interest."

"Could you count it for me, please?"

The woman began to shuffle the bills with the swift efficiency of a teller. She counted and counted and counted, and Roberta held her breath until she thought her lungs would explode. Finally the woman stopped. She had placed the notes back in neat piles. She whispered something that Roberta didn't catch.

"What?"

"Forty-five thousand dollars."

"Oh, my God." Roberta put her head in her hands. Almost enough to pay off the lien—with the life insurance, more than enough.

"He must have been ready to pay that loan. But why didn't he pay at least some of it?"

Roberta, the money towering over her pile of papers, began to go carefully through them again. More letters from Maine, threatening legal action. A letter from the town assessing interest on a late tax payment. Then a white, legal-sized envelope. Roberta broke the seal and pulled out more papers.

She read quickly, skipping again to the end. Wasn't the real stuff, the truth, always at the end? These lawyers made more money putting things off. They were worse than doctors who were afraid to give a bad diagnosis. *Get to the point,* she wanted to shout. Then she read a few more lines and stopped.

It was a will, dated 2013, just months before Alton's death. The beneficiaries were Roberta Wilcox and Paula Brown. The property bequeathed to them was Wilcox Farm—all except for a parcel also known as Roberta's Woods. That he had left only to her.

"Don't cry, honey. I'm sure it's not that bad. Why, look at all this money you didn't know he had."

"Oh, it's not bad. It's not bad." Roberta snuffled and fished in her pocket for a Kleenex. "It's not bad at all."

"I just don't understand this. How could everyone have missed this account? He had life insurance, a new will—and we didn't know. We might never have known."

"It's not up to the bank to get involved in probate," the woman said, suddenly huffy.

"Oh, I know—"

"The account wasn't in his name, you know. That might be why no one down there knew about it."

"It wasn't? Whose was it in?"

"Miller Land Company. Some company your father had started."

Was this what the town clerk had alluded to? "Why would he do that? Is this some kind of a game? I mean, this has caused serious problems in my family. You have no idea."

271

Lonnie leaned back and chewed on her lip for a moment. "Your father was awfully wary of the government," she said slowly. "I think he told me a hundred times he didn't want the IRS poking into his business. I always thought he started that company as a tax dodge."

Oh, great, Roberta thought, *next we'll have the IRS on our trail.* Did that explain the white papers with the red marks? Maybe her father had been keeping track of some illegal source of income.

"What am I going to do about this? Can I take this stuff? We're in the middle of probate. I've got to tell somebody about this."

"I can't let you take it, but all you need to do is get an order from the judge." As though she feared Roberta might suddenly stuff something in her pocket, the woman began gathering up the money and the papers and piling them back in the safe-deposit box. Roberta felt exhausted. Some trial was over, but it wasn't exactly peace that flowed through her. It was something else, something a little short of relief. The tension was gone, but the problems were not.

When she awoke the next morning, she realized Paula was gone. Ray had come to get her while Roberta was off at town hall, and Gran didn't think she'd be back any time soon. Coward's Hole was no place to be having a baby, she had said, or something to that effect. The house seemed strangely empty without her.

Gran seemed to have shrunk in the past day, and Roberta worried about the toll all this strife and upheaval was having on her. She had not thought about that when she was pulling the "for sale" stake out of the lawn and peeling out of the driveway in the Cutlass. Then she had been on a mission. As much as she wanted to stay with Gran all morning, she felt her mission was not over.

She walked to the mill without really thinking about where she was going. Ahead was the winding, rocky lane that led into the heart of the woodlot. Roberta's Woods. The path was still blocked by the old telephone poles that Maine had rolled onto the lip of the road the day after Alton had signed away the property. It had been a few weeks before she went away to school. That day Alton had driven down the woodlot road one more time, pulled out the shingle mill and his John Deere tractor, and walked away. Hours later Maine arrived with the telephone poles, and the standoff had begun.

When had she been this far in these woods last? She and Steve. They had been in high school, just kids really, sitting with their backs against the Rock of Dreams. The Indians called it that, Steve had told her, because the queen would sleep with her head against this cold pillow, and whatever dreams she had would be prophecy. She had been stoned out of her mind, but now she remembered it all with an icy clarity. And there, sure enough, was the Rock of Dreams, startling her out of her reverie. That little notch halfway up, the queen's pillow, was still there, too, rounder maybe from twenty-five years of rain, but there. Dropping to her knees she sat in last autumn's leaves, leaning her head against the rock.

She closed her eyes. She began to wander through the rooms of her mind. She thought of it that way: an upstairs, a downstairs, tiny alcoves in between where her emotions rested when they weren't needed. She saw herself running to the window, the blinds flying off like wings, the light white on her hair. Then she was swimming, more quickly this time, the tangles of weeds parting like hair, until her head bumped against it. A door? A window? She was frantically banging, pounding; her fists were bloody stumps. To be let in or let out? To break something, to break into something . . . the water was so murky, yellow almost, tinged with red. Then she saw the headlights' ghostly trail to her right. And she looked straight ahead, into the eyes of her mother.

Roberta stumbled down the woods path. Her eyesight wasn't steady. Up ahead it looked like a man standing in the path, but it must be a tree, or even a deer. But it was a man, although he stood stolid like a tree. He was blocking her way. Good God, she thought. It was Oatley.

"Did you find your answer?"

"What are you talking about?" She was dry-mouthed, hungry and tired. She had no patience for Oatley's riddles.

"On the rock. I saw you, sleeping there. When you fall asleep on the Rock of Dreams, the answers come to you, whether you ask the question or not."

"The Rock of Dreams." She repeated it, sounding stupid to herself. "Oatley. It was you watching me. You were hiding behind the rocks, weren't you?"

"I wasn't watching. I was experiencing you. I was trying to figure you out."

"There's nothing to figure out. You were trespassing. This land belongs to me now. My father left to me."

"I know."

"You know?" She studied his face. Was he laughing at her? He seemed serious, though, and there was purpose in his eyes. This meeting had not been an accident.

"Of course. But you don't own it. Nobody does."

Oh, Jesus, she thought. *Here we go.* "Look, Oatley. I appreciate your point of view. I understand none of us really owns any of this land. We're just caretakers, right? So call me the new caretaker. Whatever. But my name's going to be on the deed."

"Perhaps. If you pay off that lien."

She looked at him again. So he knew about that, too. "Well, I will. I have the money. It's just a matter of working out the details. Now could you move, please? I really need to get home."

"Roberta." He touched her shoulder; his hand, large and square, cupped her bones. "You've been given a gift this morning, haven't you?"

She looked into his face. Its intensity scared her. It was a handsome face, dark, with deep-set brown eyes and a broad nose. But it was like a god's face, on fire, all-knowing. He had watched her dreaming, and he had seen her dream. She felt goosebumps seize her arms.

Her voice had turned to a croak. "What is it? What do you want, Oatley?"

"What do you want, Roberta? Do you want this woodlot? Why? Because it was your father's, and his before him? If you possess it, will you possess him? And your mother? They are all around you, you know. They watch you far better than I ever could. They watch from above and below. They are in the dirt at my feet and in the air that's blowing through your hair. You just have to be open to them."

She felt that he was right. Her shoulder sagged beneath his hand.

"And when you have it, this land, what will you do with it? Build yourself a house? Tear down a few trees to do it? Or will you walk through here to feel that wind on your face, that ground below?" His hand moved, swiftly, to her neck. "Will you lay this head on the queen's pillow? Will you ask her to see them once again?" He was whispering now, his hand hot on the back of her hair. "I think the queen likes you. She gave you the comfort you craved. She brought your mother to you, didn't she? Why do you think that was?"

Roberta was in a trance. She knew she should be afraid, but she was listening to him now, waiting for him to tell her his secrets. "I don't know, Oatley." Her voice was tiny, like a mechanical doll's.

"You love this land. I can feel that in you. When you walk in the woods, the way you listen, the way you watch. You're not like everyone else." Abruptly he let go of her and put his hands down by his sides. "Don't pay that lien, Roberta."

"What?"

"Your father didn't owe Fred a penny. And he knows it."

"Oatley, are you sure? How do you know?"

"Because I carried every one of those payments to Fred myself. Walking through these woods with that cash in my pocket. Ha! What a funny scene, eh? The Indian errand boy, helping one white man buy land from another, as though it meant a damn. But those two hated each other so much that I had to be the go-between. Fred loved sending me out to do his bidding. I liked your father, though. He was a good man."

Roberta didn't know what to say. She took a step toward him but he turned suddenly, a slight smile on his face. "Fred wouldn't release the deed, kept putting your father off. I'm the only one who knows it. And if I keep quiet, the probate court will probably just accept the claim. It'll be like everything else Fred does."

Those pieces of paper. Were they records of payment? "Oh, Oatley, please. You can't do that. It wouldn't be right."

"So now we come to our terms and conditions." He looked around suddenly, as though he were the one being watched this time. "I've had it with Fred. I need a place where I can live without him collecting rent from me every month. I need to get away from that nuthouse over there. It wouldn't be big. Just a shack, an outhouse with it, a shed where I could dry venison. Nothing like you people build. No roads, no garages, no swing sets."

Now she understood. He wanted the land. All that talk about the Great Spirit and the birds and the wind and the dirt didn't mean he wasn't so unlike her. He wanted a corner of the earth to be alone on, a place where he could pursue his happiness without harassment. And he wanted it for the same reason she did. Because once it had belonged to his people. Once they had roamed here, camped here, hunted here, birthed here. Her parents were not the only ghosts blowing around this hollow.

She put her hand on his arm and nodded. The deal had been struck.

CHAPTER TWENTY-FOUR

The house was eerily quiet when she returned. Gran was taking a nap, and Niles was out. It was just as well. They were all curious about where she had driven off to yesterday, and now her morning walk probably was making them wonder, too. She didn't want to talk about it yet, and besides, she had things to do.

The plat of Roberta's Woods was still in Alton's dresser drawer, behind his flannel shirts. She took it up to her room and unfurled it on the bed. If everything went according to plan, Alton's more recent will would be introduced at the next probate hearing, and Paula would be forced to take the house off the market. Roberta would be granted Roberta's Woods outright, so long as Oatley lived up to his promise to testify. Oatley had said Alton had paid off the mortgage, but Maine had refused to release it. So that meant the forty-five thousand in the safe-deposit box was up for grabs—probably to be granted to Paula and Roberta to share, absent any directions in the will.

If Roberta renounced her claim to the money, would Paula sign off her share of the farm? It wasn't much, certainly less than half of what the place was worth, but it was cash in hand, and Paula had sounded desperate for money. You could buy a lot of baby clothes with forty-five thousand dollars.

"You gave me a start." Gran walked stiffly into the hall and took a ratty pink cardigan off a hook on the wall. "You've been gallivanting around all day."

Roberta started to respond, but Gran continued, almost as though she were talking to herself. "Niles was around here all morning, tailing me like that old coon cat we used to have. He just tuckered me out. Finally I told him to go ahead."

"Go ahead? And do what?"

"I don't remember." She looked as vague as she sounded, her eyes pointed beyond Roberta's head as though she were talking to someone else. "I was cold in bed. I called out for you, but I guess you didn't hear me. I was wanting that afghan, but I couldn't quite reach it, and then it fell on the floor."

The house had been quiet as death. How had Roberta not heard her? She started to apologize and reached out for her, but Gran twisted from her embrace with a sudden strength.

"You haven't been paying Niles any attention lately," she said, and then stopped, her chest rising and falling as she tried to catch her breath. "That poor boy is more mixed up than a skunk in January. All he wants is someone to pay attention to him. I'm an old woman. I can't be that boy's mother. You brought him here and, by God, you need to follow through with what you started."

Roberta felt her face redden. She had never heard Gran talk that way to anyone, and to be the object of this uncharacteristic scolding was mortifying. Worse, she knew Gran was right. "Gran, I'll go find him. Don't worry. But maybe you should go back to your nap."

She decided to walk to Steve's. She found him in the barn, his head deep in a car engine and a rag flapping from the back pocket of his jeans. "I don't like it." He wiped his hands on the rag and stared out the slit in the barn door. "Maybe you're right. Maybe May's confused, but it's not like her to be confused."

"I think she was dreaming, to tell you the truth."

"When's the last time you saw him?"

279

"He probably just went for a walk up to Lewis City," she mused.

"What's he been talking about lately? You said he was bugging May for permission to do something. Maybe that would be a clue."

"All he ever talks about is that hydroelectric project of Foley's. He was fascinated by it. I don't think I've ever seen him as animated as he was that day. And he's convinced that Maine is going to stand in his way. Oh, Steve, you don't suppose."

"That he'd go over to Maine's? I hope not. Look, I'll take a ride over there. Why don't you walk out to Lewis City. You know his haunts better than I do." He wiped his hands on the rag, then put his hands on her shoulders. "I'm sure you're right. Probably May was a little confused. But we better go round him up anyway."

A glint returned to his eyes, and he motioned to the darker recesses of the barn. "Want to see what I've been working on?"

He slinked between cars, and she followed him, her eyes gradually adjusting to the dark. He lifted a dusty green tarp, and even in the dank, dusty air of the barn Roberta could see it was a masterpiece.

The car was white. The seats were lipstick-red leather. Every inch of it had been polished and buffed to perfection. But neither the pearly gleam of its paint nor the shiny glass headlights impressed Roberta. She was too stunned by what it was, and whose car it had been.

"It's a 1961 Thunderbird," Steve finally said. She could tell her silence was making him nervous, but what could she say? "The convertible top isn't original, but I did the best I could. Everything else is original to the car. It's a showpiece, Roberta."

"Oh, Steve." The sigh escaped her; she could not help it. Would her life always be like this, a string of surprises knocking her off her feet? "Where did you get it? Was it in your junkyard all these years?"

He looked at her, puzzled. There was no disguising her reaction now.

"No, I didn't get it from the junkyard." His face had colored and his eyes were steely. "I bought it from a fellow in Massachusetts years ago. Even back then it cost me a penny. Look, Roberta, if you don't like it—"

"Steve, my mother had a car just like this. She died in it. I thought . . . for a moment, I thought this was my mother's car."

"What? What are you talking about?" He stopped and folded her into his arms. "Jesus, Roberta, whatever gave you that idea? I picked this out because of you. You always said the Thunderbird was your favorite car. I didn't know . . . I didn't know this was it." He rocked her, his mouth on her hair. "I wouldn't hurt you for anything."

Roberta felt the barn floor swaying beneath her. She could smell all the cars, a mixture of gasoline and metal and upholstery, and in the thin lip of sunlight coming through a board crack she could see motes of dust falling like spiders rappelling down a web. There were dark, mysterious things here, things she did not understand, things she had not attempted to understand. Here Steve kept what was dear to him, including his love for her, safely sheltered under a tarp in a barn where eyes had trouble adjusting to the dark.

She put her hand to his forehead and wiped away the smudge, then she reached for him, making his musky, smoky, greasy smell a part of her being.

When they parted there was just a slight curl to his lips of that old amusement, and when he spoke it was barely a whisper. "Is that a yes?"

"All this time, I've never trusted you. I can see that now. I always believed the worst about you. But it's been you all along getting us through everything. You were there for Niles, and you were there for May, and most of all, you were there for me. But it was never enough. I guess I was afraid to trust you. So many people I trusted abandoned me. I guess I was afraid you would just . . . disappear." She smiled as though at a secret joke. "But here I am, depending on you again."

"There's nothing bad about two people depending on each other." He let her go with visible reluctance. "Now we have someone else depending on us, and we better go find him."

He replaced the Thunderbird's tarp, put the hood down on the Plymouth he had been tinkering with and led her out of the barn. He would drive over to Maine's while she walked over to see Lucas, who could let her borrow a horse. Riding would be quicker than hiking. Then they would meet back at her house.

She hated to split up, but Steve's plan made sense. Niles probably was in the woods, hunkered down on his favorite rock. If he had run off, he probably was just waiting for them to discover his disappearance, and he would be expecting—nay, hoping—for her to come after him.

She banged on Lucas's back door, but there was no answer. She ran down to the stables. The horses were in. The ring was empty and she could hear them stamping in the stalls. She was about to give up when she saw Lucas headed toward the path that led in back of her farm.

When she caught up with him, she noticed his hair was aflutter and his plaid coat was unbuttoned. "I tried to call you, but the phone's dead. I was just running over to see you."

"We must have gotten behind on the bill. Listen, Lucas, I was hoping—"

He was talking over her. "No, because I'm out too. That's what I meant. My phone was dead, so I couldn't call you." He pulled his coat together and Roberta noticed his knuckles were white. "Where's Steve?"

"Steve? That's what I'm trying to tell you. He's looking for

Niles. I wanted to know if—"

"Roberta, we have to find him and warn him."

"Warn Niles? About what?"

"Not Niles! Steve!" Lucas began striding quickly back toward the house and she tried to keep up. "Piccirelli and the state," he called over his shoulder. "They're over to Fred Maine's now. They're going to arrest Maine." He stopped by the door, and she nearly collided with him as he turned around. She was trying to process everything, but it was all too much.

"Maine's been selling gasoline on the black market. They've been watching him for months. Couldn't figure out where he was getting it, how he was getting rid of it. But it was the milk trucks. Once a month a container truck would roll in here from Canada, supposedly to buy his milk. But it wasn't milk it was transporting. It was fuel."

"Canada?"

"And from Canada right down through New York state and Massachusetts and Connecticut. It was brilliant, really. Who would stop a tanker truck carrying milk? Especially in upper New York state. They're as thick as pickup trucks up there."

"What does Steve have to do with this?"

"I don't know, but I overheard Piccirelli a few weeks ago saying they spotted him out at a farm somewhere that they suspected was a selling depot. He said he was under suspicion. They knew somebody was helping Maine distribute the gas once it came here. I guess they think it was Steve. Roberta, are you okay?"

"Lucas, Niles is missing. Steve and I thought he might have gone over to Maine's, and Steve is probably over there right now. I was hoping you'd loan me one of the horses. I was going to look for Niles up to Lewis City. But we have to get over to Maine's."

Lucas started to say something, but the ground shook and

then they heard it: a blast like a mine caving in or plane crashing, and off to the west came an orange glow, like fireworks on a summer night. Roberta clutched at the wood box and another blast came, this time farther away, and the sky lit up, with terrible black smoke in a huge column piercing the sky.

They were quiet for a moment, as though waiting for another blast. Then Lucas doffed his hat and wiped his brow. "That came from over your way. If Maine had a stash of gasoline in the woods, he doesn't anymore."

"Lucas! We have to go to Maine's. That fire's going to race through here. You know how dry it is. Let's get the horses. It's the fastest way—"

"No! Roberta, I won't have you going over there. Now listen." She could see a war going on inside him. If he helped Steve, he would helping his rival, but he also would be doing what she wanted of him. He seemed to know he already had lost. "I'll drive over there," he said finally. "You go home and sit tight. You don't know. Niles might be home as we speak."

"No. He's either at Maine's or in the woods. Either way, he's in danger. Give me one of the horses, and I'll ride out to Lewis City."

"You can't take the horses in there. They'll get trapped or panic, and you'll end up getting thrown."

"Lucas, we're talking about a fourteen-year-old boy. He could be near that blast. We've got to find him."

"You have no idea where he is. We can't take the horses on some wild goose chase. Besides, I don't want you going anywhere near that fire. The best thing for you to do is to go home and sit tight."

Lucas turned away and headed toward the door. She clutched at the back of his plaid coat, her breath coming in shorter and shorter gasps. "I could take the old trail that runs into Lewis City, then head down by the mill. The horse won't smell the fire until we're on top of it."

"You get anywhere near that fire, the horse will be skittish as hell," Lucas finally said, as though he had been listening to her thoughts. "Please go home, Roberta."

Roberta spun off on her heel toward the woods. The fire at least gave her a sense of direction. When she came to the cutoff to the farm, she kept going west, toward the fire tower.

How long had it stood thus? Through that Fire of Thirty-Six that had taken everything else in its path? She began to scramble up the metal ladder. At the top she flung open the hatch and boosted herself inside.

She picked up the log, and Steve's pencil scratchings stabbed her. Roberta felt her heart begin to hammer. She picked up the binoculars and trained them to the north. A thin line of black, braided with red and yellow, wound through the treetops. It stretched on for miles from west to east, and in its wake had left a forest of smoking tree corpses. So Maine had had some kind of depot up there. How far away? West Greenwich? Coventry? Foster? That was where the Fire of Thirty-Six had started, miles from here, and it had swept from one end of the state to the other, from fresh water to salt, from the mountains to the sea.

She picked up the radio. "This is Tower Station Five in Arcadia, Tower Station Five in Arcadia, out." The radio crackled, but she heard no reply. "This is Tower Station Five in Arcadia. We have a forest fire about ten miles to the north. Explosion about fifteen minutes ago. Out."

Roberta released the button and more static came. For a heartbeat she heard what sounded like a man's voice, but then there was nothing. "This is Tower Station Five in Arcadia. I repeat: we have a forest fire ten miles to the north of the tower. The wind is out of the west, and the fire to the north of here is progressing rapidly." She paused but kept the button depressed. She could hear the desperation in her voice on her final plea.

"There are people in its path. Out."

It would take at least forty minutes to get to Lewis City. She headed down the Woodlot Road and then picked up the trail, skipping over the dry creekbed and fallen trees. She heard something, but it wasn't the crackling of a fire. It sounded like a rolling and splashing. Crows were coming. Their angry wing beats kept the rhythm of the splashing.

She rounded the bend, to see not Niles, but an older man bent over the water. He wore overalls and a dirty denim cap. He was grunting as he heaved a barrel into the river. Ahead of him other barrels lay floating, stuck in the narrow channel like logs at the end of a flume. Behind him, stacked like cordwood, were dozens more. Roberta could not take her eyes away from that tuft of silver hair sticking out of the back of his cap. She could almost smell the Brylcream on his hair and the sweat on the back of his neck. But he did not sense her. He was too intent on the effort of heaving the barrels into the water. She heard him grunt and swear under his breath. Without looking, he backed up to gain leverage and pushed the barrel again. Finally it let go and splashed into the river, bobbed once and floated along to cluster with the others.

Roberta watched him, her eyes boring into that patch of hair. He turned around as though a bug had bit him.

"Hello, Fred."

Fred Maine's face was red and sweaty. His eyes were glazed with confusion. She wondered for a moment if he was drunk. He mumbled something she didn't catch.

"What's that you got there, Fred? Barrels full of that gasoline you've been smuggling down from Ontario?"

"Get the hell out of here. You ain't got no business watching people. Go on."

"Sorry, Fred. I can't stand here and watch you endanger our environment this way. Isn't that what my mother would have said? Yes. Those old barrels look like something you used to make rotgut in. They'll get half way down the river and bust open, and every fish and frog from here to Hope Valley will die. Meanwhile you'll be holding court over at the post office, tsk-tsking over it."

"Those goddamn state people are going to bust me over this! If I didn't bring this gas in, there wouldn't be a soul in Coward's Hole getting around. Where the hell would you be, huh, if I didn't bring that gas in?"

She laughed. He really was funny, standing there with his work pants sagging, the cuffs limp from river water. "Fred, my gas tank is empty, and so is everybody else's. I don't know who you've been selling this stuff to, but it sure as hell isn't me."

"Oh, is that so? Where do you think that gas in Hope Valley comes from? Ain't been a tanker truck down there in six months. I did this for my people, you little snit. For my constituents." He stumbled over the word so it came out "con-stitch-ents." "Ain't you holier than thou. What do you think was putting food on your table? Where do you think your father was getting all that money right before he died?"

She opened her mouth, but stopped. His ridiculous accusation, his usual bravado were enough to scoff at, but she somehow couldn't get the words out. All she could see before her were those chits of paper and the bundles of cash in her father's safe-deposit box. The money that had bought Roberta's Woods had been Maine's money. It wasn't Steve who had been running gas for the old bastard. It was Alton.

"You killed him, didn't you?" Roberta spoke with icy calmness. Her voice could have been coming from the trees or the sky. "You rolled him off that mountain somehow. So he wouldn't talk."

"Naaahhh." Maine spat tobacco juice, and the plug with it. "I didn't kill him. He was a damn fool, always loadin' up that

International as high as he could. He wasn't even driving for me that day. I came over to see him in the afternoon. Had some work for him, but he wouldn't budge. Said he was out of the smugglin' business. I reminded him that I'd be just as happy to cash in that lien on your house. I suppose I got him worked up, but I didn't kill him. You Wilcoxes like to blame everything on somebody else, just like that hussy of your mother driving off the way she did. I s'pose you'd like to blame that one on me, too."

Roberta looked into his eyes and at the corners of his mouth. Somehow she believed him, although she didn't want to.

"Now get out of here," he exploded, as though remembering what she had caught him doing. "I've got that bastard Piccirelli on my tail, I've got to get rid of this stuff or won't none of us have any gas to get around in. He's been nosin' around the farm, trying to find something to hang me on."

She felt a brief stab of sympathy for him. Maybe Steve had been selling gas for him. Maybe Alton had helped him smuggle it out. But their motives would not have been to take advantage of their neighbors, but to keep them self-sufficient.

"Fred, you can't dump all your problems in this river. It's time to face up to it. Do the right thing for once."

He took a red handkerchief out of his pocket, wiped his nose and regarded her. "The only other problem I have is a nosy neighbor. I thought I told you to get out of here."

"That's interesting, considering you're kicking me off my own land."

"Not by a damned sight, you little twit. This here—"

"This here is Roberta's Woods. Oh? You never heard it called that? Maybe my father never shared his plans with you. But one thing he did share was his money. All that money you paid him to smuggle out the gas, he was sending right back to you. Something you neglected to tell the probate court. Maybe Piccirelli would like to add perjury to your other crimes."

"You can't prove it!" His nose was red, and a temple in his brow throbbed. "You can't prove a damned thing, young lady. It's my word against a dead man's."

"On the contrary, it's your word against a living man's. One who's prepared to testify that he hand-carried every last payment on that mortgage from my father to you, your own money coming back at you, and counted it out in the process. One who maybe you haven't treated so well lately. One who probably knows a lot of other things you might not want coming out in court."

His gloved hand shaking, Maine fumbled in his pockets and pulled out another plug of tobacco. The wind was picking up and Roberta could smell smoke on the breeze. Maine seemed not to notice. She watched in horrified fascination as an ember fell from the sky, just a few feet from hundreds of gallons of gasoline.

Maine inhaled, barked out a loose, deep cough and spat. "Now them's things you might call threats. I told you a long time ago not to threaten a state senator. Sometimes I think you don't know what the hell you're saying. You're always runnin' off at the mouth like that mother of yours. Your father, at least he knew when to keep his mouth shut. Now I'm going to tell you something, and I want you to listen up." He pointed a finger at her. At his foot a tiny orange dot still shone in the grass like a firefly. "Your father may have known something about the woods, but he was an idiot when it came to business. That loan was strictly business. He may've paid the principal, but he still owed me plenty of interest. Now this here land you're never going to get that backbecause the law's all about what's written on a piece of paper. Fred Maine ain't left no paper trail of his business. And I'll tell you another thing. That goddamn Indian nigger that works for me can't even write his own name. So who the hell's going to believe what he has to say? Not a damned soul, that's who."

Roberta took a step backwards, then jumped behind the stone wall. She saw him smirk as he turned his head back toward the business at hand. But the tiny trail of fire that had been marching like a line of ants to the pyramid of barrels had reached its destination.

Fred Maine flew off his feet in a blast of orange. His face, which a moment before had been twisted into a triumphant grimace, was a grisly black. The roar of the blaze, the crackling of his clothes and flesh, muffled all but a plaintive echo of the man's screams.

CHAPTER TWENTY-FIVE

May Wilcox lay fully beneath the covers, her afghan thrown crookedly over the bedspread. Her chest rattled and her white curls shook with each struggle for breath. Her eyes were closed, the lids like wrinkled prunes sunk into her face. If it were not for the woman's noisy inhalations and exhalations, it would have been difficult to tell she was alive.

Steve, Ben and Jessie Reynolds stood over her. Steve and Ben looked down at the bed with one expression, a mixture of dread and patience. Jessie stood at the headboard, threading oxygen tubing into the old woman's nostrils and adjusting the battery-operated tank. She moved deftly, keeping an eye on the dials and then May's face while her hands worked seemingly independently.

It was a moment before they noticed Roberta. She had slipped into the room like a fog, and now she stood on the opposite side of the bed facing them. It was only a sharp little cry in her throat at the sight of Gran that made them finally look up.

"Good God, what happened to you?" Steve was already ashen. His hands were folded into his armpits as though he were cold. "Did you find Niles?"

Jessie gave the oxygen tubing one more tweak and ran over to Roberta. Without a word, she led her into the bathroom and began dabbing at her face with a warm washcloth. Roberta looked down at the terry cloth wadded in Jessie's hands and saw that it ran red.

But Jessie seemed unfazed by the wound. She briskly washed and dried it, then gently but persistently began prodding Roberta's forehead with a pair of tweezers. It felt like a hot poker ramming into her temple. Roberta grabbed the rounded porcelain edge of the sink to keep from falling.

"I don't know what you've been up to, but it looks like somebody hit you with an arrowhead." Jessie was picking tiny shards of rock from the side of Roberta's head, and Roberta realized the stone wall had exploded into her face when the gas barrels went up.

"What's wrong with Gran?"

"Old age." There was a pause while Jessie picked at the wound, and Roberta squeezed at the sink to keep from screaming. "Steve found her on the floor. Came and got us. I don't mean to be facetious, Roberta. She's got the combination of problems so common to old age—her heart's weak, her lungs are full of fluid, her circulation's poor, and she might even have had a small stroke. Fortunately I was able to get her the battery tank, but she needs more than oxygen. I'd like to run some tests, but for that she'd need to be in a hospital."

"Oh, she'll never go, Mrs. Reynolds. *Aaahhh.*"

"Sorry. Call me Jessie, for God's sake. There. Whatever's left in you is too small to bother with." She walked out of the bathroom and came back with a bandage and medical tape. "Keep it dry. Wouldn't hurt to expose it to the air now and again. I treated it with goldenseal, which is an antiseptic. If you could have seen yourself, you would have thought you'd been hit by a car, or a bullet." There was just the faintest question mark at the end of her sentence, and Roberta looked up to see Steve leaning in the bathroom door. The question was on his face, too.

She told them about Maine and the fire, and as she did so,

she watched Steve's face. Was he nervous, now that the jig was up? Was he going to confess or just keep it to himself? She felt sick at testing him, but there was no other way to know. He had not seen fit to share his adventures with her.

"Maine got what he deserved," he interrupted. "Now tell me about Nile s. Did you make it to Lewis City? Did you see any sign of him?"

She shook her head. She had been hoping she would find Niles safe at home. She had run back with the image of him in her mind, and she had convinced herself he really wasn't lost at all. She hadn't believed Gran's fears. Now the old woman's outburst made more sense. She hadn't been angry at Roberta; she was sick. She had been trying to tell her it was time for her to grow up, that she wasn't going to be there for her forever. She was trying to force her to take control of the situation.

"We've got to go back there and find him," Steve was saying. "I don't believe he ever was at Maine's. Oatley said he hadn't seen him, and I believe him. There's only one place he'd be, and that's the woods. How close did you say that fire was?"

"By the river. It must have gone through. It must be through Lewis City by now," she choked out. She buried her face in her hands, and the wound beneath her bandage stung. "Jesus, what are we going to do? What about Gran?"

Jessie pressed her hand into Roberta's. "Ben and I will stay with her. There's really nothing you can do, Roberta. I gave her some digitalis for her heart and aspirin to prevent a stroke. We'll just have to wait and see how she does."

"I'm going back in the woods to look for him," Steve said and turned on his heel. "I can't see the fire yet. If it just jumped the river, I might be able to cross it by the Cook Road and circle back around."

"I'm going with you."

He looked at her, and she couldn't tell if his face was alight with the thought of company or of her company. But when he spoke he kept his voice neutral. "Suit yourself. But don't go collapsing on me out there. If we're going to find that boy, we'll have to get a move on."

She walked back into the bedroom and took May's left hand in hers. It was hot, almost torpid, and Roberta felt a strange sensation, as though some of that warmth was shooting up her arm like lightning. Although she did not know what the sensation meant, it comforted her to think that Gran had reacted to her touch. But May's eyes stayed closed, and her eyelids didn't flutter. She was already in a place of no dreams.

"Go ahead," Jessie whispered. "She would want you to take care of that boy."

Roberta kissed May's papery forehead and felt that same sensation, almost like getting burned. She stepped away and then followed Steve out the door and across the back field.

"I hear they were getting ready to arrest Maine," Steve said. He was walking in long strides. Roberta half ran to keep pace with him. "Ben said Ida told him something about smuggling in gas."

"Steve." Roberta grabbed his arm. "Maine told me something before he died." As quickly as she could she told him about the barrels, and Maine's accusation about her father. "I need to know something. It doesn't make any difference, but I need to know. Were you helping him?"

"Helping Maine? What in God's name gave you that idea?"

"Lucas said there's a warrant out for your arrest. He said you were helping Maine, helping him deliver the gas, and my . . . and my father was smuggling it out of here on the International." As she spoke, the overwhelming reality of it suddenly hit her. "That day you took me to Hope Valley. What were you doing out in the woods there, if you weren't buying illegal gas?"

He looked back at her with what seemed like pity. "Of course

I was buying gas. But what's that got to do with helping Maine?"

"That was one of his depots. At least, that's what Lucas said."

"Lucas, Lucas, Lucas. What the hell does he know about anything? Yeah, I was up there buying gas from John Woodmansee. So was everybody else around here. But that doesn't mean I was helping Maine, for Chrissakes. I told you months ago the staties raided my shed. I knew what they were looking for. They thought I was making fuel with wood alcohol. As a matter of fact I was—or trying to. But it wasn't as easy as it looks. But helping Maine? Good God. Not in this lifetime."

"Steve, if they have a warrant for your arrest, there must be some reason."

"Roberta, what's up with you? I just told you that I wasn't helping Fred Maine with his little scheme. I can't believe your father was. Jesus."

They walked on, but the subject hung between them. "What made you think I would pair up with him, anyway? Ever since you came home, it's always right there under the surface. You always think I'm up to something. Why can't you trust me?"

She had a choice. She could go back to the house. She didn't have to go with Steve. But Niles was out there, and he was their responsibility.

"Let's go." She grabbed his hand and began to pull him along, but he stayed there, holding her back.

"If you go with me, I want us to be together."

"I know that."

They came to a clearing and surprised a herd of deer. They were not running like the deer she had seen before she stumbled on Maine, but they were huddled together oddly and seemed reluctant to run off, startled as they were. "They've been driven here by the fire," Steve said as they slowly scattered. He pointed to an opening at the edge of the clearing. "Down here."

She kept pace with him. The smell of smoke was stronger,

and when they rounded the next bend she could see creeping flame, advancing on them like the edges of a flood. A few hundred yards to their west, fire was snaking to the top of a white pine. They were on the front line now.

Roberta could hear the river—or was that the roar of the fire coming at them like a freight train? In her mind she tried to place how close they were to the water, but the smoke was making her mind foggy. Behind them came a familiar crash. Without looking she knew a white pine had fallen to earth. It made a muffled sound, just as it would if Alton Wilcox had bridled it with a cable and hacked it to the ground.

"Did you hear that?" Steve turned to her, still half running through the woods.

"A pine fell."

"No, not that. Hang on. Listen." He held up his hand and she tried to quell the roaring in her ears long enough to isolate one sound from another. Birds squawking. Snapping twigs caught up in the maelstrom. The wind whipping smoke into their faces. Movement in the underbrush. Something small; maybe a mole or a shrew. A weak cry, almost human, from the trees. She couldn't place it.

"*Niles!*" Steve cupped his hand together and began to shout, sending his voice to the treetops. "*Niles!*"

"Steve!" The cry was unmistakable. "Up here!"

And there he was, in a fort whose weathered brown boards matched the tree trunk so closely that she had not seen it the first time she looked up. He dangled there, afraid to jump, his eyes trained first on the fire that sped toward them, then downward at the ground so far below.

She began to shimmy up the tree. It was an oak, probably 150 years old, with enough branches and footholds to make the ascent manageable. Niles had probably clambered up and down it a hundred times. But he had never done it with the forest ablaze below him. He had never thought one day he might want to jump rather than spend a half-hour ambling down, taking his time to pick just the right foothold.

"Niles." Roberta rested in a crotch of the tree so that her hands nearly reached him. He was crouched on a platform littered with a few dirty dishes, some magazines and a rolled-up sleeping bag. "If I can climb up here, you can climb down."

"My ladder fell."

Roberta looked down and saw an old wooden ladder lying flat on the ground about fifty yards away. So that was it. With a final push, she scooted onto the platform next to him and began throwing things down—his sleeping bag, his backpack.

"Roberta, be careful." Steve stood below with a worried expression.

She ignored him and looked up at Niles. "Now I can throw you down too, or we can go down the easy way." His hands were wound around a post he had nailed into the tree. "Come on. You've been living up here, haven't you? So you can't be afraid of heights. Now me, on the other hand . . . that's a different story. So help me out here and let's get down."

Niles looked over at her and shifted his weight so he was sitting rather than crouching. "Go down the way you came," he said finally. "Backwards. Watch the very last notch in the tree; it's always farther away than you think."

She began to inch down, keeping her eyes on him, and he followed, expertly reaching for the right handhold at the right time. Just as she was about to reach the last notch, she saw the spark come, blown by the wind into the tree house. It smoldered quickly and sent a lick of flame up the side of the platform.

Niles saw it, too. He stood there, frozen at the sight of his work going up in flame.

"Come on! Get the hell out of there!" Steve, helplessly watching from the ground, tugged on Roberta's leg. She was just

297

about to reach for Nile s when he took one last look upward and then jumped, landing with a tortured cry. Roberta leapt too, and as she hit the ground, the blazing tree house became one cauldron of flame, shooting sparks into the upper reaches of the old oak.

Niles lay crumpled in the dead oak leaves, reaching his hand toward his foot.

"Oh, shit." Roberta knew immediately what had happened: he had landed on the weak ankle and sprained it, or maybe worse. There was no time to think about it. The tree above them was blazing like a torch, and sparks flashed above as the wind blew them from branch to branch. Steve gathered up Niles in his arms and Roberta, saddled with his backpack and sleeping bag, hobbled along behind them, squinting into the haze.

They soon reached the river, and to Roberta's relief, Steve's old red canoe was still there, huddled upside down on the bank. Steve put Niles down, righted the canoe, put Niles in it with the baggage. She stood, frozen, but he pushed her into it and then jumped in, and before she knew it they were headed downriver.

"Where are we going?" she shouted above the roar of the fire.

"I don't know. Away from here. And we've got to warn people on the Cook Road."

But what about Niles? She wanted to say it aloud, but Steve seemed so confident, so in control, that he seemed to take every question as a challenge to his authority. She looked over to where Niles was holding his ankle and muttering to himself. He looked more distressed than he had the night of the blizzard.

"Steve, we've got to get him to Jessie," she whispered. "Look at him. He looks horrible."

"It hurts, it hurts, it hurts," Niles was saying, like an incantation.

"I know, baby," Roberta called to him, trying to sound soothing. "I know."

"It hurts, it hurts."

"His ankle is the least of our problems." Steve bit off the words like a plug of tobacco. "If that fire doesn't slow down, river or no river, we're going to be right in the thick of it."

Up ahead the first underpass loomed. So they were past the Whitford land and about to go under Cook Road. The concrete bridge, so far, had acted as a natural—or unnatural—firebreak, and on the other side Steve motioned her to steer the canoe to the north bank. "I'm going to check on the Teffts. Stay here. Don't get out!" And with that he was up and out of the canoe and scrambling up the bank.

Steve came sliding down the bank so quickly the boat was jarred before he reached it. "Fire's worse over on the north side. I tried to talk sense into them, but they're going to tough it out."

"Has it crossed the road?"

"Not yet, but it will."

"Do they have a way to get out?"

"No."

Roberta was silent then. She thought of Gran and Ben, of Ida and her mother. They, at least, were on the south side, but how long before the wind shifted? She looked over her shoulder and saw only smoke beyond the disappearing bridge, but both the north and south banks were swirling in it.

The dusk was complete when they emerged onto the pond. Steve was still rowing furiously, as though the fire were nipping at their heels, and Roberta struggled to keep up. "We'll camp out on the island tonight. We could even sleep indoors, if the cabin's still standing."

It seemed unthinkable, but Steve had to build a fire. They bundled Niles up in a sleeping bag and put him near the blaze. Roberta rustled through his backpack for provisions.

"Niles, want some water?" But the boy was asleep, curled up

with only his nose and forehead peeking above the sleeping bag.

Steve came back to the fire with more logs, his eyes on the edge of the moonlit horizon. "Find anything good to eat?"

"Macaroni and cheese but no milk or butter; peanut butter but no bread; cereal but no milk."

Steve was feeding a stick slowly into the blaze and staring off into the night as though he hadn't heard. "Sounds like he intended to hunt his dinner."

"Think we'll be able to row back in the morning?" Roberta, wiping her hands on her jeans, tried to keep the question casual.

Steve didn't answer right away. "I don't think we'll be going back for a while," he said finally. "I can't see it yet, but that fire's still out there, on both sides of the river. The wind's quiet now, but it'll pick up again before morning. And unless it shifts direction big time, we're going to be right in its sights."

"Can't we hike back, on the south side? It didn't seem to be that bad on that side—"

"With Niles along? He can barely hop out of the canoe."

"But the fire department must have got here by now. I know you couldn't rouse them this afternoon, but by now they must have gotten reports . . ." She didn't want to tell him about the message she had sent out on the radio. She still felt a little like a child who's been into the old man's crystal set. "They must have heard something by now."

"Of course they know about the fire. They know because you told them, and so did I."

Roberta caught her breath, but he kept talking, as though he had said something unremarkable.

"They're not staying away because they don't know about it. They've made a choice to stay away."

"What? What are you talking about?"

"I'm talking about common sense. If you only had so many fire trucks and so much fuel, what would you do? Hike all the way up here and try—*try*—to stop a forest fire, a fire that may or may not make it to town, or marshal your forces in case it does threaten the town? The state doesn't give a damn if all of Coward's Hole burns down. Isn't that what Piccirelli was warning about all along? They can't provide the services. That was his song and dance. I guarantee you every fire truck within fifty miles is bunched down at Hope Valley, set to protect the property that really counts—and it ain't ours."

"I hate this!" Roberta kicked at the edges of the campfire viciously, sending clouds of dust into the flames. "I hate this damned fire, I hate all this . . . crap . . . that's happening, I hate everything! I wish I could get in a car and drive as far as possible away from here and never come back."

She felt drained suddenly, and found herself leaning against Steve's shoulder, her eyes half closed against the glare of the moon. Steve had begun to rub her back gently, drawing small circles in her muscles with his thumb. She closed her eyes and heard no more.

A beating sound in her ears awoke her. All around them, on the southern and western and northern edges of the pond, the trees were ablaze.

Roberta scrambled up and woke Niles. He was dopey with sleep. "Niles, you have to get up." He rubbed his eyes and sat up, his mouth falling open.

"What are we going to do?" He finally whispered.

"We're going to get the hell out of here." Roberta began packing up then, rolling up his sleeping bag clumsily and tossing his stuff in the canoe, then pouring dirt on the campfire. Niles was hobbling around, trying to help. Steve, who had disappeared behind the tree cover, came back to find they had broken camp without him. He didn't even stop to comment, instead lifting Niles into the canoe and clambering in after him.

"Take the bow. I'll steer," he said to Roberta. "There's a portage at the end of the pond, then some white water, but after that it's flat. Don't look back and don't talk. We've got to move."

As soon as they had steered east of the island, the enormity of the fire took shape. Roberta, rowing faster than she thought possible, tried not to look on either side of them. The fire had engulfed the pond on three sides, and it was racing them to the narrow channel where the pond emptied into the river. She felt as though they were animals in the circus that jump through hoops of flame. The closer they got to the opening, the louder the roaring in her ears and the hotter the wind that carried it. As she brought the oar up out of the water, she realized the hairs on her arms were singed.

"Steve, I can't—"

"Don't turn around! Close your eyes if you have to. Just row."

CHAPTER TWENTY-SIX

They had been on the water for no more than a half-hour when they saw the lights.

All along the shore by the Mill River Cemetery, pumper trucks were backed up to the river, their flashing lights turning the tree bark red. The engines strained as they sucked out the water, then roared to life as the trucks drove back up the banks. One came; another left; all headed up Route 3.

Steve lifted his oar, and the canoe drifted. "They're trying to save Hope Valley." He touched Roberta's shoulder and pointed back the way they had come. "That fire can't be a thousand yards behind us. They must have found a way into it through the woods."

The Tavern was a bustle of activity. Firefighters with blackened faces drifted in and out of the water, and men in shirtsleeves huddled at tables. "She's headed to the sea, like in thirty-six," one fireman said to another, and a woman with a clipboard was trying to get her cell phone to work, wandering on and off the porch. Jack Foley seemed lost in it all, gazing out the window at his freshly painted mill houses whose white clapboards were already flecked with stray soot.

From the edge of the crowd, just inside the door, Roberta finally spotted a familiar face. Behind the bar, dispensing glasses of water was Paula, her face flushed either from the closeness of the crowded room or the bloom of pregnancy. She must have

303

felt eyes upon her for she turned and rushed over to them, ripping off her apron as she came.

"My God, what happened to you?"

Roberta could not explain any of it, but merely fell into her sister's arms with a whimper.

"Did the house go? Where's Gran?" Paula shouted the questions over the Tavern hubbub. "How on Earth did you get here?"

"Gran's with Jessie and my father." Steve quickly described their journey. "I think the fire missed the house, but . . . I tried to get your grandparents to leave, Paula, but they wouldn't come."

"Oh, God."

Roberta found her voice then. "Lucas is still up there, and he has the horses. I'm sure he'll help them if they need it." She didn't believe what she was saying, but it was the only solace she could offer. "Gran is very sick, but Jessie's with her. She's in good hands."

"This never would have happened if she had come home with us." Paula had pulled away from Roberta as though she suddenly remembered all their differences. "Now look at this mess. We'll be lucky if they save the Tavern."

Foley came over and quickly assessed the situation, finding a room where they could clean up and a bed for Niles. Somewhere, he said, a nurse was on duty, checking on the firefighters. He would bring her to Niles as soon as he could. But he made it clear that he would need Steve and Roberta. As soon as they had a bite to eat and washed up, he could use them in the pub, where more and more people kept drifting in.

The rest of the day passed in a blur of serving food and water to firefighters and refugees of the blaze. Roberta made up beds, provided minor first aid, wrapped sandwiches to take to the fire crews and washed dishes. Steve, Ray and Foley were on the riverbank, beating back advancing flames that had escaped the firebreak the volunteers had dug upriver. Foley was so proud of his little village, and the social experiment it represented was about to go up in flames.

Paula worked with grim efficiency. "After this, then what? Are you going back?" Paula was drying glasses with a linen cloth, clinking them together as she set them back onto the bar shelf.

"Yes." Roberta plunged in. "Steve and I are going to get married. We want to do it as soon as possible, because of Niles. If his mother does come back and make trouble, it will help if we're married."

"And where are you going to live?"

She hesitated. "If there's a farm to come back to, I guess we'll live with Gran. I'm not really sure."

Paula had stopped wiping glasses and looked at her, as though she knew there was more.

"Dad had a will, a newer one. He was keeping it in a safe-deposit box in Coventry. He left the farm to both of us."

She told Paula about the tuition lot, about Oatley's information and the plans for Roberta's Woods. Then, her voice in a whisper, she related Maine's fate, telling her about his accusation about Alton and his bootlegging operation. The more often she told the story, the more she hoped the general population of the area wouldn't hear it. It was one thing to confide in Steve and the family; it was another to imagine the community thinking of Alton Wilcox as a criminal.

Paula said nothing at first. Roberta felt her old suspicion resurface: that whatever their father had been up to, Paula had at least had an inkling about it.

"I knew Dad owed Maine money, but I never dreamed he'd go that far to pay him back." Paula was playing it straight, Roberta thought. "I could tell he was in some kind of trouble. But we may never know the whole truth. At least it sounds like he had good intentions. He never could bear to part with that land."

She had found no fault with Roberta, and for that Roberta was grateful. "I don't think we should sell the farm. I hope you can understand that, Paula."

"You'll have to buy me out." Paula's tone was matter of fact. "Half of the farm was left to me. You could mortgage the place, you and Steve. Gran might help you."

She would have to take that as a victory. "There's more. Dad had quite a bit of cash in his safe-deposit box. I'd be willing to let you have it if we can work something out." She made the connection between Alton's illicit work for Maine and the money, and Paula agreed with her theory.

"Maine was probably trying to get back every dime he'd paid him, claiming it was interest, and that's why he filed the lien. He knew Dad wouldn't be telling a judge about their arrangement. And after he died no one would know the difference." Paula hung up the dishtowel and looked out the window. "Now I have some news for you. Ray and I didn't just get stuck on the way home. We've decided to buy one of Jack's houses and settle here."

Roberta beamed. "That's great."

"It seemed like a good middle ground. Jack's done a lot with the village. He's generating electricity now, and by next winter the steam turbines will be heating those houses. And we won't be so far away from Gran, and you, after the baby comes."

"But what about your house? And Ray's job?"

"Jack's hired him to manage the rentals. He's got his hands full at the Tavern. And I'll be working a few shifts over here when the baby's old enough. For now we'll stay in Westerly, so I'll be near the hospital." Paula turned back to her as they heard Ray and Steve coming in the back door. "So I guess things are working out after all."

By the time evening came, the blaze had been contained. The firebreak, at last, seemed to have stopped the onslaught, and droves of firefighters filled the pub and Tavern rooms, looking for a hot meal and a place to crash for the night. Roberta worked to a point long past exhaustion, then snatched a momentary lull to sit with Niles.

He was in a downstairs room lying on a coverlet on a white metal bed. From his room he could see all the activity around the mill houses, but now that dusk had fallen there was little to hold his interest. Roberta chatted for a while about the fire, Paula's plans and the meal preparations, but after a while her voice wound down and died. He was not listening.

"Niles." He turned to her with defiance still written on his face. "Tell me why you ran away."

He looked away and then, some struggle in him having been overcome, he said, "I wanted to show you I could do it, that's all."

"Do what?"

"Live on my own. Everybody kept talking about me like I wasn't there. About what was going to happen when my mother gets back, about where I would go and who should take care of me, like I was somebody's pet dog. I just got sick of it. Nobody bothered to ask me what I wanted. I stayed by myself before, I figured I could do it again."

"Oh, Niles. I am so sorry. Steve and I care about you very much. We want to make sure we do what's best for you. But we would never make a decision like that without involving you." She got up and walked to the window, absently closing the curtains. "I know these last few weeks I haven't been paying that much attention to you. I had a lot of questions I needed to get answered, questions about my father, and what would become of the farm. I didn't mean to push you away."

"Is Gran going to be okay?"

"Oh, I hope so, Niles. I hope so."

Later Paula invited her to her room.

"There's something I want to show you." She dragged out a steamer trunk with a rusted lock, and Roberta gazed at in puzzlement.

"That's Gran's old trunk. What are you doing with it?"

"She made me take it with me. It's full of baby clothes." She laughed conspiratorially. "Some of them must be a hundred years old. Look at this." Paula lifted up the top, and the room filled with the smell of mothballs. She picked up a yellowed christening gown. "Some of this stuff must have belonged to the first Wilcoxes. It's unbelievable."

"You're not going to use it, I hope."

"Of course not! I think some of the cloth would disintegrate if you handled it too much." She carefully replaced the dress and dug deeper into the trunk. "But that's not why I brought you in here."

Paula unfolded a crinkly pile of tissue paper. Underneath was a wedding dress. The color was ivory, the material, silk. The sleeves Roberta recognized as leg-o'-mutton, and the bodice she knew to be embroidered with seed pearls. In fact, she could close her eyes and picture every inch of the sumptuous material and silky folds.

It was the most beautiful wedding gown she had ever seen. It was her mother's.

Roberta said nothing for a moment. Paula was holding it aloft, and Roberta walked up to it slowly, reaching out to feel the fullness of the skirt. The material fell off her palm like pudding sliding off a spoon. She touched it again, her fingers this time lighting on the scalloped edges that had touched her mother's throat, then the shiny pearls that had fallen in cascades at her breast. Then the defined waist, which exploded in dozens of silky pleats. The skirt seemed to go on forever, sweeping the floor and finally ending in a pool of white at their feet.

"I couldn't believe it, either," Paula said. "I was rummaging through the trunk the first night we got here, and there it was."

Roberta said nothing, just continued absently stroking the pleats that fell to the floor without a wrinkle.

"I know it will fit you. You're built just like her. Of course, I couldn't have worn it. Gran must have been saving it for you."

"You don't suppose she forgot it was here?"

"Gran? Forget something? I doubt it. And there's something else, Roberta." Paula carefully laid the dress on the couch and returned to the trunk. She rummaged to the bottom and pulled out a black composition notebook. Paula handed it to Roberta, who opened its worn cover slowly. The pages inside were covered by an elegant but hurried hand. She had seen this handwriting only a few times before. It, too, had an almost exotic beauty.

"I started to read it, then I realized what it was," Paula said. "I had no idea she kept a diary. I can understand if you don't want to look at it, but it really belongs to you."

Roberta sank into a chair and opened the notebook randomly. Paula slipped out of the door without a word.

Worked late today at school. It's getting harder to get around. I just want this to be over. May says I'm all out in front, so it will be a boy. Alton wants to name the baby after himself. Isn't that just like him? Once he said he had hoped Paula would be a boy. It's easy to see what's wrong with that poor little girl.

Roberta flipped a page. The entries were mostly like that, clipped, a paragraph or two, usually once or twice a week.

I'd like to get out of this infernal house. May says it's not good for the baby, going out in the cold. I don't care. She thinks Dr. Spock

309

has new ideas. If only she knew what the current books were saying.

After a while the entries slowed, sometimes coming months apart. *Want to go back to work, but Alton doubtful,* read one and, *The farm seems lonely this winter. Snowed in for two weeks.*

Roberta turned the pages slowly, combing them for mentions of her, but she found few. Jackie had dutifully recorded her daughter's first smile, her weight and height every six months, but sometimes her progress amounted to little more than pencil jottings in the margins. Years were passing, but her lonely mother didn't seem to have time to pour her heart into her journal. Then came the last entry, longer than the rest, scrawled in a hurried hand.

I've made up my mind. I'll have to leave in the afternoon, get Roberta at school before the bus comes, and then head out. Alton will be at the mill, and May won't suspect anything. It won't be safe to go to Worcester. That's where he'll look first. We'll head west. California. I have to get away from here, and I have to get Roberta away too—somewhere she'll have the possibility to be anything her heart desires.

The writing stopped in the middle of the page. Roberta found herself thumbing through the dozens of pages that had stayed blank, though she knew she would find nothing there. So her mother had been coming for her, that day in 1988. She had been rushing—trying to get to school before the bus left? Perhaps something—someone—had held her up? And she had never made it.

Roberta closed the black and white notebook. Her mother had loved her enough to take her along. Perhaps that was why Gran had saved the diary all these years, hidden under the wedding dress her granddaughter might someday wear. That was what she must take from the saga of a young and lonely woman who wasn't meant to settle on an isolated farm or bond with a soul as independent and distant as Alton Wilcox. Jackie had tried, with what she had and what she thought was right, to express that love. That was all anyone could do—work with what they were dealt, and stay true to who they were.

Roberta got up and hastily replaced the notebook. She had to tell Paula what she had decided; they had a lot of plans to make and not much time.

It was late, past eleven, but the bustle in the pub seemed to have picked up again. A rowdy crew of utility workers was in the corner, drinking what looked suspiciously like John Woodmansee's whiskey. Steve was manning the bar; Foley must have finally taken a well-deserved break. Roberta sighed. She wished everybody would either go home or pass out, but she dutifully joined Steve at the tap.

"Where have you been?" He seemed relieved to see her, as though she really had been lost.

"Shopping for my wedding dress."

"What?"

She gave him a coy smile. "Never mind. How much longer do you think we'll be here?"

"A day or two, maybe. If Ida ever shows up we could hitch a ride back with her. Unless you want to row home."

"No, thank you. But that sounds like time enough to plan a wedding."

"Here? Now?"

"Here and now. I've got the dress. We've got a captive audience of wedding guests, even if we don't know half of them." She stopped smiling. "I think the sooner we do this, the better. Mrs. Porter could still show up, you know. It wouldn't hurt to present a united front."

"Is that the only reason we're getting married?" He was teasing, though, and he swept her into a kiss. "Whatever you say. There's got to be a preacher around here somewhere."

The door opened, and they looked over as though a minister was about to walk in on cue. But it wasn't a man of the cloth who had burst into the pub. It was Anthony Piccirelli.

Flanked by two state troopers, he was scanning the crowed in search of someone. Roberta felt Steve squeeze her hand. In her relief at the fire being out, she had forgotten that Piccirelli supposedly had a warrant for Steve's arrest. He looked so harmless—he had on a blue suit jacket and a tie covered in bumblebees—but the troopers were standing at the ready, and one had a hand on his service revolver.

It looked as though he were about to speak, but before Piccirelli spotted his man, someone in the crowd spotted him. A grizzled volunteer tanked up on John Woodmansee's rotgut whiskey was standing on a table pointing to the doorway, and he whistled loudly to get the crowd's attention.

"Here's the man we have to thank for losing our homes," he yelled, and the noise in the bar subsided as all eyes turned toward the state official and two police officers. "Thanks to him, we had no phones to call the fire department, and they had no gas to get to us. Thanks to him, we lost everything we had."

There was a general echo of discontent from the audience. The man seemed to be about to go on, but Piccirelli motioned with his hand to quiet him.

"I've just come from up north," he said, and the crowd grew even quieter. Roberta held her breath. "Yes, there has been quite a bit of damage, but because of all your valiant efforts, the fire was stopped before it reached Hope Valley."

"We know that," came a catcall from the back. "Like he said, no thanks to you."

"You have a right to be upset, but I didn't start that fire. It was a natural disaster over which no man had any control. Unfortunately, it was made worse because Senator Maine chose to risk his own life and that of his neighbors to hide his criminal activities."

A murmur went through the crowd, and one of the troopers called for quiet. "The senator is dead," Piccirelli announced flatly. A ripple of "I don't believe it" and "I'll be damned" went through the room. "He blew himself up trying to get rid of gasoline he was smuggling up in the woods. We found his body this afternoon."

Piccirelli went on to give a long and detailed explanation of the senator's exploits, almost as though he were trying to prove a case in court. The crowd sat through this for a while, but finally the grizzled man in the back—who had since stepped down from the table—called out, "But what about The Ring? What about it, Piccirelli? All that time you were trying to convince us to leave, you were just trying to get the goods on old Maine, weren't you?"

"Not exactly." Piccirelli was looking more and more uncomfortable. He had loosened his bumblebee tie and slung his jacket on the back of a nearby chair. "I was only involved in this investigation near the end, and only because I happened to have such close contact with the residents of this area. I am not a police officer, and I do not work for the attorney general's office. I am a servant of the governor, and I was simply trying to help."

His shoulders were slumped, and for the first time she believed he was not trying to sell them anything.

"The Ring is dead," he declared flatly. "The New England Council of Governors met on this very issue last week. The states have been unsuccessful in their efforts to concentrate the population. As much as I believed in the idea, I must concede, ladies and gentlemen, that it was flawed from the start. No matter how dire your suffering, you people would not be relocated, and I honestly . . . well, I can't say I blame you."

The residents met this admission with a respectful silence, and Piccirelli continued, his voice regaining a little of its enthusiasm. "While we were trying to herd you all down to the fairgrounds, a wonderful phenomenon was taking place under our very noses. The man who owns this tavern, Mr. Foley, set about to create his own self-sufficient village. He got permission from the federal government to use the river's dam to generate electricity and steam heat. He remodeled the mill houses across the river that had been in such poor shape. He did all of this without help from the government."

A few people wondered aloud where Foley was, but he apparently was asleep, missing this tribute to his ingenuity.

"That is why the government has shifted its priorities," Piccirelli said, and his voice had risen now and taken on that familiar oratorical quality. "The money that was devoted to The Ring will be reallocated, to help citizens like Mr. Foley create their own villages, where they want to. We imagine a string of such self-sufficient communities all along the Mill River— Alton, Ashaway, Shannock, Carolina. For those of you living up in the woods, you'll have a closer place to buy your goods. For those of you who want to live in a town, you'll have an alternative to Cranston or Warwick. These will be small towns in the finest sense of the word."

Steve spoke up then, and Roberta's heart quaked. She wished he would hide under the bar. Instead he stood front and center, commanding the attention of Piccirelli and everyone else in the pub.

"But what about gas, Tony? Where will we get the gas? Man's still got to get around."

"The gas crisis isn't going to go away, Steve." Piccirelli cleared his throat. "I understand from the state police that you had a few ideas on alternative fuels. Well, the government's changed its mind about that, too. There will be grant money available for research. The university's going to get involved. There's no overnight answer, but obviously we've learned that rationing alone won't solve the problem."

Roberta relaxed then. If Piccirelli was telling the truth, and there was no reason to doubt him, the state had decided if you can't beat 'em, join 'em. She had no anticipation that their lives would get easier immediately. But with everyone working toward the same goal, it was possible they could find a way to keep a way of life that seemed about to be extinguished.

Steve and Roberta's wedding day dawned foggy, and although no one had seen a weather report, Roberta smelled rain in the air. It didn't matter. Although they had planned to exchange vows on the riverbank, they could move the ceremony and reception inside to the upstairs ballroom if they had to.

Neighbors, friends, and strangers had spent the day before getting ready. Jack Foley was making a feast worthy of any New York restaurant but composed entirely of ingredients scrounged from nature. A half-dozen fishermen had caught enough river trout for a crowd, and some local church ladies had spent the afternoon before digging up dandelion greens to be sautéed. Foley had a root cellar full of potatoes to be boiled and mashed. The only thing that had flummoxed him was the cake, and the ladies from the Baptist church had found enough confectioner's sugar, flour, and cocoa between them to whip up three tiers of chocolate cake. John Woodmansee had agreed to play his fiddle, and the Baptist minister would perform the service. Foley had loaned Steve his only suit, which was a tad short in the sleeves but would do. Paula, Ray, and Niles made up the rest of the wedding party. Niles already was putting pressure on his ankle, and his cheeks were full of color.

By noon the fog had burned off and the dew was gone from the grass, and everyone marched solemnly out to the shore, accompanied only by a few trills from some songbirds in the lilac bush. A freshening breeze was coming off the water, and it blew

Roberta's veil into her face while the roar of the river over the dam threatened to drown out their vows. Paula, who had made her dress out of a linen tablecloth the night before, held the net fabric away from her sister's face.

"Do you, Roberta Wilcox?"

Do I? I do. I do take Steve, in partnership with all he is and hopes to be. He was standing stiffly next to her, his hands crossed in front of him. He hated the suit, she could tell, but he was wearing it for her.

"Do you, Steve Reynolds?"

He was biting his lip. She knew despite the cool breeze he was sweating under Foley's tight white shirt. She was torn between pity and an absurd urge to laugh.

They had no rings. Steve had jokingly suggested using a cigar band, but there was a limit to how much improvisation she could tolerate. As it was, she was thankful the rich folds of Jackie's gown hid her sneakers. They would get rings later, they had agreed, and he had hinted that his mother had one that had been handed down in the family. That was fine, Roberta said, but she wondered if his mother might not be putting it back on her finger one of these days.

"By the power vested in me by the State of Rhode Island and Providence Plantations."

The great State of Rhode Island. It was their home, after all, even if those who ran it had put them through so much in the last few months.

"For all the rest of your days, amen."

They kissed, and the veil danced, winding itself around Roberta's neck and then Steve's. Steve looked handsome in the white collar and black coat, but not nearly as handsome, Roberta thought, as he had a few days ago when they pulled alongside the Tavern in the canoe, his face covered in soot and his hair sticking up in dozens of directions.

Then it came on the wind. It was a scent she knew so well that it was almost too familiar to place. Rosewater and mint, with a touch of something else—cold cream? It was Gran's scent, coming at them across the river on a restless zephyr. It filled her at once with longing and alarm. This was all so lovely. But they really had to get home.

The next morning John Woodmansee gave them a ride as far as the Route 95 underpass, where they waited for an hour for Ida's postal Jeep. It nearly buzzed up the entrance ramp without seeing them, but when it stopped they saw that Lucas, not Ida Kenyon, was at the wheel.

They piled in, Steve in the front and Roberta and Niles squeezed in the back with the bags of mail. They were almost to the first exit before Lucas explained. "Ida and her mother didn't want to stay. I brought them both down to South County in the Jeep the day of the blaze, then I got stuck in Kingston for almost a week. No gas. That's why the Jeep's so full—almost a week's worth of mail."

"What have you heard from home? Is everyone okay?" Roberta wished he wouldn't rattle on so; she had to hear that Gran was safe.

"Not much, I'm afraid." He took a deep breath. "The day of the fire I let all of the horses go, all but one, and headed on that one to Hope Valley. I was making great time, as a matter of fact, but something made me stop. My conscience, maybe. Maybe what you had said, Roberta."

Steve looked back at her quizzically, but she shushed him.

"So I came back. I stopped at Ida's and I decided it might be best if they came to my house. When we got there the blaze was on the other side of the river. That's when I realized I hadn't seen the Teffts anywhere."

"We tried to get them to come with us," Steve interrupted. "But they wouldn't budge."

"It was too late when I got there. I guess I should have gone there first. Would've, had I known. Their house was totally engulfed. I could barely get over the bridge at that point. I managed to get their animals out. I heard—" He stopped and something caught in his throat. "Well, it wasn't pretty. I hope I never hear or see anything like it again in this lifetime."

Roberta began to sob quietly. Bud and Amy, stubborn to the last. At least they had perished together, and they had died in their own home. That was what they had wanted. That was why they had stayed. Poor Paula; she would be devastated.

"After that, I knew we had to get out," Lucas concluded. "The fire already had taken my barn and the sugar house, and it was coming on strong. I piled Ida and her mother into the Jeep and headed for Kingston."

"What happened to your horses?" It was Niles, who had been listening intently.

"That's what I'm about to find out. Frankly I'd trade the lot of them to be able to have saved my neighbors."

The Jeep slowed as it met the final rise in the road. Around the bend Roberta could see the white of the old Wilcox house beyond the oaks, waiting there as it had so many times before. The slumping roof, the green shutters, the chimneys jutting out—it was still there, an island amid a sea of blackened stubble, the nearby barn flattened and the outbuildings scorched. But the house still stood, its tidy white paint a beacon calling them home.

Ben and Jessie Reynolds must have heard the Jeep's gears winding down. But the reconciled couple had no joy on their faces. Ben was waving, waving, waving, hailing them from up the road, too far away for them to hear him, to close not to see him call. The house had survived the fire, an island of white in the blackness left behind, and so had Ben and Jessie Reynolds.

But May Wilcox had passed before.

As they pulled in the drive, Roberta felt a soft perfumed breeze wash against her cheek. Slowly she raised her arm to wave back, a traveler who has sighted home at last.

ABOUT THE AUTHOR

Betty J. Cotter was named the 2006 fiction fellow of the R.I. State Council on the Arts and is a student in the MFA in Writing program at Vermont College. This is her first novel. A newspaper editor, she lives with her husband and three children in Rhode Island, where she traces her ancestry to the 1600s.

DATE DUE		
JUL 0 / 2008		
JUL 1 / 2008		
JUL 2 / 2008		
AUG 2 2008		
SEP 0 2 2008		
SEP 1 7 2008		
OCT 0 9 2008		